Rosie Hendry lives by the sea in Norfolk with her husband and two children. She is the author of the East End Angels series, an uplifting and heart-warming saga that follows the lives and loves of Winnie, Frankie and Bella, who all work for the London Auxiliary Ambulance Service (LAAS) during the Blitz. Listening to her father's tales of life during the Second World War sparked Rosie's interest in this period and she loves researching further, searching out gems of real life events which inspire her writing.

Keep up to date with Rosie by following her on Twitter, becoming her friend on Facebook or visiting her website:

@hendry_rosie
rosie.hendry.94
www.rosiehendry.com

Secrets of
the East End Angels

ROSIE HENDRY

SPHERE

First published in Great Britain in 2018 by Sphere
This paperback edition published in 2018 by Sphere

5 7 9 10 8 6 4

A CIP catalogue record for this book
is available from the British Library.

ISBN 978-0-7515-6684-0

Typeset in Bembo by M Rules
Printed and bound in Great Britain by
Clays Ltd, Elcograf S.p.A.

Papers used by Sphere are from well-managed forests
and other responsible sources.

Sphere
An imprint of
Little, Brown Book Group
Carmelite House
50 Victoria Embankment
London EC4Y 0DZ

An Hachette UK Company
www.hachette.co.uk

www.littlebrown.co.uk

For David, with love.

Elen sila lumenn' omentielvo

Dear Reader,

Welcome to Secrets of the East End Angels. If you've met Frankie, Winnie and Bella before in East End Angels, I hope you'll enjoy reading more about their lives, but if you haven't, then welcome to their world — I hope you'll enjoy meeting them here.

East Ender Frankie's been working at London Auxiliary Ambulance Station 75 since the previous summer and loves her job, especially as it means she can stay living at home in Stepney with her family — her grandad and her adopted younger brother Stanley (who's now been evacuated to safety in the countryside) — shielding them from her awful step-grandmother, Ivy. She's fallen in love with Scottish doctor Alastair Munro, who she met in a bombed-out Anderson shelter.

Upper-class Winnie's parents disapprove of her working as an ambulance driver, but it hasn't stopped her; she likes doing things her own way, if necessary bending or breaking rules at times, including those of Station 75, which has caused her to clash with her boss, Station Officer Steele, on many occasions. She's given a home to Trixie, a golden-haired little dog who was dug out of a bombed-out building and who now goes everywhere with her, including out on calls in the ambulance. Her new relationship with fellow driver and conscientious objector Mac might help to tame her wild side.

Former housemaid Bella's home was bombed out at the start of the Blitz and she has found a new one with Winnie at her godmother Connie's grand house – the sort she used to work in before the war. She works as an attendant while Frankie drives their ambulance, but their boss has been making her take driving lessons in the hope that one day she'll become a driver too, though Bella's not so sure she's capable of that. She's worried about her brother, Walter, who threatened to go AWOL from the army until she and Station Officer Steele helped him to think again. Bella's love of books has brought her together with Winnie's brother James.

The huge air raid of 29 December 1940 – when infernos swept through London, and St Paul's Cathedral stood surrounded by smoke and fire – pushed the three young women to the limit, testing their bravery and courage. Winnie ignored the rules and drove through flames to rescue injured firemen, Frankie had the shock of finding and rescuing her injured grandfather, and Bella was forced to overcome her fear and drive him to hospital while the bombs rained down.

Now, with a new year upon them, what does 1941 have in store for Frankie, Winnie and Bella?

I do hope you enjoy reading their story as much as I enjoyed writing it.

With warmest wishes,
Rosie

Chapter One

January 1941

Clutching her ticket in her hand, Frankie dashed out of the booking office doorway, dodging around more leisurely passengers, and ran for the train, desperately hoping that it wouldn't leave without her.

'Wait!' she shouted, waving her arms as she sprinted the last few yards along the platform.

The guard had almost reached the last open carriage door and was about to slam it shut and then wave his green flag to signal to the waiting driver at the far end of the train. 'Come on then.' He shook his head, raising his eyebrows as he waited for her.

'Thank you very much,' she gasped as she climbed aboard and he shut the door firmly behind her. Leaning against the wall of the corridor while she caught her breath, her heart gradually returning to its normal rhythm after her anxious dash here from Station 75, she watched through the window as the guard waved his flag with a flourish and blew a piercing blast of his whistle. The engine responded, belching out great chuffs of smoke that drifted through the cold air, and they began to slide smoothly out of London Bridge station. Frankie sighed and finally allowed herself to smile; she was on her way at last.

'Where are you off to in such an 'urry, then? On yer way home?'

Frankie turned around to see that the guard had come through from the adjoining guard's van.

'No, I'm goin' to Wyching Green. My grandad's in 'ospital there.' She handed him her ticket. 'I was working the late shift – 'ad to run all the way to the station.'

'Have you been there before? Know where you're goin'?' he asked as he punched the ticket and handed it back.

'No.'

'Well, I'll let yer know when we get there. It's only a little place and yer'll miss it otherwise now all the station signs 'ave been taken down.' The guard smiled at her. 'Go on, find yerself a seat. I dare say yer could do with a rest if you've been on shift all night.'

'Thank you.' Frankie smiled back at him.

The guard touched the peak of his cap, then opened the sliding door of the nearest compartment and began checking the other passengers' tickets.

As the train slid out of London, Frankie made her way

along the carriage looking for an empty seat, glancing every now and then out of the corridor window as they passed through bomb-damaged areas where so many buildings had been destroyed, the gaps where they had once stood like missing teeth in a smile. Everything was covered in a dusting of snow, some of it still in neat white patches, other parts already turned to a dirty grey – snow never stayed pristinely white for long in London.

Near the far end of the train, she found a compartment with spare seats and went in, smiling at the other passengers: an elderly woman sitting by the window knitting, and a mother who was cradling a tearful young child on her lap, doing her best to soothe him, while an older girl sat close beside her reading a book. She settled herself down opposite the older woman in the corner seat next to the window.

Sinking back into the springy seat, Frankie closed her eyes and tried to relax, but her stomach seemed to have other ideas. It felt like it had twisted into a tight knot, sitting hard and tense inside her, and it would probably stay like that until she arrived and could see whether her grandad was truly all right.

It was just over a week now since he'd been injured on that terrible night when it seemed as if the whole of London were ablaze, and the shock of finding him injured and the gut-wrenching fear that he might not survive still lingered painfully inside her. But he was alive and would recover, and now that he had been moved to Kent, he was in a much safer place, she must focus on that.

Kent. It was a place full of good memories for Frankie. Every year her gran used to take her there for the hop picking. They'd get an early train – the Hopper Special – from London Bridge, with all they needed for the weeks away stuffed in a trolley, and would stay in one of the little huts on the farm, spending days picking the bitter yet sickly-sweet-smelling hops. They had been such happy times, her gran enjoying talking and laughing with the other women as they worked. Frankie liked the space and the fresh air; it was a world away from the cramped, squashed houses of the East End, the dirt and the grime.

Thinking of that time gave Frankie a warm glow inside. She needed to remember those times when life was normal and there was no fear of bombs falling and people never knowing if they would live to see the next morning. That was real life, not like it was now.

The rocking of the train must have lulled her to sleep, and she woke with a start, opening her eyes and then quickly shutting them to block out the bright sunshine. Slowly she opened them again, and as they adjusted to the light, she stared out of the window at a world blanketed in snow stretching as far as the horizon. The Kent countryside was sparkling white under the crystal-clear blue sky. It was stunningly beautiful.

'It's quite a picture, isn't it?' said the elderly woman sitting opposite.

Frankie tore her gaze away from the window and nodded. 'I ain't ever seen it like that before . . . so clean

4

and bright and going on for miles. Snow never looks like that in London – you can't see it stretching out so far in the distance, and it never stays clean and white for long.'

The woman nodded, gazing out of the window. 'I love the snow.'

Frankie smiled. 'It's beautiful.'

'You need to wrap up warm in it, though, but I can see you're doing that. That's a fine-looking scarf you're wearing; did you make it yourself?' the woman asked.

'This?' Frankie plucked at the scarf she was wearing wrapped several times around her neck – a Christmas present from Bella. 'No, my friend made this for me. I ain't much of a knitter, I always drop stitches. I sew, though; made these dungarees for work.' She pointed to the legs of her navy dungarees, which was all that could be seen as she was wearing her thick navy-blue woollen coat. 'It saves me getting my normal clothes dirty until we get a uniform.'

'What do you do?' the woman asked.

'I'm an ambulance driver. They've promised us uniforms like the Auxiliary Fire Service have, but we ain't got them yet.'

'From what I've seen in the newspapers, you young women are out in the thick of it. They jolly well ought to hurry up and get you kitted out properly.'

'It's a bit of a sore spot at our ambulance station, and often talked about, but there ain't much we can do about it. We just 'ave to wait till they sort it out.'

'Do you really drive an ambulance?' The girl who'd

been silently reading up till then suddenly piped up, staring at Frankie with her big blue eyes.

'Ruby! Don't interrupt the lady, asking questions,' her mother chided her, smiling apologetically at Frankie.

'It's all right, I don't mind. Yes, Ruby, I really do drive an ambulance.'

'Even at night, in the blackout?' Ruby asked.

Frankie nodded. 'Yes, even in the blackout and during air raids.'

'Do you get scared?' the girl said.

'Sometimes.' Frankie smiled at her. 'But we're always careful and we look out for each other.'

'What's your name? My name's Ruby, and that's my brother Jack.' She pointed to the little boy, who was now fast asleep, his head leaning on his mother's chest, his cheeks rosy with sleep.

'I'm Frankie,' Frankie told her.

Ruby frowned. 'Isn't Frank a boy's name? There's a boy in my class called Frank.'

'Ruby!' her mother said.

Frankie smiled at the woman. 'I don't mind. Yes, you're right, Ruby, Frank *is* a boy's name. My real name is Stella, but everyone who works at our ambulance station gets called by another name. My surname's Franklin so I got called Frankie. One of my friends is called Winnie, because her surname is Churchill, and another is called Bella because her last name is Belmont.'

'Why do they do that? Isn't it confusing?' Ruby asked.

'Not really. We just know each other by our nicknames –

in fact I ain't sure what the real names of some of the crew members are.' Frankie smiled at the girl. 'I don't know why they do it, they just do.'

Ruby considered what Frankie had said for a moment and then asked, 'Where are you going now? Is it to drive another ambulance?'

Frankie shook her head. 'I'm going to visit my grandad, who's been evacuated to an 'ospital in Kent.'

'We've been evacuated to Kent,' Ruby told her. 'We're staying with Auntie May in her house. It's a bit crowded.'

'With what's happening in London, we're very grateful she took us in,' Ruby's mother said, her eyes meeting Frankie's and a look of understanding passing between them.

'You're lucky to be living in Kent, Ruby. It's beautiful out 'ere and a lot safer. I . . .' Frankie paused as the guard appeared in the corridor and pulled open the compartment door.

'Next stop Wyching Green,' he said.

'Thank you.' Frankie smiled at him, picking up her bag and standing up, feeling the train beginning to slow down. 'This is my stop. It's been nice talking to you all.'

'Goodbye, Frankie,' Ruby said. 'I think that name suits you.'

'Thank you,' Frankie said. 'You look after yourself, and enjoy living in Kent.'

Frankie's ears were tingling from the cold, so she tugged her knitted green beret down further over her auburn hair.

She'd followed the directions given to her by a porter at the station and was now out in the middle of the snow-blanketed countryside, trudging her way to the hospital, which wasn't actually in the village at all but a couple of miles outside. Doing her best to keep to the tracks already printed into the snow by previous travellers going this way, she couldn't help admiring the beauty of the landscape, even though the cold was nipping at her toes and fingers. She loved the way the snow was sculpted into drifts and had moulded itself around objects, softening their outlines and casting a gentle, muffled hush over everything. This place seemed like another world after war-torn London.

As she rounded a bend in the road, the imposing hospital building came into sight at last, its red-brick walls standing out against the white background. Frankie felt a jolt of joy run through her: her grandad was somewhere in there and in a short time she'd be able to see him again, talk to him and finally satisfy herself that he was fine.

Hurrying the last few hundred yards to the hospital, she stamped the snow off her boots before she went in and asked directions to the ward her grandfather was on. Then, with the excitement mounting inside her, like a child on Christmas morning, she made her way along corridors and up stairs until she found the place she wanted. Pausing to tidy herself up as best she could after her journey, smoothing down her hair and brushing out the creases in her coat, she opened the doors of the ward and walked in. She'd only gone a couple of yards when a nurse emerged from a side door.

'Can I help you?' she asked.

'I've come to see my grandfather, Reginald Franklin,' Frankie said.

The nurse looked uncomfortable and sighed. 'I'm sorry, but visiting hours are only on a Sunday from two till four.'

Frankie's heart plummeted. Today was Wednesday, and by Sunday she would have switched shifts again and be working during the daytime. She wasn't going to give in that easily, though, not now she'd come all the way from London. 'But I ain't goin' to be able to come then, 'cos I'll be working. I'm an ambulance driver for the London Auxiliary Ambulance Service.'

The nurse bit her bottom lip. 'I . . .' She stopped at the sight of the ward sister bearing down on them, her uniform so crisp and crease-free it could probably have stood up on its own.

'What's going on here, Nurse?'

'This is Mr Franklin's granddaughter; she's come all the way from London to see him.'

'Has she now? Well I'm afraid you've had a wasted journey,' the sister said, not looking the least bit sorry. 'Our visiting hours are Sundays, two till four sharp, and *only* those hours. You'll just have to come back then.'

'But I can't; I'll be on duty myself then. Please can I just . . .' Frankie began but was silenced by the withering look the sister gave her.

'Rest assured your grandfather is doing well and receiving the best possible care here under my watch.' The sister's smile didn't reach her eyes. She turned to the nurse. 'If you can see to observations now, Nurse.'

The nurse nodded, and satisfied that her commands would be obeyed, the sister swept away to her room.

Frankie did her best to blink back the sudden tears that threatened to spill out. It was so frustrating to get so near and yet not be able to see her grandad because of some ridiculous, unbendable, unsympathetic rule. In her excitement and desperation to come and visit him, she'd never imagined she would be thwarted just yards away from his hospital bed. It wasn't fair. But there was nothing she could do if they wouldn't let her in. Reaching into her bag, she pulled out the newspapers she'd brought for him, and the paper bag of humbugs, his favourite sweet.

'Would you please give these to my grandad, tell him I was 'ere but couldn't come in 'cos of the rule.'

The nurse nodded and went to take them, but changed her mind. 'Listen, Sister goes for her tea break in fifteen minutes.' She spoke in a hushed tone. 'You could come back then – just for ten minutes, mind, no more or she'd have my guts for garters and no mistake if she came back and caught you. Then you can give him these yourself.'

Frankie's heart lifted. 'Really?'

'Yes. Go and wait down the corridor somewhere Sister won't see you – she'll come out of here and turn left and then go down the stairs to the canteen. When she's gone, come back in; your grandfather is the third bed along on the right. Remember, ten minutes only.' The nurse smiled. 'He'll be right pleased to see you.'

Frankie reached out and touched her arm. 'Thank you, I really appreciate this.'

'I know. It's not right not letting you in when you've come so far. Just don't let Sister see you waiting or she'll know something's up.'

'I won't.' Frankie held out the newspapers and sweets to the nurse again. 'Please take these to 'im – make it look like I've gone just in case Sister checks. And tell him I'm still 'ere and comin' in for a few minutes as soon as the coast is clear.'

'All right then.' The nurse smiled at her as she took them. 'Now go.'

'I'm going.' Frankie grinned.

Tucking herself into a little alcove she found at the far end of an adjoining corridor but with a clear view of the stairs, Frankie waited. The minutes that ticked by seemed like hours, her heartbeat pounding in her ears as she watched for the sister to appear. It was like when she used to play hide-and-seek as a child, the bittersweet thrill of waiting to be found, but this time the reward for remaining unseen was far greater.

At last she heard the sound of quick footsteps coming along the corridor and was relieved to see the sister turn and make her way down the stairs. She checked her watch and waited for a few more moments to ensure the woman was gone, then slipped out of her hiding place and hurried along the corridor to the ward. Reaching the doors, she paused and took a deep breath to calm her nerves, which were jangling about inside her like a bunch of keys, then opened the door and went in.

'What kept yer so long?' her grandad's voice called out to her as she covered the few yards to his bed in record time. She threw her arms around him as best she could given that he was propped up in bed with his leg suspended in the air on a pulley system.

'Shh!' The nurse who'd been kind enough to let Frankie in popped her head out of the curtains surrounding a nearby bed. 'You need to keep the noise down, Mr Franklin, this is a hospital ward.' She smiled and winked at Frankie. 'Remember, just ten minutes, and not a minute more.' She tapped her watch and then disappeared back behind the curtain.

'By golly you're a sight for sore eyes,' Grandad said, beaming widely as Frankie kissed his cheek.

'How are yer?' she asked, looking him up and down.

'All the better for seein' you. I couldn't believe it when the nurse told me you were 'ere and Sister wouldn't let you come in. Don't she know it ain't easy for you to get 'ere working around your shifts? I would 'ave crawled out after you if the nurse hadn't said she'd fixed it for yer. I'm going to 'ave words with that sister.'

'No you ain't.' Frankie sat down on the edge of the bed and took hold of his hand. 'You don't want to get the nurse into any trouble, not when she's 'elped me. I'm 'ere now, so let's make the most of it.'

'How are things in London?' he asked.

Frankie shrugged her shoulders, 'You know, about the same. It's been fairly quiet: a few air raids, but nothin' like that night, you know ...'

'I ain't going to forget that one in an 'urry.' He looked troubled and then smiled. 'I've 'ad a letter from Stanley; he told me you'd written to tell 'im where I was.'

'We did the right thing sending him to safety in Buckinghamshire.' She was grateful that they'd evacuated ten-year-old Stanley to the countryside a few months ago. He might not have been a blood relative, her grandparents having taken him in as an orphan after his mother died, but he'd become like a brother to her. Frankie missed him terribly, but it was worth it to know he was safe from air raids. 'Have you 'eard about the Dead End Kids?'

'No. What's 'appened?'

'Two of them got killed that night. Made me think of 'ow Stanley wanted to join them, and 'ow he might 'ave ended up injured or worse if we hadn't had 'im evacuated again. There's a bit about what happened to them in the papers I brought you.'

She shivered at the memory of how shortly before he'd been evacuated, Stanley had run off in the middle of a raid to try and join the Dead End Kids, who extinguished fires and rescued people during raids but were several years older than he was. It had been that which had spurred them on to send him away for his own safety.

Grandad shook his head. 'Poor blighters, they didn't deserve that to 'appen to them.' He sat lost in thought for a moment. 'How's Ivy? She's written to me, but her letters don't say much really. Is she keepin' all right?'

Frankie did her best not to pull a face at the thought of her step-grandmother, who was keeping perfectly fine. Having her husband injured and sent to Kent hadn't seemed to bother Ivy very much at all. She'd made no attempt to visit him, claiming it was too far to go, though that was just an excuse, as she hadn't even gone to see him when he was in the London hospital before he'd been evacuated.

'She's all right.' Frankie shrugged. 'You know Ivy.'

She could have said a lot more but didn't want to upset her grandad, who remained loyal to his second wife even though she really didn't deserve it. Ivy had wormed her way into his heart after Frankie's beloved Gran had died far too early, pretending to be kind and caring and seemingly the perfect wife to care for Grandad and look after Stanley, but once they'd got married, her mask had begun to slip, revealing a woman who was lazy and selfish and only interested in herself.

'I do.' Grandad squeezed Frankie's hand. 'If anything 'appens to me, will you promise me somethin'?'

Frankie's eyes met his. 'What?'

'That you'll look out for Ivy, make sure she's all right. Take care of her.'

'Me?'

Her nodded. 'She is family.'

Frankie dropped her gaze to his hand in hers. What on earth was he thinking? she wondered. The last thing she'd ever want to do was look after Ivy.

'Well?' he prompted her. 'What do you say?'

Frankie knew what she wanted to say – no, never, not in a million years – but Grandad's blue eyes were filled

14

with concern. That was the way he was, kind and caring. He took his responsibilities seriously, and when he'd married Ivy, he'd taken it upon himself to look after her. Now he was thinking about how to make sure that still happened, even if he died. Frankie swallowed hard to ease the thickening in her throat. He wasn't going to die; she didn't want to think of that.

She squeezed his hand. 'But nothing's going to 'appen to you, is it? You're safe 'ere in hospital.'

'I 'ope so, for now anyway, but I mean when I come 'ome and get back on the beat. You never know these days if your number's going to be up in a raid, and I'd rest easier if I knew that if the worst 'appened, you'd be looking out for Ivy for me. It worries me, keeps me awake at night.'

What could she say? She didn't have it in her heart to let him down when it was what he wanted. If it would make him happy, make him feel better sitting in this hospital bed miles from home and his family, then she really didn't have any choice, did she?

'All right then, I will.'

'Is that a promise?' he asked, his eyes meeting hers.

Reluctantly, Frankie nodded. 'I promise.' Saying those two words sent her stomach plummeting into her shoes, and she quickly sent up a silent prayer that there would never be the need for her to fulfil her promise. Looking out for someone who didn't trouble herself about others – not even a child, Frankie thought, recalling how Ivy had left Stanley alone in the shelter in the middle of a heavy air raid – would be difficult.

'Good girl, thank you.' Grandad smiled, looking relieved. 'I knew I could rely on you.'

For the remainder of their too-short time, they chatted easily, until the nurse put her head around the curtain again. 'Two minutes left.'

'All right, thank you,' Frankie said. 'I'll come again as soon as I can, Grandad, during proper visiting hours so I can be here for longer.'

'You look after yerself, and be careful when you're out in an air raid.' He squeezed her hand in his. 'Don't go taking no risks.'

'I won't. You know we look after each other and always keep our tin 'ats on our heads.' She kissed his cheek and smiled at him. 'You keep gettin' better.'

Her grandad nodded, eyes bright with unshed tears.

'I 'ave to go.' Frankie reluctantly let go of his hand and walked to the door, turning back to give him a final smile and a wave before she left the ward, then hurrying away before the sister returned to catch her.

Visiting her grandad had soothed her worries about him. He was safe, well looked after and on the mend, everything she'd hoped for. She should have felt like skipping out of here, but the weight of what he'd asked her to promise weighed heavily on her. She'd agreed only to make him feel better, and she hoped with all her heart that she would never have to carry out that promise, because if she did, she honestly had no idea if she would be able to do it.

*

16

Bella winced at the crunching noise as she changed gear too hastily. 'See, I'm not ready to take the test!'

Mac touched her arm. 'Relax, Bella. You are ready, more than ready in fact. Remember, you've already done the job under fire in the middle of a massive air raid.'

She sighed, wriggling her shoulders to try and ease the tension that had curled itself into a tight, hard knot right in the middle of her back.

'I know, but that wasn't real, you know, being a proper driver. I . . .' She paused while she stopped at a junction to wait for a bus to pass, and then turned left. 'I only did it because I had to. Frankie was in no state to drive, so it was up to me to get her grandfather to hospital.'

She'd had several nightmares replaying that awful night when they'd found Frankie's grandfather badly injured. Terrified that he was going to die, Frankie had begged Bella to drive, and there'd been no other option but to agree. Bella had done it, but it had been excruciatingly difficult and frightening, and to make matters worse, when she'd confessed to Station Officer Steele what she'd done, the boss had insisted that it proved beyond any doubt that she was definitely ready to become a proper ambulance driver. Now here she was, just minutes away from taking a test that she was incapable of ever passing.

'It sounds to me like you did the real thing,' Mac said. 'You couldn't get more real than that. Bombs raining down, massive fires engulfing London and injured casualties in the back of your ambulance; after that, today's test should be easy.'

'Don't!' Bella snapped, and then glanced at Mac. 'I'm sorry. It's just I'm nervous, and when I get like this when I'm driving, everything falls apart. Having slushy snow on the roads isn't going to help either.' She swerved to avoid a car that suddenly slid towards them. 'See.'

'They'll take the weather conditions into account, Bella. If you drive carefully to suit them, you'll be fine. Remember, Station Officer Steele wouldn't have insisted you take your test if she didn't think you were capable. If you become a driver, it helps Station 75.'

'All right, I know what you're saying, Mac, I'll take the test, but don't go blaming me if I fail.'

'You won't fail.' Mac frowned. 'I don't understand why you think you're such a terrible driver when you're not at all.'

Bella sighed. 'I just feel I am. Right at the start, when I first had lessons with Sparky and he used to criticise everything I did, it made me nervous and I got even worse . . .' She paused, feeling her heart beat faster at the memory of those awful lessons, which used to leave her pale and shaking. 'It was much better after you came to Station 75 and took over my instruction.'

'Don't tell him I said this, but Sparky's a bit stuck in the past about some things. I don't think he really approves of women driving.'

'What?' Bella glanced at Mac. 'But we're just as capable of driving as men.'

18

Mac laughed. 'Of course you are. So prove it and pass your test. Show Sparky what you can do, squash his ridiculous old-fashioned notion. You can do it, Bella. Honestly you can.'

'I wouldn't be quite so sure.' She wished she had his faith, but if she drove as badly in the test as she had done so far this morning, then no examiner would pass her fit to drive an ambulance full of casualties, would they?

Bella sat on her hands to stop them shaking as the examiner placed the full pail of water in the footwell of the passenger seat and then carefully climbed in behind it.

'No doubt you'll have heard from other drivers that this pail of water represents your injured patient. Your job is to drive this patient to hospital as smoothly as possible.' The examiner smiled at her. 'A rough ride will spill the water. So when you're ready, turn left out of the gate and we'll be on our way.'

Bella nodded, her mouth dry and heart thumping hard in her chest. She took a deep breath and started the engine. Think of the pail of water as an injured patient, she told herself; that was easy enough – she'd seen plenty of those over the past few months, riding beside them in the back of the ambulance, often holding their hands and talking to them. That was what she had to do: imagine she had a badly injured casualty lying beside her, and it was her job to get them to hospital without hurting them.

The examiner coughed beside her. 'Off we go then.'

'Yes, sorry.' Bella put the car into gear and pulled away

slowly and smoothly, heading for the gate, taking her imaginary patient to hospital.

Everything was going well. Bella hadn't crunched the gears once, she'd driven with the greatest of care, slowing gently and taking bends carefully, and she was pretty sure she hadn't spilt a drop of water from her imaginary casualty. She was just beginning to believe that she could really do this when the sound that Londoners dreaded suddenly began to wail its mournful cry. The examiner started in his seat, knocking into the pail, sending water sloshing out over the side.

Bella eased her foot off the accelerator. 'What would you like me to do?'

'Right, um . . .' The examiner tapped his pen rapidly on his clipboard.

'Do you want to stop and find a shelter, or shall I head back to where we started? Do you have a shelter there?'

'Yes, there's one there.'

'So what should I do?'

The examiner peered up through the window, scanning the wintry blue sky. 'I can't see any planes yet . . . Take us back, please. It's not that far; turn left at the end of this road.'

Bella did as she was asked, doing her best to drive as carefully and smoothly as she had before, all the while aware that the examiner was anxiously peering out of the window looking for planes, tapping his pen on his clipboard and willing them onwards.

'Would you like me to go faster?' Bella asked. 'Though it might not be such a smooth ride.'

'Yes, yes, I think that would be a good idea. You've already proved to me that you can drive very well . . . Oh!'

Bella felt sorry for the examiner as he jumped and groaned at the sound of the crump and thud of bombs falling in the distance. She was used to being out in the middle of air raids, but the examiner, like most people, wasn't.

'Our shelter's over there, not far from the garages.' The examiner pointed to the brick-built structure and Bella turned in through the gates and headed towards it, stopping close by. 'We'll go straight in there and we can sort out the paperwork inside,' he added, quickly opening the door and climbing out. 'You've passed, by the way, very well; you kept a cool head on you after the siren went. I've no doubt you'll be an excellent ambulance driver.'

Bella was smiling broadly as she followed him into the shelter, where she saw Mac sitting on one of the benches waiting for her.

'How was it?' he asked, shuffling along to make room for her to sit down.

'I did it, I passed. Didn't crunch a single gear change, even when the air-raid siren went off.'

'She did extremely well,' the examiner said, coming over and handing Bella the form that he'd signed. 'She kept very calm and didn't spill a single drop of water from the pail, unlike me.' He lifted up one leg to show a wet patch on his trousers.

Bella smiled at him. 'I'm used to being out in air raids, it's our job. You get used to it, and at least the bombs weren't falling nearby today; that's when it gets tricky.'

The examiner held out his hand to her. 'Good luck to you, and well done, your ambulance station has just got itself an excellent driver.'

'Thank you very much,' Bella said, shaking his hand.

She looked at Mac, who smiled at her, his dark blue eyes crinkled at the corners. 'See, I told you you could do it. All you need now is a bit of practice to get used to driving an ambulance instead of just a car, and then you'll be out there doing it for real.'

Bella nodded, trying to ignore the unpleasant thought that had crept stealthily into her mind. If she was now going to be working as an ambulance driver, would Station Officer Steele pair her with an attendant instead of another driver? The thought of not working with Frankie any more took the shine off passing her driving test. She'd spent enough lonely hours when she'd been a maid; she loved working with people like Frankie and Winnie, who weren't just loyal, considerate colleagues but had become dear friends to her as well. Bella hadn't known such friendship since she'd left her home village to go into domestic service in London, but she'd found it again at Station 75 and it was utterly precious to her. She would far rather have stayed an attendant than split up her and Frankie's team. What had she done?

'I would have been quite all right on my own, you know,' Harry said, raising his arm to catch a taxi driver's attention as they walked out of East Grinstead station.

'I know you would, but I wanted to come with you to make quite sure that you're settled in and have all you need.'

Winnie squeezed her brother's arm where she had her own linked through it, her chest tightening as she recalled the moment she'd heard that he'd been shot down during the Battle of Britain, and the agonising hours that had followed until news came through that he was alive but badly burned. Fire had put him in hospital for months, robbing him of his handsome features and leaving his fingers curled into claws.

Harry looked at her and smiled, the tight, shiny skin on his face doing its best to stretch.

'Do you want the hospital?' the driver asked, holding the back door of his taxi open for them.

'That's the place, thank you.' Harry stood back to let Winnie climb in first. 'They've got a bed there with my name on it apparently.'

'They'll look after you all right there,' the taxi driver said as Harry got in. 'Don't you worry.' He closed the back door, then climbed into the driver's seat and started the engine. 'They're a good bunch of fellows being fixed up, too,' he threw back over his shoulder as he pulled away from the station. 'Mr McIndoe lets his patients come out into the town to enjoy themselves.'

'Really?' Winnie asked. 'Is that wise?'

The taxi driver nodded. 'You should know that where you're going, sir, it's no ordinary sort of hospital ward. They do things differently there.'

Harry laughed. 'Good thing too. I've had enough of being in an ordinary one to last me a lifetime. Somewhere out of the ordinary sounds just the ticket.'

The rest of the journey passed in a haze of banter,

Winnie listening as her brother chatted to the taxi driver, grilling him for details of what the patients did when they were out and about in the town.

'Will you drop us at the gate, please?' Harry asked.

Winnie turned and stared at her brother. 'Why on earth do you want him to do that? It's cold today and you don't want to catch a chill.'

'Don't fuss, old girl. I'm not going to catch a chill walking a few yards up the drive. See, I've got my coat on.' Harry's fire-damaged fingers plucked at the thick wool of his blue Royal Air Force greatcoat. 'I just want to walk in there on my own two feet.'

'Right you are, sir.' The taxi driver pulled up at the gate, switched the engine off and jumped out to open the back door.

'How much do I owe you?' Harry asked, fumbling for his wallet, his curled fingers making it difficult for him to reach into his pocket.

'Here, let me help,' Winnie said.

'No, no.' The taxi driver held up his hand. 'There's no charge. It's my privilege to bring you here, and I hope everything goes well for you, sir.'

'No, no, I must pay you,' Harry said.

The taxi driver shook his head. 'I won't take it.'

Harry smiled. 'Thank you, that's jolly decent of you.'

Standing at the gates of the Queen Victoria hospital after the taxi had driven off, Winnie put her arm through Harry's and waited for him to move, but he stood quite still looking ahead, his breath steaming out in visible puffs

24

in the cold air. It was as if he was poised on the edge of something and was taking a moment to prepare himself for what came next.

'Harry, are you all right?' Winnie asked, looking at his face, remembering how it used to look, so handsome and confident; now it was mask-like and she wondered how he really felt underneath it, how he coped with what had happened to him.

He didn't answer for a few moments; then, taking a deep breath, he stepped forward on the path, which had been swept clear of snow. 'Come on, old girl, I thought you were coming with me, not standing there dilly-dally daydreaming. Haven't you got to make sure I'm settled in all right?'

Falling into step beside him, Winnie looked up at his face again. 'You haven't answered my question, dear brother. Are you all right?'

'I'm perfectly all right, thank you.' His grey eyes met hers. 'Just needed a moment to get my bearings, prepare myself . . . ' He paused. 'I must confess to being a bit nervous, but I will be fine.'

'Of course you will. From what the taxi driver told us, this sounds like a wonderful hospital, nothing like the other one you were in. Mr McIndoe will sort you out with some new eyelids and you'll be able to flutter your eyes at young ladies again.'

Harry grinned. 'Yes, we've got that date to go dancing at the Café de Paris when I'm fixed, remember?'

'Of course. I'm looking forward to it very much.'

*

25

Ward Three, where Harry was to stay, was in a long, low hut about fifty yards away from the main hospital. From the outside it looked like any ordinary ward, but from the moment Winnie went inside, she could see that it was anything but ordinary. There were the usual beds along each side, each separated by a locker, but in the middle of the ward stood a grand piano and at the far end a barrel of beer. The patients, some of them in bed, others out of it, were busy doing their own thing. One man was tapping away on a typewriter, another listening to the wireless, another learning to read Braille, but they all had one thing in common: they all bore the scars of fire.

'You must be Harry Churchill,' a smiling nurse said, coming up to them. 'Welcome to Ward Three. I'll do some checks, then get you settled in.' She turned and smiled at Winnie. 'I'll take that for you.' She held out her hand for the small suitcase that they'd brought with Harry's belongings in. 'It won't take long.'

Standing by the entrance, Winnie wasn't sure what to do while the nurse dealt with Harry, but was saved from awkwardness by a badly burned man coming over and pulling out a chair for her to sit on. 'Take a seat while you wait.' He smiled at her as best as he could, his burned face not moving in the way it would once have done.

Winnie smiled at him and sat down. 'Thank you very much.'

'So what's your husband in for then?' the airman said, pulling up another chair and sitting down beside her.

'Oh, Harry's not my husband, he's my brother. He's come for some new eyelids.'

The airman laughed. 'New eyelids, noses, lips – this is the place to get them. He'll be just fine here, we look out for each other. How'd he get fried?'

'Fried?' Winnie asked, and then smiled as it dawned on her what he meant. Clearly these injured airmen didn't go in for euphemisms when talking about their injuries. 'His Spitfire was hit, but luckily he managed to bail out and landed in the North Sea.'

'Well at least he had a soft landing.'

'I see you've met George, one of our resident charmers,' said the nurse, bringing Harry over to where Winnie was sitting.

'Welcome,' George said, standing up.

Harry smiled. 'Thank you. This place certainly looks a jolly sight better than the last hospital I was in. Never seen a ward with a beer barrel in it before.'

'They like to keep us happy.' George studied Harry's face carefully. 'Once you get some new eyelids like mine, you'll be more comfortable.' He paused to blink slowly. 'When's he going under the knife, Toots?'

'Tomorrow morning, I believe,' the nurse said.

Winnie looked at Harry, who appeared as surprised as she did. 'Forgive me for asking, but did I just hear George call you Toots?'

The nurse nodded, smiling. 'Yes you did. The matron at my old hospital would have kittens if she was here to see it, but things are rather more informal here. The patients like to call us nurses by nicknames.'

'She's called Toots because she never stops talking,' George added. 'Who fancies a glass of beer?'

'Don't mind if I do,' Harry said. 'Thank you.' He followed George to the other end of the ward, where they helped themselves to beer and were asked to join in a rowdy card game.

'The taxi driver told us this ward wasn't like an ordinary one, and he was quite right about that,' Winnie whispered to the nurse.

'It's what the boys need. They've been through a heck of a lot and it's not easy for them.' The nurse put her hand on Winnie's arm. 'I can assure you that the treatment they receive is first rate. Mr McIndoe is a top-class surgeon.'

Winnie nodded. 'I think my brother will be quite happy here.'

'And that will make you happy too,' the nurse said.

'Exactly. He'd hate me to tell him this, but I do worry about him. Still . . .' she smiled, watching as her brother threw his head back, laughing at something one of the other men had said, 'I can see he's right at home here already.'

Bella turned the steering wheel, feeling the back of the ambulance sway to one side, then the other, and gradually settle back into its usual gentle rhythm as she straightened up. It was starting to feel normal now, and she was no longer terrified that it was going to tip over.

'You're doing really well.' Mac was sitting beside her in the darkness of the cab. 'You're not going to need much more practice before the boss gives you the go-ahead.'

'I'm just glad there's hardly anyone about.' Bella peered out into the gloomy street. It felt other-worldly driving around in the dark while most of London slept, the city free of the danger of bombs so far tonight. Driving in the darkness of the blackout was tricky, with only the thin, faint sliver of light coming through the covers on the headlamps to guide her. She had to concentrate hard to see where she was going, keeping her speed low, one foot hovering near the brake just in case.

She'd hoped Station Officer Steele might wait until they swapped around to the daytime shift before she ordered Bella to get some practice driving an ambulance, but the boss was having none of it, her argument being that Bella would eventually have to drive at night so she might as well get used to it now. The sooner Mac was satisfied she was safe to drive on her own, the sooner she'd be able to share the driving with Frankie – that was, if the boss didn't swap her to work with someone else. That worry was gnawing away at Bella, knotting her stomach, and she knew she'd have to do something about it. She had to ask. Find out one way or another what was going to happen. She could always try arguing her case, she thought, although once Station Officer Steele had made her mind up about something, she was loath to change it.

'That'll do for tonight. Let's head back to the station.' Mac yawned, stretching his arms out. 'Excuse me. I'll never get used to working shifts; it's hard to sleep in the day.'

'If we're lucky and it stays quiet, you might get a chance to catch up on some sleep back at the station later on. It's such a relief when the air-raid siren doesn't go off around its usual time, but I still feel on edge wondering if it's going to come later.' Bella sighed. 'I always think they're just trying to lull us into a false sense of security, and then *bam*, they come in and catch us on the hop.'

'After last month's big raid, it's a wonder they've got any bombs left.'

'Their munitions factories must be working flat out like ours, I suppose.' Bella braked at the junction and carefully checked for any sign of traffic before turning right, back towards Station 75.

'So much effort is being put into killing people and destroying things,' Mac sighed. 'I know Hitler has to be stopped, but it's a hell of a price people are paying, Germans included.'

'Do you know, I forget sometimes that you're a conscientious objector,' Bella said. 'You get on and do the same as everyone else, and you don't shirk danger, do you?'

Mac laughed. 'Course not. I'm a CO because I couldn't kill another person – my conscience won't allow it – but I'm not against helping in any other way I can.'

'I think you're brave to stand up for what you believe in. I wish my brother was a CO. At least he'd be here in England instead of off in North Africa or wherever he is.' Not knowing exactly where Walter was was frustrating and worrying.

'Have you heard from him lately?'

'He never was the best of correspondents. His letters come every now and then, sometimes none for weeks and then a few together. I just like to know he's all right, that's all.'

'We're nearly back,' Mac said. 'Remember to take it really slowly going through the archway back into the station. There isn't a lot of clearance and it'll be harder to judge in the dark.'

'Oh blimey, maybe you should do this bit for me,' Bella said. 'Can you imagine what the boss would say if I bashed in the side of the ambulance?'

Mac laughed. 'So don't, then.'

Bella dropped down to first gear and slowly turned the ambulance, lining it up as best she could with only the thin beams of light from the headlamps to help, then drove through the archway back into the yard. She winced as they passed through, waiting for the sickening noise of the ambulance scraping the wall, but none came.

'Park in front of the garages so it's ready to go out,' Mac said.

Bella did as he asked and sighed with relief as she turned off the engine.

'See, you did it,' Mac said. 'I knew you could.'

'Well I'm glad you thought so, because I didn't.' Bella put a hand on his arm. 'Thanks, Mac, you're a good teacher. I think we both deserve a cup of cocoa after driving about London in the dead of night. Winnie's promised us toast as well – a feast awaits us.'

Up in the common room of Station 75, Winnie was already making the toast when Bella and Mac went in, holding two long toasting forks, each speared with a slice of the brown National Loaf, in front of the bars of the small electric fire, carefully keeping an eye on them to make sure they didn't burn.

She glanced up smiling, her lips painted with her usual pillar-box-red lipstick and her honey-blonde hair twisted into neat rolls at the nape of her neck. 'We heard you drive in; how was it? Is the ambulance still in one piece?'

'Very funny.' Bella plonked herself down in an armchair close to the fire, holding out her hands to its warmth. 'Of course it is.'

'I'm glad to hear it.' Winnie checked the sides of the bread nearest the fire and, satisfied that they were toasted enough, loosened them on to a waiting plate before re-threading them the opposite way around and resuming the toasting. 'Frankie's in the kitchen warming up the milk for the cocoa.'

Station Officer Steele appeared in the doorway of her office. 'Everything went well, did it?'

'Perfectly,' Mac said, patting Trixie, Winnie's golden-haired little dog, who had left her vigil by the toast and was skipping around his legs in welcome. 'Bella's a very capable driver.'

'Of course she is,' the boss said. 'One who just needs to believe in herself, and now perhaps you do . . .' She raised her arched eyebrows, her brown eyes twinkling behind her horn-rimmed glasses as she smiled at Bella.

Bella shrugged and tried to ignore the warmth rushing to her cheeks.

'Well, you'll soon be taking your turn as driver out on call. Winnie, if there's a spare piece of toast going, please do send it my way.' Station Officer Steele smiled again and, turning on her well-polished lace-up shoes, went back into her office and a pile of paperwork that needed attending to.

'I want to ask her something, so I'll take her the first one that's ready,' Bella said, grabbing a clean plate and taking the piece of toast off the fork that Winnie held out to her. She quickly spread it with scrapings of margarine and jam, each layer equally thin because of rationing, and then headed for the office.

'Here we are, toast and jam, just what you need to keep you going through the night shift.' She put the plate down on the desk.

'Thank you.' Station Officer Steele looked up from the paper she was writing on and snapped the lid back on her fountain pen. 'Please sit down for a moment.'

Bella perched on the edge of the chair beside the desk and prepared herself. The boss only asked people to sit down when she had something to say, something that perhaps they might not like. She decided to get her view in first, argue her case if necessary.

'I was wondering what's going to happen once Mac's happy that I can drive an ambulance on my own.'

'Well you'll work as a driver, of course,' Station Officer Steele said, picking up her piece of toast. 'Please excuse me if I eat this now, I like my toast still warm.' She bit into it and chewed slowly.

'Who will I be partnered with?'

Station Officer Steele swallowed. 'Do you wish to change who you're partnered with?'

Bella shook her head. 'No, definitely not. I want to stay with Frankie. We work well together and could share the driving. I really don't want to change.'

'Well I don't see why you should then.' Station Officer Steele smiled. 'I see no reason to change something that works well.'

'Really?'

'You and Frankie are a good team; it's my job to make sure my ambulance crews are the best they can be, so as long as you keep on working well together, then you'll stay together.'

'Thank you.' Bella beamed at her, feeling the burden slide off her shoulders. 'I was worried you might pair me up with someone else. Frankie's good to work with.'

'Yes, she's come a long way since she first started here and is an excellent crew member.'

'Talk of the devil,' Bella said as Frankie appeared in the doorway with a tray of steaming mugs.

'Are you talkin' about me? 'Ave I done somethin' wrong?' Frankie asked, holding out the tray.

'Not at all.' Station Officer Steele took a mug and cradled it in her hands. 'I was just reassuring Bella that I am keeping the two of you working together as a crew. Now you'll be able to share the driving.'

'Good.' Frankie grinned, her blue eyes meeting Bella's. 'The toast is ready, so you'd better come and get some or there won't be any left.'

Bella stood up and followed Frankie to the door, then turned and looked back at her boss. 'Thank you.'

Station Officer Steele raised her mug of cocoa to her. 'Believe in yourself, Bella, because I believe in you.'

Sitting around eating toast and jam and sipping milky cocoa in the early hours of the morning, surrounded by people who were not just colleagues but also good, dear friends, was something she would never have dreamed of before the war, Bella thought as she leaned against the back of the old sofa and chewed on her mouthful feeling happy and content.

Winnie was sitting at the other end of the sofa, cuddled up against Mac, who had his arm around her shoulders while Trixie sat on her lap, watching each mouthful they took with her liquid brown eyes, willing them to share more toast with her. Frankie sat opposite them in the over-stuffed armchair, her plate of toast balanced on her lap while she sipped at her cocoa. It was one of those rare moments when they had the common room almost to themselves, as many of the crew members had gone to try and get some sleep while they could, making good use of the mattresses that were kept in the rest rooms.

'There aren't many ambulance drivers who've had to cope with an air raid during their driving test,' Winnie said, holding out a titbit of toast crust to Trixie, who took it daintily and swallowed it down without chewing. 'You did magnificently, Bella.'

'You should have seen the poor examiner's face! He knocked the pail of water in fright, slopping it out, but I didn't spill any.' Bella laughed. 'Poor man. We're used to being out in raids; he obviously wasn't.'

'You proved you can drive in 'em, that's for sure, but you've already done it for real anyway.' Frankie's eyes met hers as she referred to that dreadful night when Bella had had to drive their ambulance.

'Well congratulations, Bella.' Winnie held up her mug in salute. 'We knew you would pass.'

Bella chinked her mug of cocoa against Winnie's and then leaned forward to do the same with Frankie and Mac.

'Here's to Station 75's newest driver,' Frankie said.

'Thank you.' Bella took a sip and settled back against the sofa once more.

Mac yawned. 'Excuse me. It's no good, I'm going to have to get some kip. It's been a long day.' He kissed Winnie's cheek. 'Goodnight for now. Wake me up if I'm needed.'

'Go on, sleepyhead.' Winnie smiled at him, squeezing his hand as he stood up. 'Don't worry, I'll come and wake you if you're needed.'

'You make such a lovely couple,' Frankie said after Mac had gone to the men's rest room. 'Though it took you long enough to work out you were made for each other.'

Winnie's cheeks flushed. 'All good things come to those

who wait.' She grinned, her grey eyes twinkling happily. 'And Mac was well worth waiting for.'

'He's a good man,' Bella said. 'I'd never have passed my test without his patience during my lessons. If I'd had to stick with Sparky, I'd have given up.' She took a sip of cocoa. 'Did you get to see your grandad, Frankie?'

Frankie nodded. 'In the end. I nearly missed the train, and then when I got to the 'ospital, the sister told me it wasn't visiting day and to come back on Sunday.'

'What?' Winnie said, looking indignant.

'Luckily a nurse took pity on me and let me in for ten minutes when the sister went on her tea break,' Frankie explained.

'How is he?' Winnie asked.

'Fine. 'E misses being at 'ome, of course, but his leg's mending and 'e's well cared for and safe, and that's what matters. It was good to see 'im again. I miss him.' Frankie smiled, but it didn't quite reach her blue eyes.

Bella leaned forwards and touched her friend's arm. 'Are you all right?'

'Course I am,' Frankie said, busying herself by breaking off a piece of toast crust and tossing it to Trixie, who caught it expertly with a gentle snap of her jaws.

'Only you look a bit … unhappy. Is there anything wrong?' Bella probed gently. 'We might be able to help you.'

'You read too many Sherlock Holmes stories, Bella. You ought to be a detective.' Frankie paused a moment. 'Grandad asked me to do something for 'im, something I don't really want to do but I 'ad to promise. He's worried

37

about what might 'appen in the future ...' Her face clouded and she stopped.

'What do you mean?' Winnie asked.

Frankie sighed. 'Getting injured has scared 'im; he's worried what will 'appen if he gets killed next time.'

'That's not necessarily going to happen, though, is it?' Winnie said. 'None of us know what tomorrow will bring, so we have to enjoy the now. It's no use worrying because there's nothing we can do apart from the obvious precautions – you know, tin hat on and all that.'

'I know.' Frankie twisted her mug round and round in her hands. They all knew about the risks: every time they went out in a raid they could be injured or worse. She preferred not to think about it, because if she did, it might be impossible to do the job she loved. 'He wasn't worrying about 'imself.'

'It's only natural he's worried about you,' Bella said. 'It's what parents do, and he's been as good as a father to you, hasn't he?'

'It ain't me he's so particularly worried about.' Frankie bit her bottom lip. 'It's Ivy. He asked me to promise to look after 'er if anything 'appened to him. I really didn't want to say yes, but I had to, for him.'

Winnie spluttered on her mouthful of cocoa. 'Shouldn't it be the other way around? The grandmother – sorry, I mean *step*-grandmother – looking after the granddaughter?'

Frankie shrugged. 'Yes, for any normal person perhaps, but not for Ivy.'

Bella's eyes met Winnie's. They'd heard enough about Ivy to know what sort of person she was; not one that any decent, kind person like Frankie should be lumbered with caring for.

'I 'ad to say yes, didn't I? I couldn't worry 'im any more. He looked so relieved when I agreed. She's a weight on 'is mind.'

'And now a weight around your neck too,' Winnie said.

'Winnie!' Bella glared at her. 'You did what you had to do, Frankie. Hopefully you'll never have to look after her, but the fact that you've agreed to will have helped your grandfather rest easy, that's all.'

Frankie's eyes met hers. 'I 'ope so, I really do. She'd be a nightmare to look after. Knowing her, she'd do as little as possible and expect everything to be done for her. She's like a parasite on our family, taking all she can and giving nothing. I'd hate to have to be responsible for her.'

'Best to forget about it,' Winnie said. 'Your grandfather will be home before you know it.'

Frankie nodded, and all three of them sipped their cocoa in silence for a few moments.

'How's Harry?' Bella asked.

'Oh, he grumbled about me going with him and then admitted he was glad I had,' Winnie said. 'He was a bit nervous before we got there – rather unusually for him – but I think he'll be all right there. It's not like any other hospital ward I've seen before.'

'What's different about it?' Frankie asked.

'It's got a barrel of beer in it for starters, known as "the barrel that never runs dry". And the patients ...' She paused. 'Poor fellows, they're terribly injured, but they're very upbeat.'

'It will probably help Harry to know he's not the only one who's going through it,' Bella said.

'I agree. He'll be having his operation later today. I'll try and get down to see him in a few days' time. They're very happy for the men to have visitors.'

'They could teach that sister in my grandad's ward a thing or two,' Frankie said.

Winnie drank the last of her cocoa and stood up. 'I'm exhausted. I'm going to try and get some sleep. Are you two staying up?'

Frankie yawned. 'I 'ope we don't get a call-out.'

'Go and have a nap, both of you,' Bella said. 'I'm going to stay here and read for a bit. James sent me a list of books to read from Connie's library, and I'm keen to get started on another.' She looked at Frankie and smiled. 'It's a Sherlock Holmes story.'

Bella had first connected with Winnie's brother James through their mutual love of books, and since then their relationship had grown and blossomed into a romance.

Frankie rolled her eyes and shook her head. 'We'll leave you to solve the mystery while we get a bit of kip.'

'Sweet dreams,' Bella called after them.

Chapter Two

The cobbles of Matlock Street, Stepney, where Frankie had lived all her life, were dusted with a covering of snow, which had fallen in the night and hadn't yet been turned to a dirty grey colour by the tramping of many feet. Frankie smiled to see a familiar figure, dressed in her usual crossover paisley-print pinny, busy outside number 5. Her neighbour, Josie, who kept an eye on all the comings and goings of Matlock Street, was sweeping the snow off her front doorstep, and the pavement either side of it.

'Morning, Josie,' Frankie called out to her, dismounting her bicycle with care. 'How are you?'

Josie stopped sweeping and smiled, her plump cheeks creasing with a welcoming beam. 'I'm fine, ducks. You just come off shift?'

Frankie nodded. 'Thankfully there was no air raid, so it was a quiet night. I went to see Grandad yesterday.'

'What, in Kent?'

'Yes, I caught a train there after my shift and then went straight to the ambulance station when I got back. It took a while to get back to London so there weren't time to come 'ome in between.'

''Ow is he?'

'He's all right.' Frankie smiled. 'I 'ad to go and see 'im to make sure. I miss 'im, but at least he's being well looked after there.'

Josie reached out and squeezed her arm. 'Course you miss 'im, ducks. We all do. It ain't right, Matlock Street without Reg walking around in his smart police uniform.'

'He'll be back as soon as they let 'im.'

'Has Ivy been to see 'im?' Josie put her hands on her ample hips.

Frankie shook her head. 'No.'

Josie tutted. 'I know the 'ospital's not on our doorstep, but . . . ' She left the words unsaid, but Frankie could see from her neighbour's face that she thought Ivy's lack of effort to visit her husband showed a poor attitude, especially as she wasn't working and had no child to care for now Stanley had been evacuated to the countryside.

'That's Ivy.' Frankie shrugged. 'Anyway, I'd better get 'ome.' She started to walk away but Josie came hurrying after her, grabbing hold of her arm.

'Wait a minute, I wanted to ask you something. Did you 'ear what Herbert Morrison said on the wireless about calling for volunteer fire-watchers? If every street has their own fire-watchers then we can protect our 'omes from burning down if they drop incendiaries on us. He don't want another great firestorm like what 'appened last month.' Josie paused while she took a breath and then quickly hurried on. 'There's going to be a meeting at the church 'all about setting up volunteer groups. I'm goin', and I wondered if you'd come with me.'

'When is it?'

'January the thirteenth, at seven o'clock.'

'All right, I'll come, but I'll 'ave to leave before the end if it goes on too late so I can get to work for the night shift.'

'Thank you, ducks.' Josie beamed at her. 'I knew I could rely on you. Do you think Ivy might come too?'

'You could ask her.' Frankie grinned. 'But I'm not sure she'd say yes. You know Ivy.'

Josie nodded, her lips thinning for a moment before she shrugged and patted Frankie's arm. 'Never mind 'er; we need people we can rely on if the worst 'appens and we need to put out fires to save our 'omes.' She paused for a moment. 'What about your young man, would he be interested?'

'Alastair.' Frankie sighed. 'Only if you can magic up another few hours in the day. He's workin' flat out at the hospital. It's 'ard enough for us to snatch any time together. If our shifts coincide, we sometimes get a few minutes when I take casualties into the London, but most of the time either he's workin' and I'm not or it's the other way round. I wish I could see more of 'im.'

'At least he ain't far away, not like some fellows. Being a doctor's an important job.'

43

'I know, it's just it ain't the best time to be courting.' Frankie smiled. 'But it makes the time we do spend together all the sweeter.'

'Where 'ave you been?' Ivy pounced the moment Frankie walked into the kitchen. 'Where were you yesterday?'

Frankie didn't respond and took off her coat and hat, slowly unwinding her scarf and doing her best to ignore the feeling of anger rising inside her. She refused to get into an argument. Ivy wasn't worried about her, she knew, but she wasn't going to say so, knowing that would be the spark to ignite the older woman's temper.

'Well? I asked you a question. Where were you? I was 'ome here all on my own.' Ivy stood, hands on hips, her cold blue eyes blazing in her heavily made-up face.

'I didn't plan to not come 'ome, only the train was delayed and I had to go straight to work or I'd 'ave been late. There wasn't time to get back 'ere and I couldn't let you know.' Frankie felt the teapot and looked inside. It was still warm, but empty apart from the dregs of tea leaves at the bottom. She filled the kettle at the sink and put it on the stove, lighting the gas with a match.

'What train? What are you talkin' about?' Ivy snapped.

'After work yesterday morning I caught a train to Kent. I went to see Grandad in hospital.' Frankie watched the blue flames of the gas licking around the base of the kettle.

'You went to see Reg?' Ivy's voice came out in a high-pitched shriek. 'Without telling me?'

Frankie turned to face her. 'Did I need to tell you?'

'I might 'ave come with you.' Ivy patted her peroxide-blonde hair, which was carefully styled into waves like the Hollywood starlets she spent so much time admiring in *Picture Post* magazine.

'He's wondering why you 'aven't been.'

'Well it ain't easy from 'ere, is it?'

'Ivy, you didn't even go and see 'im when he was still at the London, did you?'

Ivy's cheeks flushed. 'I only knew he was there for a few hours before they shifted 'im.'

'Most wives would have gone to see their 'usbands if they only had a few minutes before they might be moved. They'd have snatched any chance they 'ad.'

'I needed time to get ready . . .' Ivy picked up her packet of cigarettes from the table, then, finding it empty, threw it down again in annoyance. She chewed on her bottom lip before asking, 'How is he?'

'He's fine. They're looking after 'im well.'

'When's he comin' 'ome? Did 'e know?'

Frankie shrugged. 'When they say he can; when 'is leg's mended, I suppose. There's plenty of time for you to go and see 'im in the meantime. He won't be back for some weeks yet.'

Ivy glared at her, then, without saying another word, stomped out of the room and up the stairs. And that is the woman my dear, kind grandad is worried about should anything happen to him, Frankie thought. A cold, self-ish, heartless piece who didn't deserve his love and care.

Frankie hated the thought that she had promised to look out for her if the time ever came.

Winnie was doing her best to ignore the sound of the enemy planes passing overhead. Their engines always ran out of sync, giving the bombers their distinctive steady 'voom voom' beat that even now, months after she'd first heard it at the start of the Blitz, still had the power to make her skin prickle and her heart gallop. She took several long, slow breaths, focusing her thoughts on just doing that and nothing more, because it simply wouldn't do to give in to fear when she might have to go out on call at any moment.

Like everyone else sitting in Station 75's air-raid shelter, she was waiting, nerves taut, for the telephone to ring and for Station Officer Steele to grab it, scribble down the details and then choose who would be going out, leaving the comparative safety of the shelter and venturing out into the midst of the raid.

'Come on, your move.' Mac nudged her arm.

With her attention brought back to the game, Winnie smiled sweetly at him and then swiftly moved one of her draughts pieces, putting one of his in danger. 'There.'

Mac quickly moved his threatened piece and smiled back at her. 'Still no sign of Hooky, then?'

'No, she's taking a while to get over her flu, apparently.' Winnie didn't wish her usual attendant ill, but it was a relief sometimes not to have to work with her; putting up with Hooky's whingeing and general air of unpleasantness often tested her patience to the limit.

The telephone suddenly rang, and as Station Officer Steele snatched it up, there was a subtle change in the atmosphere of the crowded shelter. They all carried on with what they were doing – reading, knitting, playing cards or, in Bella's case, scribbling away in her notebook while Frankie worked on a sketch – but like Winnie, all of them had one ear on what Station Officer Steele was saying.

The boss replaced the telephone receiver, then, without looking up while she hurriedly wrote down the information on a chit, called out, 'Winnie. Mac. You can pair up for tonight and this one's for you.'

'Do you want to drive?' Mac whispered to Winnie as they stood up, abandoning their game. 'Or should I?'

'I will.' Winnie bent down and scooped Trixie up into her arms from her blanket under the bench they'd been sitting on. 'Get the chit and I'll be ready.'

Leaving him waiting to find out where they were going, Winnie went outside. She was halfway across the moonlit courtyard, heading for the garage, when a loud crump from a few streets away made her flinch and Trixie whine as she buried her head in her mistress's neck.

'It's all right, Trix. Everything's all right,' Winnie crooned, stroking the little dog's head as she hurried the final few yards to where her ambulance stood waiting. Was she crazy to be doing a job that sent her out in the middle of an air raid, when most sensible people were safely tucked away in a shelter? Perhaps, she thought, smiling to herself as she climbed into the cab and settled Trixie on the passenger seat beside her before starting the engine; but she loved it anyway.

Pulling out of the garage, she waited with the engine running for Mac to join her, stroking Trixie's silky soft ears.

'It's Bishopsgate,' Mac said, climbing into the cab and slamming the door shut. 'Near the police station.'

'Shouldn't take long to get there.' Winnie put the ambulance in gear, drove under the archway and turned left along Minories, heading for Houndsditch and then on to Bishopsgate. 'Has the police station been hit?'

'No idea. All it says on here,' Mac waved the chit in his hand, 'is what I told you. You know they never give more details than that. We'll find out when we get there.'

'I'm always impatient to find out, you know me.'

Mac reached across and put his hand over hers on the wheel. 'I do, and to know you is to love you.'

Winnie laughed. 'You really are a much, much nicer crew member than my usual partner, have I told you that before?'

'Once or twice, but I don't mind you telling me again. Watch out!' Mac shouted as an incendiary bomb suddenly clattered down on the road a few yards in front of them and started to sizzle, sending a fountain of greenish-white sparks up into the air.

'Bloody hell.' Winnie reacted quickly, swerving the ambulance sharply to the right to avoid it. 'That'll teach me to keep my thoughts on the road and not on sweet-talking. We'd better save the lovey-dovey stuff for after work, or I might end up crashing the ambulance and the boss will never send us out together again.' She glanced quickly at Mac, his face shadowy under the brim of the steel helmet that all the ambulance crew had to wear. 'I do very much enjoy going out on jobs with you, though.'

'Likewise,' Mac said.

Winnie wished they could work together all the time instead of only on the odd occasion like tonight. She'd asked Station Officer Steele about it, but the boss had said no and Winnie had had to bite back her desire to argue with her in case she stopped them working together at all.

It wasn't just because she enjoyed working with Mac so much more than with Hooky; it was also that while she was out with him she could look out for him, do her utmost to keep him safe. Being in love was wonderful, but it brought worries too. Winnie was scared that something might happen to Mac while he was out in a raid, and she'd do everything she could to keep him safe.

Bishopsgate was already busy with rescue workers when they arrived, with rubble and glass strewn across the road and the acrid smell of cordite hanging in the air. Liverpool Street station, adjoining it, had taken a direct hit, and the blast had thrown a passing bus across the road, slamming it into the wall of the police station opposite. The red bus lay there like a wounded beast, crumpled and twisted beneath a wall that was threatening to topple over on to it.

'Wait here, don't go any closer.' An ARP man threw his arm out to bar Winnie and Mac from advancing any nearer the stricken bus with their stretcher. 'They'll bring the injured out to you.' He looked up at the wall the bus had hit. 'It could come down any time.'

'We could—' Winnie began but was cut short by the ARP warden.

'Not now. If you go in there and that wall comes down, we'll be an ambulance crew down, so you stay right here by me and when they get people out then you can do your bit. Understand?'

Winnie nodded, not liking what he'd said but knowing that it made sense. Their job was to take casualties to hospital and not to go wading in trying to rescue the injured when there were people already there who were properly trained to do just that. The ARP warden said the same thing a few minutes later when two more ambulance crews from a different station arrived.

Patience had never been one of Winnie's virtues, so the clattering sound of something hitting the ground not far behind them was a welcome distraction. Turning round quickly, she saw it was another incendiary bomb, but before she could do anything, a volunteer fire-watcher appeared, grabbed one of the sandbags left at a nearby lamp post and efficiently extinguished the bomb before it could do any harm. Herbert Morrison, the minister who'd appealed for more fire-watchers, would be delighted, Winnie thought.

Mac's hand on her arm brought her attention back to the plight of the bus passengers. 'Here they come.' Rescue workers had managed to free some of the injured and were ferrying them towards them on stretchers.

'Now it's over to you,' the ARP warden said, nodding at Winnie and the others.

With practised ease, Winnie got to work, quickly assessing a woman's injuries, while Mac did the same with another casualty.

'Hello, I'm Winnie.' She gently put her hand on the woman's shoulder and smiled at her. 'I'm here to help you. What's your name?'

'Elsie. Elsie Carter.' The woman's face was ghostly pale and she groaned with pain. 'Me leg's hurt.'

'I'm going to have a quick look, all right? I'll be as careful as I can, but please do feel free to shout at me if I hurt you. I really won't mind, I promise you.' Winnie gently felt along the length of the woman's leg, recognising the telltale sign of a bone being out of line. 'Looks like you've got a broken leg. I'll have to splint it to the other one, and then we can get you to hospital, where they can fix it for you properly.'

Taking out some bandages from her kitbag, she carefully bound the woman's ankles together to keep her broken leg as still and supported as possible. Then, with help from Mac, and with the greatest of care, they gently transferred her on to an ambulance stretcher and Winnie tucked a blanket securely round her to keep her warm.

'I just need to fill in a ticket for you and we'll get you in the ambulance. I've got some hot-water bottles in there to keep you warm and snug.'

She took a label out of her kitbag and filled in the details of the injury, time, date and place of incident and the casualty's name, then threaded the label's string through a buttonhole on Elsie's coat.

'There we are,' she said, tucking the blanket back in place and securing the stretcher straps. 'They'll know who you are now and what's happened to you.'

'Thank you.' Elsie managed a smile even though she was clearly in pain.

'You're welcome. Right, we'll get you in the ambulance and whisk you off to hospital.'

Driving to the London Hospital on Whitechapel Road a short while later, with Elsie and three other casualties in the back of the ambulance with Mac, Winnie had to remind herself to keep her speed down. Her instinct was to get them there as quickly as she could. Out on the road, they were still vulnerable to falling incendiaries, shrapnel, and the high-explosive bombs that were still being dropped from the bombers droning overhead, but she had to stick to the regulation sixteen, excruciatingly slow miles an hour. She checked the speedometer: it was seventeen, that would do; she dared not go any faster because if she ruined the tyres on the glass-strewn roads, Station Officer Steele would be after her. New tyres were in very short supply these days.

'How far off are we?' Mac called through the grille behind the cab.

'Five minutes,' Winnie replied. 'Is everything all right back there?'

'Get us there as quick as you can.' Mac's voice sounded strained. One of the men who'd been pulled out of the bus had been in a bad way; he was still alive but badly injured, and getting a patient like him to hospital was

52

always nerve-racking. Winnie desperately hoped that he'd survive the journey and at least have a chance of treatment at the hospital.

By the time they arrived and Winnie opened the back doors, she could tell by the look on Mac's face that they were too late. The blast had already claimed the lives of the bus driver, conductor and several passengers, and now this poor man too.

Winnie put her hand on Mac's arm as he jumped out of the ambulance and began to slide a stretcher out bearing a still-living casualty. 'Are you all right?'

Mac nodded. 'We should be used to it happening by now, but it still gets you.'

'We did our best for him.' Winnie briefly laid her head on his shoulder. 'It's a bloody, bloody war.'

He nodded and kissed her cheek. 'I know. Come on, grab hold of the handles. We need to see to these people, get them into Casualty and get back to Bishopsgate again.'

Winnie straightened up and smiled at him. This was no time for flagging or getting emotional; there was work to be done, people who needed their help. 'Ready then, chin up, stiff upper lip – now's not the time for crumbling.'

She took hold of the handles. 'One, two, three.' They slid the stretcher out and carried the casualty into hospital.

Bella read through what she'd written in her notebook again, but just like the first time, the words failed to sink in, her eyes skipping and skimming over them while her mind stubbornly refused to focus. She usually found writing while she waited for a call-out calming, recording funny anecdotes or incidents that she'd seen that day at Station 75 or elsewhere. It was her way of trying to make sense of wartime, but tonight her mind stubbornly preferred to fret about what was to come. Tonight, for the first time, she would be the one doing the driving when they went out on call. And she was scared.

Giving up writing, she closed her notebook and looked across to where Frankie sat opposite her, completely engrossed in drawing, her pencil deftly adding more strokes to the picture. Knowing how much this helped her friend while she waited, Bella didn't want to disturb her, so she turned her attention to the game of draughts that Winnie and Mac had abandoned when they'd gone out to an incident a short while ago.

She began to idly play around with the pieces, moving them to make patterns on the chequered board, grateful to lose herself in the mindless activity for a few minutes, but when the telephone suddenly rang again and was snatched up by Station Officer Steele, Bella's full attention switched to her boss, her stomach knotting in case this call-out was for her and Frankie.

As usual, her boss replaced the telephone receiver and started to scribble on a chit as she called out the names of those she was sending out. 'Sparky and Paterson.' Bella felt a surge of relief wash through her, but the station officer hadn't finished. 'Blackie and Jones and Frankie and Bella.'

Bella looked at Frankie. 'All of us?'

'Looks like it.' Frankie stood up.

'You'll get the chit?' Bella asked, tucking her notebook and pencil into her dungarees pocket, trying to ignore the way her stomach had started to somersault inside her.

Frankie smiled at her. 'Of course.' She reached out and touched Bella's arm. 'I'll be out as quick as I can.'

Bella swallowed hard and nodded, doing her best to look confident while her legs felt as if the bones had been replaced with jelly.

Leaving Frankie to find out where they were going, she followed the other drivers outside into the night, where the courtyard was bathed in the cold, ghostly mono-chrome of moonlight. She glanced up at the sky, and the sight of a squadron of bombers passing across the face of the almost full moon sent an icy shiver trickling down her spine.

'Must be something big to send out three ambulances in one go,' Sparky said as they hurried towards the garages.

Bella's hands were shaking as she started the engine. With the greatest of care, she drove out of the garage into the courtyard and positioned herself at the end of the convoy of waiting ambulances behind Blackie, with Sparky at its head. She took some slow, steady breaths to try and calm herself down. She could do this, she told herself. She had to do it. Station Officer Steele was satisfied that she'd had enough practice driving ambulances over the past week, when thankfully there'd been no raids and time for Mac to take her out on drives, and of course she'd passed her test in the middle of an air raid, so there really was no reason why she shouldn't be sitting in the driving seat now, waiting for Frankie and the instructions about where to go. The only doubt came from Bella herself, and she had to stop that right now, she told herself sternly.

Drumming her fingers on the steering wheel, she silently urged Frankie to hurry up. The waiting and not knowing where and what she was going to wasn't helping. This was nerve-racking enough, and now she was out here she wanted to get going, but the uncertainty was part of the job and she should be used to it by now, never being able to predict what a shift would bring, what incidents they'd be sent to.

Her relief at Frankie's arrival was short-lived.

'It's Bank station,' Frankie said, climbing in and shutting the passenger door. 'Must have had a direct hit.'

Bella felt sick. 'But hundreds of people would be sheltering down there, wouldn't they?'

'Yes. There must be a lot of casualties to send all of us out.' Frankie sighed. 'Nowhere's safe from the damn bombs.'

Ahead of her, Blackie's ambulance started to move off behind Sparky. Trying not to think about what they were going to, Bella put her ambulance in gear and followed behind, out through the archway and on to the road, turning left along the Minories. She was glad that Sparky was leading the way tonight; with him navigating to the incident, it was one less thing for her to think about. She could have done it herself, of course, as Station Officer Steele made sure all her drivers had an almost encyclopaedic knowledge of Station 75's patch. They had to know their way around without the aid of street signs, as these had all been taken down, and even if they had still been there, it would often have been impossible to see them in the blackout. For tonight, Bella was thankful for any help she got.

Sparky led them the most direct way he could, but it still took them longer than usual to reach Bank station, as so many of the roads around the area continued to be blocked to traffic after the huge raid at the end of December. When they finally got there, the sight that met them made Bella feel utterly sick.

In the middle of the road, which was usually a busy intersection where several streets met, a place that she and Winnie had bicycled across just a few hours earlier on their way to Station 75, was a huge, gaping crater, its yawning shadowy depths visible in the moonlight.

'Look at that!' Bella was shaking. 'Could anyone survive that?'

'I 'ope so.' Frankie touched her arm.

Bella looked at her friend, glad of her calmness and unflinching support. It helped so much to have Frankie by her side at times like this. They had a job to do, and sometimes it was hard and they saw sights that came back to haunt them in their dreams, but if there were injured people down in that hole, then they needed help to get to hospital and it was her job to do it.

Carrying a stretcher each, with their bags of first-aid equipment slung across their shoulders, they made their way to where the other crews from Station 75, and some from other ambulance stations, had gathered near one of the entrances to the Underground.

'The bomb exploded in the booking hall,' an ARP warden explained. 'The blast ripped through the tunnels and down to the platform; it's killed a lot of people sleeping on the stopped escalators . . .' He paused, wiping his sweating brow with his sleeve. 'The rescue workers and stretcher-bearers have gone down to look for survivors, and will bring up any injured. The poor blighters on the escalators didn't stand a chance, but further down they might have been luckier.'

'We're ready for them when they get here,' Sparky said, looking around at the other Station 75 crew members, who nodded their agreement.

Everyone was quiet, listening out for any sound of approaching footsteps coming up from the depths, but it was hard to hear anything with the cacophony of noise – the drone of bombers still going over, the crump of bombs exploding, shrapnel clattering to the ground and the clanging of fire-engine bells as they raced along.

As the anxious minutes ticked by, Bella's mind tormented her with the thought of what it must be like down there. She didn't like the Underground at the best of times – going down into tunnels below the earth always felt unnatural to her – so she rarely used it, much preferring to walk, go by bus or on her bicycle. Since the Blitz had started, she'd only ever spent one night sheltering in an Underground station; that had been last autumn, when they'd been out at a dance at the Lyceum and had fled to the safety of Aldwych station when the sirens had wailed. She remembered not liking it but at least thinking it was safe, and had been distracted by helping out when a woman had gone into labour and Frankie's Alastair had delivered the baby there on the platform.

Now people had died sheltering in a place they'd believed would protect them. It seemed that nowhere was completely safe from the bombs.

'Here they come,' the ARP warden suddenly said as the sound of voices and the beams of torches emerged from the dusty, darkened station. 'The ambulance crews are here waiting,' he shouted to them.

Moments later, several teams of stretcher-bearers emerged carrying out the injured from the depths of the Underground, and the crews quickly got to work. The injured were gently transferred on to the ambulance stretchers, and while Frankie examined the unconscious man on her stretcher, Bella quizzed the men who'd brought him up.

'What happened to him? Where did you find him?' she asked.

'He was in the tunnel not far from the platform; probably got hit by something. There's a lot of tiles come off – must have knocked him out,' one stretcher-bearer explained.

'Are there many injured down there?' she asked.

He nodded, his eyes shaded under the brim of his steel helmet. 'Plenty. It's going to be a long night. We'll go and get some more for you.'

'Did you hear that?' Bella said, crouching down beside Frankie.

'Yes, so we'd better hurry up and get this man ready and loaded into the ambulance before the next lot arrive,' Frankie said, tucking a blanket around the injured man while Bella filled in the label, adding an X for his name as he wasn't awake to tell them.

As more casualties were brought to the surface, news of what had happened down in the depths of the station filtered up. Bella was dressing an old woman's head wound when she overheard a stretcher-bearer talking to Sparky.

'There's more dead on the tracks. The blast blew people off the platform straight into the path of an incoming train.'

Bella stopped winding the bandage around the woman's head and stared at the stretcher-bearer, who was now helping Sparky transfer an unconscious casualty on to an ambulance stretcher. Swallowing hard, she turned her attention back to her job, her eyes locking with those of the old woman, who gave the briefest nod of her head in confirmation of what they'd just heard. Tears filling her eyes, Bella carried on with the dressing, trying hard to suppress the horror of the tragedy. It wasn't fair what had happened down there, not to innocent people seeking shelter, but then war wasn't fair. It didn't play by any rules; she'd seen enough working as ambulance crew to know that much was true.

By the time their fourth patient had been loaded into

the ambulance and Bella was back in the driver's seat, her earlier worry over driving had paled into insignificance. The terrible destruction that had befallen Bank station and the innocent people sheltering there had put it all into perspective, and as she started the engine she was just grateful that she was doing something to help the victims of the bombing.

Coming off duty the next morning after a prolonged, exhausting shift, Bella had one thought in her mind: Bank Underground station. She wanted to go back and see it in bright daylight, when the ghostly moonlit shadows would have been burned away, to see if it was really as bad as it had seemed.

'I'm going to have a look at what's left of Bank station,' she said to Winnie as they pedalled slowly away from Station 75, both of them achingly tired after a busy night ferrying casualties to hospital.

'What on earth do you want to do that for? After what you've told me, I'm not sure I'd want to go and see it so soon,' Winnie said.

'It's on our way home and I ...' Bella paused. 'I want to see it in daylight. I want to put my mind at rest ... otherwise it's going to give me nightmares.'

Winnie reached her arm across between their two bicycles and touched Bella's arm briefly. 'All right, if you're absolutely sure about this, we can try to have a look, but I doubt we'll get through; the road will be shut and they won't let us past.'

'We can get off and walk as close as we can. We've got our steel helmets on – they'll help us look like we should be there.'

'God bless Station Officer Steele for insisting we wear our helmets,' Winnie whispered to Bella a short while later. They'd managed to walk through a roadblock on Cornhill after leaving their bicycles leaning in a doorway further back down the street. Even Trixie being carried in Winnie's arms didn't catch anyone's attention, as the rescue workers and ambulance crews were too busy with their own work to pay them much heed. Wearing their helmets, they blended in perfectly.

As they walked past the Royal Exchange, their boots crunching loudly on the broken glass strewn across the road, the full horror and scale of the damage came into view and brought them to a halt.

'Bloody hell,' Winnie said. 'I didn't expect it to be this big.'

Bella grabbed hold of her friend's arm as she stared at the gaping hole in the road, the tarmac buckled and broken like huge jigsaw pieces around the edge of the crater. Inside its gaping mouth, steel girders were exposed to the air, bent and twisted by the force of the blast. Something that had seemed so solid and strong was pulverised and crushed.

'It's worse than I thought. God have mercy on the souls of those poor people who died sheltering down there.' Her voice cracked and she bit her bottom lip while she composed herself. 'But they weren't safe, were they?'

Winnie put her arm around Bella's shoulders, hugging her friend to her. 'No, they weren't, but it would have been terribly quick. They wouldn't have known what was happening, they wouldn't have suffered.'

Bella leaned her head on Winnie's shoulder. 'I hope not. Some of them were killed while they slept on the escalators; there wasn't a mark on them, so the stretcher-bearers said.'

'Come on, let's go home, we need some sleep.' Winnie linked her arm through Bella's.

'Last night's shift wasn't a good one, was it?' Bella said as they walked away. 'January the eleventh is a day I won't forget in a hurry.'

Chapter Three

Station Officer Violet Steele felt dreadful. Her head was pounding and she was shivery cold, her skin feeling as if it was being pricked by thousands of icy needles. She wrapped her thick woollen cardigan more tightly around herself and adjusted her scarf to try and stop any little draught sneaking its way on to her neck. Whatever had got into her today was making her legs and arms feel heavy and achy. She wiggled her fingers and toes, trying to rid her limbs of the leaden throbbing that had been there since she'd woken up this morning. But it didn't help.

Sighing heavily, she slumped forward in her chair, folded her arms on her desk to make a pillow and rested her head on them. A few minutes' rest and she'd be all right, she told herself. She closed her eyes and didn't even try to fight the welcoming sense of drifting into a sleepy haze that quickly engulfed her.

'Are you all right?' She was vaguely aware of a voice and the feel of a hand on her shoulder. She turned her head away from whoever it was who had come to disturb her and tried to ignore the voice, but it came again. 'Are you feeling unwell?'

Annoyed at being dragged back, she opened her eyes and immediately snapped them shut again as a black dizziness spun her head around. 'I'm ...' Her voice came out in a strange croak from her sore and scratchy throat.

'It's fine, take your time. I'm just going to check your temperature; you look like you're burning up.' A soothing, cool hand rested gently on her forehead. 'No doubt about it, you've got a fever. How do you feel?'

With a supreme effort, Station Officer Steele pressed her hands down and pushed herself up into a sitting position. When she opened her eyes, Winnie was peering down at her, a look of concern on her face. She felt a warm, wet nose nudge at her hand and saw that Trixie was there too. The little dog jumped up, resting her forelegs on her arm.

'Hello, Trixie.' She ruffled the dog's ears, then looked at Winnie, doing her best to sound normal when she felt anything but. Being upright was requiring a great deal of effort when all her body wanted to do was lie down and sleep. 'I'm fine.'

'No you're not.' Winnie put her hand on Station Officer Steele's arm. 'You look awful, if you don't mind me saying so, and you've got a high temperature.'

'It's just a headache, that's all.'

'Let's add that to the list of symptoms then: fever, head-ache, what else?'

'What's going on?' Bella appeared at the office doorway, her brown eyes wide with concern. 'Are you all right, boss? You don't look very well at all.'

'That's just what I've been telling her,' Winnie said. 'I don't think you are well enough to be at work. We'd better take you home; you need to be tucked up in bed.'

'No, I need to be here, I . . .' Station Officer Steele stopped talking, the effort of trying to carry on becoming too much.

'It's probably flu, it's going round. Hooky's still off with it,' Bella said. 'We'll take you home in one of the cars and I'll stay with you and look after you.'

Could she go home? Station Officer Steele wondered. The thought of being tucked up in bed, warm and snug under her eiderdown, with the chance of drifting off into a blissful sleep, was so tempting. But what if there were incidents to deal with? There needed to be some-one in charge. 'I can't leave the station. If there's an air raid . . .'

'We can manage, we know what to do,' Winnie said. 'Look, how about if Sparky takes charge. I'll go and ask him.' She went out of the door into the common room, returning a few moments later with Sparky, who was carrying a half-eaten sandwich.

'You needn't worry about the station, boss,' Sparky said kindly. 'We're all more than capable of doin' what needs doin'. If Winnie stays by the phone, she can answer any calls and write them on the chit – 'er 'andwriting's better than mine and I expect her telephone manner is as well. I can organise who goes where and make sure all the vehicles are prepared. You don't 'ave to worry about a thing – just go 'ome and concentrate on getting better.'

'Me in here?' Winnie glared at Sparky. 'I don't know if that's a good idea.'

That could work, Station Officer Steele thought; she trusted them both to do a good job and look after Station 75 and its crews. 'Oh, I think it is. I think you'd do an excellent job, Winnie.' Tears suddenly pricked the back of her eyes. 'I do feel rather dreadful.'

'Right, that's sorted then. Winnie, you take over in the office and I'll go and organise Mac to get a car ready to drive you 'ome,' Sparky said.

'We shouldn't use an ambulance station car, not for personal use. I'll—' she began.

'Don't be so stubborn,' Sparky said. 'How else are you going to get 'ome? You're in no state to catch a bus or go on the Underground. Just accept our 'elp, will you? You'd do the same for us.'

'And I'll go with you and stay to look after you,' Bella said.

'But your job is here. If there's a raid, we need all the crews ready,' Station Officer Steele protested.

Bella put her hands on her hips. 'I'm coming with you and will stay with you as long as you need me. If there's a raid and Sparky needs me, then he can telephone your flat.'

Station Officer Steele sighed, holding up a hand in submission. 'Very well then, I know when I'm beaten. Bless you all for being such caring people. Thank you.'

Ten minutes later, she was tucked up in blankets in the back of one of the ambulance cars and Mac was driving her home, with Bella beside her in the back.

'If there's an air raid, you will make sure everyone gets to the shelter, won't you, Mac?' she asked.

His eyes met hers in the driver's rear-view mirror. 'Of course. You're not to worry about Station 75; we'll manage. All you need to do is focus on resting and getting better.'

She nodded and closed her eyes, and must have drifted off to sleep, because the next thing she knew, someone was gently shaking her shoulder to wake her.

'We're here.' Bella's voice seemed to come from far away, and it took a supreme effort to rouse herself and open her eyes.

She didn't protest when they helped her out of the car, and with Mac supporting her on one side and Bella on the other, they walked her inside and almost carried her up the stairs to her flat.

Slipping into a bed warmed with hot-water bottles by Bella a short while later was absolute bliss. Station Officer Steele sighed as she let her body relax and sink into the soft cocoon of sheets, blankets and eiderdown, while her head rested on the downy feather pillow. She closed her eyes and quickly drifted off to sleep.

*

Winnie stared at the telephone on Station Officer Steele's desk. Would it ring? And when? She picked up a pen and fiddled with it before putting it down again. Glancing up at the clock on the wall, she sighed when she saw that the hands had only moved on a couple of minutes since the last time she looked; it was still only three o'clock in the morning. Pushing her chair out noisily behind her, she stood and started to pace up and down the small office like a caged animal. Trixie, who was sleeping on a cushion in the corner, opened her eyes, looked at her and then shut them again.

'Sorry, Trix. You get some sleep while you can.' Winnie bent down to pat the little dog's head, then straightened up and started to prowl around again, peering at notices pinned up on the wall in an effort to distract herself.

When Sparky had suggested that she take charge of the office, she never thought it would be like this. She'd never seen Station Officer Steele looking anything other than calm and composed in here when they were on shift, apart, of course, from the occasions when she'd had to chastise Winnie over some misdemeanour or other. The boss didn't pace about waiting for that phone to ring. Winnie glared at it. It remained silent. She was grateful that the air-raid siren hadn't gone off tonight, because that would have made things so much worse.

'What are you doing?' Winnie turned at the sound of Mac's voice. He was standing in the doorway looking at her, his eyebrows raised. 'You look upset – what's happened?'

'Nothing.' Winnie did her best to smile and went over and wrapped her arms around him, resting her head on his chest. 'I'm just a bit on edge waiting for the telephone to ring with an incident.'

Mac kissed the top of her head. 'There's nothing you can do to make it ring. Getting anxious about it isn't going to help. Just be glad things are quiet. I'll go and make you a cup of cocoa, shall I?'

Winnie nodded. 'In a minute. Tell me about the boss first. Is she all right?'

'She is now. Bella's got her tucked up in bed with hot-water bottles and is there to look after her. The boss didn't give in without a fight, though; she's certainly dedicated to her job.'

'And she's put her trust in us, so we mustn't make a mess of things.'

'Don't worry, Winnie, we're not going to.' He looked down at her, his dark blue eyes meeting hers. 'Station Officer Steele has trained us to run this place like a well-oiled machine. We can manage without her until she's better.'

'It's just the waiting for it to ring . . .'

'Winnie, for goodness' sake sit down and read a book, or knit some of your socks or something – anything. Just keep nearby so you can get the telephone when it rings . . . *if* it rings.' Mac hugged her tight and then let go. 'I'll go and make some cocoa.'

She stared at him for a moment and then smiled at him. 'There was I thinking Station Officer Steele was bossy, but it seems you can be too. In fact, perhaps you should take over and *I'll* go and make the cocoa.'

'Oh no.' Mac held up his hand. 'The boss left you in charge of the telephone, not me. Nice try at wriggling out of it, though.' He winked at her and went off to make the drinks.

'How about a cup of tea?' Bella asked, plumping up the pillows before helping Station Officer Steele lie back against them. It was late afternoon and her boss had just woken up.

'Yes … please.' Station Officer Steele's voice was scratchy and hoarse and she still looked pale and sickly.

Bella laid her hand gently on her patient's forehead. 'You're not as hot as you were, that's good. Do you fancy anything to eat? Some toast, porridge, anything?'

Station Officer Steele shook her head. 'Not hungry. I'll get up in a minute or two.'

'No you won't. You're still far from well and need to rest. You must keep drinking. I'll go and make some tea. Stay right where you are.'

'I never thought you were quite so bossy,' Station Officer Steele said croakily. 'Now Winnie …'

'Well we could always swap over: she could come and look after you …'

Station Officer Steele held up her hand in surrender.

Bella laughed. 'Don't worry, I'm staying here. Winnie's not the nursing kind; she wouldn't last very long looking after you. I'll be right back with your tea.'

It was strange being back in Station Officer Steele's flat, Bella thought as she put the kettle on the cooker to boil. It reminded her of the time she'd stayed there after she'd been bombed out at the start of the Blitz. That was only a few months ago, but it felt like a lifetime. Things had changed so much since then: many parts of London looked different now, so many buildings gone or damaged, and its people were used to a strange existence, their lives ruled by the wail of the air-raid siren and their nights spent in uncomfortable shelters hoping they would still have a home to go to in the morning.

The image of her former home, reduced to a pile of brick dust and rubble in which her dear, sweet landlady had been killed, flashed into Bella's mind, along with the awful, gut-wrenching pain it had brought her. But she wasn't the only one who had lost her home – there were plenty of others – and she was perfectly fine now, living in a lovely home with Winnie and her godmother. She had a lot to be thankful for.

She had just poured the hot water on to tea leaves in the china pot when there was a knock at the door. Leaving the tea to steep, she went to answer it.

'I come bearing gifts.' Winnie held up a basket as Bella opened the door. 'How's the patient?'

'Still very poorly, but she's had a good long sleep, which will help her.' Bella stood to the side and ushered Winnie in. 'I'm just making tea – would you like some?'

'Yes, please.'

Bella led the way into the kitchen and took another cup out of the cupboard. 'What are these gifts, then?'

Winnie put her basket on the table and began to unpack it. 'Connie sent this.' She held out a jar of honey. 'She recommends the boss has a spoonful in a hot toddy with some whisky.'

'Thank you.' Bella took the jar that Winnie's god-mother had so generously given. Connie had never met their boss, but it was typical of her kind nature that she'd wanted to help.

'I've brought you some clean clothes,' Winnie added, 'and these.' She held out a bundle of letters, smiling. 'Came for you this morning all the way from ... some-where in North Africa.'

Bella took them and looked at her brother's familiar writing on the envelopes.

'At last. I'd begun to think he'd given up writing to me. Thank you for bringing them, I'll read them later.'

'I wasn't sure how long you'd be here, and I thought you'd like to read them as soon as possible.'

'I'd better get this tea ready.' Bella poured out three cups and put Station Officer Steele's on a tray along with the jar of honey and a spoon. 'Come and say hello.'

Station Officer Steele sat up straight as Winnie walked into her bedroom. 'How's Station 75? Did you ...' She started to cough.

'You shouldn't be thinking about work.' Bella put the tray down on her bedside cabinet.

'Everything was fine. We only had one incident all night and it was dealt with by the book.' Winnie patted the boss's hand. 'You just focus on getting better.'

Station Officer Steele looked hard at Winnie, her eyes seeming to search her face for any sign of untruth, but finding none, she was satisfied and rested back on her pillows once more. 'I'll be back tonight.'

'No you won't!' Bella and Winnie chorused, and then looked at each other and smiled.

'You're in no fit state to get up, let alone work an eight-hour shift,' Bella said. 'Sparky and Winnie can keep things running smoothly for another night. Come on, drink this cup of tea and then you can have a spoonful of the honey Connie sent to ease your throat.'

'I'm the one who usually tells people what to do,' Station Officer Steele grumbled.

'Indeed you are, but right now you need to concentrate on getting better,' Bella said, handing her a cup.

Later, when Winnie had gone home and her patient had fallen asleep once more, Bella finally got to read her brother's letters. As usual, they were short, but they did at least give her an idea of what life was like for him. He glossed over what he'd actually been doing, probably because he knew the censor would just black it out, and talked about the things that bothered him, like the heat, the dust and the flies. It was a world far removed from the English countryside where he'd grown up. Holding the letters in her hand, Bella sent up a silent prayer that the heat, dust and flies would be all Walter had to deal with; better those than the wrath of the German army.

'Cooeee! Only me. Are you ready to go?'

Ivy looked up from the *Picture Post* on her lap as Josie walked into the kitchen of number 25 Matlock Street. 'Ready for what?'

'The meeting at the church 'all – remember I told you, Ivy, it's about becoming volunteer fire-watchers.'

Frankie, who was drying up the last of the plates by the sink, watched as Ivy shrugged. 'Do you want to come with us?'

Ivy turned to look at her, her eyes narrowing. 'No.'

'Why don't yer, it'll be fun,' Josie encouraged her.

Ivy shook her head. 'Why would I want to do that? It ain't for me.' She went back to reading her magazine.

Josie looked at Frankie. 'You're still comin', ain't yer?'

'Of course, I'll be ready in just a moment.'

'Wait till yer see what I've got outside.' Josie smiled enigmatically.

Outside, Frankie stood and stared at what was parked in the street near number 25.

'What d'yer think?' Josie spread her arms wide, as proud as if she were showing off a Rolls-Royce.

Frankie walked around the vehicle, admiring the way her neighbour had cobbled together an old wooden soap box on a pram chassis; inside it were metal pails of sand, a spade and a rake, and painted on the side in white splotchy letters, 'Matlock Street Fire Engine'.

'I think it's marvellous, Josie.'

'Well it's a start. I'm 'oping to learn a lot more tonight, but at least if we've got this with our equipment in it, we'll be ready for any incendiaries that fall 'ere. They can be put out before they get a chance to burn the street down.'

The church hall was packed with local people who'd answered Herbert Morrison's plea to become volunteer fire-watchers. Josie had left Matlock Street's fire engine parked outside and pushed her way through to the front row, where she'd found them two empty seats. Now she sat quite still, her eyes fixed on the fire officer as he explained all they needed to know about organising their own street fire parties.

'You never know where incendiaries will fall; some streets may get them, others not. The best defence against them is if fire parties not only look after their own street, but go to the aid of the neighbouring streets if they need help.'

'I ain't leaving my street to go and 'elp the next one,' a man shouted from the back of the hall.

Josie swung around in her chair to see who had spoken.

'What would happen if *your* street was badly hit and you needed more help, and a fire service pump couldn't get there for some time? Wouldn't you be glad of your neighbouring street's help then?' the fire officer reasoned.

Josie leapt to her feet, hands on her ample hips. 'I ain't goin' to stand by and do nothin' while the next street burns. Ain't there been enough destruction already without makin' it worse 'cos you won't 'elp other people?' She pointed back in the direction of the man who'd spoken, waggling her finger at him. 'You ought to be ashamed, thinking only of yerself. The best way of beating Hitler is workin' together. Hands up if you're willin' to 'elp your neighbouring street?'

A show of hands went up, with nearly everyone nodding in agreement with Josie. She beamed back at them, satisfied, and then sat herself down again, her cheeks flushed.

Frankie squeezed her arm. 'You told 'im. I'm proud of you.'

'Mean-spirited bugger,' Josie whispered.

'Well thank you very much, madam.' The fire officer smiled at Josie. 'Looking out and being prepared to help your neighbouring streets is an extra backup.'

'Hear, hear,' a woman's voice cried from the back, and everyone laughed.

'The next thing I need to tell you about is the forms that each fire-party leader will be given. They'll need to be filled in with date, time and address of any incident you have to deal with. Keeping records is an important part of the job.'

After he'd explained about the paperwork, the fire officer moved on to talking about equipment.

'Fire-watchers will be issued with one of these.' He held up a white steel helmet with a black band painted around it and the letters 'FG'. 'Madam, if you'd like to come and model this for me,' he said, nodding to Josie.

'Me?' she said, her cheeks flushing pink.

'Yes please.' He waited for her to get out of her seat and join him at the front, and then gently placed the hat on her head so that the letters were positioned at the front.

'You'll notice that these helmets have a higher dome than most steel helmets; that's to allow for some indentation should something hit you on the head.' He took a dark blue armband with the words 'Fire Guard' printed on it out of his uniform pocket and handed it to Josie to slip on over her sleeve. 'And the final piece of fire-watcher's uniform, such as it is, is an armband to identify you to the public.'

'Give us a twirl then,' someone shouted from the back of the hall, and Josie obliged, twirling with her hands on her hips like some fashion model, making the hall erupt with laugher.

'Now for the equipment,' the fire officer said. With Josie helping him to hold up the various items to show the audience, he quickly ran through what they would need to fight fires: spades, rakes, scoops, pails of sand and the important stirrup pump. 'I could stand here all night telling you how to use these, but the best way for you to learn is to do it yourself. So after hearing what I've said, those of you who still want to sign up, please follow me outside for a demonstration.'

Almost the entire audience followed the fire officer outside and watched as he showed them how to put out a fire using a stirrup pump, with another volunteer pumping water out of a pail while he directed the hose at a small fire he'd started on the ground in the garden of the church hall.

'Now it's your turn, working in threes, one of you holding the hose, another pumping and the other keeping the water level topped up.'

'Come on.' Josie grabbed hold of Frankie's hand. 'And will you join us to make up a three?' she asked another woman Frankie recognised from the neighbouring street. The woman nodded and they collected their equipment ready to start.

'The most effective pumping is thirty-five double strokes per minute,' the fire officer called once everyone was organised.

'Hear that?' Josie asked Frankie, who was poised ready to pump while Josie held the hose and the other woman was in charge of keeping the pail topped up.

'Make sure that you all have a go at each job,' the fire officer said.

The next five minutes passed in a blur, Frankie using the stirrup pump first, then swapped to handling the hose and finally working at keeping the water level topped up. It felt good to be working as a team to battle the fire. It was fun, but she knew that going out in raids tackling actual fires would be much harder and far more nerve-racking. Being part of Matlock Street's fire party would challenge her in a different way to working as an ambulance driver. She hoped that when it came to it, she could do what was needed and not let Josie and Matlock Street down.

The fire officer blew his whistle to stop them. 'Very

good, well done, everyone. Next we'll move on to practise dealing with incendiaries.'

'So,' Frankie said as she and Josie walked back home after the meeting had finished. 'How does it feel to be the official fire-party leader of Matlock Street?'

'I weren't expecting that. You'd 'ave been a much better choice.'

'Not at all. You have the enthusiasm and the fire engine.' Frankie looked back at the cart Josie was pulling behind her; it had been much admired by the fire officer after they'd finished practising how to put out incendiaries safely. He'd been impressed by Josie's commitment and had suggested that she take on the role of fire-party leader when they were organising people into street fire parties near the end of the meeting. 'I ain't here all the time so I couldn't do it, though I will 'elp when I'm around.'

'It's funny, 'ere I am lookin' forward to the next raid in case there are incendiaries to put out. It's a whole new way of looking at air raids. We'll all 'elp each other even if it's not in our street.'

'You'll be wonderful, Josie, unflappable and very capable. You put that man to rights in the meeting and no mistake.'

'I did, didn't I?' Josie grinned. 'I was shakin' like a leaf inside but I wasn't goin' to let that selfish bugger get away with it. That ain't the East End way. We 'elp each other round here.'

*

'Incendiaries are falling like bleedin' rain tonight. Frankie's on fire-watch duty up on the roof for an hour, and I'll stay out in the yard doubling up picket duty and fire-watching,' Sparky said hurriedly. 'I'll leave it to you to organise who goes where. All right?'

Winnie stared after him, getting no chance to protest before he disappeared out into the night, leaving her in charge of the telephone in Station 75's air-raid shelter. So much for her just answering the phone and neatly writing out the chits. She smiled at a few of the crew members who'd stopped what they'd been doing to listen to Sparky, trying her best to appear confident when she felt anything but.

Images of the last time she'd been given responsibility for others flashed into her mind. She'd made a complete hash of being sports captain at school, mixing up practice times and team lists. The school had lost its previously unbroken triumphant record at the interschool games and her captaincy had been swiftly removed. She'd been given responsibility and failed miserably, only all that mattered then was missed hockey practice or coming second in the hundred-yard dash. Being in charge at Station 75 was far more important: here, people's lives were on the line. Winnie's insides quaked in fear; she couldn't afford to mess up this time.

The telephone suddenly started to ring, its sound seeming to bounce off the brick walls of the confined space, waking Trixie from her sleep on the blanket underneath the desk. Winnie snatched the receiver up and listened hard to the faceless voice on the other end giving out instructions, and hurriedly wrote the address down on the chit, mentally going over it again and again to make sure she'd got it right. A mistake now could cost someone their life.

Carefully replacing the receiver, she thought about who to send out to the incident. The decision weighed heavily on her. She was aware that she was deciding her fellow crew members' fates – she could be sending them into danger, into the path of a bomb . . . She remembered how distraught Station Officer Steele had been after the Jones sisters had been killed on their way to an incident. How did the boss cope with doing this all the time; did she feel the same way?

'Winnie?' Mac grabbed her hand. 'I'll take this one.'

She stared at him for a few moments. 'I . . .'

He smiled at her and squeezed her hand. 'I'll go and start the engine. Hooky can come with me.'

Winnie nodded, watching him go out the door.

The sound of someone clearing their throat made her turn around. Hooky stood there looking at her, her arms folded and a pained, haughty expression on her face. 'I knew it would be like this, favouritism setting in.'

Winnie frowned at her. 'What do you mean?'

'I notice you're not sending Frankie; no doubt she'll be the last to go, with you using your position to keep your friend safe,' Hooky sneered.

A flame of annoyance flared up in Winnie. Hooky had been very off with her ever since she'd returned to work and found out that Winnie had been put on phone duty while Station Officer Steele was off ill. Her crewmate clearly resented her temporary promotion and would be delighted if she wasn't up to the job. But the stubborn streak that ran through Winnie like writing through a stick of rock wouldn't let her fail.

'Now look here, Hooky, it was Mac who suggested you, not me. I will allocate incidents as fairly as Station Officer Steele does. Right now, Mac's out there waiting for you.' She wished that he hadn't volunteered to go; at least while he was here in the shelter she knew he was safe and wouldn't have to worry about him. But it was exactly the sort of thing he'd do to help her out when she'd been floundering at the unwanted responsibility. She handed the chit to Hooky, smiling sweetly. 'So get to it, then. Good luck.'

Hooky held the piece of paper as if she'd been given a hot potato, then, without saying a word, she stalked out of the shelter, slamming the door behind her.

Several other crew members who'd been watching gave Winnie sympathetic smiles before returning their attention to whatever they were doing to pass the time. They'd all fallen foul of Hooky at one time or another, and most of them had very little to do with her. At least while she was manning the telephone she didn't have to go out on call with the woman, Winnie thought; every cloud had a silver lining.

'Take no notice of Hooky,' Frankie said to her a few minutes later when she brought her a cup of tea. 'Everyone knows you'll be as scrupulously fair as the boss is about sending crews out.'

'Thank you.' Winnie smiled at her friend. 'I don't know how the boss keeps so calm doing this.'

'You're doing a fine job, Winnie,' Paterson, Sparky's crewmate, called from behind his newspaper.

Frankie laughed. 'See.'

Tonight's shift was turning out to be a busy one. The telephone had hardly seemed to stop ringing, and Winnie had had to send so many crews out to incidents that she'd gradually got over the worry about who to choose; everyone was getting a turn at going out tonight. So when it had finally gone quiet for a while, she was relieved. The all-clear hadn't gone yet, but the need for ambulances seemed to have died down.

'Cup of tea?' Mac, who'd returned from his incident, handed her a steaming mug, which she gratefully wrapped her hands around; tea seemed to be the fuel that kept them going through the long nights. 'Are you all right?'

She nodded. 'Thanks for earlier. It was a bit of a shock Sparky putting me in charge of who goes where. It's not what I agreed to when the boss went off sick.'

'He wouldn't have done it if he didn't think you'd manage, and clearly you have.' He raised his mug to her in salute. 'It's busy out there tonight.'

'It's gone quiet now, thank goodness.' Winnie took a sip of tea.

Mac picked up the telephone receiver and listened to it, frowning, then passed it to Winnie. She put it to her ear and listened. There was silence, no hum as there was usually. Her stomach felt as if it had just plummeted to her feet.

'Bloody hell, the line's gone down.' How could she have been so foolish as not to check? Control could have been ringing for help but not getting through, and all the while there were casualties needing to get to hospital. She had to act quickly; there could be lives at risk.

When the phone line had gone down before, Station Officer Steele had always sent someone to run to the nearest ARP post and ask them to telephone Control to let them know what had happened and receive instructions through them.

'I'm going to the ARP post.' Winnie stood up.

'You can't!' Mac said. 'You've been told to stay here coordinating the crews; you need to stick to that order. Whose turn is it to go out next?'

Winnie looked at the list she'd kept to make sure that every crew member took their turn at being sent to an incident. 'It's Taylor and Pip.'

Hearing their names, the two volunteer crew members looked up from their game of cards. Winnie quickly explained the situation to them.

'I'll go first,' Taylor said, checking the strap of her steel helmet was secure. 'I'll let them know what's happened and get instructions, and then Pip can go next. It'll be like a relay race.'

Some relay race, Winnie thought. Sending crew members out in an ambulance was bad enough, but in the open with incendiaries and shrapnel falling, it could be a dance with death. 'For goodness' sake be careful,' she said.

Taylor grinned at her. 'Don't worry, I will be.'

Winnie watched her go out of the door and glanced at her watch. It was almost half past two; how much longer would the raid go on for? How long would it take Taylor to run to the warden's post along the Minories? Five minutes at the most.

Mac took hold of her hand. 'She'll be all right, try not to worry.'

'I can't help it!' she snapped and immediately felt awful. 'I'm sorry, Mac, I feel so anxious every time I send someone out. I thought I was getting used to it, but . . .'

'It's our job to go out. You do it without a thought when the boss tells you it's your turn. You never question her decision, do you?'

'I know, but that feels different.' She shrugged. 'Being the one giving the orders . . . it feels so much more responsible.' She grinned at Mac. 'And I'm not always the most responsible of people, am I?'

'You can be if you need to be.' He squeezed her hand. 'You've done really well stepping into Station Officer Steele's shoes.'

'I'll be glad when she comes back and I can return to just being an ambulance driver.' She sighed. 'I thought my job could be hard at times, but I'd rather that than this any day.'

'They say you never know what it's truly like for someone until you walk in their shoes.'

'I'm just finding that out!' Winnie glanced at her watch. Five minutes had passed since Taylor left.

'Drink your tea before it goes cold,' Mac said. 'I'm going to see if Sparky wants to come in for a break. He's been out there for ages.'

'Be careful.' Winnie watched him go, feeling that she was turning into the mother hen of Station 75 and wouldn't be able to relax until all the crew members were back safe and sound.

It was another long five minutes before Taylor came bursting in through the door, her cheeks flushed with the cold air.

'Look at this, it's still hot.' She held out a piece of shrapnel.

Winnie was tempted to snap at the young woman for stopping to pick it up when she should have been hurrying as quickly as she could to get back to the safety of the shelter, only she knew that she'd very likely have done the same thing herself.

'Have you got any incidents for us?' she said, doing her best to keep her voice calm.

'Yes, just the one.' Taylor handed her a piece of paper. 'If Pip goes to the ARP post now, she can stay there till they get another one in.'

Winnie nodded and set about writing out a chit for the incident and instructing the crew whose turn it was to go out to get ready.

*

Half past seven seemed to take an eternity to arrive that morning. Winnie had never known a shift to last so long, not even during the worst raids, when she'd been out in the thick of it rescuing casualties. Being confined to Station 75, and being the one responsible for sending the crews out was emotionally exhausting and she felt completely wrung out, her nerves stretched like the wires in the piano up in the common room. The shift had passed successfully, with all incidents properly dealt with and every crew member back safe and sound.

Her admiration for Station Officer Steele had grown even more in the past few hours; the woman was a marvel. As she collected her bicycle from the garages, with Trixie settled into the basket in front, she sent up a silent prayer that her boss would be back at work very soon.

'That was quite delicious.' Station Officer Violet Steele put her spoon into her empty bowl and leaned back in her armchair. 'Thank you.'

Bella smiled at her as she took the tray off her lap. 'It's what my mother always used to make for us when we'd been ill; she said it would help us get better.'

'I think she was quite right.' Station Officer Steele sighed happily, enjoying the simple act of sitting in her armchair by the fire with her legs and arms free of the gnawing ache that had plagued them, and a sense of strength slowly returning to her body. It was a joy to be upright, rather than sprawled out in bed. She was very rarely ill, and having to give in to the dreadful flu hadn't been easy with so much work to be done, but in the end she'd simply had no choice.

'Are you warm enough?' Bella asked.

'Perfectly, thank you.' She patted the blanket tucked around her legs and wiggled her slippered toes that rested on the stone hot-water bottle Bella had put there for her. 'You've looked after me so well, you've been very kind and patient. Thank you, my dear, I do appreciate it very much.'

Bella shrugged. 'I know you'd do the same for me, in fact for any of us at Station 75.'

'I appreciate you putting yourself out to stay here.' Station Officer Steele leaned forward and patted Bella's arm. 'I know I'm not the easiest of patients. I'd rather be doing the looking after than receiving it.'

'Well nobody can help getting the flu, and it's been nice to be back here again – reminded me of when I stayed with you before.'

'I remember when your brother stayed a night too. Have you heard from him lately?'

'Nothing for weeks, then Winnie brought me a pile of letters from him the other day. He seems all right as far as I can tell; he's never been the best of correspondents. The heat, dust and flies seem to be his problem.'

'Goes with the territory.' Station Officer Steele smiled at the young woman. 'My sister, Lily, found the heat hard to bear when she first arrived in Singapore.'

Bella looked surprised. 'I didn't know you had a sister.'

89

'Oh yes, she's much younger than my brother and me; she was a surprise addition to our family when I was fourteen. Her husband's in the RAF and was posted to Singapore two years ago. Lily and her two daughters followed on a few months later. I still miss them.'

'How old are your nieces?'

'Ten and twelve now. I used to see as much of them as I could when they were still in England. They'll have grown a great deal since I last saw them. That's them, in the last photograph my sister sent at Christmas.' She nodded to one of the photo frames on the sideboard.

'Can I see?' Bella asked.

'Of course, bring it over.'

Bella handed it to her.

'That's Helena,' she pointed to the taller girl, 'and this is Grace.' She smiled at the younger girl's beaming face. 'And my sister and her husband, George.' Looking at their dear faces, she wished she could see them again. 'I suppose the one good thing about them being so far away is that they're out of this war, safe from the bombing, so I'm thankful for that. It's Lily who worries about us over here, wanting to know what's happening.'

'She must be proud of what you do,' Bella said.

Station Officer Steele batted the idea away with her hand. 'I'm just doing my job, same as everyone else, pulling together to get us through.' She sighed. 'It's much worse this time because the war's on the home front, not just abroad. No one has escaped and nowhere is completely safe.' She shook her head and then smiled at Bella.

'Look at us talking about the war; let's move on to a more cheerful subject. You choose.'

Bella looked thoughtful. 'Can I ask you something?'

'Why not?'

'Well . . . we've wondered – that's Winnie, Frankie and me – what you did before the war. You know about us, but we have no idea what you did.'

Station Officer Steele raised her eyebrows and looked at Bella, whose beautiful brown eyes suddenly looked worried.

'You don't have to tell me if you don't want to; we were just being nosy.'

She laughed. 'So I'm the object of your curiosity, am I? It probably won't surprise you to learn that I was a grammar school teacher, English and history. When war was declared I signed up for the ambulance service thinking my experience driving ambulances in the Great War was more use to the war effort than trying to stuff the brains of young girls with Shakespeare and the important dates of the Civil War. I can go back to all that when this is finished.'

'Did you always want to be a teacher?' Bella asked.

'That was what I wanted to do before Father died.' She sighed. 'Then I had to forget that and go into domestic service.'

'It was a job I could do, and very well as it turned out, but it wasn't my dream.' She paused as the image of her beloved fiancé filled her mind. Being with him, being his wife had been her dream, but it hadn't happened: he'd been shot during the Great War, leaving a hollow sadness inside her that she still felt even now. She took a deep breath and went on. 'It's been a good way to earn a living. I have no complaints.'

'Where did you teach?'

'In Exeter, not too far from where I grew up.' She paused, aware from Bella's eager expression that she was keen to know more. 'My father was the rector of a rural Devon parish not far from the sea, so my brother, sister and I had an idyllic upbringing. My father came out of retirement and went back to the same parish when the present incumbent left to join the army. My mother is there with him, busying herself helping with evacuees.' She smiled. 'So there you have it, mystery solved. I'm a rector's daughter and a teacher who now runs an ambulance station in London. Nothing so terribly interesting. What did you think I'd done?'

'Well ... Winnie thought you must have done something where you had to be bossy.' Bella suddenly clamped her hand over her mouth, her face flushing.

Station Officer Steele laughed. 'She was right there. I was a bossy teacher, I had to be, and it's taught me how to deal with young ladies.' She raised her eyebrows, smiling at Bella. 'One of the things I like most about my job is working with you all, even if some of you do the silliest things. I have secretly laughed about many of Winnie's scrapes – her soaking poor Frankie on her first day was priceless – only I can never let on to her how funny I find them.' Her lips twitched at the thought of what she'd seen from the common room window that morning. 'So please don't tell her.'

'Don't worry, I won't. We'd never hear the end of it, and Winnie needs no encouragement, though she's been much more sensible of late.'

'Indeed. I think Mac has a good steadying influence on her. I'm not sure I would have been happy about her helping Sparky to run the station a few months ago, but now ... she's proven herself many times over. The war has brought a new side to Winnie, and to all of us.'

Chapter Four

'We're nearly there.' Winnie struggled to open her eyes, wanting to ignore the voice and drift away again into blissful sleep. 'Come on, Winnie, wake up.'

With a mighty effort, Winnie opened her eyes. It took her a few moments to recall where she was, her head resting on Mac's shoulder, his arm around her in the railway carriage compartment whose gentle rocking had lulled her to sleep. Smiling at him, she sat up and stretched. 'How long have I been asleep?'

'Nearly the whole way. You dropped off not long after we left Victoria,' Mac said. 'Thought I was going to have to kiss you awake like Sleeping Beauty.'

'I'm sorry, I haven't been terribly sociable, have I?' She did her best to stifle a yawn. 'I'm still tired.'

'That's not surprising when you've been awake all night. You didn't get to have a lie-down like the rest of us.'

'Station Officer Steele never gets to do that.' Winnie had dropped off a few times sitting at the boss's desk, but what little sleep she did snatch was fitful, as she was always on edge waiting for the telephone to ring. Luckily last night, like the past couple of nights, had been quiet, and the air-raid siren hadn't gone, but she still couldn't rest just in case a call came in.

The train started to slow, pulling into East Grinstead station.

'The fresh air will wake me up.' Winnie stood up and slid open the door into the corridor that ran the length of the carriage. 'I couldn't not come and see Harry, not when I'd promised to visit him.'

'You're a sight for sore eyes,' Harry called out to them as soon as he spotted them walking into Ward Three. 'Come and admire my new eyelids.'

'Hello, Harry. Let's have a look then.' Winnie bent down for a closer inspection, and as she did so, Harry fluttered them at her and she burst out laughing. 'They are absolutely lovely, you must be delighted with them.'

'I certainly am, they make a lot of difference. It's so wonderful to be able to close my eyes properly again.' Harry held out his hand to Mac. 'Good to see you, Mac.'

Mac shook hands. 'And you. How much longer are you going to be here?'

'Not sure. The boss, Mr McIndoe, wants to do some more ops on my face but will give me a break before he does them. I'm looking forward to getting out and about again.' He turned to Winnie. 'And it would be good to go out dancing. I've been dreaming about going to the Café de Paris and dancing the night away. Are you still coming with me, old girl?'

Winnie smiled at him. 'Of course I am.'

'Though you might want to catch up on some sleep first.' Harry stared at her, his grey eyes fixed on hers. 'If you don't mind me saying, you're looking awfully tired. Have you been keeping her out on the tiles, Mac?'

'Chance would be a fine thing. We've been on the late shift for the past week or so and Winnie's had to take over Station Officer Steele's job.'

'Ah, your headmistressy boss. What's happened to her?' Harry asked.

Winnie told him about Station Officer Steele's illness and how she'd been asked to step into her place. 'I never knew how exhausting her job is. I can't rest at all in case the telephone rings, and having to make decisions about who goes where and does what is such a worry. I'd rather be a driver any day than be in charge.' Harry started to laugh. 'What's so funny?'

'You being put in such a responsible position, the girl who hates rules and regulations.'

Winnie did her best to keep a straight face, fighting back the urge to laugh that tingled and twitched at her lips. 'I'll have you know, dearest brother, that I have done an extremely good job and been very conscientious, haven't I, Mac? It hasn't been easy but I haven't given up.'

Mac smiled at her. 'You've done an excellent job, Winnie.'

'See!' Winnie finally let her mouth smile widely. 'Though I fully admit that I'm not what you'd call a naturally responsible person and I'll be jolly glad when the boss comes back and I can go back to driving an ambulance.'

'Well it just proves what you're capable of if you try. Mother will be delighted to hear about it,' Harry said.

'Oh I haven't told her,' Winnie said. 'And I wasn't planning to, either.'

'Well you should.' Harry looked at Mac. 'Have you met our dear mother yet?'

Mac shook his head. 'Not yet.'

'She doesn't know about him, Harry, you know that, I hope you haven't gone and said anything to her.'

'Of course not, old girl, calm down. So you're still keeping Mac a secret then; how long are you going to keep that up?'

Winnie sighed. 'For as long as I choose. You know what she's like. If she gets wind of our relationship, she'll do her best to split us up one way or another. I'm not going to subject Mac or myself to her vindictiveness. She wants me married to that awful Charles Hulme, but that will never, ever happen.'

'She's bound to find out sometime,' Harry warned her.

'Not from me she won't, unless I decide to tell her, and not from you either, I hope, not if you know what's good for you.' Winnie narrowed her eyes and gave him a hard stare.

Harry held up a hand. 'Never fear, she won't hear it from my lips, you can be assured of that.' He looked at Mac. 'Does your mother know about Winnie?'

'Yes.' Mac smiled. 'But I think my mother and yours are quite different, from what I've heard.'

'Then you are indeed a fortunate man,' Harry said.

Opening the door of the pie-and-mash shop, Frankie breathed in deeply, savouring the delicious smell, her stomach rumbling loudly in response.

'I heard that – you need to get some food inside you,' Alastair said in his warm Scottish accent before planting a kiss on her cheek.

'Yes, Doctor.' Frankie grinned at him. 'Happy to oblige.' Her gaze met his striking blue eyes. 'It's good to see you.'

Alastair squeezed her hand. 'And you, Frankie. Us both working shifts isn't making it easy to see much of each other. I miss you.'

'I know, I miss you too, but we're together now, so let's make the most of every precious moment.' Seeing so little of Alastair over the past weeks had been frustrating, but Frankie kept reminding herself that they were lucky compared with many couples who were separated by thousands of miles of land and sea, not knowing when they'd see each other again. She smiled at him. 'Pie and mash all right for you?'

'Absolutely.'

*

'I needed that,' Alastair scraped the last few crumbs of pastry and drops of parsley liquor from his plate. 'It's been a long day.'

Frankie smiled at him, finishing off her own meal, her stomach now feeling pleasantly full. 'You need to go straight 'ome and get some sleep after this. You look tired.'

He ran a hand through his brown hair, making it stick up. 'I am, but being with you is good for me. I enjoy it very much, and if I hadn't met you, I may never have ventured into a pie-and-mash shop.'

'Then you would have missed a treat, so it's just as well we met.' She put her knife and fork down on her empty plate. 'Don't they 'ave pie and mash where you come from?'

'Alas no, but we do have neeps, tatties and haggis. Pie and mash is nearly as good as them, but not quite. I'll take you home one day and you can try them for yourself.'

'I'll 'old you to that, Dr Munro. We seem to have a habit of introducing each other to new things. I'd never been to a fancy classical concert before I met you, remember?' She still thought about the day they'd been to see Myra Hess playing in the basement of the National Gallery; it had opened up a whole new world for her. Girls like her from Stepney didn't usually go to classical concerts; a band playing in a local dance hall was the most live music she'd ever experienced before then.

'Of course I do.' He reached out his hand and took hold of hers. 'And I've been wanting to take you to another one ever since, but our shift patterns haven't allowed that.' He frowned. 'I want to spend a whole day with you, Frankie, not just snatched meetings or a quick word when you bring casualties into the London.'

Frankie squeezed his hand. 'I know.' She sighed. 'I'll ask the boss if I can work an extra shift and earn a day off, and you see if you can sort somethin' out too.'

'I'll do my best and let you know. So tell me more about your visit to your grandfather.'

Frankie fiddled with the knife on her plate. It was only ten days ago that she'd gone to see him, but now it felt like an age since she'd rushed to catch the train to Kent and walked through the snowy lanes to the hospital, where he'd asked her that question.

'Frankie?' Alastair's beautiful Scottish voice interrupted her thoughts. 'He is all right, isn't he? You said he was when I saw you bringing patients in last week.'

She looked at him, her eyes holding his. 'Yes, 'e's fine. Like I told you, 'e's on the mend and well cared for.'

Alastair arched his eyebrows. 'Something's wrong, isn't it?'

Frankie nodded. 'He asked me somethin' I couldn't tell you about the other day.' She sighed. 'He's worried what will 'appen to Ivy if he gets killed.'

'He won't, he's much safer where he is.'

'He means when he gets 'ome and is fit enough to go back out on the beat again.' She paused, biting her bottom lip and looking down at the chipped Formica table. Taking a deep breath, she returned her gaze to Alastair. 'He asked me to promise to look after Ivy if he dies.'

Alastair's eyes widened. 'What did you say?'

Frankie's throat suddenly thickened and she had to fight back the rush of tears that threatened to spill over. 'I 'ad to say yes.' She looked down at the table. 'I couldn't let him down – it was important to 'im and I could see how worried 'e was.'

Alastair took both her hands in his. 'Oh Frankie, you're a dear, sweet, kind person. He shouldn't have asked you, it wasn't fair – he knows what Ivy's like.' He shook his head. 'Your grandfather's a decent man and he feels responsible for his wife, but he shouldn't have put it on your shoulders. Ivy is a grown woman and is quite capable of looking after herself if she wants to. Do you want me to speak to him about it?'

'No!' Frankie shook her head. 'I'm sorry, I shouldn't 'ave snapped at you, but I gave 'im my promise and I can't go back on it now.'

'You'll probably never have to honour it anyway, and it made your grandfather feel better.'

She rubbed her hand across her forehead. 'But imagine what it would be like if I did 'ave to do it. It would be like dragging a heavy weight behind me.' She sighed. 'And think about when Stanley comes 'ome. I wouldn't be able to trust her not to be unkind to 'im again.'

Alastair squeezed her hands. 'Try not to upset yourself over something that might never happen.'

Tears smarted in Frankie's eyes. 'I know, but it's tormenting me. I can't 'elp worrying about it.'

'Just take one day at a time. We've got enough to deal with each day as it is without worrying over the what-ifs.

Whatever happens, Frankie, I'm here for you as much as I can be.' Alastair smiled, his kind eyes meeting hers.

'Thank you.' Frankie glanced at the clock on the wall. It was almost time to go or she'd be late for work. She sighed and stood up.

Alastair followed her outside, wrapping his arm around her shoulders, and they walked a little way along the street till they reached the corner where they'd have to head their separate ways, Alastair to the doctors' home to get some much-needed sleep and Frankie to Station 75 to start her shift.

Stopping, Alastair turned to face her and took her in his arms. 'Even if I can't see you as much as I want to, I'm always thinking of you.' He hugged her tightly, resting his chin on the top of her head where it leaned on his chest. Frankie wished they could stay like that for ever.

After giving him an extra squeeze, she loosened her arms, stood on tiptoes and kissed him on the mouth. 'And I'm thinkin' of you too.' She smiled at him. 'Take care, Alastair.'

'You too.'

Frankie walked off towards Station 75, turning to look back when she reached the end of the street. Alastair was still standing there watching her. She waved at him and he waved back, and Frankie thanked her lucky stars that she'd met him. The war had done a lot of harm to so many people, but it had also brought some good things too, and without Alastair, her life would have been the poorer.

*

'I want to offer you a promotion, Winnie. I was very impressed by the way you handled things here while I was ill – you kept a calm head and did everything the way it should be done. You were an asset to the station. So ... I would like you to become deputy station officer.'

Winnie stared at her boss, not quite believing what she'd heard. 'Me? Deputy station officer?'

'That's correct. I think you would make an excellent one. You have experience of being out in raids and you've had to deal with my work in here. I would be very happy to know I had you to rely on if I needed you again. You'd keep working as a driver for the rest of the time.'

Winnie shook her head. 'I appreciate the offer, I really do, but honestly, I don't think I'm the right person for the job. If you're looking for a deputy, then Sparky or Mac would be a much wiser choice than me.'

'Oh, I beg to differ with you there, Winnie. Both of them have their strengths, but I need someone I can trust in here.' The older woman threw her arm wide to encompass her office. 'You have the aptitude for dealing with incoming calls and sending out crews.' She smiled. 'You've proved to me that you can do it and are perfect for the job.'

Winnie sighed. She wished the boss hadn't even considered such a thing; the thought of having to take over again and deal with telephone calls and decisions made her stomach quake. She'd been lucky to get through it while Station Officer Steele was ill, but she was in no hurry to repeat it.

'Thank you for offering, I'm truly surprised, but honestly, I really don't think I'm the right person for the job.'

Station Officer Steele reached out and touched her arm. 'I understand this must come as a shock to you.' She smiled. 'After all, there have been quite a few instances when I've had to speak to you in here about various misdemeanours, such as squirting poor Frankie with the stirrup pump on her first day here.'

Winnie felt her cheeks grow warm at the memory of that day. 'That's precisely why I'm not right for the job; a deputy station officer would never do that.'

Station Officer Steele's brown eyes were twinkling behind her owlish glasses. 'I know, but you've changed, Winnie. The past few months have been difficult and you've risen to the occasion magnificently to become a crew member I am truly proud to have at my station.'

'I like my job driving an ambulance,' Winnie said.

'I know, and you would keep doing that most of the time, but if needed, you could step in and help me. Just think about it, will you?'

Winnie sighed. 'All right, but I don't think my answer will change.'

Bella looked across to the statue of the Duke of Wellington sitting astride his horse in front of the Royal Exchange, where a banner declaring 'Dig For Victory' was strung across its tall columns. Everything over there looked normal, but in front of the building, what had once been a busy intersection was now opened up into a massive crater, and looking down into it, she could see the remains of Bank station. She bit her bottom lip, fighting back the tears that threatened to spill over as she remembered the night of the raid three weeks ago, when she and Frankie had been sent here to help take the many casualties to hospital.

'They're nearly ready.' Winnie nudged her arm.

'What?'

'To cross the bridge, of course.' Her friend looked at her. 'Are you all right?'

Bella nodded. 'It's still a shock seeing this ... I know we've been watching it being cleared up over the past few weeks, but it still makes me shiver when I think of all those people down in the Underground imagining they were safe.'

Winnie tucked her arm through Bella's and hugged it close. 'It doesn't pay to think about some things too much, you know. We see a lot of truly awful things doing our job that in normal life would be ... Well, wartime puts a different slant on things, and we mustn't let ourselves get too upset by it or it will all become too much.' She smiled sympathetically. 'Let's look on the bright side. We're here to celebrate the opening of a wonderful new bridge that will make our journey to work much quicker, since we'll be able to go right over the crater instead of detouring around.'

Bella nodded. 'It just gets to me sometimes, all the destroying and killing and maiming.'

'That's what happens in war. It's not nice, but what choice do we have? We have to keep on going, not let it get us down, keep a stiff . . .'

'Upper lip,' Bella finished for her. 'You're a real tonic, Winnie, did you know that?'

'That's a new one for me. I can't recall being called that before, but thank you, I appreciate your sentiment, Bella.' Winnie squeezed her arm again. 'I'm just looking out for you – you're my darling friend and it makes me sad to see you downhearted.' She lifted her chin and took a deep breath. 'So come on, old girl. And look, here comes the first lorry.'

They watched as the first of a convoy of army lorries, all packed to the brim with smiling, waving soldiers, drove out on to the bailey bridge that now spanned the width of the crater, clapped and cheered by the crowds that had come to see the opening.

The Royal Engineers had spent weeks working here, first clearing away the debris, then putting down strong steel girders and beams to support the bridge. Bella and Winnie had watched their work with fascination, often stopping to see what was happening on their way to or from Station 75. It was only fitting that the men who had worked so hard to build the bridge should be the first ones to cross when it opened.

'See, some good rising out of the ghastly stuff,' Winnie said, clapping enthusiastically as more lorries rumbled across the crater.

*

Opening the front door of 25 Matlock Street, Frankie could hear her grandad's voice in the kitchen and the sound of it brought tears rushing to her eyes. He was home at last. He'd been away for nearly eight long weeks since he'd been injured at the end of December, and how she'd missed him. Home hadn't been right without him. It had felt emotionally cold and heartless with just Ivy there spouting her malice and selfishness.

Taking a deep breath, she blinked away her tears and pasted a smile on her face as she went into the kitchen, her forced smile immediately turning into a genuine one at the sight of Grandad sitting at the table in his usual place, holding court, while Ivy flitted around looking like the perfect wife as she refreshed the teapot. She'd clearly made an effort: the table was spread with a clean cloth, and there was a plate of his favourite currant buns.

'There you are!' his deep voice boomed. 'I was thinkin' you'd be 'ome from work soon.' He held out his arms to Frankie and she bent down and kissed his cheek.

'Welcome 'ome.' She smiled at him, her eyes locking with his. 'It's good to have you back.'

'I'm delighted to be 'ere, I can tell you. They were very good at the 'ospital, but there's no place like yer own 'ome.'

'How's your leg?' Frankie asked, noticing the walking stick hooked over the edge of the table beside him.

'Comin' on a treat. I've got to walk with this,' he tapped the crook of the stick, 'for a week or so, but I'll soon be back on the beat.' He smiled.

'You'll need to take it easy, Reg. Your leg'll need building up again before you can go walkin' miles each shift,' Ivy said, fitting the tea cosy over the brown earthenware pot.

'I'll be fine, don't worry about me, Ivy. I ain't finished with policing yet, not while there's still breath in my body and they need me.'

Ivy put a hand on his arm. 'You shouldn't go doin' any more than you need to, Reg. Keep to yer own beat from now on – remember, it was goin' off doin' more what got you in trouble in the first place.'

Frankie remembered her shock at discovering him injured in the City of London, far off his usual beat. If he'd stuck to his own patch, he wouldn't have nearly been killed. He wasn't even supposed to be on duty that night when London had burned, just days after Christmas. For once, she agreed with Ivy's sentiment.

'There's a war on, Ivy. 'Ow could I just sit there in the Anderson and do nothing while London was being pounded? I couldn't, could I? My conscience wouldn't 'ave allowed it,' he said. 'And I'll carry on doin' what's needed.'

Ivy opened her mouth to speak, but shut it again as her husband reached out and took hold of her hand. 'The best thing for everyone would be for the war to be over, but that ain't likely to 'appen just yet. We've got to keep fightin' in any way we can. I know you worry,' he said gently, squeezing her hand, 'but I'll be all right. They ain't goin' to get me.'

Ivy shrugged, doing her best to smile, but Frankie noticed that although her lips might have curved into what passed for friendliness, it wasn't reflected in her eyes, which were hard and cold. She didn't like not getting her way, but Frankie knew her grandfather wouldn't be shifted: he would do what he could to help, and she could only hope that he didn't get hurt again, or worse.

'Do you know what I thought about while I was in 'ospital?' Grandad asked. 'Fish and chips with mushy peas.' He smiled. 'Dreamed about it, even. Shall we 'ave some for tea?'

'If you like. I'll go and get it,' Frankie offered.

'No, sit yourself down, you've only just got back from yer shift. Ivy'll go, won't yer?'

Ivy glared at Frankie for a moment and then nodded.

'Thank you.' Her grandfather smiled at his wife. 'We'll get the plates ready for when you get back.'

As soon as Ivy had gone, slamming the front door on her way out, Grandad stood up and began to pace slowly up and down the room, using his walking stick to support him. 'Got to keep movin', so they told me at the 'ospital.'

'Do you 'ave to go back on the beat?' Frankie asked.

He stopped walking and smiled at her. 'Course I do, as long as they need me. I know Ivy ain't 'appy about it, but as I said, there's a war on and we've all got to do our bit. Being a policeman's what I know, what I love doin'.'

'It nearly got you killed.'

'Driving your ambulance ain't the safest of jobs, is it?'

109

'I know, I know.' Frankie held up her hands. 'I worry about you, that's all.'

He nodded. 'And vice versa. We'll just both 'ave to be careful, won't we?'

'I always am,' Frankie said. She didn't want to argue; she knew there was no point. He wouldn't change his mind and she didn't want to spoil his homecoming. For now, everything felt right in her world. Grandad was home and she was happy.

'Winnie, Mac. The boss wants to see you both in 'er office.'

Winnie wiped the oily dipstick clean on an old rag and returned it to its place in the engine, then turned to look at Sparky. 'What for?'

He shrugged. 'I don't know, I'm just the messenger. You ain't done anything daft lately, 'ave yer?'

'Not as far as I know.' Winnie looked at Mac, who was doing the checks on his own ambulance. He shook his head and shrugged at her.

'Well go on then,' Sparky urged them. 'Don't keep 'er waiting. If it is bad news, you don't want to make it any worse.'

'Keep an eye on Trixie for me.' Winnie nodded to where the little dog was curled up asleep on the driver's seat in the cab of her ambulance.

Sparky nodded. 'Will do.'

'Come on.' Mac wiped his hands and together they headed for the stairs leading up to the office.

'Feels like school all over again, being suddenly summoned to the headmistress's office,' Winnie said, tucking her arm through Mac's.

'Did that happen a lot?'

Winnie looked at him and grinned. 'A time or two, most of them thoroughly deserved, I might add. Rules and I have never really seen eye to eye, especially stupid ones that seem like they're there just to make things unpleasant for those who have to follow them.'

'I wouldn't like to have had to teach you.' Mac held the door open for her.

'Thank you very much, oh sweetheart of mine.' Winnie pretended to look hurt by his remark.

'Am I wrong in thinking you were the best-behaved, most attentive pupil in your school, then?'

'Well ... yes. I was very good and well behaved in games, though.' Winnie grinned at him and went up the stairs, Mac following on behind.

'Ah, Winnie, Mac, do come in, please,' Station Officer Steele said as they arrived at her office door. 'Take a seat.' She gestured to the two chairs lined up ready in front of her desk, and then sat down herself.

Winnie looked at her, trying to read her face for any clue to what this was about, but it was pleasantly neutral-looking. At least she didn't seem angry, so that was something, wasn't it?

Station Officer Steele looked at them both for a few moments and then spoke. 'No doubt you've been wondering why I sent for you … It certainly isn't the first time.' She smiled. 'Don't look so worried, Winnie, I haven't summoned you to give you a dressing-down. You haven't done anything you shouldn't have, have you?'

'Certainly not. I've been a model crew member, especially after having to do your job when you were ill,' Winnie said. Experiencing life at Station 75 from Station Officer Steele's point of view had been something of a revelation to her. Perhaps if she'd done the same with the teachers at school, she might have tamed her behaviour there. In fact she definitely would.

'Good.' Station Officer Steele picked up a piece of paper from her desk. 'As you'll recall after that terrible raid on the twenty-ninth of December, when you drove through fire to rescue casualties, I told you that the two of you were going to be recommended for a medal. Well this,' she held out the paper for Winnie to take, 'confirms that you are both to be awarded the George Medal for your brave actions.'

Winnie took the paper and quickly scanned through what it said, and then promptly read it again, only more slowly this time.

'Congratulations, both of you.' Station Officer Steele held out her hand and shook Winnie's hand and then Mac's. 'I'm very proud of you. You'll be awarded your medals by the King at Buckingham Palace in the next few months.'

Winnie turned to Mac and smiled at him. 'I'd forgotten all about this. I didn't think what we did was that brave.'

'We were only doing our job,' Mac agreed.

'Well it *was* brave,' Station Officer Steele said. 'Your families will be very proud of you too.'

The thought of her mother and what she would say flashed into Winnie's mind. Perhaps now she'd finally accept that Winnie's job was worthwhile and stop pestering her to leave it.

'I expect they'll be able to go with you to the palace when you get your medal,' Station Officer Steele said.

Her mother would love that, Winnie thought, but whether she would love taking her was another matter.

'Winnie, could you stay behind a moment? I need to speak to you about something else,' Station Officer Steele said.

Mac stood up. 'I'll see you back downstairs. I won't tell anyone what's happened, keep them guessing for a bit, especially Sparky.'

'Yes, it'll do him good to stew for a while,' Winnie said.

Station Officer Steele closed the door behind Mac and then sat down again facing Winnie. 'I wanted to know if you'd come to a decision about that job offer I made you, now that you've had a couple of weeks to think about it. I honestly think you would make an excellent deputy station officer, otherwise I would never have suggested it.'

Winnie winced. She should have known this was coming. 'I was rather hoping you'd forgotten all about it, actually.'

'Was that likely?' Station Officer Steele's warm brown eyes were twinkling behind her spectacles.

'Not really, no.' Winnie sighed. 'I appreciate you asking, but I honestly don't know if it's the right thing for me. I'm not exactly known for keeping to the rules, am I? I like to go my own way too much.'

'Indeed, though there are sometimes occasions when rules need to be bent; it's about knowing when that's appropriate. You *can* do the job, Winnie, and do it very well.'

'It would feel rather … a bit like poacher turned gamekeeper.'

Station Officer Steele laughed. 'I suppose it would, but isn't that a good thing? You know all the tricks and short cuts from experience, and would bring that knowledge to the job.'

'Doing your job for a few days was one thing, but any longer probably wouldn't be right for me. I'd just end up getting things wrong.'

'I very much doubt that. You're an extremely capable young woman.'

'The last time I was given responsibility like that, at school, I messed up badly.' Winnie threw her hands wide. 'Messing up here would be utterly terrible; it could mean the difference between life and death.'

Station Officer Steele nodded. 'I suspect you are very different now to how you were as a sixteen- or seventeen-year-old. You've been through a lot since the start of the Blitz – it's changed you, Winnie, made you face up to things. You've shown great courage and resilience.' She smiled. 'I understand your reluctance, but I honestly believe you are extremely suited to this role. How about a trial period, say three months, and if after that time you decide that it isn't for you, then fair enough.'

'Just for three months, and no more if I don't want it?' Winnie asked.

Station Officer Steele nodded.

Should she give it a try? Winnie wondered. Do it for the boss, whom she admired greatly? The idea both terrified and strangely enticed her. She could look on it as a challenge, and that was something Winnie always liked to rise to.

'Very well then. But don't be cross when I mess up.'

'You still don't know exactly where he is then?' Sparky asked.

'No, only that it's somewhere in North Africa. He can't say exactly because of the censor.' Bella was poring over the latest map of troop movements and action in that area in the newspaper spread out on the table in the common room, something she often did now, ever since her brother had been sent abroad. Keeping an eye on what was going on out there, no matter how distant it was, helped her feel a little bit closer to him.

'It's bleedin' difficult fighting in the desert,' Sparky said. 'We just ain't used to it.'

'But they must be getting used to it by now,' Bella said. 'Getting better at knowing how to survive out there and dealing with all the problems.'

'You mean the heat, the sand, which gets into everything

and makes the food all gritty, the "gippo guts", and all the blasted flies?' Sparky shook his head. 'You only had to put your cup of tea down for a moment and there'd be a dozen of the blighters in there helping you drink it. Of course there was the enemy who might come attacking yer at any time as well.'

Bella looked at him and smiled. He'd told her a little about how he'd been sent to Egypt in the Great War to defend the Suez Canal from possible attack by the Turkish army. 'It wasn't all bad, was it? Surely there was something even you liked?'

Sparky shrugged his shoulders and took a slow sip of tea, then grinned at her. 'Flyless tea, delicious.' He paused for a moment. 'I've never seen such beautiful skies as I did there. When evening came, a cool breeze would start to blow and the earth seemed to still and the sky would take on a glorious hue. Never seen such sunsets as the ones in the desert.' His face took on a faraway look. 'It weren't all bad, and I know I was luckier than many who were sent away and never came back.'

'Did you ever ride on a camel?'

'I certainly did, and I saw the pyramids an' all.'

'What were the local people like?' Bella asked.

'They were nice. We used to barter with them – we gave them tea and sugar and they gave us eggs and toma-toes.' He looked at her, his keen brown eyes meeting hers. 'You're worried about your brother, ain't yer?'

Bella nodded. 'He seems a long way away and there's nothing I can do to help him. I just hope he's all right.'

'Just keep writing to 'im. Letters from 'ome 'elp a hell of a lot, that contact with real life and family when you're away and not knowing what the next day's going to bring.'

'Walter's not so good at writing letters.'

Sparky waved his hand dismissively. 'That don't matter. You keep on writing to 'im, that's the important thing. He might not write back as often, but I can guarantee you that he appreciates 'earing from you about what you've been doing. From all the writin' you do in that notebook of yours, I bet you write a smashing letter.'

Bella shrugged. 'Well I try, but it's only about what I've been doing and seeing; nothing fancy, just describing life really.'

'Exactly!' Sparky nodded. 'When you're stuck in a trench living an odd existence, that's what you want to 'ear – it'll transport 'im out of there for a bit, so keep at it.'

'I'll tell him what you said, ask him if it's true, shall I?'

'Go right ahead. Take it from an old soldier who knows what 'e's talkin' about. Letters from my wife 'elped keep me going and reminded me of 'ome.'

'Thanks, Sparky,' Bella said.

'Any time, ducks. We've all got to 'elp each other if we can. You can make me another cup o' tea if you want.' He grinned at her. 'Or I could just make me own.'

Bella laughed. 'Go on, I'll make you one.'

Chapter Five

'Here we are, old girl, twenty feet below ground in "the safest and gayest restaurant in town – even in an air raid".'

Winnie laughed as her brother quoted the Café de Paris advertising slogan to her. They'd just arrived and were standing on the balcony looking down at the dance floor, which was surrounded by tables where people were already seated and enjoying themselves. 'You've been looking forward to this, haven't you?'

'It's been like a light at the end of the tunnel.' Harry grinned at her. 'A celebration of my new eyelids.' He paused, fluttering them up and down at her. 'And of you being awarded the George Medal. Tonight, dear sister, we enjoy ourselves.'

'What are we waiting for then?' Winnie slipped her arm through his and led him down the curved staircase.

*

Seated at a table near the dance floor, Winnie sipped her delicious cocktail and relaxed back in her gilt chair, toes tapping along to the jaunty song being played by the band.

Harry smiled at her. 'Enjoying yourself?'

'Absolutely! It feels wonderful to be dressed up and out on the town.' She loved the feel of her favourite dark blue silk gown against her skin, a stark contrast to the sensible, hard-wearing slacks and blouses that she spent so much time in these days.

'Shall we dance?' Harry stood up and held out his hand to her.

'Thank you, kind sir, I'd be delighted.'

Winnie took hold of her brother's hand and they joined the throng of dancers moving around the floor, everyone smiling and enjoying themselves in the lively, fun atmosphere. If it weren't for the fact that some people were wearing uniforms, it would be impossible to tell there was a war on, thought Winnie. The Café de Paris was like an oasis in the horror of wartime London, a haven of fun for a few hours, and she was determined to enjoy every moment.

'I've dreamed about doing this again,' Harry said, twirling her round and round.

'Steady on, twinkletoes,' Winnie said, increasing her pace to keep up with him. 'I'm rather out of practice.'

'Utter rot, you never forget how to dance. Remember how Connie taught us in the summer hols?'

'I remember how sore my toes were where you and especially James trod on them.'

Harry laughed, the shiny skin on his scarred face stretching. 'Our dear brother isn't the best of dancers.'

'No, but . . .' She paused, her attention drawn to the man who'd just come down the staircase. 'Look who's arrived.' She nodded over Harry's shoulder and he spun her round so he could see.

'Snakehips Johnson.' He grinned at her. 'Now *he's* a man who really knows how to dance.'

Rotating around the floor, Winnie watched as the dance-band leader took up his place by the microphone ready for the next number. She recognised the song as soon as the band struck up the opening bars – it was 'Oh Johnny, Oh Johnny, Oh!'. Snakehips Johnson began to sing, his beautiful voice caressing the words.

Winnie closed her eyes and let Harry sweep her around. It was bliss; they should do this more often.

'Are you joining in?' Harry asked. 'Only your lips are moving but there's no sound coming out.'

Winnie looked at him and smiled. 'It's the best way. In my mind my voice sounds wonderful, duetting along with Mr Johnson's in the most beautiful way, but unfortunately my real singing voice doesn't live up to my imagination. The music teacher at school was most unkind about it, told me to mime whenever we had to sing . . .'

Snakehips had just moved on to the second verse when there was a sudden blinding blue flash. Winnie was blown off her feet by a force that felt like a giant hand pressing her down as the room was plunged into pitch darkness. Unseen things crashed and clattered, the air filled with powder and dust and there was a strong smell of cordite. Winnie would recognise that smell anywhere.

Moans and cries started in the darkness. A few small sparks of light flickered on as people lit their cigarette lighters, the thin globes of light they threw out revealing a shadowy world of twisted, broken bodies lying scattered like rag dolls. It was stiflingly hot; sweat trickled down Winnie's back.

Just moments ago she'd been dancing with Harry, singing along ... Where was her brother? She pushed herself up into a sitting position and groped around in the semi-darkness, trying to find him, calling out his name, but there was no reply. Something warm and sticky trickled down her face. She put her hand up to touch it, and her fingers came away wet. It was blood.

As suddenly as the lights had gone out, another, lower-level light came on – the emergency lighting. Winnie shielded her eyes for a moment until they adjusted to the brightness, and then her stomach roiled as she looked about her. What only minutes ago had been a stylish, beautiful room packed with people enjoying themselves was now a scene of destruction, ruin and death.

Standing upright, her legs feeling strangely wobbly, like a newborn foal's, she began to search for Harry, carefully stepping over bodies littering the floor. She was looking for his blue RAF uniform, but people's clothes were so covered in dust and plaster that their colours were dimmed and obscured. Then she spotted him. He'd been blown across to the far side of the dance floor and was lying on his side near a table where, she noticed, a bottle of champagne stood perfectly intact while all the people who'd been sitting around it were dead, their bodies slumped awkwardly on their chairs.

Crouching down beside her brother, she gently felt for a pulse in his neck, desperately watching his soot-blackened face for signs of life. Her own heartbeat raced along in terror that he had suffered the same fate as those sitting around the table. But it was there, a steady bumping against her finger; he was alive. Winnie started to shake, and tears stung her eyes. She swallowed hard and bit down on her lip. This wasn't the time to become emotional. Harry needed her help, and there were plenty of others, too. Taking some deep, steadying breaths, she told herself that this was just another incident, and she knew what needed to be done.

Thankfully her training instinctively kicked in. She quickly examined Harry, checking for bleeding and broken bones. His left arm was twisted into an awkward position and he was unconscious, but there was no sign of any bleeding. She needed to splint his arm but had no medical kit with her, no bandages. She'd have to improvise. Looking down at her silk dress, she noticed that the skirt was hanging in tattered ribbons. Giving the material a sharp tug, she tore off strips and quickly got to work, all the while aware of other people stirring and helping the injured. Help had also started to arrive from the outside, and rescuers were beginning to carry people up the stairs on their backs. Ambulances would have been sent for.

Harry would need to be stretchered out; he was far too heavy for Winnie to carry on her own.

Satisfied that she'd done all she could for her brother, she looked around her, quickly assessing the situation. Many people were beyond assistance, their bodies lying lifeless, some with parts missing, but there were those who were still alive and who needed help, and fast. She spotted a woman sitting on the floor nearby, weeping silently, tears making tracks through her soot-blackened face as she stared at her hands, which dripped blood on to her pale-lavender dress. All her fingers were gone, blown clean away.

'Let me help you.' Winnie quickly tore more strips from her tattered skirt, then crouched down in front of the woman and gently began to bandage her hands. 'What's your name?'

'Philippa.' The woman's voice came out in a whisper. 'Are you a nurse?'

'No, I'm an ambulance driver. Thought I was having a night off tonight, but looks like Hitler had other ideas.'

'The Café de Paris was supposed to be safe.' Philippa's face crumpled and she began to shake.

'It seems that nowhere is completely safe. Are you here with someone?'

Philippa nodded and looked around her. 'With Peter, there.' She pointed to a man lying a short way off, quite still.

Winnie didn't need to check his pulse to know that he was dead.

123

'Let's get you upstairs, and then I'll see to Peter.' She helped Philippa to her feet and put her arm around her waist, supporting her across to the bottom of the stairs, where she handed her over to one of the rescuers. 'I'll go back and see what I can do for your friend.'

'Thank you.' Philippa smiled at her, and allowed herself to be helped up the stairs.

Going back to where Peter's body lay, Winnie checked for a pulse, but her instinct had proved right: he was gone. Poor Philippa had lost her fingers and her friend in one cruel blow.

Planes were still droning overhead when Winnie emerged from the Café de Paris and made her way to the Rialto cinema next door, where stretcher cases had been taken to wait for ambulances. Harry had been carried out of the devastated basement a while ago, and she had stayed down there helping till all the injured had received first-aid treatment. The dead would be brought out later.

Spotting her brother, she crouched down to check on his condition.

'Harry, can you hear me?' She gently shook his shoulder.

His eyes flickered open and he winced. 'What . . . what happened?'

'We were bombed. You're injured and we're just waiting for an ambulance. It won't be long. I'll go with you.'

'You're hurt too. You've been bleeding.'

'It's nothing. Head wounds bleed a lot.' Winnie gingerly

felt the gash on her head. Her hair was matted with blood, and it had dripped down on to the bodice of her dress.

'Is it bad down there?' Harry asked.

Winnie nodded. She was grateful for the arrival of two ambulance crews so she didn't have to elaborate. There'd be time enough for that later.

'What have we here?' the ambulance driver asked, taking out a label and pencil.

Winnie quickly told her the details of his injuries.

'You a nurse?' the woman asked, tying the label on to Harry's RAF tunic.

'No, I'm an ambulance driver, like you. Can I go with him in the back?'

'You look like you need some patching up yourself. You can help my crewmate here keep an eye on the casualties, if you'd be so kind. It's been a hell of a night. Never thought the Café de Paris would get hit, what with it being twenty feet below ground.'

'Nor did we,' Winnie said.

'I needed that.' James put his spoon down in the bowl, which he'd scraped clean of spotted dick and custard.

'Do you want some of mine?' Bella offered. She was only halfway through her pudding.

'No, but thank you for the kind offer. I'm quite full up now.' He leaned back in his chair and smiled at her, his grey eyes crinkling at the corners. 'It's so lovely to see you, Bella.'

'And you. It was a wonderful surprise to find you

waiting for me when I left work, and now to be treated out to a meal as well.'

'It's not the grandest of places, but I rather like it, and the food's good.'

'It's perfect.' Bella glanced around her, where many others were enjoying their British Restaurant meal in the homely atmosphere. 'Winnie and Harry will be pleased to see you, too.'

'I keep thinking what might have happened to them. It was pure chance they got out alive when so many didn't.' He shook his head. 'Sends a shiver down my spine thinking about it.'

Bella reached out and took hold of his hand. 'Try not to dwell on what could have been; focus on the positives. Whether someone survives a bombing is down to chance – something as simple as where they were standing can make all the difference: a few inches in one direction and they live, a few inches in the other and they don't. There's nothing you can do to stop it; you just have to hope a bomb hasn't got your name on it.'

James winced. 'It's frightening, Bella. You just don't know.'

She squeezed his hand. 'No, you don't. I'm used to seeing what bombs can do, so please don't think I take it lightly, but it's no good living your life worrying about if one is going to fall on you. If you did that here in London, you'd go crazy with worry. Just be glad they're all right.'

'I don't know how you cope, Bella. You're so strong and calm about it.'

'Not always. I write about it, get my thoughts and

126

feelings down in my diary or notebook, and that helps me. Capturing it on paper . . . it's a way of making sense of things, and finding the right words to describe something is a challenge . . . I love it.'

'It sounds like an excellent idea, and one day you can read them back and marvel at what you went through.' He sighed. 'I'm sorry to be such a grump, Bella. I live in a cocooned world in Bletchley, just pushing bits of paper around. We don't get bombed, and . . . ' He shrugged. 'I think too much sometimes.'

'I like it that you think a lot, but trust me on this, don't go dwelling on bombs, concentrate on something more interesting instead. Tell me about the book you're reading at the moment.'

'They're probably in the sitting room,' Bella said as she and James walked up the stairs from the basement kitchen of Connie's house a short while later. 'They'll be delighted to see you.'

Stepping out into the black-and-white-tiled hall, James stopped, his face paling. 'What's the matter?' Bella linked her arm through his.

His grey eyes met hers. 'Can you smell it?' he whispered.

Bella sniffed. 'Perfume.'

'My mother's here. That's Chanel No. 5, her perfume. I'd know it anywhere.'

'Ah.' Bella squeezed his arm. She'd heard enough about their mother from James and Winnie to know that a visit from her could be difficult.

'Perhaps we could ...' James turned to escape back down to the kitchen, but the door to the sitting room opened and Connie stood there.

'I thought I heard something. James, how lovely to see you.' She strode across the hall and kissed him on the cheek. 'Your mother's here,' she whispered. 'Brace yourself.' She looked at him sympathetically, then said in a loud, cheerful voice, 'Do come through and see everyone.'

Bella sensed a strained atmosphere the moment she walked into the sitting room. Winnie sat on the edge of the velvet-covered sofa, so upright that she looked like she had a steel rod in her back. She glanced up at Bella and James and did her best to smile, but her eyes had a startled look about them, like a cornered rabbit. Trixie sat very close to her mistress's legs, leaning against them as if to give support. Only Harry seemed unaffected, sitting on the other end of the sofa, lounging against the back, his broken arm in a sling.

The woman causing this change in the usually happy atmosphere of Connie's home sat perfectly still in the winged leather armchair, dressed in a powder-blue suit, a string of pearls around her neck, with her feet neatly aligned in their spotless shoes.

'James, I wasn't expecting to see you here too. What a treat to have all my children together.'

'Hello, Mother.' James bent down and kissed her proffered cheek. 'My shift pattern changes today, so I had a chance to come to London for a few hours, see how everyone is after the ...' He looked at Winnie and Harry.

128

'Cynthia, I don't believe you've met Bella, have you?' Connie made the introductions. Bella held out her hand to the older woman, who ignored it.

'No, I don't believe I have, though I have heard about you. How do you do?' She smiled, but Bella noticed it didn't reach her eyes, which remained like chips of blue ice as they looked her up and down. She felt as if she were being assessed and found distinctly lacking.

The room fell into silence for a few moments before James, who looked more uncomfortable than Bella had ever seen him, began to speak. 'How are you both?'

'We're fine, thank you.' Winnie smiled warmly at her brother. 'A few cuts and bruises, and a broken arm for Harry, but it could have been a whole lot worse.'

'Bella said you got caught by some shrapnel,' James said.

'It's fine.' Winnie put her hand to her head. 'A couple of stitches put it right and I'll be back at work tomorrow.'

'Hitler's going to have to try a lot harder to get rid of me,' Harry said, taking a cigarette out of his silver case. 'Tried frying me, then blowing me up – I'm like a cat with nine lives.' He grinned.

'Let's hope he doesn't have another go at you,' Connie said. 'I'll go and make some tea.'

'I'll do it, and Bella can come and help me.' Winnie stood up. 'It'll be quicker with the two of us.' She put her hand through Bella's arm and hurried her out of the door. 'I'm so sorry about my mother treating you like that,' she said as they went downstairs to the kitchen. 'She was appallingly rude ignoring your hand.'

'Please don't upset yourself over it, Winnie. It doesn't matter,' Bella reassured her as she filled up the kettle and put it on to boil.

'Oh but it does. You are one of my best friends, you're James's girl and you live in Connie's house, all of which should garner you respect and good manners. She ... she ...' Winnie's grey eyes filled with tears. 'She makes me so bloody uncomfortable and terribly angry at times.'

'I noticed. I've never seen you sitting to attention like that before.' Bella caught her friend's eye and they both giggled. 'And poor James, he smelled her perfume in the hall and was about to turn tail and make a run for it when Connie came out and caught us.'

'Mother has that effect on both of us.'

'But not on Harry.'

Winnie shook her head. 'He seems immune to her, goes his own way, and she doesn't challenge him over it, unlike me and James.'

Bella started to put a tray of tea things together, taking cups and saucers off the dresser. 'Why is she here?'

'She came to see how we were after the incident at the Café de Paris. I didn't know she was coming or I'd have gone out.' Winnie poured some milk into a jug and set it on the tray.

'She was probably worried about you.'

Winnie shrugged. 'Perhaps, but I can't help thinking there's an ulterior motive behind her visit.'

Bella laid a hand on her arm. 'Try to look on the positive side, Winnie, she'll be gone again before you know it.'

Winnie sighed. 'I'll try my best, but she just brings out the worst in me.'

The kettle began to whistle and Bella turned off the gas. 'Come on, let's get this tea made and up to them. James will need a cup to soothe his nerves.'

Bella had never known half an hour pass so slowly or so awkwardly. Everyone had focused keenly on their tea, and the conversation had been stilted, stopping and starting despite Connie's valiant efforts to keep it going. Bella couldn't help thinking that if Cynthia Churchill really had come to see her injured children, it was very odd that she should say so little to them.

The woman was the most unmaternal person Bella had ever met; she seemed to exude a sense of haughty displeasure. For all the wealth and privilege of Winnie's family, there seemed to be little love between the mother and her children. Thankfully Winnie and her brothers had a far more caring relationship with each other, which her friend had told her was all down to Connie's kind, nurturing influence during the many school holidays that they'd spent with her.

Bella's family may have been far poorer in material terms, but she and her brother had grown up with something infinitely more precious, something money couldn't buy – the wholehearted love of their parents.

'I really must be going if I'm going to make the seven o'clock train home.' Winnie's mother stood up. Nobody protested. 'I'm sure Bella will be kind enough to fetch my coat for me,' she added regally.

Winnie opened her mouth to protest, but Bella shook her head at her friend. 'It's fine, I'm happy to fetch it for you.'

'I'll be out in the hall in just a moment,' Winnie's mother told her.

Glad of an excuse to avoid having to watch the awkward goodbyes, Bella fled from the room and found the elegant dark red coat with its extravagant silk collar neatly draped over the back of a chair in the hall.

A matter of moments later, Winnie's mother emerged and closed the sitting-room door firmly behind her. She came over to Bella and stood in front of her, making it quite obvious that she expected her to help her on with the coat, as though she were the maid. Bella could easily have handed it to her and left her to put it on herself, but she preferred to show good manners, even if Cynthia Churchill hadn't afforded her the same courtesy.

'I suppose "Bella" is another of those ridiculous nicknames the ambulance crew use,' the older woman said, her back to Bella.

'Yes, it is,' Bella said. 'It comes from my surname, Belmont. My first name is—'

'Indeed,' Mrs Churchill interrupted, swatting the subject away with a flick of her wrist before marching to the door without a word of thanks. Before she opened it, she stopped, turned around and beckoned Bella closer. 'I think it best to point out to you that you are wasting your time with James.' Her voice was little more than a whisper, but it was loud enough for Bella to hear that it was laced with venom. 'He's not right for you, not for your sort, and is never going to be serious about a maid, is he now, *Belmont*?'

Bella stared at her. The use of her surname, just like when she'd worked as a housemaid, had stunned her, pulling her back to those days when she'd been an invisible member of a wealthy family's household clearing up behind them.

Sensing Bella's reaction, Mrs Churchill pressed her point. 'James comes from a good family and will make a worthy marriage with someone far more suited and from the correct sort of background.' She narrowed her icy blue eyes. 'If you really care for my son then you will do the right thing for him and put an end to your ... relationship.' Her final word was spoken as if it left a disgusting taste in her mouth. 'I hope I have made myself clear, Belmont?'

Bella opened her mouth to protest, but Winnie's mother gave her no chance to have her say, opening the door and striding through it, her head held high and her back poker straight.

As she stared after her, Bella's stomach was knotting tightly and her legs were trembling at the woman's nerve, her mean-spiritedness and her utter snobbery. Winnie had been right: Cynthia Churchill hadn't just come here to see her injured children, she'd come to warn Bella off her son.

'You've done a good job looking after the 'ens.' Frankie's grandfather threw some corn down to the chickens, which

133

they'd let out on to the vegetable bed to have a scratch around.

'I like them, they're funny creatures. I enjoy seeing them scraping about and always so busy, and their eggs are a bonus.' Frankie stamped down on the spade and turned over a clod of soil, revealing a fat pink worm, which a hen quickly spotted, rushing over to gobble it up. 'They've gone off the lay a bit 'cos it's winter, but we're still getting more eggs than on the ration.'

'It's good to see them and be out in the fresh air again. Didn't like being cooped up in the 'ospital – I'm not used to it after years walking the beat.'

'It's good to 'ave you 'ome again. It wasn't the same here without you.' Frankie leaned on the spade and smiled at him. 'Gave me a right proper scare you did that night.'

'You weren't the only one who was scared. When they shouted *run*, I thought that was it, I was a goner. I could 'ear bricks raining down and I was runnin' for me life . . . I was thinking how I didn't want to leave you and Stanley, but if it was the end then at least I'd see your gran again, we'd be reunited.'

Frankie stared at him, astonished to hear that what might have been his final thoughts had been about her, Stanley and her gran, but not his current wife. She couldn't stop herself, she had to ask. 'What about Ivy, didn't you think about her?'

Her grandad glanced back at the house. 'Not then.' He rubbed his ear. 'Course, when I came to, later on, I thought about 'er. Got me thinking about what would 'appen to her if I 'ad been killed. It made me realise I needed to make sure that she'd be all right, that ... you know ... I needed to ask you ...' he paused and looked at her, 'if you'd be prepared to look after her.'

Frankie didn't need reminding. She hadn't forgotten her promise, and often wished she hadn't made it, but she didn't have much of a choice, did she?

'You don't want to worry about it,' she told him. 'You ain't going to get killed; you'll die of old age in your chair many years from now.' She was trying hard to sound cheerful, but there was a sick feeling of dread in her stomach.

'Whatever 'appens, I feel a lot better knowing that everyone will be cared for and there'll be an 'ome waiting for Stanley to come back to. Your gran would 'ave wanted that – you know she thought the world of him.'

But what would she think of Ivy as your wife? a voice whispered in Frankie's mind. 'It's a shame Ivy never came to visit you in 'ospital,' she said. 'Not even before you were sent to Kent.'

'Oh, she don't like 'ospitals. She told me they make her feel ill, and that's why she couldn't come.' Grandad didn't meet Frankie's eye as he spoke. 'Said it would 'ave upset her too much as well. Don't matter, I'm home now.'

Frankie thrust her spade into the soil and stamped down hard on it, biting back a retort. Ivy had an excuse for everything; she would never put herself out for anyone. Frankie didn't know what was worse, the woman's behaviour, or seeing her grandad accepting it and making excuses for her. He showed her care and consideration, but there was none in return, and this was who Frankie had promised to look out for. Damn and blast it. She turned over a sod of soil and watched through tear-blurred eyes as the hens fought over the exposed worms.

The tide was out, exposing the muddy banks of the Thames, the barges keeping to the middle of the channel. Winnie watched them ploughing their way upstream against the current, leaning her head back against Mac's chest, his arms wrapped around her. They'd come down by the Tower of London to spend a bit of time together after their shift had ended at half past three. It had been a quiet one, with no raids, for which Winnie was grateful. Her usual energy and joyfulness was distinctly lacking today although the boss had kept her busy doing thorough checks on all the ambulances.

'Are you going to tell me what's bothering you?' Mac said quietly in her ear. 'Something is most definitely wrong with you; you've lost your spark somewhere. It's not working as deputy station officer, is it?'

She shook her head. 'No, I don't mind that, it keeps me busy, and I'm getting more used to having to send people out if the boss puts me on telephone duty, though I wish I could keep you at the station all the time and never send you out in the middle of an air raid.'

Mac frowned. 'You can't do that, Winnie. You have to do it fairly.'

'I know.' She turned to look into his eyes. 'But it doesn't stop me wishing.'

'I wouldn't want you to, even if you could.' He ran a hand through his dark hair. 'I appreciate you feel like that for the right reasons, and I feel the same way about you, worrying about you when you go out to an incident, but this is what we do, Winnie, what we signed up for. With me being a CO ... well, sometimes I feel I have to prove I'm not a coward.'

'But you're not!' Winnie reached up and cupped his cheek. 'You are a brave, honourable man and I love you, Mac.'

He pulled her into a tight hug and they stood wrapped in each other's arms for a few minutes before he said, 'So if it's not your new role that's upsetting you, what is it?'

Winnie looked up at him. 'I'm tired, Mac. I'm not sleeping well. Every time I drop off, I dream I'm down in the Café de Paris drinking cocktails with Harry, and then there's a flash ... Sometimes when the lights come on I can't find him, or he's been blown apart like some of them were ...' Her voice broke and she bit down on her lip to try to compose herself.

Mac gently stroked some stray hair from her face. 'It's just a dream. You both got out of there.'

'I know!' she snapped. 'I'm sorry, I can't help thinking what would have happened if we'd stayed at the table instead of getting up to dance when we did, or what if we'd been nearer the band when the bomb went off, what then?'

'There's nothing any of us can do about the what–ifs. You shouldn't dwell on them, because you can't change the past.'

'It reminds me of that night the Jones sisters were killed. I went a different way, remember?'

Mac nodded. 'Of course. I followed you and we didn't get blown up like those poor women.'

'I don't know why I went the other way ... or why Harry and I were dancing at that particular spot when the bomb exploded in the Café de Paris. Both times I could have come out of it badly injured or dead. Will I be so lucky next time?'

Mac took hold of her face gently and looked straight into her eyes. 'There are no answers to your questions, Winnie. None of us knows what tomorrow will bring, so don't waste today worrying about what might or might not happen.'

'I've been wondering again if it's time I left the ambulance service, did what my parents want for once. Sometimes it's hard to keep going when I see so many innocent people getting injured and killed. It's difficult to keep my chin up.'

Mac smiled and hugged her to him. 'You've really got it bad, haven't you? Remember we talked about that on Christmas night? You love what you do, so stay put and get on with it. It's what *you* want, not what your parents want. We do an important job, Winnie, take heart from that, because what we do really matters.'

Winnie squeezed him tightly. 'Thank you.'

'What for?'

'For listening to me and for setting me on the straight and narrow again. I don't know what's the matter with me.'

'You had a very near miss. It would make anyone question the what–ifs. Be thankful you survived and enjoy what you have. Things like this.' Mac kissed her gently.

'That makes me feel a whole lot better.' Winnie smiled at him.

'Let's go out tonight, go to the pictures or something,' Mac suggested.

'Yes, I'd like that. We could ask Bella and Harry to come as well if you want. It would cheer her up. She's been a bit quiet since James left; she's probably missing him.'

'She told me she met your mother. When am I going to meet her?'

Winnie shook her head. 'I'd rather you didn't.'

Mac frowned. 'You're not ashamed of me, are you?'

'Certainly not! You are extremely precious to me. I'm just protecting you, Mac. You know I haven't told her about you, and James and Harry are sworn to secrecy. I know my mother, and believe me when I say she is a woman who will do her utmost to get what she wants – which if she knew about us would be to split us up. She'd be utterly vile and would direct that at you.' She squeezed his hand. 'My mother can be beastly, and I don't want you upset by her.'

'I can stand up for myself; I've had to do plenty of that since I registered as a CO. Don't you think we're serious enough about each other to withstand her disapproval? She objects to you being in the ambulance service and you're still in it; she might be against our relationship but it won't stop us, will it?'

Winnie sighed. 'Oh darling Mac, I wish I could tell her, but I know how she'd react. She would find fault with everything about you – your family, being a CO – and I don't want her cruelty targeted at the man I love. Please just trust me when I say that it's best she knows nothing about us for the time being.'

Bella stared into the darkness, wide awake and yet bone-achingly tired. She sighed and turned on to her side, bunching up the pillow to make it more comfortable, and closed her eyes, willing her body to relax and for sleep to come. But it wouldn't. Her mind would not be still, running again over what James's mother had said to her a few days ago. It had been on her mind ever since, and although she'd done her best to look at it from every angle, examine the older woman's motives and think about it logically, she couldn't shake off the fact that those cruel words had stung. They'd cracked her confidence and left her doubting whether she and James should be together. Was their relationship harming him? If she really did care for him, should she let him go?

She threw back her covers and sat up. Lying there mulling things over wasn't helping; she was no nearer falling asleep. Perhaps a warm milky drink would help – she'd go and make some cocoa.

Slipping on her dressing gown, a soft, silky garment that Winnie had given her when she had first come to live here after she'd been bombed out and lost most of her own clothes, she quietly opened her door and made her way along the landing, then padded down the stairs, feeling her way in the darkness.

Downstairs in the basement kitchen, she put on the light and made herself a cup of cocoa, enjoying the soothing routine of heating the milk, then adding the powder and whisking it smooth before pouring it into a mug. She'd just sat down at the large table when the door creaked open and Connie appeared, blinking in the light.

'I wondered who it was.'

'I'm sorry, I woke you up.'

'You didn't. I've been tossing and turning since I went to bed. Couldn't sleep.'

'Nor could I. I thought some cocoa might help. Would you like a cup?'

Connie nodded. 'Yes, but stay where you are, I'll make it.'

Bella watched as the older woman busied herself at the stove. She still marvelled that she was living in this grand house off Russell Square. Before the war, the only way she'd have been in such a house was working as a maid. Connie was unlike any upper-class woman she'd ever met: she treated everyone the same and welcomed people into her home with open arms.

Once they were both settled at the table nursing their

mugs of cocoa, Connie said, 'So what was keeping you awake?' She reached out and touched Bella's arm. 'You don't have to tell me, but sometimes it helps to talk. A problem shared is a problem halved, or so they say. I might be able to help.'

Bella took a sip of cocoa to give herself time to think. Should she tell Connie what was bothering her? Since she was part of James's family and knew his mother well, she might be able to see a way through. 'It's something Mrs Churchill said to me,' she began.

Connie looked puzzled, hooking her blonde bob behind her ear. 'She hardly spoke to you, as I recall, though she seemed to have forgotten her manners when you offered her your hand. I thought it was rather odd, as she's usually quite forceful with her opinions.'

'It wasn't while she was in the sitting room; it was just as she was leaving. Remember she asked me to fetch her coat?'

Connie nodded. 'Go on.'

Bella told her what the woman had said, watching as Connie's face clouded and her hand clasped her mug so tightly the knuckles stood out white.

'That ... that woman ...' Connie ran her hand through her hair. 'I should have known she was up to something. Cynthia doesn't do social visits in my experience; there's always a reason behind them, something she wants.' She reached out and took hold of Bella's hand in both of hers. 'I'm so sorry she said that to you. She had no right, and she is completely and utterly wrong.'

'But she's right about one thing. James and I are from completely different backgrounds. My family were servants, his family *has* servants.'

'Some of them do, not me. I judge a person by the way they are, the way they act and how they treat other people, not by who their family are or what they do.' Connie sighed. 'I think that's the right thing to do, but sadly that's not the way everyone sees things. Those in the so-called upper classes usually look down on the lower classes, assuming they are lesser or inferior, when they are nothing of the sort.' She slapped her hand down on the table, making Bella jump. She shrugged and smiled at her. 'Sorry, this has touched a raw nerve of mine. You know, Bella, I have had the supposed pleasure of spending time with people from families who are considered the cream of society, but honestly, some of them are rotten to the core. They wouldn't help anyone else, their only thought is for themselves. I've also known many people from the working classes who were the very best kind of person, kind, generous ...'

'There's good and bad in all classes,' Bella said.

'Exactly. So when James's mother spouts her rubbish that you're not the right sort for him ... well, it makes my blood boil. She knows nothing about you, she hasn't taken the time to talk to you, just judged you by a former job.' Connie leaned forward and took hold of Bella's hand again, her blue eyes wide with concern. 'I hope you're not seriously thinking of doing what she asked.'

Bella shrugged. 'Not really, but it keeps playing on my

mind. I care very much for James and I wouldn't want anything I do to jeopardise his life.'

'Oh darling Bella, James adores you. I've never seen him so happy as when he's with you. You make him glow. You two are perfectly suited. It would break his heart if you did what his mother asked. It might be what she wants, but it isn't what he wants. Or you?'

'No, of course not.'

Connie sipped her cocoa. 'You'll have realised by now that I'm a bit of a black sheep in my family, preferring to go my own way. Well once upon a time I did try to conform. I was a debutante and did the season, my parents hoping I might find a suitable husband. Of course I didn't.' She smiled. 'I was already falling in love with someone much better than the shallow fools paraded before us at balls. I loved one of the under-gardeners on my parents' estate. Bertie was a joy: intelligent, well-read, kind and understanding . . .' Her eyes suddenly filled with tears. 'He joined up in 1914 and I followed, joining the Voluntary Aid Detachment and being sent to France as well. It was wonderful. We felt free there and saw as much as we could of each other. We couldn't meet very often, but when we did, it was sheer bliss. He asked me to marry him and I said yes.' She reached inside the neck of her dressing gown and pulled out a gold chain on which was threaded a ring. 'My engagement ring. I always wear it next to my heart.' She sighed. 'But we never got the chance to marry. Bertie was killed, his life wasted like so many others.'

Bella squeezed her hand. 'I'm so sorry.'

Connie smiled, and sniffed back her tears. 'So you see, I do know that it doesn't matter what job you do, it's the person you are that counts. I wish more people could see that. The same goes for religion. Hitler could do with some lessons on that.' She paused. 'What I'm saying, Bella, is listen to your heart and ignore what other people want, especially ones with biased, short-sighted views. It's what you and James want that matters, what makes you happy, and I think that's each other. You both have my complete and utter support.'

Bella nodded, unable to speak for a few moments. 'Thank you, Connie.' Her voice came out hoarse and scratchy. 'I don't want to give up on him.'

'Then don't.' Connie suddenly yawned. 'Excuse me. All this has worn me out. I hope you'll be able to sleep now.'

'I feel a lot better. I'm going to ignore what Mrs Churchill said. It's my life and I'll do what I think is right.'

'That's my girl. I knew you'd fit in well when you came to live here.' Connie stood up. 'Come on, time for bed.'

Chapter Six

Winnie was halfway across the hall, heading for the kitchen, when the telephone started to ring, making her jump half out of her skin and Trixie bark loudly. Her first thought as she dashed across to answer it was that something was wrong. Who rang for anything other than to pass on bad news at half past six in the morning?

'Hello,' she said warily.

'Winnie, is that you? It's Station Officer Steele.'

Something was definitely wrong; why else would the boss be telephoning? 'Yes, I'm here.'

'There's an unexploded bomb at Station 75. All the crews have been evacuated and the station's out of action until it's been dealt with.'

'A bomb?'

'Yes, came down last night and thankfully didn't explode, otherwise Station 75 wouldn't exist this morning.

It's been given a category A so will be defused as soon as possible so that we can get operational again, but it could take a while.'

'How long?' Winnie asked.

'That is the question: as soon as they can. In the meantime, I'm telephoning all the crew I can to tell you not to come in for the start of normal shift. Give it a few hours and then come and see what's happening. There's no point us all hanging around waiting. You'll let Bella know?'

'Of course.'

'Jolly good. Goodbye.' Station Officer Steele quickly ended the call.

'Well, Trixie, we have some unexpected time off.' Winnie bent down and patted the little dog's head. 'Let's hope they can defuse it, otherwise ...' Her stomach tightened: she didn't want to think about the prospect of Station 75 being blown up, because it had become like a second home to her.

'You can't come down 'ere! Can't you read?' A policeman pointed to the UXB sign blocking the road leading down to Station 75, arms crossed as he glared at her.

'I'll answer your second question first,' Winnie said crisply, feeling herself starting to bristle. 'Yes, I can read perfectly well, thank you. And down there is where we work. At Station 75.'

'Winnie!' Bella hissed at her. 'Calm down, he's only doing his job.'

'Not today you don't,' the policeman said. 'No one's allowed past this point.'

'Are these two giving you any trouble, Constable?' a familiar voice said. Winnie looked round and saw Station Officer Steele striding towards them.

'I was just tellin' 'em they can't go down there on account of the UXB,' the policeman said.

'Of course they can't.' Station Officer Steele turned to the two girls. 'The landlord of the Ten Bells has kindly allowed ambulance crew to wait in the snug, so come and join us.' Not waiting for them to reply, she turned on her well-polished heel and marched across the road and into the pub.

'Well we'd better do as the boss says,' Bella said, turning her bicycle round. 'Never thought we'd be spending part of our shift in there.'

'It'll be strictly cups of tea, so don't go getting any fancy ideas about drinking on duty,' Winnie said.

Inside the pub, crew members were sitting around drinking tea, as Winnie had predicted, and occupying themselves just as they might while waiting for call-outs to incidents. Winnie spotted Frankie, who was sitting in the far corner, absorbed in her drawing.

'Frankie!' she called as she and Bella went over to her, Trixie scampering ahead of them and receiving a warm welcome.

'So you've arrived at last,' Frankie said, moving along the wooden bench to make room for them to sit.

'Didn't you get the message not to come in?' Winnie asked.

'We ain't got a telephone, so I didn't know nothin' about it till I turned into the Minories and saw the UXB sign up.'

'Do you know where the bomb is?' Bella asked.

'In the courtyard. It's a five-hundred-pounder. The bomb disposal squad are dealing with it.'

'Tea?' Station Officer Steele arrived with a cup for both of them.

'Thanks.' Bella took the cups off the tray and put them on the table, where Frankie had moved her drawing book over.

'Where's Mac?' Winnie asked.

'He's gone to find out what's happening.' The boss glanced at her watch. 'I thought he'd have been back by now.'

A prickle of worry shivered over Winnie's skin. 'He should be in here with the rest of us. What time did he go?'

'About half an hour ago.'

Winnie stood up. 'I'm just going to see where he is. Keep hold of Trixie for me.'

'Winnie!' Bella called.

Winnie ignored her and made for the door, her mind on one thing only: Mac and what on earth he was doing. Was he safe?

'Oh, it's you,' the policeman said as Winnie approached the barricade blocking off the road.

'Yes, here I am again. My station officer is wondering what's happened to the crew member she sent to find out what was going on – a tall man, dark hair.'

'He's still through there with the bomb disposal lot.' The policeman indicated towards the ambulance station.

Further down the street, opposite the turn into Station 75, a wall of sandbags had been built, behind which some soldiers were waiting. Among them, dressed in the usual dark blue overalls that he wore for work, was Mac.

Her immediate thought was to whistle to him, that high-pitched piercing whistle that Harry had taught her to do using her fingers, but it wasn't a good idea in an area where a bomb was being made safe, when any sudden noise could cause the defuser to jump and ... She didn't want to think about that; she knew what could and did happen to bomb disposal crews.

This was going to require stealth and a smidgen of rule-bending. Winnie sighed and nodded to the policeman, then turned back towards the pub. Stopping to pretend to do up her shoelace, she crouched down and looked back at the policeman, who now had his back to her, watching what was going on beyond the barricade. She stood up, adjusted the strap on her steel helmet and then ran for it, jumping over the barrier in one clean leap, one her sports mistress at school would have been proud of. She was past the policeman and halfway down the street before he shouted for her to stop, but she ignored him and kept going until she reached the sandbag wall.

'What the ...?' one of the bomb disposal crew exclaimed as she skidded to a halt behind the sandbag wall and crouched down next to Mac. 'You shouldn't be here.'

'Winnie, what the bloody hell are you doing here?' Mac said. He didn't look pleased to see her.

'I could say the same about you. The boss is wondering where you are. So I—' Winnie stopped as a firm hand gripped her arm and hauled her to her feet.

'I've a good mind to arrest you,' the constable panted.

'Don't. I'll take her back.' Mac stood up. 'She won't do it again, will you?'

For a moment Winnie had the strongest of desires to argue, to say that they couldn't tell her what to do, but she knew it wouldn't be a good idea. 'No.'

'Very well, but if I see her outside of the pub before that bomb's been made safe, then I *will* arrest her.' The constable puffed up his chest like one of the pigeons that strutted around London, and it took all of Winnie's will-power not to smile.

'Come on.' Mac took hold of her arm and marched her back towards the pub. 'What the hell were you thinking of?'

'You. I was worried about you. What were you doing down there?'

'The boss sent me down to find out what was happening.'

'But that should only have taken five minutes. She was wondering where you'd got to.'

Mac looked at her sheepishly. 'Well I got talking to the lads. They're waiting while the officer and the sergeant defuse the bomb, then they'll take it somewhere safe to blow it up. Some of them are conscientious objectors like me.'

151

'Not like you!' Winnie snapped. 'You're an ambulance driver.'

'Well not in the same job maybe, but a CO is a CO.'

Nearing the pub, Winnie stopped walking. 'Don't tell the boss about me running past the policeman, will you? It was ... well, a stupid thing to do, but I just wanted to get to you.'

Mac looked at her, then took hold of her hand and squeezed it. 'Only if you promise never to do something like that again. The barrier is there for a reason.'

'*You* went past it.'

'Winnie, let's not argue over this. We're both safe and sound, so let's just leave it there. We both went beyond the barrier and came back. All right?'

She nodded. 'Very well. Come on, the boss will want to know what's going on and if we're likely to be allowed back into Station 75 before the end of the shift.'

Only a few hours remained of their shift by the time the barrier blocking the road was removed. Station 75's crew stood outside the pub and clapped and cheered as the bomb disposal men drove away in their truck with the defused bomb loaded in the back.

'Right, let's get back to work,' Station Officer Steele said. 'We need to get the station back in operational order as quickly as we can.' She turned on her heel and strode back to Station 75, with the crews following in her wake.

'Did you see the size of it?' Bella asked, walking beside

Winnie. 'If that had exploded, Station 75 would have been no more.'

Winnie linked her arm through her friend's. 'Luckily for us, it didn't. Seeing a bomb like that . . . ' She shivered. 'Horrid thing.'

'The bomb disposal teams know what they're doing,' Mac said, joining in the conversation. 'They've got a lot better at it since the start of the Blitz, only the Germans keep changing the types of fuses to try to catch them out, so they have to keep up with them and learn new ways of defusing the bombs safely.'

'How do you know all this?' Frankie asked.

'Just by talking to them when I went to find out what was happening,' Mac replied.

'They do a terribly dangerous job,' Winnie said. 'I'm glad we just drive ambulances for the war effort.'

'Bella, Frankie, can you come into my office for a moment, please?' Station Officer Steele called across the common room from the door of her office before disappearing back inside again.

'What's going on?' Bella quietly mouthed to Frankie, who was relaxing in the armchair opposite her.

Frankie shrugged. 'Only one way to find out.'

Bella left the paper she'd been reading on the arm of her chair and followed Frankie to the office, where they saw that their boss was not alone. Sitting in the chair beside her desk was a tall, thin man, who immediately sprang to his feet as they walked in.

'Bella, Frankie, this is Mr Dawson, he's a journalist who wants to write a piece about the work of the London Auxiliary Ambulance Service and has chosen Station 75.'

Mr Dawson held out his hand to shake both of theirs. 'Pleased to meet you,' he said.

'Hello.' Bella couldn't help noticing how yellow and nicotine-stained his fingers were as she shook his hand.

'I thought it would be best to send Mr Dawson out with you two,' Station Officer Steele said. 'You can answer any questions he has and show him how you deal with incidents.' She turned to the journalist. 'Of course my crew will be carrying on with their duties as normal; there'll be no time to pose for photographs at an incident, not when casualties need getting to hospital. Any photos you do take will have to be real-life action shots, but,' she smiled, 'I'm sure your readers would prefer that to a posed picture.'

'Right you are,' Mr Dawson said. 'I'm here to get an idea of the real thing. People want to know what's happening out there when your gallant crews go out in the middle of air raids to rescue the wounded.'

Bella caught Frankie's eye and she knew her friend was thinking the same as her. Gallant crews indeed! Having a journalist along with them was going to be an interesting experience.

'So, Mr Dawson, Bella and Frankie will give you a guided tour of our station and explain how we do things. If the air-raid siren sounds, you must go with them to our shelter out in the courtyard where all the crews wait to be called out,' Station Officer Steele explained. 'Frankie, can you make sure that Mr Dawson is given a steel helmet to wear when you go out, please?'

'Of course,' Frankie said.

'Jolly good.' The boss smiled. 'I look forward to seeing your write-up about us, Mr Dawson.'

'I'll make sure you're sent a copy.' Mr Dawson picked up his hat. 'Shall we make a start, then?' He smiled at Bella and Frankie. 'If you'll show me the ambulances first ...'

Bella nodded. 'If you'd like to follow Frankie, she'll lead the way.'

Down in the courtyard, Mr Dawson had a good look at Station 75's fleet of ambulances, which as usual had all been prepared at the start of their shift and were ready to go at a moment's notice. His close examination of each one reminded Bella of a sniffer dog on the trail of something.

'What are all these pockmarks?' he asked, trailing his hand over the dented bonnet of one ambulance, his fingers feeling the pits in the metal.

'They're where bits of shrapnel hit it,' Frankie said. 'All the ambulances have got them, and there are plenty of dents and bumps from falling debris as well. Our vehicles are battle-scarred veterans.'

'They're an odd assortment,' Mr Dawson said, scribbling something down in his notebook. 'I'd wrongly assumed they'd be all the same.'

'It's a case of needs must,' Bella said. 'We've got a few pre-war ambulances, but this one,' she put her hand on the grey bonnet of the nearest vehicle, 'is a converted car: a box van fitted on a saloon car chassis. It does the job.'

'I've seen a converted Rolls-Royce ambulance,' Frankie said. 'But we ain't got one of them 'ere.'

'Where'd they get a Rolls-Royce from?' Mr Dawson asked, writing in his notebook.

'A lot of fancy cars have been donated. They can't be used by their owners because of petrol rationing, so they've given them to the ambulance service instead,' Bella explained.

By the time the air-raid siren started its mournful wail over the rooftops, Bella felt like she and Frankie had been thoroughly quizzed. It seemed there was nothing Mr Dawson hadn't discovered about Station 75 and the job the ambulance crews did. She'd found it fascinating to see how he worked, asking hundreds of questions and winkling out information for his article. He was definitely thorough in his research, but he needed to see them in action to fully understand what they did.

'How long before we get called out?' he asked, sitting next to Bella in the shelter.

She shrugged. 'There's no telling. It depends where the bombs fall; if they're in our patch or whether another area gets hit hard and we get called in as extra help. We just have to be patient and wait.'

Mr Dawson nodded, twiddling the pencil that was permanently in his fingers as he looked at the other crew members, who had settled down and were occupying themselves with various distractions.

'We try to relax and rest while we wait,' Bella told him, thinking that the journalist didn't look like someone who ever did a lot of relaxing. In fact he seemed even more fidgety now that they were cooped up in the shelter. He was probably nervous, she thought.

'So what do you usually do to pass the time in here? Do you draw like your friend?' Mr Dawson nodded to Frankie, who sat opposite drawing in her sketchbook.

'No, not me, I'm no artist,' Bella said. 'I write, just bits and pieces, recording stuff.'

Mr Dawson looked interested. 'What sort of things?'

'Just things I've noticed or heard. I like to get it down on paper, try and find the best words to describe it, like painting a picture with words. I really enjoy it.'

He nodded appreciatively. 'A writer's choice of words can make all the difference.'

'How long have you been a journalist?'

'Oh, years.' He paused for a moment. 'I joined my local paper as a cub reporter when I left school and have been doing it ever since, so about thirty-five years.'

'Have you always been in London?'

He nodded. 'It's a good job, I like it. When—' He stopped, his mouth still open, as the telephone started to ring, its shrill sound echoing around the shelter before it was cut short when Winnie picked it up. 'Is it a call-out?' he whispered to Bella, his eyes not leaving her friend, who was listening intently to whoever was at the other end of the line.

'Possibly.'

Putting down the receiver, Winnie called out, 'Frankie, Bella and Mr Dawson.'

Bella stood up. 'Time to go.'

Mr Dawson looked up at her, his face suddenly drained of colour. He swallowed hard and then nodded, rising to his feet.

'Frankie's going to get the ambulance ready to go, and we'll collect the instructions.'

'Good luck, Mr Dawson, and do be sure to keep your steel helmet on at all times,' Winnie said as she handed over the chit to Bella. 'It's not just there to look good.'

'Don't worry, I will,' Mr Dawson said, checking the chin strap of his helmet was securely in place.

'Ready?' Bella asked him.

'Yes,' he said, doing his best to smile, still grasping his pencil tightly in his fist.

Outside, Frankie was waiting with the engine running.

'Ensign Street, off Cable Street,' Bella said as she climbed in, sitting in the middle with Mr Dawson nearest the window.

'Do you know where that is?' Mr Dawson asked Frankie.

'Of course I do.' Frankie smiled at him as she put the ambulance into gear and drove them out of Station 75's courtyard. 'We have to know our patch well; there's no time for getting lost when people need to get to hospital.'

'Have you been out with any of the other civil defence services?' Bella asked.

'No, you're the first. I'm not usually out in the middle of an air raid.' Mr Dawson cleared his throat. 'It's a—'

A bomb exploded at the far end of the street they were driving along, the flash and roar startling them and making Mr Dawson leap up in his seat, letting out a loud yelp. Dust and rubble rained down on the ambulance as Frankie brought it to a safe halt.

'Are you all right there, Mr Dawson?' she asked.

'Yes, made me jump, that's all,' he said, his voice strained. 'Is it always like this?'

'Like what?' Bella asked. Frankie had started to turn the ambulance around as the road ahead of them was blocked.

'You know, bombs going off . . .' Mr Dawson said.

'Well it is an air raid . . . This isn't too bad; we've been out in a lot worse, incendiaries raining down and fires burning on both sides of the road.' Bella patted his arm. 'You'll be all right.'

'You girls are made of stern stuff,' Mr Dawson said. 'I'm not sure I could do this every night.'

When they reached Ensign Street, the rescue workers were busy digging in the remains of a house that had collapsed into a pile of rubble, beams sticking out like matchsticks.

'You just do your job and ignore me,' Mr Dawson said as Frankie parked the ambulance where an ARP warden directed her to. 'I'll keep out of your way and take photographs.'

'It's not light enough for them to come out, is it?' Frankie asked.

'I've got a special infrared flash light to use, so they'll come out just fine,' Mr Dawson assured her.

With three casualties to tend to, Bella forgot about the journalist being with them. He'd kept his word and stayed out of their way, not bothering them with questions as she and Frankie carried out their examinations and basic first aid, applying field dressings and loading the wounded into the ambulance.

'Can I ride with you in the back?' Mr Dawson asked as Bella climbed into the ambulance ready to take care of the casualties on their way to hospital.

She looked at Frankie, who shrugged. 'If you want to, but it's not very comfortable. You'd be better off in the front.'

'No, no, I want to experience it for myself, see what you do,' he said.

'All right then.' Bella held out her hand to help him climb in. 'I need to keep a close eye on the casualties, so you'd better stay down that end near the door.'

'Who's 'e?' asked the old woman they'd loaded in last as Frankie closed the ambulance doors and Bella switched on her torch to illuminate the inside with its dim light.

'He's a journalist, he's writing a piece about the ambulance service,' Bella explained, holding on to the side of the frame in which the stretchers were loaded as Frankie started the engine and pulled gently away.

'Are we goin' to be in the paper?' the old woman asked, before starting to cough.

'I'm not sure.' Bella laid her hand on the woman's fore-head. 'You just relax and try not to—'

'Goin' ter be sick,' the old woman suddenly said, turning on her side and making retching noises.

Bella whipped out one of the buckets kept ready for such events, putting her hand gently on the woman's shoulder as she vomited noisily into it. The acrid smell quickly filled the confines of the ambulance, and Bella had to ignore the horrible feeling of nausea it evoked in her. She couldn't be sick herself with injured people to care for.

As soon as the old woman had finished, slumping flat on her stretcher again, Bella clanged the lid on the bucket to seal in its foul contents and stowed it away to deal with later.

'Are you all right there, Mr Dawson?' she asked.

He turned round to look at her. 'Yes,' he replied, his voice muffled by the handkerchief he was holding over his mouth and nose.

'Frankie? How long till we get there?' Bella called through the grille to the driver's cab.

'Nearly there, a few more minutes,' Frankie called back.

Just as well, Bella thought, looking at Mr Dawson, whose shoulders were hunched as he sat on the floor facing the back doors. He was probably wishing he'd sat in the front with Frankie now, but he had said he wanted to experience a call-out for himself so that he could write about the real work of the ambulance crews. At least it was only vomit and she'd managed to contain it, rather than blood or other bodily fluids dripping on to the floor as sometimes happened. She had the feeling the journalist wouldn't be writing about the less palatable side of the ambulance crews' work – it wasn't the sort of thing readers wanted to hear about, she suspected.

'Can't you give me a clue where we're goin'?' Frankie asked as she strolled along Oxford Street, arm in arm with Alastair. 'Not even a little one?'

'No, I can't, otherwise it won't be a surprise.' Alastair smiled warmly at her, his blue eyes twinkling with amusement. 'You'll know soon enough.'

'Will I like it?'

'I hope so. I've heard good things about it.' He stopped and turned her towards him, planting a kiss on her lips. 'No more questions, we're nearly there.'

Frankie laughed. 'You can't blame me for tryin'.' It didn't matter where he was taking her, she thought. She was just happy to have a whole afternoon to spend with him, their differing shift patterns finally allowing them more than just a snatched half-hour together.

She was momentarily lost for words when they arrived outside the London Palladium, with its colourful posters advertising its popular variety show *Apple-Sauce!*. 'Is this it?'

'Yes.' Alastair smiled at her. 'I've got tickets for the matinee.' He reached inside his jacket pocket and pulled them out. 'I thought you might enjoy seeing the show.'

Frankie threw her arms around him and hugged him

tightly. She'd read about the popular variety show in the paper but never thought she'd get to see it herself. 'Thank you, I've been trying to guess where we were goin', but I never expected this.'

'I thought you'd like it.' Alastair hugged her back. 'It's nearly time for curtain up, so we'd better go inside or they'll start without us.'

Sitting in her seat in the stalls, Frankie gazed around the theatre, taking in every detail: the ornate decoration, the boxes high up at the sides with only a few people sitting in each, and the heavy curtain hanging in swathes across the stage. The discordant sound of the orchestra running through its final tuning sent a shiver of anticipation down her spine.

'It's lovely.' She squeezed Alastair's hand then lowered her voice to whisper in his ear. 'I ain't ever been to the theatre before.'

'Then it's a good show to start with.'

It felt different to the pictures she usually went to, Frankie thought; there was an expectant atmosphere, with everyone in the audience waiting for the show to begin. She had a tingling of excitement in the pit of her stomach, not knowing what to expect.

'Let's see who's on first.' Alastair opened the programme he'd bought and held it so they could both read it.

Frankie quickly scanned down the list of acts. 'There's Vera Lynn.' She could hardly believe she was about to see the famous singer with her own eyes. She'd heard her on the wireless many times, her beautiful voice filling the common room at Station 75, where crew members often joined in.

'And there's Max Miller, the comedian.' Alastair pointed to where his name appeared several times in the list of acts.

From the moment the lights dimmed, the orchestra began to play and the curtains opened, Frankie was transfixed, her feet tapping to the music, laughing at the jokes and sketches and bowled over by Vera Lynn's singing. It was all quite wonderful, and when the curtain finally fell at the end of the show, she felt as if she'd been carried away for a while.

'Are you all right, Frankie?' Alastair asked.

Nodding, she turned to him and smiled. 'Yes, I am, it's like I've been off out of myself for a while, forgetting about the everyday, like on a holiday.'

Alastair took hold of her hand. 'Good, I think we needed that. I certainly feel better for it. My sides were aching laughing at Max Miller. Do you want to go and have something to eat? There's time before we need to start heading back.'

'Yes please.' Frankie was in no hurry. She wasn't due back on duty until half past eleven that night and wanted to spend every moment she could with Alastair. 'Let's go to a Lyons Corner House.'

Frankie loved the atmosphere of the Lyons Corner House on the Strand, with its orchestra playing, the gentle hum of conversation, the chink of cutlery on china, and the nippies weaving their way between the tables in their smart black-and-white uniforms.

Sipping her tea, she suddenly remembered she'd brought something to show Alastair. She reached into her bag, bringing out the cutting she'd taken from the paper and handing it to him. 'Recognise anyone?'

Alastair looked at the photograph that accompanied the piece. 'You and Bella.' He smiled at her. 'This was when you took that journalist out with you.'

'Yes, he had a special camera for takin' pictures in poor light, and it worked.' The picture of her and Bella carrying a casualty on a stretcher wasn't as clear as a photograph taken in daylight, but it was still clear enough to see them properly.

Alastair read through the article. 'He's full of praise for Station 75.'

'Station Officer Steele was pleased with it; she's pinned a copy up on the noticeboard in the common room. 'E makes it sound a lot more glorious and noble than it really is. There's no mention of the 'orrible bits. No gory injuries or people dying before we can get them to hospital.'

'I don't suppose the readers want to hear about that. It's got to be morale-boosting to keep us going.' Alastair reached across the table and took hold of her hand. 'You do a good job, Frankie. I know it's not always easy and you see things that . . . ' He shrugged. 'I'm proud of you.'

'I'm proud of you too.'

They both knew how hellish it could be out in the air raids, and their aftermath when broken bodies needed urgent help. Seeing people so badly injured day after day was hard, especially when it was little children. It could get you down, make you wonder whether the bombing would ever end.

Frankie gave herself a mental shake. She had to keep her chin up, as Winnie was so fond of saying. Here she was with Alastair on a much-longed-for afternoon out, and she shouldn't waste a precious second of it on gloomy thoughts.

She smiled at him. 'So shall we go dancing? I like the idea of spending time wrapped in your arms.'

'Aye, that sounds good to me.'

Bella was kneeling on top of the ambulance, washing the grey paintwork, pools of suds puddling in the dents made by shrapnel and debris. Pausing to dip her rag into the bucket of soapy water, she sat back on her heels and looked up to admire the April sky, which was a beautiful blue, bringing with it a promise of a long-awaited spring after the cold days of winter.

'Oy! That ain't the way to get the job done,' a voice called from above.

Bella looked up to see Sparky smiling down at her from the open common-room window. 'There's a telephone call for you.'

'For me?'

'Yes, for you, so shift yerself and come and see to it. The boss is keeping them talkin' till you get there. Gawd knows what she might be sayin', you'd better 'urry up.'

'Who is it?'

Sparky shrugged. 'I ain't got a clue, she just said "Fetch Bella", that's all I know.'

Hurriedly climbing down the ladder, Bella's mind flicked through the possibilities of who might be telephoning her here. The only answer she could come up with was her mother, and that would be because something was wrong. As she raced up the stairs to her boss's office, her heart was pounding, and not just because of her haste. Was her mother ill, or had something happened to Walter? She was dreading what she might be about to find out; she wanted to know and yet she didn't.

Station Officer Steele looked up as Bella arrived at her office doorway. 'Ah, here she is now. I'll pass you over to her,' she said into the receiver, then held it out to Bella, smiling. 'It's nothing to worry about, my dear.'

Taking the telephone gingerly, Bella held it up to her ear. 'Hello,' she said.

'Ah, Bella, it's Eric Dawson here, you remember I went out to an incident with you and Frankie a few weeks ago.'

'Of course I do. Hello, Mr Dawson.' Why was he telephoning her? Did he want to come to another incident?

'I hope you liked the piece I wrote in the *War Illustrated*. I thought it came out rather well.'

'Yes, I did, we've got a copy of it pinned up in our common room, as a matter of fact.'

'Excellent. Now the reason I'm telephoning you is to offer you a little job. Your station officer is quite happy for you to do it.'

Bella glanced at the boss, who nodded at her, smiling. 'What is it?'

'You might recall that you told me you like writing, said it's "painting pictures with words", as I recall. Well, my editor wants you to write a piece about working for the ambulance service, something along the lines of an interesting or amusing thing that happened that would give our readers a flavour of what it's like to work as ambulance crew. About four hundred words, ready for the next edition.'

Bella didn't know what to say. She liked writing very much, but writing for her own amusement was different to writing for a national newspaper that would be read by thousands. 'I don't know if I can.'

'Nonsense,' Mr Dawson said. 'Station Officer Steele thinks you are the perfect person for the job, and I trust her judgement. It's only four hundred words, not a whole novel, and you have a week to deliver.'

Bella felt a hand on her shoulder. 'You *can* do this, Bella. I know you can.' Her boss's eyes were sincere behind her owlish glasses.

'Very well then.' The words were out of her mouth before she had time to realise what she was saying.

'Excellent. I look forward to getting your copy in one week's time. Goodbye then.' Not waiting for her answer, he disconnected.

Slowly replacing the receiver, Bella felt slightly dazed. Had she really just agreed to do it? She'd have to telephone him back, say it was all a mistake, she couldn't possibly do it, he'd have to find someone else.

168

'I know what you're thinking, Bella, and you are wrong,' Station Officer Steele said, gesturing for her to sit down. 'This is something you can do, and do well. It's a great opportunity for you; who knows what it could lead to?'

'But what would I write?' Bella asked.

'There are plenty of tales you could tell, some sad, some funny. The only thing I ask is that you don't use the real name of any crew member; we need to respect their privacy.'

To Bella's surprise, some ideas started filtering into her mind. Perhaps she could do this after all. 'I don't want anyone else to know what I'm doing. If it goes wrong then it doesn't matter, no one will be any the wiser.'

'Not even Frankie and Winnie?'

Bella shook her head. 'No, not even my best friends.'

Her boss frowned. 'But why ever not? They'd be thrilled for you.'

Bella sighed. 'I know, but … It's just I'm not highly educated like Winnie, I didn't go to a fancy school like her. I had to leave when I was fourteen. I—'

'Stop right there.' The older woman held up her hand. 'Just because Winnie went to an expensive boarding school does not mean she is any better educated than you. In fact from what I've gathered from Winnie herself, she wasn't the best of pupils, excelling on the sports field far more than in the classroom. Frankie would only have gone to her local school in Stepney. Out of the three of you, I suspect that you are actually the most highly educated – you might not have stayed at school as long as Winnie, but you have educated yourself greatly since then by reading so extensively.' She paused and smiled. 'You are a very intelligent young woman who given the chance could go to university.'

Bella's cheeks grew warm. 'I don't know about that, but I really don't want to tell them yet. I will in time, but only once I've proved to myself and Mr Dawson that I can do it.'

Station Officer Steele nodded. 'Very well, I understand, but you do undersell yourself. You need to believe in yourself more.' She reached out and touched Bella's arm, smiling warmly at her. 'I have no doubt that you will do an excellent job and I look forward to seeing it in print.'

Bella did her best to smile back, hoping that she could live up to Mr Dawson and Station Officer Steele's faith in her. This was an unexpected, wonderful chance to do something different, something that might lead on to other things, something that was making a small spark of excitement squiggle and squirm in her stomach.

'Are you feeling all right?' Winnie asked Bella as she was doing the washing-up that evening. 'Only you've seemed a bit distracted since we got home.'

Bella finished drying the plate she was holding and smiled at her friend. 'I'm feeling perfectly fine, just a bit tired. It takes me a while to adjust when we switch shifts around. I'll probably have an early night.' She ignored the twinge of guilt that poked at her for not telling Winnie what was really distracting her.

'Sounds like a good idea. I might turn in early as well after my bath,' Winnie said.

Bella was grateful that Winnie had been down at the allotments with Frankie when Mr Dawson had called, so knew nothing about the fact that she'd had a phone call. Had her friends been there, she might not have been able to keep what had happened from them. Until she'd actually written the piece, it really was best to keep it a secret, wasn't it?

Sitting cross-legged on her bed a short while later, with paper and pencil at the ready, Bella thought through what she was going to write. She'd decided on something that had surprised her when she'd started working at Station 75, something Mr Dawson hadn't picked up on and written about in his article, but was what made it such a good place to work.

She started to write, and to her surprise and utter delight, the words poured out of her as if they'd been there waiting all along. When she'd finished, she read it through, altering a word here and there, tightening a sentence to make sure it was the best she could make it and counting the words to make sure she hadn't gone over the limit Mr Dawson had asked for. Satisfied, she put it down. Although she knew that she'd come back to tinker around with it again tomorrow before she handed it in, for now she was happy, surprised at how it had flowed out of her, and thrilled with how much she had enjoyed writing it.

Chapter Seven

'I think Station Officer Steele sent me here on purpose,' Hooky said, tears glinting in her eyes as she surveyed the scene of carnage before them. 'She could have sent any of the crews and yet she picked *me*.'

And me too! thought Winnie, getting a body bag ready on the stretcher and doing her best to ignore the metallic tang of blood in the air, but Hooky would never consider that, only herself. Winnie didn't say anything. She was too tired, and it was going to be hard enough keeping her own emotions in check without having to deal with Hooky's tantrum as well.

'I can hardly bear to look at them.' Hooky pulled a face.

Winnie rounded on her, hands on hips. 'For God's sake show some respect and thought for these poor people,' she hissed. 'Just get on with it and stop whingeing.'

Hooky stared at her, tears filling her baby-blue eyes. Winnie instantly felt guilty for snapping. Hooky was understandably scared and revolted by the terrible sight. It was Winnie's job to encourage and support her, as Station Officer Steele would do if she were here.

'Look, I'm sorry.' She put her hand on Hooky's shoulder. 'I know this is beastly but it needs to be done. Imagine if these poor people were members of your family; you'd want them to be treated with respect and dignity in death, wouldn't you?'

Hooky nodded, sniffing loudly.

'So come on, let's do what we can for them, and if you need to take five minutes' break at any point, I'll quite understand.'

'Thank you.' Hooky managed a weak smile.

Winnie left her to gather herself together as she started her own grim task. Last night's air raid had been hellish, bombs raining down for hours on end, and the day shift had been called out to deal with the consequences this morning. Normally their ambulance carried the living, but not today: these poor souls were gone. They hadn't stood a chance last night, and now Winnie and Hooky had the gruesome but necessary task of collecting up the body parts and attempting to sort arms, legs and torsos into body bags ready to be taken to the hospital so they could be certified dead.

All these people snuffed out in an instant, Winnie thought as she spotted an arm with a sleeve that matched the material of the coat on a torso that she'd already put

173

in a body bag. She picked it up and laid it carefully in the bag, then began her search for the other arm.

By the time they'd loaded four pieced-together bodies into the back of the ambulance, Winnie felt strung out, her patience worn thin as she despaired at what the war was doing to innocent people. Trixie had picked up on her sombre mood, sitting close by her mistress, leaning against her as if to comfort her.

As she started the engine, her mind was awhirl. These poor people who'd been blown apart hadn't been responsible for starting the war, she reflected, but they had paid the ultimate price. Sometimes it was hard to keep doing this job, which exposed her to the horrors of what war could do. Just keep going, she told herself, get the job done. Take them to hospital so they could be declared officially dead, then on to the morgue, and then go back to pick up more bodies and do the same all over again.

Arriving back at Station 75 after a difficult few hours' work, she parked the ambulance and was climbing out when Sparky came over to her with one of those looks on his face, the one he wore when he was about to tease her.

Winnie put her hand up to stop him before he could say anything. After what she'd faced this morning, she wasn't in the mood for any of his silliness. 'Please don't aggravate me, Sparky, not today.'

He frowned. 'Gawd, what's the matter with you?'

Winnie told him what they'd been doing.

'That ain't nice. I've done that and it . . .' He shook his head. 'I weren't goin' to upset you, Winnie, it's just I 'eard somethin' I thought you'd want to know.'

'And what would I want to know?' Winnie demanded.

'St Paul's was bombed last night.'

Winnie stared at him, not wanting to believe what he'd just said. Her day had just become even worse. 'How bad is it?'

Sparky shrugged. 'That's all I know, 'eard it from a fireman when I was out at an incident a little while ago. Didn't you see anything on your way here this morning? You usually go past it, don't you?'

'Not today we didn't. We came a different route because of the roads closed in Holborn,' Winnie explained.

'You'd better go and 'ave a look on yer way 'ome then. I'm sorry to tell you that, I know how much you like that old cathedral.'

She sighed. 'I'll definitely go and look.'

'But not before you've reported back and signed off the job.' Sparky patted her shoulder. 'Go on, the boss'll be waiting, she'll have 'eard the ambulance come back.'

Winnie nodded. Finding out about the state of St Paul's would have to wait for the moment.

'It's no good, I've simply got to go and find out what's happened.' Winnie threw the broom she'd been using to sweep the garage floor back into its place in the corner and hurried over to where she'd left her bicycle propped against the far wall.

'Winnie, wait!' Bella, who was on her hands and knees sweeping up the pile of dirt with a dustpan and brush, yelled after her. 'Don't be so bloody stupid.'

Winnie stopped in her tracks. Bella never swore. She spun around to face her. 'You just swore.'

'I did, and if you go off now, you deserve it.' Bella had climbed to her feet, her hands on her hips and a furious look on her face. 'You could end up in a whole lot of unwanted trouble from the boss.'

'I don't care,' Winnie said mutinously, throwing her arms wide. 'I need to find out what's happened; I can't get it out of my mind. It's been a horrid shift and finding out about St Paul's made it even worse.'

Since Sparky had told her the news, thoughts of how badly damaged the cathedral might be had been tormenting her. She hadn't been able to get it out of her mind; she was worried about the charming, exceptional building that had come to mean so much to her since she first came to London. It symbolised the city for her, and the thought that it had been bombed was agonising. It didn't help either that she was dog tired after a night of little sleep because of the huge air raid.

Bella came towards her. 'I know you're worried.' She linked her arm through Winnie's. 'But if you wait until the end of the shift –' she glanced at her watch, 'that's only another twenty minutes to go – then I'll come with you and you won't upset the boss.'

Frankie came into the garage carrying a pile of clean folded blankets to go in the ambulances and stopped at the sight of them, her eyes narrowing. 'What's going on?'

Bella quickly explained what Winnie wanted to do.

'Well I wouldn't do anything to upset the boss right now if I were you. She was givin' Hooky a right good tellin'-off a few minutes ago. Last night and the amount of incidents we've had today 'as taken its toll on 'er, so don't push it, Winnie – don't go lookin' for trouble when you don't 'ave to.'

'See,' Bella said. 'So just wait a little longer and I'll go with you when we're finished here.'

'So will I.' Frankie smiled at her. 'But you might not be able to see anything; they won't let anyone in if it's damaged.'

Winnie blinked away sudden tears. 'After what I've dealt with today, I really don't give a fig about waiting another twenty minutes. It's been utterly beastly, so I'm going to St Paul's now.' She bent down, scooped up Trixie and put her in the basket at the front of her bicycle.

'But you might lose your position as deputy station officer, or even your job,' Bella said, her brown eyes anxious.

'I don't care.' Winnie started to push her bicycle out of the garage.

'Wait!' Bella shouted. 'I'm coming with you. Frankie, can you try and cover for us, please?'

Frankie nodded. 'I'll do my best. I'll come along to St Paul's straight after the shift. Wait for me there.'

*

Several times they had to take detours because of roads closed due to bomb damage from last night's raids, or get off and push their bicycles over rubble spilled across the street.

'It looks fairly all right from out 'ere,' Bella said as they arrived and propped their bicycles up against the wall of the cathedral. 'Are you sure Sparky wasn't having you on?'

'He wouldn't be so foolish as to wind me up about my beloved St Paul's. He might play the joker, but he's not stupid,' Winnie said, standing with her hands on her hips as she stared up at the building. She couldn't spot any damage from here, but the roof was many feet higher than she could see.

'We'll have to go in,' she said.

'But we can't!' Bella grabbed her arm. 'We'll have to ask someone, there must be someone we can ask.' She looked around helplessly.

'My dear Bella, sometimes you have to push at the boundaries of life to get what you want,' Winnie said. 'I haven't worried myself silly just to turn back at the first obstacle. Look at me, what do you see?' She flung her arms wide. 'Well?'

Bella stared at her. 'A woman.'

'Come on, you can do better than that,' Winnie encouraged. She pointed to her steel helmet. 'What's this?'

Bella frowned. 'An ambulance service helmet, of course.'

'Exactly. And ... ' Winnie pointed to Bella's own

helmet, 'you're wearing one too, and . . .' she gestured down the street to where she could see Frankie pedalling fast towards them, 'here comes another one. So here we are, an ambulance crew come to rescue a casualty in St Paul's.'

'But we haven't,' Bella said.

'They don't know that, do they? There could have been a mix-up and we were told to come to St Paul's instead of . . .' Winnie shrugged. 'We have the perfect reason to go in there: we are civil defence workers and are here to do our job.'

She quickly explained her plan to a breathless Frankie as she propped her bicycle against theirs.

Frankie started to laugh. 'You've got a lot of gall.'

'Needs must and all that.' Winnie picked Trixie up and tucked her under her arm. 'Heads up and look confident, that's all you need to do, and leave the talking to me.'

'I'm not sure we should do this,' Bella said.

'Please stop worrying, Bella, there's no harm in goin' in to 'ave a quick look, and we *are* ambulance crew, genuine civil defence workers,' Frankie said. 'Ain't you just a little bit curious to see what's 'appened in there?'

'Well, yes,' Bella admitted. 'Wait! Did Station Officer Steele discover we'd gone?'

Frankie grinned. 'No, luck was on your side. She had a telephone call from regional office and was still talking when I left.'

Bella sighed. 'Thank goodness for that.'

'Jolly good, so come on, girls,' Winnie said. 'Follow me.'

It was surprisingly easy to walk in through one of the doors. No one stopped to challenge them, although a few of the St Paul's fire watch did glance as they walked by, their heads held high, looking confident and as if they had every right to be there. Winnie quickly homed in on a pile of rubble lying in the north transept under a hole in the roof through which she could see the cloudy April sky.

'Look at it,' she heard Bella whisper behind her.

'Keep walking, don't stop,' Winnie hissed back over her shoulder, heading straight towards it for a closer look.

The sight of the masonry piled up on the floor, from large chunks to bricks and dust, made Winnie's heart drop into her shoes. Beams protruded from the rubble like broken bones, and columns lay toppled in the dust. Getting closer, she could see that a crater had been punched through the tiled floor into the crypt below, so that the under-storey's arched ceiling was visible through the hole. She couldn't help thinking how odd it seemed to see the chairs still standing in their neat rows just a few yards from the crater and its surrounding chaos.

Bella came to stand beside her, slipping her arm through Winnie's, while Frankie stopped on her other side, putting her hand on her shoulder. 'Thank you,' Winnie whispered, her voice coming out in a croak.

They'd barely been there a minute when a voice

intruded on them. 'What are you doing in here? You shouldn't be there, it's not safe.'

Taking a deep breath, Winnie glanced quickly at both of her friends, who had suddenly stiffened at the sound of the voice. Poor Bella's face had gone pale, so Winnie winked at her before turning around to see who was talking to them.

'Could you direct us to your casualty, please?' she said.

The man, a senior member of the St Paul's fire watch from the look of him, frowned. 'There are no casualties here, except for the poor old cathedral, and there's nothing you can do for her. You sure you've got the right place? We didn't call for an ambulance.'

Winnie raised her eyebrows, shaking her head, and gave an exaggerated sigh. 'We've been sent to the wrong place then. It's been such a hectic shift after last night, it's not surprising we don't know if we're coming or going sometimes.' She took a step towards him, smiling. 'I'm most terribly sorry to have bothered you.'

The man smiled back, completely disarmed by Winnie's charming apology. 'No harm done. I hope you sort out where you need to be.'

Winnie nodded, looking down into the crater. 'Do you think the cathedral will be all right? Can it be repaired?'

'Of course it will. We're not going to let a bomb get us down, and holes can be mended.' He looked around, his eyes drawn to the soaring heights above him before returning to the three girls. 'We'll be watching over her till the end of the war. Hitler's not going to get St Paul's while we're here to fight for it.'

'Thank you.' Winnie beamed at him. 'London wouldn't be the same without it.' She turned to Frankie and Bella. 'Come on, we need to get a move on.'

They nodded and followed her without a word as she strode confidently back down the nave towards the door they'd come in through. She smiled at the fire-watchers, who returned her smile and touched the brims of their own steel helmets.

Outside in the fresh air, Winnie didn't stop walking till they were back where they'd left their bicycles, then she spun around and beamed at her friends, who stood staring at her shaking their heads.

'You were so cool and collected,' Frankie said. 'Astonishing. They should parachute you in to France as a secret agent.'

'I wanted to confess all,' Bella said. 'I'm surprised you didn't hear my heart thudding when that man asked us what we were doing in there.'

Winnie beamed at them. 'I told you we could do it. It just takes a bit of confidence and belief in yourself. I . . .' She stopped as a bubble of laughter welled up inside her and burst out.

Frankie and Bella joined in too, the three of them soon bent double holding their aching sides. It was several minutes before they managed to calm down without one of them setting the others off laughing again.

'Thank you for coming with me. I'm not sure I could

have done it without you, you know. I probably wouldn't have dared,' Winnie admitted. 'You really are both such darling friends.'

'Right, I'm all set.' Josie put her white fire-watcher's helmet on her head and beamed a wide smile at Frankie. 'Hitler can drop his nasty ol' incendiaries, but we'll be waiting for 'em. They ain't goin' to burn down Matlock Street on our watch.'

Frankie smiled warmly at her neighbour, who had thoroughly embraced her role as a fire-watcher, even fashioning a uniform of sorts for herself, abandoning her usual dress and crossover apron for a pair of her husband's trousers and one of his shirts, saying that if she was going to be climbing up ladders putting out fires, she didn't want her drawers on show for all to see while she did it.

'You're a force to be reckoned with, Josie.'

The older woman laughed, her eyes twinkling. 'Just doing my duty same as a lot of people. Come on, ducks, we need to give the fire engine the once-over and then we're ready.' She hurried out of her front door and started inspecting the grandly named Matlock Street Fire Engine, which was parked outside.

They were still using Josie's original creation made from a soap box attached to a pram chassis, but it had been further equipped with ladders hung along each side, and was filled with pails of sand, spades, scoops, hoes and rakes as well as the essential stirrup pumps. Satisfied that everything was as it should be, Josie turned to Frankie and smiled. 'Time to watch and wait then, ducks, see what the night brings.'

It was just after half past eight. The light was beginning to fade and the blackout would soon be in force. Would there be a raid tonight? Frankie wondered. The moon was on the wane, the last bomber's moon a week ago, so perhaps they would be lucky and London could sleep safe tonight.

The heavy raid three nights ago had left everyone feeling a bit jittery. It had been a hellish raid, and she and Josie had been out with the rest of Matlock Street's fire party dealing with the deluge of incendiaries. Thankfully they'd managed to limit the damage and the street had survived.

She hoped tonight would be a quiet one and that the air-raid siren would remain silent. It was the not knowing that got to you. Frankie knew she should be used to waiting and wondering by now, since they did it all the time at Station 75, but when she was doing her fire-watch duty it felt different, as though they were more vulnerable somehow. She knew what to do with incendiaries and had had plenty of practice dealing with them lately, but she still felt as if she was very much an amateur doing her best to keep Matlock Street from burning. Working on the fire party was a world away from being ambulance crew, where they were well trained and equipped and used to performing like a well-oiled machine.

'I'll go and put the kettle on and we'll 'ave a cup of tea,' Josie said, looking more relaxed now that she knew everything was in order and ready in case they needed it.

'I could do with one, thanks,' Frankie said.

Josie turned to go inside, but stopped as she spotted the figure walking down the street towards them. 'Reg, you must have 'eard I was puttin' the kettle on. Do yer want a cup?'

Frankie looked round and saw her grandad walking towards them from number 25, wearing his police uniform.

'I'd love to, Josie, but I'm on duty,' he said, smiling at them both.

'We're on duty too.' Josie laughed. 'But it ain't goin' to stop us havin' a cup of tea while we wait.'

'Good luck to yer. Let's 'ope it's a quiet night tonight for us all,' he said.

'Let's 'ope so.' Frankie smiled at him. 'Watch that leg of yours; make sure you rest if it starts to ache.'

'I'm all right, don't you worry.' He patted her shoulder. 'I'll look in on you if I'm this way later, take you up on that offer of a cup of tea.'

'Right you are, Reg, we'll see you later.' Josie linked her arm through Frankie's and led her into the house. 'Don't worry about 'im, love,' she said. 'He ain't daft and won't overdo it. He loves 'is job, and knows that if he wants to keep walking the beat, 'e's got to keep well.'

'Thanks, Josie.'

'What for?' the older woman asked, pulling out a chair for Frankie before lighting the gas under the waiting kettle.

'For knowing the right thing to say.'

'I've known you since you were a little girl and I know when you're worried.' She put two cups on the table and patted Frankie's shoulder. 'Your grandad'll be all right. 'E's a Stepney man and made of tough stuff.'

Frankie nodded, knowing full well from the number of people she'd seen killed and maimed in raids that the bombs were indiscriminate. It didn't matter who you were, young, old, rich, poor or born of tough East End stock, if one fell on or near you, then you'd had it, but she couldn't say that to Josie, who was only trying to help and keep her spirits up. It was time to change the subject. 'I ain't told you where Alastair and I went last week, 'ave I?'

'Where'd you go?'

'To the Palladium to see the *Apple-Sauce!* show. Vera Lynn was wonderful, 'er voice is like an angel's.'

'Gawd, I'd love to see that.' Josie pulled out a chair at the table and sat down while she waited for the kettle to boil. 'Tell me everything.'

Frankie had regaled her neighbour with every detail she could recall about the show – the costumes, the songs, the jokes – and they'd almost drunk the teapot dry when the mournful wail of the siren started up, sending her stomach plummeting into her boots.

Josie looked at her. 'Looks like we're in for it tonight, ducks.' She stood up and put her helmet on. 'Come on, action stations.'

Outside in the darkness of Matlock Street, they could hear the boom of the ack-ack guns firing in the distance and the drone of approaching bombers getting steadily louder. Frankie's stomach clenched tight as she scanned the sky, where searchlights were moving back and forth, trying to catch a plane in their beam. Josie paced up and down the cobbled street. For someone who was never short of something to say, her silence spoke volumes.

The first falling incendiaries made Frankie jump as they landed with their characteristic clatter, like the sound of tin cans falling on to the street. Stunned for a few seconds, she quickly leapt into action with Josie, grabbing one of the sandbags from where they were kept in readiness at the bottom of a street lamp and throwing it over the nearest incendiary, smothering it before it started to burn.

Further down the street, other incendiaries began to sizzle into life, erupting into bluish-white flames that glowed with an eerie light and gave off a fierce heat, filling the air with acrid smoke that made their eyes water. Hauling pails of sand out of the fire engine, they rushed over and doused the flames, and then on to the next one, and the next. Frankie felt a rising tide of panic threatening to engulf her, and her heart was thudding hard as she heard still more incendiaries rain down. It was more than they could cope with.

'We need the others to help,' Josie shouted. 'There's too many for just us.'

But before Frankie had a chance to rouse the other members of Matlock Street's fire party from their shelters, they began to emerge into the street to help. She'd never been so grateful to see her neighbours.

"Heard 'em comin' down,' Mr Thomas from number 18 yelled to her, grabbing a pail of sand and a hoe from the fire engine and setting to work.

Frankie had just emptied the rest of her pail of sand over an incendiary when she felt someone grab her arm.

'There's one landed in our back yard.' It was Vera, who lived next door to Frankie. 'Can you come? Quick.'

Frankie grabbed a spade out of the fire engine and ran after Vera, through her house and out to her back garden, where an incendiary was sending up its bright flames dangerously close to the Anderson shelter. She drove her spade into the soft earth of Vera's vegetable plot and dug out a good clod, which she threw over the bomb with a mighty heft before pushing the spade in to get more.

''Ere, watch out for my radishes,' Vera shouted at her.

Frankie stopped, wiping her brow with her sleeve; the fierce heat from the bomb was making her sweat. 'Radishes or Anderson shelter, make up your mind.'

Vera looked stunned for a moment. 'Anderson,' she muttered.

Frankie nodded and resumed her battle with the incendiary, digging fast and throwing soil over it till it was finally out.

'Thank you, ducks,' Vera said. 'I shouldn't 'ave shouted at yer like that, I'm sorry.'

Leaning on her spade while she caught her breath, Frankie smiled at her. 'Won't take long to grow some more radishes.'

A whistling sound from above followed by a loud crump from a few streets away made them both duck down.

'Bleedin' 'eck!' Vera raised her fist and shook it at the sky. 'Bugger off and leave us alone.'

'I don't think they can 'ear yer.' Frankie looked up at the sky, where squadrons of planes were flying over. As she did so, a flicker of orange caught her eye, making her feel sick. It was coming from the back bedroom of the house next door. The elderly woman who lived there adamantly refused to go to a shelter, and now her house was on fire and she was in there.

Frankie grabbed hold of Vera's arm and pointed to the glowing back window. 'Go and tell the fire party Mrs Davies's is alight. I'm goin' in to get her out.'

'But it's on fire.' Vera's voice was panicky. 'You ain't goin' in there.'

'Just go!' Frankie shouted at her as she scrambled up and over the wall separating the two gardens. 'And 'urry up about it.'

Not waiting to see if Vera did as she was told, she opened the back door of the house and went into the scullery. 'Mrs Davies?' she called, but there was no reply.

Whipping out her handkerchief, she quickly drenched it in water under the scullery tap and tied it over her mouth and nose bandit style. Then she made her way through the kitchen into the hall, forcing her feet forward step by step, ignoring the jelly-like wobbliness of her legs. As she went upstairs, the smell of smoke was strong, but thankfully the fire was still contained in the back bedroom. Reaching the landing, she could hear the hiss and crackle of flames, and putting her hand near the door she could feel it was getting hot.

'Mrs Davies!' she shouted again, opening the door of the front bedroom. The old woman was lying in bed fast asleep, her hair in iron curlers under a net, completely oblivious to the fact that her house was on fire. 'Mrs Davies!' Frankie shook her shoulder and the old woman woke with a start and screamed.

'It's all right, it's me.' Frankie pulled the handkerchief down to show her face. 'There's a fire in your back bedroom, I need to get you out.'

Mrs Davies stared at her for a few moments in the confusion of suddenly being woken up.

'We need to go now,' Frankie urged her, pulling back the bedclothes and helping her out of bed. 'Come on, quickly.'

They were halfway across the room when Mrs Davies turned around and hurried back to the bed, scrabbling under the pillow and bringing out her handbag. 'I ain't goin' anywhere without this.'

Checking to see what it was like outside on the landing, Frankie saw that the smoke was much thicker now, seeping through the gaps around the door. It might only be a matter of seconds before the fire broke through the wood. Turning back to Mrs Davies she said, 'Take a deep breath and follow me down the stairs, and keep hold of my hand.' She grabbed hold of the old woman's gnarled hand. 'Ready, one, two, three.'

Together they went out on to the landing, the acrid smoke immediately making Frankie's eyes water. She was grateful for the fact that this house was a replica of her own home just two doors away, so she instinctively knew where the stairs were and how many, and was able to use touch more than sight to guide Mrs Davies down.

They'd just reached the bottom step when the front door burst open and three of Matlock Street's fire party rushed in with a stirrup pump and pails of water.

'We didn't see the fire from out in the street,' one of them said. 'Incendiary must have gone through the roof.'

'It's getting hot up there,' Frankie said. 'Be careful.'

Leaving them to deal with the fire, she guided a shocked Mrs Davies out into the street. She'd only taken a few steps outside when Josie pounced on her.

'Thank Gawd you're all right.' She looked Frankie up and down. 'You ain't burnt or anything?'

'No, I'm fine, and so's Mrs Davies, just a bit shocked at being woken up like that.' Frankie spotted Vera in the street. 'Can you take Mrs Davies to your shelter, please?'

'Course I will. Come on, ducks, I've got a Thermos in there so we'll 'ave a nice cup o' tea.' She put her arm through Mrs Davies's and led her away.

'You shouldn't 'ave gone in there on yer own,' Josie said.

Frankie shrugged. 'I needed to act quick.'

'It gave me a right scare when Vera appeared saying you'd gone in a burning 'ouse.'

Frankie was about to reply, but the clatter of more incendiaries falling at the far end of the street drew her attention, and smiling at Josie she grabbed a pail of sand and hurried over to put them out.

By the time the all–clear sounded a little after four in the morning, the sky over London was glowing orange, lit up by flames. Many of the thousands of incendiaries that had dropped that night had done their job and started numerous fires. Matlock Street had received its fair share, but all of them had been successfully dealt with. The fire in Mrs Davies's back bedroom had been extinguished and all the houses were still standing, though some now had holes in their roofs.

'That was a bad 'un,' Josie said as the last wail of the all-clear died away. 'I dread to think what would 'ave happened if we didn't have our street fire party, 'ow many houses would 'ave gone up in smoke.'

'We did a good job,' Mr Thomas said. 'And you were a brave young woman.' He patted Frankie's shoulder. 'Another few minutes and the fire would have spread out on to the landing and we'd 'ave had a devil of a job getting Mrs Davies out.'

Frankie's cheeks grew warm. She hadn't felt in the least bit brave; she'd been frightened but had to do something.

'You go 'ome and get some sleep,' Josie said, taking her arm and turning her towards number 25. 'You're back on duty driving ambulances in a few hours' time. Go on, we'll sort the fire engine out; we can always 'ave a nap this afternoon.'

Frankie didn't argue. She was exhausted – the shift had pushed her to the limit – but she was grateful she'd spotted the fire in Mrs Davies's house. The thought of what might have happened if she hadn't sent a shiver through her. As hard as she found fire-watch duty, that was why she did it, and she would carry on with it as long as she was needed.

Chapter Eight

'Well, what do you think? I hope you're very proud of it, because you should be. You've done an excellent job.' Station Officer Steele beamed at Bella.

'It's a . . . ' Bella didn't quite know what to say. Seeing her words there in print was extraordinary, something she'd never dared dream might happen. She shrugged.

'You've captured the essence of what makes a good ambulance station, and that could only have been written by someone who works in one. No journalist could have gleaned that from a fleeting visit.'

'I wasn't sure if it was the right thing or . . . ' Bella began.

'Let's put it out in the common room for the rest of the station to read, see what they think.' Her boss picked up this week's copy of the *War Illustrated* and walked out of her office to put it on the table, opened at the page with Bella's article.

Bella frowned. What would the others think? She was grateful that at least they wouldn't be able to tell it was written by her, as it didn't have her name on. She'd asked Mr Dawson to publish it under a pen name so there was no way to trace it to her or Station 75.

'Don't look so worried,' Station Officer Steele said when she saw Bella's face. 'It really is very good.' She raised her eyebrows. 'You know I wouldn't say that if I didn't think it. Just watch and listen today and see how people react to it.'

Bella did her best to smile, hoping that the boss was right.

After last night's heavy raid disrupting everyone's sleep yet again and bringing a heavy workload today, any breaks brought crew members up to the common room for a much-needed rest, and inevitably it wasn't long before someone spotted her article in the paper.

'Blimey, 'ave you seen this?' Sparky said. 'There's someone who works as ambulance crew writing about their station in 'ere, and they've got it spot on talking about all the different sorts of people who work for the service.'

'Let's see.' Winnie leaned on the back of Sparky's armchair and peered over his shoulder to look at the article.

'Read it out for us,' Mac said.

Sparky handed Winnie the paper. 'Here goes. *Imagine yourself in a tight spot: you're doing your job out in the middle of an air raid, bombs are falling thick and fast and there are people depending on you to get them to hospital. Who would you want out there with you? Someone you can trust and who will do what's needed. That's exactly the type of person I work with at my London Auxiliary Ambulance station.*

'We're a mixed bunch, and if it hadn't been for the war it's unlikely that our paths would have crossed the way they have. Pre-war you wouldn't find many market traders working alongside debutantes, sharing a cup of tea and a chat in their break time, but here it happens often. Nobody cares what you did before, whether you worked in a factory, sold fruit from a stall, drove a taxi, mixed with royalty or served in a shop – none of that matters because we've gelled together to become a strong team.

'But surely there must be some differences of opinion from such a varied bunch? you might ask. Of course there are. In any workplace people have their own opinions and don't always agree with each other, but that makes for many interesting discussions. Take the other night, sitting in our shelter waiting for the telephone to ring: one of our crew members was commenting on the latest reports in the newspaper, which sparked off a lively discussion with everyone chipping in with their opinion. There was a lot of laughter too.

'However, when it comes to doing our job, we all have one common goal – and our aim is to do it well. Casualties depend on us to get them to hospital, and when the call comes for us to go out, we are ambulance crew first and foremost, supporting each other to do our job.

'Everyone brings their own experiences and strengths to work and together they've combined to make a strong

ambulance station. We learn from each other and pride our-
selves on working as a team and doing a good job in difficult
times. So when the air-raid siren goes and I head to the shelter
to wait for a call-out, I know that whoever I'm sent out with,
I'll be in good hands. My fellow crew members are exactly the
sort of people you'd want beside you in a tight spot.'

'They're quite right,' Mac said.

'Makes a change from the general view of how it is in
the ambulance service, like the piece that journalist wrote
after coming here,' Winnie said. 'Didn't you say he missed
out the bit about the woman being sick in the back of the
ambulance, Bella?'

She nodded. 'Yes, he didn't like that.'

'Well jolly good show to ... er ... ' Winnie peered at
the paper again. 'P. Harper, whoever he or she is. It doesn't
say which station they're at. I'll have to keep an eye out
for them at incidents, ask around and see if I can find out
who they are.'

Bella felt her face grow warm. She hoped Winnie
would soon forget about that; it was only one article
after all, and wasn't today's news tomorrow's fish–and–
chip paper?

Station Officer Steele caught up with her a little while
later as she was putting clean mugs back in the cupboard
after the common room had emptied out again. 'Now
will you believe me?'

Bella smiled and nodded. 'I'm pleased.'

'So you should be. If you can satisfy our varied bunch,
who certainly aren't backwards in coming forward with

their opinions, then you have indeed succeeded. Writing about the wide variety of people who work in an ambulance station was inspired. It's the sort of thing that goes unnoticed but it's what makes it work so well. Look at our mixture of different classes – we've all been thrown together and have gelled, and on the whole work very well together. Before the war, most of us would never have mixed, but now . . .' She smiled warmly. 'And you captured that beautifully in your article, Bella. I knew you could do it.'

'Aye, aye, what's going on 'ere?' Frankie said as she drove the ambulance along Whitechapel Road and saw a crowd of people hurrying along in the same direction. 'Has the greengrocer got some bananas in, do you think?'

'Seems a lot of people in a hurry just for bananas,' Bella said. 'Something's happening.'

Frankie brought the ambulance to a halt at the side of the road.

'What are you doing?' Bella asked.

'Finding out what's goin' on.' Frankie cranked down her window and leaned out, calling to a woman hurrying past, 'What's goin' on?'

The woman halted, her face flushed. 'The King and Queen are 'ere. I'm goin' to 'ave a look. Why don'cha come?' She didn't wait for an answer but hurried off.

Frankie looked at Bella. 'What do you think? Do you want to see the King and Queen?'

'Do you think we should? We ought to be getting back to Station 75 in case there's another incident.'

They were on their way back from the hospital, where they'd taken some casualties who'd been dug out of the ruins of their house after it had been reduced to rubble in last night's raid.

'It's not as if we're in the middle of a raid, and it'll only be for a few minutes. Come on, Bella, let's go and 'ave a look at them,' Frankie urged her. 'We're not Station 75's only ambulance crew; the boss has got plenty more to send out if she needs to.'

'All right then,' Bella said. 'It'll be something to tell my mum about when I write to her.'

Leaving the ambulance parked at the side of the road, they joined the throng hurrying along the street. Turning into a side street, they saw the royal couple's car standing there, polished and gleaming in the April sunshine, surrounded by crowds of people, many of them standing on piles of rubble to get a better view.

'There they are.' Bella grabbed hold of Frankie's arm.

The King was dressed in naval uniform, while the Queen was wearing a smart blue coat with fur on the sleeves and a matching blue hat. They were flanked by a group of dignitaries – Frankie recognised the mayor from his picture in the paper. Their majesties were talking to people and shaking their hands, and looking around at the destruction surrounding them.

Standing to one side on a pile of rubble that crunched and shifted under her feet, Frankie thought it was one of the strangest sights she'd ever witnessed. People she'd only ever seen in the Pathé news at the pictures were suddenly here in the middle of the East End, amongst the devastation of bombed buildings with gaping holes in the walls and broken beams like matchsticks poking into the air. They looked so smart, their expensive clothes contrasting sharply with those worn by the people who'd come to see them. The crowd were smiling and cheering, and someone had hung a Union Jack flag out of the window of a nearby house that was still standing.

'We're not downhearted, your majesty, it'll take more than this to get us down,' an old woman with a shawl over her head shouted not far from where Frankie and Bella were standing. The Queen smiled and walked over to her as the crowd cheered.

'Have you been bombed out?' she asked. Frankie could hear her clearly, and couldn't help thinking that her voice was even more plummy-sounding than Winnie's.

'Yes, your majesty,' the old woman replied. 'Twice, but I ain't goin' nowhere. I'm all right as long as I can get a cup o' tea and a bit of bread and butter.'

The Queen smiled again. 'I think you are marvellously brave. God bless you all.'

'Are we downhearted?' a man standing nearby shouted out.

A unanimous chorus of 'No!' was called out in reply, making the Queen smile again. Then she spotted Frankie and Bella, who were still wearing their steel helmets with the bright white 'A' painted on the front, and came right up to them, holding out her hand to shake theirs.

'Have you come to take someone to hospital?' she asked.

Frankie shook her head, not quite believing that she was shaking hands with the Queen. 'No, we've just been; we're going back to our station.'

'You do a marvellous job.' The Queen shook Bella's hand.

'Thank you.' Bella's voice came out in a squeak.

'Keep up the good work.' The Queen smiled at them and then moved on.

'That's something to write and tell your mother about,' Frankie said, nudging Bella's arm as they watched the Queen speaking to more people and shaking hands.

A few minutes later the visit drew to a close and the King and Queen made their way back to their waiting car. As they were driven away, a few people ran after them, cheering and waving. The crowd slowly dispersed, and Frankie and Bella walked back to where they'd left the ambulance.

'It was strange seeing them here amongst the rubble,' Bella said. 'It didn't seem real somehow.'

'I know,' Frankie said. 'But you really did shake hands with the Queen of England, I saw it with my own two eyes.'

Bella laughed. 'I did, didn't I?'

Back at Station 75, Bella was listening to Frankie entertaining crew members sitting outside in the spring sunshine with the tale of seeing the King and Queen when Station Officer Steele appeared at her side.

'Could I have a word with you, please?' She spoke quietly. 'It's nothing to worry about.'

Bella followed her boss to the other side of the courtyard, out of earshot of the others. 'I have a message for you. Mr Dawson came while you were out on call; he wants you to write a fortnightly piece for the *War Illustrated* about working at an ambulance station.'

She stared at the older woman for a few moments while what she'd told her sank in. 'But why?'

Station Officer Steele laughed softly. 'My dear girl, and ye of little faith in yourself,' she put her hand on Bella's arm, 'your article was a hit. The paper had lots of letters about it and readers want to know more.' She reached into her pocket and took out a folded piece of paper, handing it to her. 'Here, he left you specific instructions so you know when to deliver your copy.'

Bella was stunned. They wanted more, much more. Writing a one-off piece was one thing, but to write an article every fortnight – could she do it?

'It's a marvellous opportunity for you. Just look where writing the first piece has led you. Remember to keep real names and places out of it, that's all I ask.'

'I don't know what to say . . . I never expected this.' Bella shook her head. 'It's astonishing.'

The older woman frowned. 'You are going to do it, aren't you?'

Bella nodded and beamed at her as a warm glow of excitement spread through her. 'Of course I am, I'd be a fool to turn it down.'

'Good. We must celebrate, toast your success.'

'Oh, but I don't want anyone else to know. Not yet.'

'They'd be proud of you, you know.' Station Officer Steele's eyes met hers. 'I hope you'll tell them sometime.'

Bella nodded. 'I will, when the time's right.'

Chapter Nine

Winnie warmed her hands around her mug of tea and leaned back against the wall of Station 75's air-raid shelter, thinking she had never seen it so empty. She and Hooky were the only crew members here; they'd only got back from their third call-out this shift some ten minutes ago, and all the rest were still out at incidents.

Whatever was going on out there tonight was big and bad. London was taking another massive pounding from the bombers that had been streaming over in squadrons, using the light of the full moon to their advantage, though they hardly needed it now as the city was burning fiercely, lit up like a beacon to guide them in.

'You can see the barrage balloons it's so light out there,' Hooky was telling Station Officer Steele. The older woman looked haggard, her face pale and drawn from the strain of tonight's raid.

Not wanting to join in the conversation as she'd already had enough of Hooky's company this shift, Winnie finished her tea then picked up Trixie, who'd been sleeping at her side, and cuddled her on her lap, taking comfort in the little dog who had brought such joy into her life since she'd been dug out of a bombed-out building last autumn. Trixie lapped up the attention, leaning her head against Winnie's chest and looking up at her with her adoring liquid brown eyes.

The telephone suddenly burst into life, its jangling echoing loudly around the almost empty shelter. Station Officer Steele snatched it up and went through the routine she'd done countless times before. Winnie watched her, knowing for the first time ever who would be sent out to this incident. Usually it was a guessing game which crew it might be, but this time there was no choice in the matter: there was only her and Hooky here.

Winnie stood up with Trixie in her arms, not waiting for the boss to call her name.

'I'm sorry, but you'll have to take this,' Station Officer Steele said. 'I've never known it as bad as this; we're stretched to our very limits tonight.' She shook her head wearily. 'If another call comes in, I've got no crews left to send out.'

Winnie put her hand on the older woman's shoulder. She knew how hard the boss's job was, and tonight it was a hundred times worse than anything she'd had to deal with before. 'It's all right, we'll go.' She glared at Hooky, who was looking obstinate but who gave in and finally nodded her agreement as well.

Back on the road, driving towards the Tower of London, Winnie's heart sank at the sight of the solid sheet of leaping flame on the other side of the river, its colour reflected in the Thames, which had taken on the hue of burnished copper. Hadn't London suffered enough bombing and destruction in the past months? When would it end – when there was nothing left standing?

Giving herself a mental shake, Winnie did her best to block out the sights and sounds of the city in distress, the urgent clanging of fire-engine bells, the hungry tongues of flame writhing out of windows and doors, and the crump and tremor of the earth as bombs fell. It was hellish and it would be so easy to crumble, but now was not the time; she had to keep going. Gripping the steering wheel hard, she focused on driving, on just getting the ambulance to where it was needed.

'Are you all right?' Hooky's voice broke into her thoughts.

Winnie quickly glanced at her crew mate, not quite believing what she'd just heard. Hooky was looking at her, her face clearly visible in the light from the many fires burning across the city. She had never once asked that question of her before; Hooky was always far more interested in herself than anyone else.

'I beg your pardon?' Winnie said, before turning her attention back to the road.

'I said, are you all right?'

Winnie couldn't help smiling. Here they were in the middle of what seemed to be the worst raid to hit London, and Hooky was suddenly enquiring after her well-being. 'Yes, I'm all right, thank you.' She wasn't going to admit that she was feeling ... what was she feeling? Scared, spooked, anxious. None of them were nice emotions, but they were probably being felt by many of the people out here tonight: the rescuers, the ARP wardens, the firemen. It was natural to feel that way; even after months of raids, you never got used to it. On top of that, she was worried about Mac, who was out here somewhere, terrified that something would happen to him.

'Well *I'm* not!' Hooky's voice was petulant. 'I never should have volunteered for the ambulance service, I'm going to leave and find something else that doesn't require me to do this ... ' Her voice went up in volume and pitch, making Trixie whine and shift closer to her mistress, resting her head in the crook of Winnie's arm.

An immediate and unsympathetic response jumped into Winnie's mind and she had to rein it in hard before it spilled out. Now wasn't the time to antagonise Hooky, when she was clearly in rather a state. Winnie had to keep her fellow crew member going, as she needed her help and wouldn't be able to manage casualties on her own.

'All right, I understand if you feel you need to change your job, but right now we have to keep going and get *this* job done.' She reached out and briefly patted Hooky's arm.

Hooky grabbed hold of her hand. 'We will be all right, won't we?'

'Of course we will. We've been through tricky times before, haven't we?' Winnie did her best to smile. 'If you don't mind, I do rather need my hand back to steer properly.' She tugged her hand out of Hooky's tight grip.

Hooky suddenly started to cry, sobs making her chest heave and her breathing shuddery.

Winnie sighed inwardly. A hysterical crew mate wasn't going to be of much use. 'Now look here, Hooky, it's no good getting all het up when there are people out there waiting for us to get them to hospital. Imagine how awful they must be feeling, frightened and in pain. If we don't do our job, it could be hours before another ambulance is available to take them there, that's if they survive that long. Do you want that on your conscience because you had a bit of a wobble?'

Hooky stopped crying immediately, and when Winnie turned to see what had happened, her crew mate was glaring at her, eyes narrowed. 'Of course not,' she snapped.

'Well then, it's time for a jolly good dose of stiff upper lip, isn't it? After this shift you can do what you want and leave the ambulance service, but for now you have a job to do and you should do it with a good heart.'

'If you say so,' Hooky said curtly, and then fell silent.

Sometimes, Winnie thought, she was challenged as much by working with Hooky as by being out in the middle of an air raid. If nothing else, putting a positive light on it, Hooky's outburst had taken her mind off her own discomfort, and for that she was grateful, though she'd never admit that to her prickly crew mate.

Turning a corner, Winnie had to brake sharply at the sight of a body lying in the road.

'Bloody hell.' She stopped the ambulance. 'Wait here, Hooky, while I go and have a look.'

Approaching the body, she could see it was a young lad of about fourteen or fifteen and he was unconscious. Kneeling down beside him, she checked for a pulse. He was alive, but he had congealed blood on the side of his head from where it had hit the ground. How he'd been injured she couldn't tell; he might have been thrown by the force of a blast.

She hurried back to the ambulance. 'He's badly hurt; we need to pick him up.'

'But we're only supposed to get casualties from the incident we're sent to, you know that,' Hooky said, folding her arms.

'Normally, yes, but we're the last ambulance from our station, and there's no one here to telephone for help for him. I'm not leaving him here. By the time someone else finds him, it might be too late. So get out of the cab and come and help me.'

'But it's against the rules,' Hooky protested.

'Stuff the rules! If we leave him, he might die. I don't want that on my conscience when we can help him, do you? Think of it as just bending the rules, given this hideous raid and the fact that everyone is stretched to their limit. You can tell the boss about it later if you want, I really don't care.'

By the time Winnie had got a stretcher from the back, Hooky was out of the ambulance ready to help. It didn't take them long to load the unconscious lad, and she was grateful that Hooky said no more about broken rules. Sometimes common sense dictated that rules had to be bent, and tonight was one of those occasions.

When they reached the incident they'd been sent to, they found two casualties waiting for them who'd been rescued from the wreckage of a block of flats that had collapsed from a bomb blast. Working together, they quickly examined them, gave the necessary first aid and loaded them into the back of the ambulance, with Hooky in there to keep an eye on them while Winnie waited outside for the rescue team to bring out any more survivors.

'Shouldn't be long now till they get the last one out,' an ARP warden said, taking out a soot-stained handkerchief and wiping his face with it.

'It's a wonder anyone survived in there at all.' Winnie could see the hole where the rescuers had tunnelled down into the wreckage and crawled in looking for people. Their bravery never failed to amaze her, because the whole lot could cave in at any moment, and the situation wasn't helped by the earth trembling every now and then from bombs exploding in the neighbouring streets.

'Look at that.' The ARP nudged her arm and pointed up to where a bomber had suddenly been caught in the cross-beams of searchlights, though luckily for the crew of that plane, the roiling clouds of smoke blew over and quickly blotted it from sight. 'Dammit.'

'Just one of many up there,' Winnie said, listening to the unsteady beat of the bombers' engines above the blanket of smoke, which reflected the burning fires lighting up the night with a strange orange glow. Tiny cinders drifted down from the inferno like grey snow.

'Wish they'd bugger off and leave us alone. Ain't they done enough damage already? I—' The warden stopped talking as a figure emerged from the tunnel.

Winnie grabbed the stretcher she'd left leaning against the ambulance and hurried over to where the rescue worker was gently laying the survivor down on her back, unlooping her arms from where they'd been tied together and slipped over his neck. It was the wheelbarrow technique; Winnie had seen it used several times before, when the rescuer straddled the survivor and carried them out lying beneath them.

'Over to you,' the rescue worker said to Winnie as she knelt down in the rubble beside the woman, who was conscious and doing her best to smile. 'She's the last one.'

'Thank you.' Winnie smiled at the man, who was filthy, covered in dust and dirt, and then turned her attention to the casualty. 'Hello, I'm Winnie and I'll be taking you to hospital,' she said, beginning to examine her for injuries.

Five minutes later, with the woman safely in the back of the ambulance with the other survivors and the lad they'd picked up on the way, Winnie was back behind the wheel and heading for the London Hospital. The roads were in a bad way, many of them blocked by falling rubble or holed by craters. What should have been a fifteen-minute journey was going to take much longer because of the detours she kept having to make.

Turning left, she kept a careful eye on the speedometer, making sure it didn't creep over the permitted sixteen miles an hour. The roads were littered with broken glass and the last thing she needed was a puncture; she'd had one of those before and wasn't keen to repeat the experience, especially tonight.

She didn't hear it coming. She just saw something large plummet to the ground fifteen yards ahead of her and then vanish. She braked and brought the ambulance to a halt, staring ahead through the windscreen, a prickling sensation crawling up her spine.

'What's going on?' Hooky called through the grille from the back of the ambulance.

'Something's in the road, I just need to look. You stay here, Trixie.' Winnie patted the little dog's head and opened the door very gently, taking care not to slam it shut. Slowly she walked towards where the object had vanished. She didn't need to go far to realise it was a bomb, which had buried itself in the ground without going off, like the one that had landed in the courtyard of Station 75 a few weeks ago.

Her heart was hammering hard. If this bomb had exploded, she and Hooky and all the casualties would have been blown to bits. She hadn't heard it falling; it was true that the ones you could hear whistling down were all right, it was the ones you didn't hear that got you. This one hadn't, not yet anyway. But it still could.

Winnie turned and walked back to the ambulance, adrenalin surging through her. She was painfully aware of every step she took, moving as gently as she could, not wanting to make any vibration that might set the bomb off.

Climbing back into the ambulance, she wondered if she should say anything to Hooky, but decided against it for now.

'The road's blocked up ahead, I'm going to have to reverse,' she called through the grille.

'Not again,' Hooky moaned.

Ignoring her, Winnie started the engine, wincing as it juddered into life, but nothing happened: there was no blinding flash, no bang. Putting the ambulance into reverse, she edged it backwards slowly, using her wing mirrors to keep her straight, grateful for every inch of road she gained between her and the unexploded bomb.

Reaching the end of the street, she carefully turned out into the adjoining road and headed off taking a different route, one she hoped would get them safely to the London without further mishaps. Once she'd got these casualties to hospital, she'd stop at the nearest ARP warden hut and tell them about the unexploded bomb. She had a feeling it wouldn't be the only one dropped tonight.

Frankie knew there was a beautiful butter-yellow full moon up there, shining out above the city, but it was impossible to see it now as the sky was choked with thick, billowing smoke. Tonight's air raid was massive; London was taking a vicious pounding, the bombing heavier than anything that had come before. Frankie was scared.

Normally she just got on with the job, but tonight something felt out of kilter, and she had a bad feeling in the pit of her stomach. But there was no time for dwelling on something that might be nothing when there were casualties in desperate need of help.

Forcing herself to focus and concentrate, Frankie gripped the wheel hard as they headed for the docks, where fire was engulfing buildings, forked tongues of flame leaping into the sky from rooftops where incendiary bombs had rained down, and the Thames mirrored the orange glow of the burning warehouses that lined its banks.

'Shall I open up the back and get a stretcher out while you go and find out how many casualties we've got?' Bella asked when they arrived at the incident, where the front of a building had been bombed out.

'Good idea,' Frankie said. Working with Bella was like being part of a smoothly oiled machine, she thought, checking that the chin strap of her steel helmet was securely in place. The two of them worked so well together, often instinctively knowing what the other needed, probably because they weren't just colleagues but good friends too. On a night as bad as this, it really helped having her friend working beside her.

Outside, the air was acrid with smoke, making Frankie's eyes smart. She ducked her head to shield her face from flying sparks, which were drifting in the air like miniature fireworks, and made her way over to where an ARP warden was talking to a policeman, stepping carefully so that she didn't trip on the rubble strewn across the ground, her boots crunching on broken glass and debris. All the while, the drone of bombers' engines went on above her. She loathed the sound of their engines, which were so different from the sweeter hum of the British planes. She'd heard them enough over the past months, but the sound still got to her, made her stomach twist and an icy finger of fear run down her spine.

'What have you got for us?' she asked the warden.

'Three casualties—' The ARP warden suddenly stopped, his attention caught by something further down the wharf. 'What the devil?'

Frankie turned, and saw what looked like a large khaki-coloured tarpaulin drifting downwards, lit up by the orange glow from the fires. It fell like a pocket handker-chief, then collapsed into the shadows, where she couldn't see it any more.

'Stay here,' the policeman ordered, and hurried towards it, but he didn't get far before he did a quick about-turn and ran back towards them shouting loudly, 'Run!'

Before Frankie could move, a loud swishing noise like a giant fuse spluttering into life filled the air. She knew it was going to be bad, but she couldn't outrun it. Instinctively she dropped down, but she hadn't quite made it to the ground when she glimpsed a large ball of blinding white light with two concentric rings, the inner one lavender, the outer one violet. Her head was jerked back as a heavy blow hit the dome of her steel helmet and another smashed into her forehead and the bridge of her nose. A horrible growling noise filled the air and a blast of pressure like a tornado rushed past. Her ears throbbed with an agonising pain and she couldn't hear anything other than a singing noise.

She felt herself beginning to slip away. *Hold on!* a voice shouted inside her head. *Just hold on.* Responding, she lay as flat as she could, face down on the ground, with her chest slightly raised to protect it, as she'd once been told to do in a blast by a fireman, her hands covering her ears, trying to ease the pain.

Another blast wave hit and the ground heaved beneath her. It felt as if it was trying to rip her away from where she lay to toss her into the air. She pressed herself harder into the ground, using her feet to anchor herself against the kerb. More waves came, and Frankie was hit hard by something on her arm, sending waves of excruciating pain slicing through it. She was vaguely aware of the blast waves decreasing and a shower of dust and rubble pattering down on her. She felt dizzy and a terrible weakness flooded through her as she gladly sank into a painless blackness.

Bella lay quite still, not daring to move a muscle in the darkness. She could hear shouts from outside and opened her mouth to call out, but no words came, her throat feeling hoarse and dry. She reached into her dungarees pocket for her torch and switched it on, her eyes squinting as they adjusted to the light till she could see that the ambulance was lying on its side, the contents of the back spilled everywhere. She was wedged under the bottom stretcher; thankfully the stretchers were still in their runners and hadn't moved, otherwise she could have been impaled on one.

She started to wriggle her way out from where she'd been thrown, but winced as pain sliced through her ribs. She stopped and gingerly felt her ribcage; she knew she'd probably cracked some ribs, but if that was all that was wrong with her then she was lucky. Whatever it was that had gone off outside had been big, sending the ambulance toppling like a domino flipped over, the blast waves pushing it along the ground. Something warm ran down her face and she dabbed at it, her fingers coming away sticky and red in the torchlight: blood.

Frankie! Bella suddenly thought. Where was she? She'd been out there in it, not protected inside the ambulance. Bella felt sick – she had to find her friend. Easing her way to the back of the ambulance, she tried to open the door. She just needed to lift it up enough to crawl out, but the doors were buckled and bent, and pushing on them sent pain searing through her ribs. She was trapped.

She lay still, fighting the surge of panic that was bubbling up inside her. Keep calm, she told herself, help would come, she just needed to be patient and bang on the door so that someone would know she was in there.

'Help!' she shouted. 'Help!'

Lying on the stretcher, a blanket tucked securely around her, a label tied to the front of her dungarees and hot-water bottles warming her, Bella started to shake. Shock had finally hit her. While she'd been trapped in the damaged ambulance she'd kept calm, calling out and banging on the door until help had come. It had seemed to take forever, but time had been stretched and distorted and she couldn't be sure how long she'd been in there. Now, being on the receiving end of help from an ambulance crew seemed odd; she was used to being the one doing the helping.

Breathing slowly, aware of the pain in her ribs, she did her best to keep calm, but it was difficult when thoughts were charging around her mind, all centred on the same question: where was Frankie? She'd asked but they hadn't been able to tell her; the crew was busy collecting the final casualty before they left for the hospital. On the stretcher below hers was a policeman, who was groaning with pain. On the other side at the bottom was an ARP warden; he was unconscious, blood covering his face.

As the ambulance crew started to load up the last stretcher, sliding it into its runners, Bella looked over and gasped, tears suddenly clogging her throat.

'Frankie,' she called out. 'Frankie.'

But there was no reply.

'Is this your crew mate?' the attendant asked, checking that the blankets were securely tucked in around Frankie's still form.

Bella nodded. 'Her name's Stella Franklin, Frankie.' The attendant pulled the label out from under Frankie's blanket and quickly wrote her patient's name on it.

'Ready?' the driver called from outside.

'All set,' the attendant said, and the back doors were closed on them as Bella had seen so many times before.

'How is she?' Bella asked.

'Unconscious, must have been hit on the head; the brim of her helmet was pushed back, though it would have been worse if she hadn't been wearing it. And a broken arm by the look of things.'

As the engine started and the ambulance began to move off, Bella tried to turn to have a better look at Frankie, but the pain in her ribs caused her to wince.

'Just lie still.' The attendant gently put her hand on Bella's. 'We'll get her to hospital as soon as we can and they'll look after her.'

Tears filled Bella's eyes. If anything happened to Frankie . . .

'You're from Station 75 then? Saw it painted on the side of your ambulance.'

Bella nodded. 'Not far from the Tower of London.'

'We're from Station 77, near Bishopsgate.'

'Where are you taking us?'

'The London.'

Alastair was there, Bella thought; he'd be able to help Frankie, he'd do everything he could to save her.

The journey seemed to take forever, and all the while Bella watched Frankie's still face, hoping for signs of her coming round, but by the time they got to the hospital she still hadn't regained consciousness.

*

Station Officer Steele took the piece of paper that Winnie had just completed to sign off her last incident and added it to the pile on her desk. 'Go home now and get some rest. Don't worry about cleaning the ambulance; it'll get done by the day shift.'

Winnie stretched out her arms and wriggled her shoulders. 'I need a long soak in a hot bath first.'

'Make it a quick one, you need sleep.' Station Officer Steele gently stroked Trixie's ears as the little dog leaned against her legs, glad of the moment of contentment that being with Winnie's faithful companion always gave her.

'So do you, if you don't mind me saying so,' Winnie said. 'It's been one hell of a night.'

The heavy raid had once again stretched their shift way beyond its usual eight hours. The bombing had made it difficult for many of the next shift's crew to get to the station, and so they'd all had to just carry on working, dealing with the calls that came in one after another, the telephone seeming to ring constantly all night.

'There are just a couple more crews to come back and then I'll be done.' Station Officer Steele glanced at her list. All the crews had been crossed off on their return except Frankie and Bella and Sparky and his attendant Paterson. She wouldn't leave until they were all back safely.

'I'll wait for Bella, we always bicycle home together,' Winnie said. 'I'm sure she won't be long.'

'I think you'd best get home while you can; there's no telling how long Bella will be. I'll tell her I sent you home.'

Winnie yawned, putting her hand over her mouth. 'Oh, I do beg your pardon.'

'Go home, dear,' Station Officer Steele said. 'You've done your bit for now. Get some sleep, and that's an order.'

'Very well, I'm going. I'll see you later. Come on, Trixie.'

Station Officer Steele watched her leave, glad that she and the young woman had settled into a more comfortable relationship, where they understood one another better. The Blitz had changed Winnie; she was far less like a naughty schoolgirl these days and didn't clash against rules as much as she once did. She deserved her role as deputy station officer, and the older woman hoped she would continue with it after her three-month trial was up.

Leaving her desk, Station Officer Steele went into the common room and stood at her usual post by the window to watch out for the return of her two last crews. Down in the courtyard, the members of the day shift were busy making the necessary checks to the ambulances, cleaning them of the dirt and debris from last night's raid.

It wasn't long before another ambulance nosed its way in under the archway and came to a halt in the middle of the courtyard. Unusually, it didn't reverse back into line with the other ambulances; instead, the driver's door flew open and Sparky jumped out. He looked up at the window, and the expression on his face caused a shiver to slide down her spine, like an icy finger drawn over warm skin. Something was wrong. She abandoned her lookout post and made for the stairs, meeting Sparky halfway down.

'What's happened?' she asked.

'Frankie and Bella got caught in a blast.' Sparky's face was filthy with dust, his eyes standing out against the grey.

She had to take a deep breath to steady her voice. 'Are they alive?'

'Yes, they were when I left 'em.'

'Where are they?'

'In the London.'

'Right, I'm going there. I'll take one of the cars.' She turned to go back upstairs to fetch her bag.

Sparky grabbed her arm. 'We ain't supposed to use vehicles for our own use. It's against the rules.'

'Well I'll change the bloody rules,' she snapped. 'They're my crew and I need to find out what's happened to them.'

'Then I'll come with you,' Sparky said. 'You mustn't go on your own.'

'I can.'

'I know you can, but I *want* to come with you, I know which roads are shut; it'll be quicker if I take you, and I can tell you what 'appened on the way. All right?'

Station Officer Steele sighed. 'Thank you, Sparky. I appreciate that.'

He nodded. 'Meet you downstairs in a few minutes.'

Back in her office, she grabbed her bag and then stopped, steadying herself with her hand on the back of her chair, and sent up a silent prayer that the two young women would be all right. She might be their boss, but she was very fond of them too.

*

'Tell me everything,' Station Officer Steele said as Sparky drove under the archway and out on to the road.

'We'd just delivered our injured to the London's casualty department and were goin' out through the doors when we met another ambulance crew coming in with a stretcher. They asked if we were from Station 75 – I suppose they'd seen our ambulance parked outside – and said they'd got a couple of our crew with them.' Sparky paused for a moment as he steered carefully around a crater in the road. 'It was 'er 'air I recognised first, that lovely auburn colour; it was Frankie lying there on the stretcher, unconscious. They said they'd got her crew mate waiting in their ambulance.'

'How badly injured was she?'

'Unconscious, like I said. I only saw her for a moment before they hurried her through. I asked them later and they said it was her arm.'

'What about Bella?'

'After they told us, we 'urried out to their ambulance and found Bella on a stretcher in the back. She was awake. We pulled 'er out and took her in.'

'Did you ask her what happened?'

'Course I did. She said she was in the back of the ambulance getting some equipment out. Frankie was out-side – she'd gone to find out about the casualties – when there was an explosion and the ambulance tipped over. Frankie was caught in it outside.'

Station Officer Steele put her hand to her mouth. 'What are Bella's injuries?'

223

'Her ribs, she said. Cuts and bruises. She was lucky; it could have been a lot worse. It's a hell of a shock seeing your crew mates being stretchered in.' Sparky cleared his throat. 'You don't expect that.'

She put her hand on his arm and squeezed it gently. 'I know. We'll find out what's happened to them and do what we can. I'm glad you're with me, Sparky.'

He glanced at her and smiled. 'The crews are like family, ain't they?'

'Indeed they are.'

They drove the rest of the way in silence, Station Officer Steele staring in horror out of the window at the destruction. Her job kept her in the shelter during a raid, so it was always a shock when she came out and saw what had happened. This morning was the worst she'd seen, reminiscent of that first terrible raid of the Blitz. Like then, a thick pall of smoke hung over London, and fires still burned, ash falling like snow over the streets of the wounded city.

The casualty department of the London Hospital was packed with injured, the less badly hurt sitting huddled in blankets while they waited to be attended to.

Station Officer Steele marched up to an exhausted-looking nurse. 'Excuse me, I'm Station Officer Steele, from Ambulance Station 75. Two of my crew were brought in injured – can you please tell me what's happened to them?'

'What are their names?' the nurse asked. The station officer quickly told her. 'Wait there, I'll go and find out what I can.'

'Thank you.' She glanced at Sparky, who stood beside her still wearing his steel helmet, which she noticed was covered in a film of brick and plaster dust. 'I could write my name on your hat, it's so filthy.'

Sparky shrugged. 'It's an occupational 'azard.'

'It doesn't matter, it'll wash off.'

It wasn't the nurse who returned to speak to them a few minutes later, but an ashen-faced Alastair. 'I heard you were here. Bella's got cracked ribs, cuts and bruises; she can go home as long as she rests. Frankie ... ' He paused for a moment. 'She's still unconscious and her arm's broken; they've taken her up to a ward.'

'Will she be all right?' Station Officer Steele asked.

'I hope so.' Alastair ran a hand through his dark hair, making it stick up. 'I must get back.'

'Of course, thank you for coming to tell us. I appreciate it.'

He nodded at her and hurried back to the treatment rooms.

She glanced at Sparky, their eyes meeting. 'Let's hope they can sort her out.' Tears suddenly prickled in her eyes.

Sparky put his hand on her arm. 'I'm sure Alastair will do his best for her, make sure she gets the help she needs.'

'Yes, yes, it's lucky he's here.' She sniffed and blinked away the tears, doing her best to smile. 'In the meantime, we'll take Bella home as soon as they let her go. I can come back later and see how Frankie is doing.'

*

Winnie woke with a start. Something was wrong. Trixie was out of her basket and scrabbling at the door, whining to be let out.

'Trixie, what's the matter?' Winnie scrambled out of bed, doing her best to ignore the woozy feeling in her head and the heavy, leaden weight in her limbs from her sudden catapult from sleep to wakefulness. She knelt down and tried to calm the little dog, stroking her silky golden ears, but Trixie wasn't budging and continued her whining, frantically scratching at the door.

Winnie grabbed her silk dressing gown and flung it on, then opened the door. As soon as the gap was wide enough, Trixie squeezed through and bolted.

'Trixie!' Winnie called after her, hurrying out on to the landing. Trixie ignored her, running to the top of the stairs and disappearing down them.

Winnie rushed after her, grabbing hold of the polished wooden banister to steady herself. As she reached the bend in the stairs, the sight in the hall below brought her to a jolting halt. Trixie was there, now calm and quiet, watching as Bella slowly made her way across the hall, flanked by Connie and Station Officer Steele, each with an arm around her, supporting her.

'Bella!' Winnie ran down the rest of the flight of stairs. 'What's happened?'

Her friend looked at her and smiled wanly. Her hair and clothes were covered in dust and dirt, and her face was pale apart from the livid red scratches and bruises that were starting to bloom.

'Bella was caught in an explosion, a landmine, and she needs to get to bed,' Station Officer Steele said.

Winnie's stomach squeezed tight. She opened her mouth to speak, but was silenced by a look from Connie.

'Go and make her some hot, sweet tea,' her godmother instructed. 'Quick as you can.'

Winnie nodded and hurried down to the kitchen, her mind reeling through so many questions. What had happened? Where and when? Various scenarios swirled and teased in her mind. And what about Frankie? Had she been injured too?

She turned on the gas on the cooker to boil the kettle, but nothing happened. She sighed: the raid had damaged the gas mains again, there was no chance of tea. She raced up the stairs, across the hall and into the sitting room and grabbed Connie's emergency medicinal bottle of brandy out of the cupboard, together with a glass, and then headed up the stairs.

'Connie's helping her wash and change into her night-clothes,' Station Officer Steele said when Winnie hurried into Bella's bedroom.

'The gas is off so I couldn't make tea. I brought this instead.' Winnie put the brandy bottle and glass down on the chest of drawers. 'Is Bella all right?'

'She's got some cracked ribs, scratches and plenty of bruises, but she'll recover with rest. The doctor at the London was happy for her to come home.'

'What about Frankie? Was she injured too?'

Station Officer Steele's face paled. 'Yes, I'm afraid so,

much worse than Bella.' Winnie's heart started to thump hard in her chest. 'She was outside the ambulance and caught more of the blast. She was unconscious when they took her in and her arm's broken. She still hadn't woken up when they took her to a ward. I'll go straight back to the London once we've got Bella settled.'

'Will she be all right?' Winnie asked.

'I hope so. Alastair was on duty when they were taken in; he'll have done all he can to help her.' Station Officer Steele sighed. 'Right, Winnie, I need you to look after Bella, make sure she rests and doesn't overdo it. And please ...' she raised her arched eyebrows, looking directly at Winnie through her horn-rimmed spectacles, 'don't go quizzing her about what happened just yet. I know you want to know, but she'll tell you when she's ready. Remember, she's had a terrible shock and needs rest and quiet.'

Winnie nodded. 'Of course I'll take care of her – she's my friend and I care about her.' She held up her hand as if giving an oath. 'And I promise I won't badger her about what happened. I do want to know, of course, you know me, but I'll wait till she's ready.' She shrugged and smiled.

'Indeed I do.' Station Officer Steele patted her arm. 'I know you'll look after her very well.'

'Is that tea ready?' Connie asked as she and Bella came into the bedroom. Bella was now dressed in her night-clothes and looked a lot cleaner, but she was still very pale, the scratches on her face standing out against her white skin.

'The gas is off, so I raided the emergency brandy,'

Winnie said, pulling back the covers so that Bella could get into bed.

'That'll probably do her more good than tea,' Connie said, supporting Bella as she gingerly lowered herself to sit on the edge of the bed. Station Officer Steele gently lifted her legs and swung them round and under the covers, while Connie arranged the pillows for her to lean back on.

'Are you comfy?' Station Officer Steele asked, drawing the covers over Bella and smoothing them down.

Bella nodded and did her best to smile, her brown eyes huge. 'Thank you.'

Station Officer Steele patted her hand. 'I'll leave you in Connie and Winnie's capable care.' She looked at Connie. 'I'll telephone later to check how she is.'

Connie nodded. 'Don't worry, we'll take good care of her.'

'I can sit with her now,' Winnie said, pulling up a chair beside the bed.

'Oh no,' Connie said. 'You haven't had enough sleep after last night, so back to bed with you. I'll look after Bella for now. The best thing you can do is get some sleep so you're ready for your next shift.'

Winnie opened her mouth to argue but caught Station Officer Steele's eye and closed it again. She knew when she was beaten, and if she was honest, she was exhausted. With Bella in Connie's safe hands, Winnie should grab the chance to sleep while she could, because who knew what was going to happen next.

*

'Frankie?'

The muffled voice calling her name was familiar, it belonged to someone she liked. No, more than liked. Loved. Alastair. Frankie felt herself drifting away again, floating off to some dreamless place of peace and nothingness.

'Frankie.' A warm hand stroked her forehead. 'Wake up.'

Part of her wanted to ignore the voice and just drift off to oblivion again, but it was Alastair calling her. With a mighty effort she flickered her eyes open and then snapped them shut again as a strong urge to sleep pulled her back.

'That's it, open your eyes.' His voice was warm, with that distinctive Scottish accent that she adored, but it sounded muffled, as if she were under water.

Making a supreme effort, she opened her eyes again and this time kept them open, only letting them blink momentarily as she looked straight up into Alastair's face.

He smiled at her. 'Welcome back.'

Back? Where had she been? She couldn't work out where she was for a few moments, but judging from the beds on either side and opposite her, and the smell that she knew so well from her frequent deliveries of casualties, she was in hospital.

Alastair took her hand in his, tenderly stroking it with his thumb. 'How are you feeling?' he asked.

'Bit woolly-headed and I've got a headache.' She winced. 'I can't hear properly.'

'That's to be expected. You're concussed and your

eardrums have taken a battering from the explosion. I stitched up the cut on your head.'

She put her hand to her head and felt a bandage wrapped around it.

'Any pain in your arm?'

Her arm? Frankie was suddenly aware of a heavy solidness encasing her left arm and pulled it out from under the sheet to look at it. 'A bit. What happened to it?'

'It's broken, but it's been reset and plastered up and will be fine in time. You were caught in a landmine explosion, do you remember?'

She frowned, searching her mind, which felt as though it had been stuffed with cotton wool, 'I don't know ...' she began, but then it all came rushing back to her: going to ask about the casualties, the policeman running and shouting, and then the explosion, the roaring noise and the whoosh, the feeling of falling into welcome oblivion. She screwed up her face trying to push away the memory of fear and helplessness that had accompanied it.

'Frankie? What's the matter?' Alastair's expression was concerned.

'I remembered it, what happened.'

'It's all right, it's over and you're safe now,' he said.

She nodded, breathing slowly and deeply to try to calm her racing heart and the unsettling fluttering in the pit of her stomach. The thing she'd dreaded had finally happened – a bomb had had her name on it – but she was still here, still alive, so she'd been lucky. Something nudged at the edge of her awareness; she had an empty feeling, she was missing something, someone. Searching frantically in her mind, pushing through the woozy feeling, it suddenly came back to her and she tried to sit upright, but her head swam and the room swayed. 'Bella, where is she? Is she all right?'

Alastair smiled at her. 'Bella's fine. She's got some cracked ribs and cuts and bruises, but she came out of it much better than you. Station Officer Steele took her home this morning.'

Frankie sighed and slumped back on her pillows. 'Thank God.' The thought of anything happening to her dear friend was too awful to contemplate.

'It was bad out there last night,' Alastair said. 'There's been a lot of people hurt and killed, and London's badly damaged.'

She'd been lucky to survive her encounter with a landmine; there were plenty not so fortunate this morning. Frankie's eyes grew heavy and it was an effort to keep them open. Teetering on the edge of sleep, she suddenly realised that her grandad wouldn't know she was here.

Forcing her eyes open again, she squeezed Alastair's hand. 'Grandad'll be wondering where I am; he'll be worried because I 'aven't gone home.'

'Don't worry about that, I'll go and tell him where you are,' Alastair reassured her.

'Will you?' Tears filled Frankie's eyes. 'Thank you. Tell 'im I'm all right and I'm safe.'

Alastair smiled. 'No doubt he'll be in to see you as soon as he can.'

She nodded and let her heavy eyelids fall, vaguely aware of her cheek being kissed, and the words 'I love you, Frankie' whispered into her ear as she drifted away into sleep.

'Here we are. I want to say breakfast, but at half past one in the afternoon it seems rather odd.' Winnie put the tray down on the nearby dressing table and looked at Bella, whose face had regained some of its colour. 'Let me help you sit up more comfortably.'

Bella slowly leaned forward while Winnie plumped up her pillows and propped them up behind her, then gently helped her friend lean back against them, wincing as she moved.

'Is it very painful?'

'A bit.' Bella did her best to smile. 'It could have been a whole lot worse. Is there any news about Frankie?'

'Station Officer Steele telephoned to say that she's regained consciousness and is resting on the ward. I'm going to the hospital before work to see her.' Winnie put the tray on Bella's lap. 'The gas is still off, I'm afraid, so it's bread and honey rather than toast, and milk instead of tea. Do eat up: you need to build up your strength again.'

'I'm really hungry.' Bella picked up a piece of bread. 'It's hours since I last ate something.' She took a bite and closed her eyes with pleasure as she chewed. 'That tastes so delicious.'

'Good, it's some of Connie's friend's honey from the countryside. She keeps it for us for when we need a boost.'

Bella smiled. 'It's helping. Where's Trixie?'

'Connie's taken her for a walk around Russell Square. I wasn't sure if you'd want her in here.'

'Of course I do, she's a sweet-natured dog.'

'I'll leave her with you today – she can keep you company.'

'Are you sure?' Bella took a sip of milk.

'Yes, she made a real fuss when they brought you home. She knew you'd come back and was whining and scratching at my bedroom door to get out to you.'

'We're her family now and she likes to look after us.'

'Absolutely, I can't imagine life without darling Trixie. They should be back soon.' Winnie went over to the window and looked down into the street to see if she could spot them coming back.

'What's it like out there?' Bella asked. 'Is there anything left after last night?'

'Yes, thankfully, but there's less standing now than there was yesterday morning, that's for sure. Apparently the Houses of Parliament were hit, and the British Museum.' Winnie sighed, thinking about the beautiful building just around the corner from them, with all its treasures from centuries past. 'Several stations are closed, and a lot of roads. Dear old London's in rather a terrible state today.' She turned and smiled at Bella. 'But you mustn't worry about that, darling girl, just concentrate on resting and getting better.'

Bella smiled. 'I always knew you could be bossy.'

'Me?' Winnie smiled. 'It's for your own good, you

know, otherwise we'll have Station Officer Steele here telling you to rest, and she *really* knows how to be bossy.'

'I'd better do as I'm told then,' Bella said. 'As long as you go and see Frankie and find out how she is.'

Winnie sat down on the side of the bed and took hold of her friend's hand. 'Don't worry, I will. She's an important part of our team and we've got to look out for her. Is there anything I can get you before I go?'

'Just my notebook and pencil, they're over on the dressing table.'

Winnie got up and fetched them. 'What are you going to write about, getting caught in a landmine explosion?'

Bella smiled. 'Something like that. You know I like to write things down.'

'Make sure you get some sleep as well, you need to rest.'

'I will, I promise. Just find out about Frankie – I won't be able to rest properly till I know how she is.'

Alastair leaned his bicycle against the front of number 25 Matlock Street and knocked on the door, the news about Frankie weighing heavily on his mind.

When the door opened, it wasn't Frankie's grandfather or even Ivy. 'I recognise you – you're Stella's young man, ain't yer?' the woman said, using Frankie's real name. 'I'm Josie from number 5.' She nodded her head to indicate further down the street.

'Yes, that's right, I'm Alastair. I've come to speak to Frankie's . . . um, Stella's grandfather.'

Josie's plump face paled. 'You'd better come in.'

Alastair followed her into the hall and through to the kitchen at the back of the house, where Frankie's step-grandmother was sitting in an armchair staring at a shiny button in her hand. She looked up briefly, barely registering his presence, and then returned her gaze to the button.

'Is her grandfather at home?' he asked.

'You'd better sit yourself down, ducks.' Josie pulled out a chair from the table and motioned for him to sit.

'I've got some news for him. Frankie wanted me to come and tell him.'

'I'm afraid you ain't goin' to be able to give it to 'im.' Josie's eyes suddenly filled with tears. 'He was killed last night.'

'Killed?' Alastair looked from Josie to Ivy and back again.

'That's right, blown up, nothing left of him but that.' Josie pointed to the shiny button in Ivy's hand. 'One of 'is colleagues brought it 'ere this morning. He saw it 'appen. Reg got a direct hit, and was gone just like that.'

Alastair stared at Josie, suddenly aware of the clock on the mantelpiece ticking loudly, its sound seeming to have been magnified in the heavy atmosphere of the room. The thing that Frankie had dreaded had actually happened. She would be devastated. 'I . . . I'm so sorry, Mrs Franklin, your husband was a good man.'

Ivy looked up at him, her face ghostly white. 'What am I going to do without him?' Her voice was barely more than a whisper.

Josie went over and put her hand on the woman's

shoulder. 'We'll all look out for yer, ducks. You don't need to worry.'

Alastair cleared his throat. 'I'm afraid I've brought some more bad news – not so awful, but I'm afraid Frankie … Stella … was injured on duty last night. She's in the London Hospital. That's what I came to tell her grandfather; she didn't want him to be worried wondering why she hadn't come home.'

'I didn't even notice she weren't 'ere,' Ivy said, still staring at the button. 'He would of, though.'

'Is she badly injured?' Josie's face was full of concern.

'She was knocked unconscious and has broken her arm, but she'll be all right.'

'Thank God. Will you tell her about Reg?' Josie asked. 'She'll be right cut up about it. She thought the world of 'im.'

Alastair nodded and stood up. 'I must get back to the hospital. Goodbye, Mrs Franklin.'

Ivy ignored him and Josie shrugged. 'Come on, I'll see you out.'

Opening the front door for him, she whispered, 'Don't mind Ivy, she's in shock. I'll stay wiv her for the time being.'

'It's fine, I completely understand.' Alastair smiled.

'Thank you for coming to tell us. I'll do my best to pop along and see Frankie as soon as I can, tell her that, will yer?'

'Of course, she'd be glad to see you.' Alastair stepped out into the sunny street, where life was carrying on as normal: a woman walked past with a shopping basket over her arm, and some children were lying on their bellies on the pavement playing marbles.

'You keep a close eye on 'er, make sure she's all right.' Josie reached out and patted his arm. 'She's going to need looking after, poor girl. Reg was all the blood family she 'ad left.'

'Don't worry, I will.'

As he pedalled down Matlock Street, Alastair wondered how he was going to tell Frankie that her grandfather was dead. He had plenty of experience – far too much for his liking since the Blitz had started – of breaking devastating news to relatives, but in these cases he'd always had a professional distance. This time, though, he was very much involved, and it was going to be so much harder. Telling Frankie was going to hurt the woman he loved, but he couldn't leave it to anyone else to do. It was better that it came from him.

All the way back to the London, Alastair's mind had raced through different ways of breaking the news to Frankie, but it didn't matter how he might put it; the plain, stark truth was that her grandfather had been killed and was gone, completely and utterly, with nothing left to weep over or even bury. It was probably best to tell her straight, not drape the message in fancy words to try and disguise the horror of it. Saying it cleanly and clearly would be kindest, he finally decided as he walked along the hospital corridor towards the ward where Frankie was recovering.

But not yet. He wouldn't tell her today, not when she needed rest, because the news would tear her world apart.

Nearing the ward doors. he was surprised to see a familiar figure sitting on one of the seats lining the wall. It was Winnie.

Hearing his footsteps, she looked up, then jumped to her feet and hurried towards him, grabbing hold of his arm. 'Oh Alastair. How is she?'

'She's all right. Her arm's been plastered and her head wound stitched up, but she'll need to be kept in for a few days so we can keep an eye on her after being knocked out. How long have you been here?'

'Not long. They wouldn't let me in to see her, so I just sat down to wait until I saw someone I could ask.' Winnie looked closely at his face. 'What's the matter? You look awful. Frankie will be all right, won't she?'

Alastair shrugged. 'Physically she'll mend just fine, but I've just come from her home . . . she wanted me to go and tell her grandfather where she was.' He swallowed hard. 'He's been killed, last night in the raid . . . he took a direct hit from a bomb.'

Winnie put a hand over her mouth. 'Oh God! Are you on your way to tell her?'

'No, not yet – tomorrow or the next day, when she's a bit stronger.' Alastair ran his hand through his hair. 'Whenever she finds out, it's going to come as one hell of a shock.'

'Are you going in to see her now?'

'Yes, do you want to come with me?'

Winnie beamed at him. 'Can I?'

'As long as you behave yourself and keep the noise down, otherwise Sister will be after us.'

'I will, I promise. I just want to see her.' Winnie squeezed his arm.

Frankie's hair was spread across her pillow, the beautiful auburn shade so reminiscent of autumn bracken on the hills of home, it made Alastair's breath catch in his throat. She looked calm and peaceful, her eyes closed and her breath coming in gentle rises and falls.

'She's asleep,' Winnie whispered. 'We'll have to come back.'

'I'm not asleep.' Frankie's eyes snapped open, their blueness standing out in her pale face. 'Just resting my eyes.' She smiled at them both and held out her hand to Alastair.

'How do you feel?' He bent down and kissed her cheek.

'Still a bit groggy. Did you tell my grandfather where I am?'

'He wasn't there. I saw Ivy and told her what had happened and where you are.' Alastair looked at Winnie standing on the other side of the bed, who gave him a slight nod of encouragement.

'Wasn't he back yet? Probably still off helping after the raid, he's like that.' Frankie smiled. 'It drives Ivy mad.'

Alastair shrugged. 'She didn't look very happy.'

Frankie sighed. 'As long as he knows where I am. I didn't want him worrying. Perhaps he'll come in and see me soon.'

Alastair glanced at Winnie again, and she sat down on the side of the bed and put her hand on Frankie's shoulder.

'What happened?' she asked .

'A policeman shouted for us to run, but there wasn't time before it blew up. I got down on the ground, then there was a loud roar and a rushing and then blackness . . . ' Frankie winced and closed her eyes. 'My head's still sore.'

'You're concussed,' Alastair said. 'And it would have been worse if you hadn't been wearing your steel helmet.'

'Wait till Station Officer Steele hears that,' Winnie said. 'It justifies her nagging at us to always wear them.'

Frankie smiled. 'I'm glad she did. How's Bella? They told me she'd gone home.'

'She's tucked up in bed with Trixie, and Connie's on guard to make sure she doesn't get up.'

Frankie nodded and then yawned. 'I'm sorry, so tired.'

'You sleep.' Alastair gently stroked her cheek. 'I'll come back and see you later, before my shift starts.'

'I'll come back tomorrow if they'll let me in,' Winnie added. 'I only sneaked in this time as I was with Alastair.'

Frankie squeezed Winnie's hand. 'Thank you for coming, and send Bella my love.'

'Come on, let's leave the patient to rest.' Alastair kissed Frankie's cheek and then stood up. 'See you soon.'

Frankie smiled sleepily at them, and by the time they'd walked to the ward doors and looked back at her, her eyes were closed and she'd drifted off to sleep.

*

241

Winnie drove the spade into the soil with all the force she could muster, then stamped it further in with her booted foot before levering it up and turning the clod over. She repeated the process again and again, ignoring the ache in her muscles. If she could just keep digging, focus on the effort and the smell of the newly turned soil, then perhaps she could forget, but the images and feelings of the past few hours wiggled their way through like the worms in the earth beneath her feet.

'Bloody, bloody war!' She yanked the spade out and threw it like a spear so that it impaled a plant a few yards away, then tipped over and fell flat on the ground with a thud. Her energy spent, she dropped to her knees, her breath coming in gasps as she started to sob. Winnie very rarely cried; it felt like all the emotions she had saved up over the past months of bombing and destruction were spilling out of her, leaving her a blubbering wreck.

'I thought I might find you here.'

She swiped at her tear-stained face with the back of her earthy hand, and, keeping her head bowed, glanced sideways at the familiar pair of lace-up shoes standing beside her. It was Station Officer Steele, the last person she would want to find her like this.

'Come on, up you get.'

She felt her upper arm being pulled and didn't have the energy to resist.

'Right, let's have a look at you.' Station Officer Steele put her hand under Winnie's chin and tilted her face upwards, then fished a clean, neatly ironed handkerchief out of her pocket, shook it out in one deft flick and very gently wiped away the tears and the streaks of soil.

'Frankie and Bella will both be all right. I telephoned the hospital to check on Frankie a short while ago and spoke to the ward sister myself.' She smiled and squeezed Winnie's shoulder. 'I know you three are the best of friends and it's only natural that you're upset, but they survived and we've got to be grateful for that, because there are a lot of families out there today who lost loved ones last night.'

'Like Frankie.' Winnie's voice sounded hoarse after her sobbing.

Station Officer Steele frowned. 'What do you mean?'

Winnie explained what had happened, watching the look of horror dawn on her boss's face.

'Poor girl, she's going to be devastated when she finds out.' Station Officer Steele shook her head. 'There's her step-grandmother, of course, that's something.'

Winnie stared at her, a sickening thought rushing into her mind: Frankie's promise to her grandfather to look after the dreadful woman. What her friend had dreaded had actually happened. But perhaps she wouldn't have to stick to it; after all, she'd been cornered into giving her word, hadn't she? Winnie would talk to her about it, try and persuade her to think of herself and not live her life beholden to that horrible promise.

'How's Bella?'

'Resting in bed under my godmother's watchful eye. I left Trixie with her to keep her company.'

243

'Good.'

Winnie looked up at the blue sky, which was still tainted with smoke from burning buildings. 'Do you think they'll be back again tonight?'

Station Officer Steele shrugged. 'Who knows? I sincerely hope not. There's been a massive amount of damage and I'm not sure London can take much more.'

'Did you know they even hit the Tower?' Winnie gestured towards the walls of the Tower of London, which bordered the allotments, her voice coming out in a high-pitched shriek. 'It's been standing there for hundreds of years and those bloody Nazis bombed it.'

'Go home and get some more rest, Winnie. You look like you still need to sleep.'

'I'm all right.'

'You're not, so take that as an order. If you turn up on shift tonight without having had some sleep, I shall send you home again.'

'What?' Winnie glared at her boss, fighting the sudden tears that were prickling her eyes.

'I need my crews to be fully fit and ready for duty, and *you* clearly are not at the moment.' Station Officer Steele sighed and put her hand on Winnie's arm. 'Look, we'll be two crew members down at least, so don't make me lose another one. If they come back and bomb us again tonight, I will need you, Winnie, but only if you are fit to be on duty.'

Winnie sighed heavily. 'Very well. But I'm only doing it because I know you would send me home.'

Station Officer Steele smiled. 'You know me so well. Go on, take care of yourself.'

Winnie collected her bicycle from where she'd left it leaning on the moat wall and started to walk away, then stopped and turned back. 'What about you?' she said.

'Me?' Her boss smiled. 'Oh don't worry about me, I'm fine. I'm just going to watch the river go by for a little while.'

'Do you think he'll come today?' Frankie asked.

Alastair's stomach lurched as he put the chart he'd been checking back into its place at the end of her bed. He still hadn't told her about her grandfather. To begin with she'd been recovering from being knocked out, but now she was much improved, her face a healthy colour and her eyes bright, and she would probably be discharged soon. His excuse for keeping the dreadful news from her was that he simply wanted to protect her, because he knew the pain she would suffer the moment he was honest with her.

'I thought he'd 'ave come before now, or at least sent a letter or something. Don't you think?' Frankie stared at him. 'Alastair?'

If he didn't tell her soon, perhaps someone else would. If Josie came to visit her, she'd presume that Frankie already knew. Finding out like that would be an even worse blow. He had to do it, in the kindest way he could. And now.

'Frankie.' He sat down on the edge of the bed and took

245

both of her hands in his. 'Remember I told you the other day that your grandfather wasn't there when I went to tell him about you being injured?'

She nodded, her blue eyes fixed on his as he struggled to find the words to lessen the terrible blow. But there simply wasn't a way to diminish what he had to tell her; no words could make it less of a loss for her.

'Frankie, I'm so very, very sorry to have to tell you that the reason your grandfather wasn't there was because he'd been killed in the raid. He never came home.'

Frankie stared at him, the blood draining from her face. She began to shake her head, her eyes wide. 'No, no, that can't be right.'

'I'm sorry, but it is. He was killed by a direct hit,' Alastair told her, holding on tightly to her hands. 'He's gone, Frankie.'

'No, he can't be ...' Frankie's eyes filled with tears, which quickly spilled over and ran down her face, her mouth working silently before she suddenly let out a loud sob that wrenched at her whole body.

Alastair gathered her into his arms and held her tightly while she wept, her tears soaking into his jacket.

'They would have been here by now if they were coming, don't you think?' Winnie stopped pacing up and down and stared up at the moonlit sky, straining her ears to listen for the sound of enemy planes. But there was nothing, just the sound of a city sleeping in the early hours of the morning.

'Probably.' Mac put his arms around her and pulled her close. 'Try not to worry. There's nothing you can do to stop them if they do come. It's no good getting yourself all worked up about it.'

She rested her head against his chest and tried to calm down, to relax, because here she was sharing picket duty with Mac under a clear moonlit sky, and it could be so romantic ... 'What's that?' She shrugged off his arms, cupping her hand around her ear to help her hear. 'There, can you hear it? It's a plane, and it's getting nearer.'

'I hear it, but listen to the engines, Winnie; it's one of ours on its way home.'

Winnie concentrated hard. The engines' beat was steady, not the *voom, voom* throb of the German planes. She sighed. 'You're right.'

Mac took her hand. 'Relax, Winnie, or you'll drive yourself crazy. You've been like a cat on hot bricks since that big raid. They haven't been back since.'

'No, but they might, any time,' she snapped. 'I'm sorry, I feel so terribly on edge waiting for the siren to go. I miss Frankie and Bella, too. It feels very strange without them here.'

'I know, but they'll be back as soon as they can.'

Winnie sighed. 'I'm being an awful misery, aren't I? I'm sorry.' She kissed him gently. 'I'll try and cheer up.'

He drew her into his arms again. 'Would this help?' He kissed her passionately.

'Better not let the boss see you doing that on duty,' Winnie said when they came up for air.

Mac laughed. 'Just as well it's dark out here then.'

The remainder of the shift passed peacefully, without a single call-out, and the bombers didn't come back, so Winnie was feeling much more cheerful and relaxed as she made tea for everyone a little after seven o'clock, while the rest of the crew members did their final jobs and got ready for the handover at half past.

'Look at this!' Sparky slapped the morning's newspaper down on the table. 'I wonder what 'itler's got to say about this.'

Winnie stared at the instantly recognisable face on the front of the paper – it was Rudolf Hess, Hitler's right hand man.

'What's going on?' Station Officer Steele emerged from her office and came over to see what everyone was crowding around to look at.

'Hess flew to Scotland and 'as been arrested,' Sparky explained. 'He arrived a couple of nights ago when the Luftwaffe were dropping tons of explosives on us lot.'

'Let me see.' The boss picked up the paper and read out loud how Hess had parachuted out of his plane, broken his ankle when he landed and been found by a ploughman.

'What do you think it means?' Winnie asked.

'Well he didn't arrive 'ere by mistake,' Sparky said. 'Perhaps he's come to tell old Churchill all Hitler's plans and the war'll be over by next week.'

'Who knows?' Station Officer Steele said. 'We'll carry on as normal until we hear otherwise. If anyone's making some toast, I'd appreciate a slice before we do the hand-over to the next shift.' She nodded and returned to her office.

If Hess really had come to help the war finish early, then it would be perfectly all right with her, Winnie thought as she set about making toast.

Frankie closed her eyes and did her best to ignore the visitors coming on to the ward, because the one person she wanted to see more than anyone wouldn't be coming. Biting on her bottom lip, she tried to stem the rush of grief that was starting to build up inside her again. It came in waves, the heartbreaking sadness so heavy in her heart it often made her sob into her pillow.

''Ello, ducks.' A gentle touch on Frankie's arm made her open her eyes. 'You weren't asleep, were you?' Josie smiled at her kindly.

Frankie shook her head and sniffed. 'I wasn't expecting anyone to come.'

Josie sat down on the chair beside the bed, then reached over and took hold of Frankie's hand. ''Ow are yer?'

She shrugged. 'Me head's not hurtin' now; they've said I can go home tomorrow.'

'They ain't sending you to a 'ospital out in Kent like they did yer grandad?' Josie stopped, her face flushing. She squeezed Frankie's hand. 'I'm ever so sorry about 'im. Reg was a good, kind man and he didn't deserve to get killed like that.'

Frankie nodded, her throat throbbing painfully. 'Oh

Josie!' Tears spilled over and ran down her face. 'What 'appened to him, Josie? Tell me.'

Josie looked down at their entwined hands before fixing her eyes on Frankie's. 'He was out in the raid, 'elping out, yer know, and he got a direct hit from a bomb. One of the other constables saw it.' Her eyes filled with tears. 'He was gone in a moment – 'e won't 'ave known a thing about it.'

Frankie's breaths came in gasps as Josie's words sank in. 'What about a funeral?' She knew the answer already, but she had to ask anyway, just to be sure.

Josie looked away for a moment, then returned her gaze to Frankie, tears glistening in her eyes. 'He was completely gone, you understand? There weren't nothin' left of 'im to bury.' She took a neatly ironed handkerchief out of her pocket and dabbed away the tears that had started to run down her plump cheeks. 'They found one of the buttons off his police uniform. Ivy's got that.'

Frankie knew enough about what could happen when a bomb fell to know that Josie was telling the truth. It seemed so final, so cruel and unfair. He'd been there one moment, a man full of life and doing the job he loved, then he was gone, nothing left of him, just a button. There'd be no grave to visit, no place where she could go to feel closer to him. She started to sob, her chest heaving as she gulped for air.

''Ere, let me 'elp yer, ducks.' Josie fished another handkerchief out of her handbag and dabbed at Frankie's face until she'd calmed down.

'Thanks.' Frankie's voice was hoarse.

'So.' Josie did her best to smile. 'You must be looking forward to comin' 'ome.'

'I'll be glad to get out of 'ospital.' But as for going home, Frankie thought, that was a different matter. With her grandad gone, home wasn't going to be the same any more. It would just be her and Ivy, until Stanley came home, and that might not be for months or even years.

'Well I'll be pleased to see you back in Matlock Street, and if there's anythin' I can do to 'elp you, then you only 'ave to ask, all right?'

'Thank you, Josie. I appreciate that.'

'We all look out for each other, don't we?'

Frankie nodded. Most people did, but not everyone. Now she was supposed to be looking out for Ivy, doing what she'd promised to do.

She'd tried to block out thoughts of the promise she'd made. Inside the walls of the hospital it had been easier to ignore what the future held for her, but from tomorrow she'd be back home, facing the reality of life without Grandad, in his place a heavy, unwanted responsibility. The future looked bleak.

Bella loved the library in Connie's house. It had drawn her in and made her feel at home from her very first day there. Its shelves, crammed with books, were a constant source of joy to her, giving her hours of pleasure as she escaped to different places and times, something that had become increasingly precious to her as a diversion from the horrors of the Blitz.

Now, sitting in a shaft of summer sunlight streaming in through the large French windows, she settled back in the winged leather armchair and lost herself in a book, drifting off to another place. She had no idea how long she'd been reading when the door opened and Connie came in, closely followed by a familiar figure.

'Bella, you've got a visitor,' Connie said.

It was Station Officer Steele. 'Hello, Bella.'

She went to stand up, but the older woman waved for her to stay sitting and settled herself down in the chair opposite.

'I'll bring you some tea,' Connie said, and left the room.

'How are you?' Station Officer Steele asked, her keen brown eyes searching Bella's face. 'You're certainly looking a lot brighter than when I last saw you.'

'I'm not so sore now, thankfully. I'll be back to work in a day or two.'

'Oh no you won't.' Station Officer Steele smiled. 'I have other plans for you. I've made arrangements for you and Frankie to go and convalesce at one of the Red Cross country hospitality scheme homes.'

Bella stared at her boss for a few moments. 'But there's no need for that. I'm fine, honestly.'

'I think there is.' Station Officer Steele leaned forward in her chair, fixing her eyes firmly on Bella's. 'I need you to go for Frankie's sake as well as your own. She definitely needs to convalesce, rest and be looked after properly, and from what Winnie's told me, there's no chance of her getting that if she goes home. That step-grandmother of hers isn't going to help her.' She pursed her lips in a look of disapproval. 'But if you go with Frankie you can help her, make sure she's all right and get some rest yourself as well.' She reached out and put her hand on Bella's arm. 'I'd feel much happier if you were there with her. Frankie's had two hard knocks and I need to give her the best chance to recover. So I hope you'll agree to go.'

Bella nodded. 'Of course I'll go for Frankie. It's terrible what happened. She adored her grandad and must be devastated. I'll do everything I can to help her.'

'Jolly good. And you'll be delighted to know that the home you're being sent to is in Buckinghamshire, not far from your mother. I expect you'll be able to meet up with her, and Frankie can see young Stanley, which will help her immensely.'

'Buckinghamshire?' Bella beamed at her boss. 'Thank you very much.' The thought of being able to see her mother again soon was wonderful. 'When are we going?'

Station Officer Steele smiled at her. 'Tomorrow.'

Winnie bumped her bicycle over the cobbles of Matlock Street, looking at the numbers on the doors as she pedalled along. She was aware that her arrival in the street had been noticed by the woman who'd been vigorously cleaning the front windows of number 5. Winnie had the feeling that if she looked back, the woman would still be watching her, like some guard dog keeping an eye on any strangers who dared enter the street.

Spotting number 25, she dismounted and leaned her bicycle against the front of the house, then glanced back.

Sure enough, the woman was staring in her direction, her hands on her ample hips, her window cleaning forgotten for the moment. Aware that her every move was being scrutinised, Winnie undid the straps attaching Station Officer Steele's brown leather suitcase to the carrier at the back of her bicycle and then knocked on the door of number 25. There was no sound from within; perhaps they hadn't heard. She knocked again, louder this time.

'She ain't goin' to answer,' a loud voice called.

Winnie turned to see the guard–dog woman homing in on her, her slippers slapping on the pavement. 'She's just been widowed and ain't up to 'aving visitors.'

'Yes, I know. I've come to get some clothes and things for Frankie.'

The woman eyed her up and down. ''Ave you now, and why's that?'

Winnie held out her hand. 'I'm Winnie. I work with Frankie at Station 75.'

The woman's face broke into a smile and she shook Winnie's hand hard, squeezing it tight in her roughened, meaty hand. 'Why didn't yer say? Any friend of Frankie's is a friend of mine. I'm Josie from number 5.' Her eyes narrowed. 'So you say you've come to get some clothes for 'er? Ain't she supposed to be comin' 'ome tomorrow? That's what she told me when I went to see 'er this afternoon.'

'There's been a change of plan. Our station officer has arranged for her to go away and convalesce somewhere in the country where she'll be well cared for and get plenty of rest and fresh air.'

'When's she goin'?'

'Tomorrow. I've been sent by our boss to get her clothes and anything else she might need. I was hoping Frankie's step-grandmother might help me.'

'What, Ivy?' Josie pulled a face, shaking her head. 'I doubt it.' She smiled suddenly, her plump cheeks dimpling. 'But I'll 'elp yer. We can't 'ave Frankie going away without her clothes and things.'

'Thank you, that's awfully kind of you. I'd appreciate your help very much.' Winnie had the feeling that Josie would enjoy organising Frankie's things for her.

'Come on, you'll 'ave to meet Ivy first, explain what's 'appening.' Josie opened the front door and called out as they walked in. 'Cooee, Ivy, it's only me.'

Inside, the air smelled stale with smoke, and when they reached the kitchen at the back of the house, Ivy was puffing away on a cigarette. Evidence of many more already smoked lay stubbed out in an overflowing ashtray on the table amidst a clutter of unwashed teacups. Ivy glared at Winnie, her eyes narrowing and lips puckering around the butt of her cigarette as she sucked in another lungful of smoke.

'This is Winnie, she's a friend of Stella's,' Josie introduced her, referring to Frankie by her real name. 'She's come to collect some clothes for her 'cos she's going away to stay at a convalescent home in the countryside.'

'It's in Buckinghamshire, not far from where Stanley's staying,' Winnie added. 'She'll hopefully be able to see him while she's there.'

255

'Stanley will like that. I wrote to 'im for Ivy and told 'im about Reg bein' killed,' Josie said. 'He 'ad to be told, poor lad.'

Winnie nodded. 'He must have been upset.'

'The lady that looks after 'im wrote back and said he was, but he'll get over it in time – you 'ave to, don't yer?'

'It's all right for some, swannin' off to the countryside,' Ivy snorted, tossing her head so that her untidy peroxide-blonde hair fell over her face. 'Wish I could go away from 'ere.'

'Would you rather Frankie came back here?' Winnie asked. 'She'll need a lot of care while she recovers from her injuries.'

'What for?' Ivy sneered. 'I ain't missin' 'er, if that's what you're wonderin'. And I ain't lookin' after her either if she does come 'ome.'

'Then it's just as well that she's going to the convalescent home, isn't it?' Winnie said sweetly, doing her best to stay calm when she'd much prefer to give the woman a good shaking. 'So if I may, I'd like to get Frankie's clothes and things for her to take with her.'

Ivy stubbed out the butt of her cigarette. 'Do what you want.' She swatted her hand towards them. 'I don't care.'

Josie's gaze met Winnie's. 'Come on, ducks, I'll give you an 'and. Back bedroom's hers, ain't it, Ivy?'

Ivy nodded and grabbed her cigarette packet off the table, then, finding it empty, swore and threw it on the floor.

'This way.' Josie pulled at Winnie's sleeve and led her out of the kitchen and up the stairs to Frankie's room.

Chapter Ten

Frankie had never been in a trap before, but she liked the way it bobbed and swayed along, gently mirroring the rhythm of the grey pony's movements, accompanied by the satisfying clop of its hooves on the road.

Bella sat opposite her chatting to Bertie, the old man who'd met them at the station and who now sat at the front of the trap, the reins held loosely in his gnarled hands. They were talking about where Bella had grown up in Buckinghamshire, not that far from here.

Leaving them to it, Frankie looked around her, struck by how green and lush the countryside was. It was as if it was bursting with life, the trees verdant with fresh green leaves and everywhere filled with a sense of expectation and growth. It felt so different to the grey, drab London that they'd left this morning, and the pristine world of the hospital where she'd spent the last few days since she'd been injured.

She marvelled at the brightness of the colours, the sounds of birds singing and the simple fact that she could see off into the distance across hedgerows and fields. After what she was used to in London, it was a shock to her system, a whole new world, but one that she welcomed. She breathed in, enjoying the freshness of the air, grateful for the chance to come somewhere that was so different for a while and put off returning home, where she'd be forced to deal with the massive hole left by her grandad's death, and with it the fulfilment of her unwanted promise.

'Nearly there,' Bertie said. 'If you look past them trees you'll see the gateposts of Beechings House.'

Frankie didn't know what to expect, but as Beechings House came into view, she was astonished that this was where she'd be staying. It was so different to the terraced houses of Matlock Street, built of a mellow honey-coloured stone with large windows looking out like eyes on to the wide lawns and driveway. It was beautiful.

'What's happened to the owners?' Bella asked as they turned in through the gates and drove along the drive lined with beech trees.

'They're still here, just moved into the west wing to make room for the country hospitality home,' Bertie told them. 'You'll probably see them.'

'Do you live 'ere?' Frankie asked.

Bertie nodded. 'In the gardener's cottage with my wife. I'm the gardener as well as the coachman.' He gave a throaty chuckle. 'So you'll be seeing me around the place.

My wife helps in the kitchen. You'll be well fed while you're here – she's a good cook.'

Arriving outside the front door, with its pillars on either side, Bertie brought the pony to a halt and helped them both out, mindful of Frankie's broken arm.

'Thank you.' Frankie smiled at him.

Bertie touched the brim of his cap. 'My pleasure. I hope you'll enjoy your stay here.'

'We will,' Bella said. 'Do we just go in?'

Before Bertie could answer, the front door opened and a pleasant-looking woman stepped out, smiling at them. 'Welcome, I hope you've had a good journey. I'm Joan Bartlet, I work for the Red Cross and help run our country hospitality home here.' She held out her hand to each of them.

'I'm Peggy Belmont, or Bella,' Bella said, shaking her hand.

'Stella Franklin, Frankie,' Frankie said.

Joan smiled. 'Ah yes, I know you ambulance crews go by other names; we've had quite a few come and stay here. Shall I call you Bella and Frankie, or would you prefer your real names?'

'Bella's fine by me.'

'And Frankie for me.'

'Jolly good. Now let me take your luggage and I'll show you to your room.'

She bent down and picked up their cases before they could protest and led them inside to the wide hallway, which had a beautiful grand staircase leading up to the next floor.

'Off to your left is the drawing room, where you are welcome to relax, meet with the others staying here, join in the games evening as you wish.' She indicated to the right. 'Over there is the library; again please use it, but do make sure you return any books before you leave.'

Bella caught Frankie's eye and grinned.

'You'll be happy,' Frankie said.

'Further along is the dining room – breakfast is at eight, lunch at twelve thirty and dinner at half past six. We don't eat late in the evening as many visitors like to retire early – not sure if it's the country air making them sleepy or the simple need for sleep after all they've been through in London.' She looked at them both. 'You do a splendid job, you know.' She nodded, smiling. 'Right, let's show you your room and you can settle in.'

She led them up the grand staircase, opening a door at the top and stepping aside for them to go in first.

Frankie looked around her, hardly believing that she would be sleeping in here. There were two beds, both made up with soft-looking pillows and silky eiderdowns. The carpet was a pale dusky pink and the walls were painted a soft cream. Velvet curtains to match the carpet hung at the window either side of a deep cushioned window seat. 'It's beautiful.'

'I'm glad you like it,' Joan said, putting the cases down near the beds. 'The bathroom is through here.' She opened a door leading off the room that Frankie hadn't noticed. 'There's plenty of hot water, so do use it – baths are very relaxing – though please remember to stick to the four-inch limit; there's a ring painted around the inside of the bath so you'll know how deep you need it.'

Frankie and Bella peered in through the door.

'If you'd like to come over here . . . ' Joan led the way to the window. 'You can see the kitchen gardens to the back of the house, and beyond that the orchard. Please feel free to go wherever you wish.'

'Thank you,' Bella said.

'Now I'll leave you both to settle in. There'll be tea in the drawing room at four o'clock if you'd like it, and you can meet some of our other guests; we've got fire service crew and ARPs staying as well.'

'Thank you, we'll be there,' Frankie said.

The moment Joan had gone, closing the door quietly behind her, Frankie and Bella looked at each other and grinned.

'Did you think it would be like this?' Frankie asked, twirling around and looking at the room again.

'I wasn't sure what to expect. Station Officer Steele didn't tell me anything other than where it was. I've read a bit about country hospitality homes in the paper. Some are much smaller and you stay with a family. We've hit the jackpot here.' Bella reached out and took hold of Frankie's hand. 'It'll be good for you here, give you time and space to begin to come to terms with what's happened.' She paused. 'I know how hard it is to lose someone so suddenly. When my dad died, it was such a shock and hurt so much . . . but time helps, it really does. It will be all right, Frankie, I promise.'

Frankie squeezed her friend's hand. 'I'm glad you're here with me, Bella.'

'Me too.' Bella smiled and pulled Frankie into a very gentle hug, mindful of her cracked ribs, then stepped back. 'Come on, let's try out the beds, see if they're as comfy as they look.' She threw herself down on top of the nearest bed and let out a loud sigh. 'I can feel myself relaxing already.'

Frankie lay down on her bed more carefully, mindful of her broken arm, and felt herself sink into the soft mattress as if she was being gently cradled in protective arms.

'I think I'm going to enjoy staying here,' Bella said.

'Me too,' Frankie said, closing her eyes and slowly beginning to drift off. Aware that sleep was claiming her, she didn't fight it, but let it come. She was here to rest and recuperate, and it might as well start right now.

'The investiture's next week,' Winnie said, scanning through the letter that had arrived in the post. 'At Buckingham Palace, where it says I will be presented with the George Medal by the King.' She held up two tickets that had been enclosed with the letter. 'And I can bring two guests with me.'

'Your mother will certainly enjoy herself,' Connie said, sitting down on the sofa next to her and looking at them. 'Perhaps she'll finally accept that being an ambulance driver is an acceptable occupation, recognised and endorsed by the King himself.'

Winnie pulled a face. 'I'd rather you came with me. Would you?'

'Darling girl.' Connie put her arm around Winnie's shoulders and hugged her. 'I would love to come, but I think it only proper that you should invite your parents. If for any reason they can't make it, then of course I'd be delighted to accompany you, but you really must ask them first.'

'I suppose you're right.' Winnie sighed. 'But Mother is bound to make an awfully big fuss over it, and after how downright unpleasant she's been about me being an ambulance driver, it seems rather hypocritical that she should come to see me get a medal for doing it, whereas you have always supported me.'

'I know, but look on it as a way of proving your point, and with any luck she might come to finally approve of her daughter driving ambulances around London.'

'I very much doubt it. Mac must have got his letter today as well. I expect he'll invite his mother along.'

'So will you introduce him to your parents?' Connie asked.

'Only if I have to, and then as a colleague, nothing more. I don't want Mother knowing and turning her spite on him. I intend to keep our relationship a secret for as long as possible.' She sighed. 'It's too precious to risk it being ruined by my mother.'

Connie smiled. 'I think you're wise, but you do know you won't be able to keep it from her for ever, not if you're serious about each other and might want to marry. She'll have to know eventually.'

'Hold on there, Connie. We're not thinking of getting married, you know.'

'Perhaps not yet.' Connie grinned. 'But you might do, and sooner than you think. This war is speeding up relationships. Courtships are shorter because there's so much uncertainty in life now; people are grabbing at happiness while they can.'

'Well Mac and I have no plans to be anywhere else other than Station 75. It's not as if he's in the army and is going to be sent overseas. We're quite happy as we are.'

'If you say so.' Connie laughed. 'I haven't forgotten what it's like to be young and in love in wartime.'

Winnie took hold of her godmother's hand and squeezed it. 'I wish you'd had your chance to marry your fiancé.'

Connie nodded and did her best to smile. 'So do I, but it's in the past and I have happy memories of the time we had together.' She took a deep breath. 'Enough sad talk; let's think about what you're going to wear for the investiture. You'll need to look smart.'

'If we had a uniform, I'd be able to wear that,' Winnie said.

'Well you don't, so you're going to have to look wonderful in your own clothes. Come on, let's go and sort through your wardrobe for the perfect outfit for receiving the George Medal.'

Frankie had found this spot the morning after they'd arrived at Beechings House. She loved how cosy and tucked away it felt, cocooned in the peaceful orchard where the trees were swathed in pink blossom and gently humming with the busyness of bees at work.

Sitting on a wrought-iron bench, bathed in blissfully warm sunshine, she watched a mother hen shepherding her chicks under the trees, stopping now and then to scratch for insects, sending out a joyful 'tuk, tuk' call to her babies when she found some tasty morsel, which sent them running to her, their little legs whirring. It made Frankie smile. She was happy to be there witnessing the little scene, but then the thought that her grandad would have enjoyed it too suddenly sliced into her mind, sending a chill through her body despite the sunshine, and firmly reminding her that he wasn't here any more.

Tears stung her eyes and she felt guilty that she'd forgotten, even for a short while. She'd enjoying watching the mother hen and her babies, and it had felt good to be normal again. But the heavy weight of her loss had returned, sweeping in on a wave of grief. Wiping away escaped tears with the back of her hand, Frankie knew that wherever she went, she would take the sorrow with her; there was no avoiding it. It would always be there to haunt her. She might have escaped from London for a while, but she'd most definitely brought the pain with her.

The past week had shaken her to the core. She'd come face to face with her own mortality after surviving the landmine explosion. Luck had been on her side, but it chilled her to think that if she'd been just a few feet closer, the outcome could have been so different. She breathed in a deep, shuddering breath, her heart banging hard in her chest. She couldn't ignore what had happened. She'd looked into the abyss and survived, and though part of her felt eager for life, to grab at it, live it, love it, in another way her world had crumbled. Grandad was dead. Gone. Snatched away in an instant, leaving her existence colder and more drab, as if the colour had leached out of it. She wanted the world to stop, to still for a while in acknowledgement of the hole he'd left. But it wasn't going to. Life went on. It didn't stop because you'd lost someone.

Her eyes returned to the hen and her chicks as they went about their business. Grandad wouldn't want her to be miserable; he'd expect her to carry on, enjoy life because it was so very precious and the war could snatch it away at any time. One of the chicks had strayed too far from its mother, and the hen gave a sharp, cross-sounding call, sending it barrelling towards her, nearly tripping over its spindly little legs in its haste. Frankie laughed, glad to be here and grateful for Station Officer Steele's decision to send her and Bella here to rest and recuperate.

'There she is. Frankie!'

She turned to see Bella walking towards her, and at the sight of the blond-haired boy at her friend's side, Frankie's heart seemed to leap out of her chest. She quickly stood up and held her uninjured arm out wide as the boy rushed to meet her.

'Stanley.' Frankie wrapped her arm around him and squeezed him tight. Looking over his head, she saw that Bella was beaming at her.

'I thought you might enjoy a visitor,' she said.

'How did you know I was 'ere?' Frankie asked, pulling

back and looking at Stanley, studying his face carefully after months of not seeing it.

'Bella wrote and told her mother you were here and invited us to visit,' Stanley explained.

'Where's your mother?' Frankie asked.

'She's waiting at the house, you can meet her later, I thought you and Stanley might like some time together first.' Bella smiled. 'I'll leave the two of you to catch up.'

Frankie nodded. 'Thank you, Bella, this is . . . ' Her eyes started to fill with tears and she shrugged, unable to speak.

Bella touched her shoulder. 'It's my pleasure. I'll see you in a bit.' She turned and walked back to the house.

'I can't believe how much you've grown since last autumn.' Frankie put her hand on Stanley's head, smoothing his hair. 'Must be all this good country air and fresh food.'

Stanley looked at her arm in its sling. 'Are you all right? Bella said you were in an accident.' He reached out and gingerly touched her hand.

'It's nothing to worry about, honestly. I'm fine. The bone just got broken, that's all, and it's getting better now. Once the plaster's off, it'll be as good as new again.'

'What 'appened to Grandad? He said he'd be all right, but he wasn't, was he?' Stanley's chin started to wobble and he quickly hung his head.

Frankie swallowed hard against the lump that had suddenly wedged itself firmly in her throat. What should she tell him? Not the whole truth; she should spare him the details.

'Let's sit down.' She sat on the bench and patted the space beside her.

He lingered for a moment, poking at the grass with the toe of his shoe, and then came over and sat down beside her, swinging his legs back and forth, his knobbly knees showing beneath the hem of his shorts.

'Well, he was unlucky, Stanley, a bomb fell too close to 'im and it killed 'im. He was out doing his job and was very brave.' She put her arm around the boy's shoulders. 'He didn't suffer at all.'

Stanley didn't say anything, just kept swinging his legs.

'Grandad did his best to survive, but it's tricky out in an air raid. You can't tell where the bombs are goin' to land; it's just chance if it's where you are. He wouldn't want you to go on being sad about it forever, you know. It's all right to cry, but you 'ave to keep on living and enjoying things.'

Stanley turned to look at her. 'I miss 'im. He used to write to me.'

Frankie squeezed his shoulders. 'I miss 'im too. I think about 'im every day and I try and remember some good memories.'

They sat quietly for a while, both lost in their own thoughts. Frankie was doing her best to picture some of the good times with Grandad: how he'd spent time with her when she was little, had shown her things around Stepney, pointed out the ships at the docks, told her tales about where they came from.

'How long will you be 'ere?' Stanley asked, breaking the silence.

'We're 'ere for a whole week, so I've got four more days before I have to go back to London.'

'Will you come and see me so I can show you where I live? It ain't that far away, a couple of stops on the train; it won't take long to get there.'

'I'd like that very much. You can show me round and I'll be able to picture you there when I'm back in London.'

Stanley grinned at her. 'Bella can bring you and talk with her mother while we look around.'

'I'm sure she'd like that. Our station officer arranged for us to come to this convalescent 'ome because it's near where you and Bella's mother live. I'm glad she did that.' She leaned her head against his. 'Seeing you again is the best medicine I could 'ave, Stanley. It makes me feel a whole lot better.'

Picket duty with someone else was much better than being out in the darkness all on your own, Winnie thought. She and Mac always did theirs together now, one going out with the other even when it wasn't their turn, as it gave them a chance to spend some time alone while they were at work.

'Will your mother come to the investiture?' she asked.

'I hope so, though she's never been to London before so it'll be a whole new experience for her. I'll have to find somewhere for her to stay; she couldn't get here and back home again in one day.'

'She can come and stay at Connie's house. There's plenty of room and she'd be most welcome.'

'All right then, thank you, as long as Connie agrees, of course. It would be a treat for her to stay in such a grand house.' Mac put his arm around her shoulders and pulled her to him.

'It's not that grand,' Winnie said.

'Oh it is, Winnie, compared with where most people live. My mother's cottage would fit inside it easily several times over.'

'Don't, you make me feel embarrassed. You know Connie's not stuck up and shares her home with people freely and happily,' Winnie said. 'It's how people are and how they treat others that matters, not where they come from.'

'In theory, yes.'

Winnie turned to look at him, the lightening sky as dawn approached making it possible to see his face. 'What do you mean by that?'

'In an ideal world people would be judged on how they behave and not on how rich they are or what class they were born into, but it doesn't work like that most of the time.'

'I think like that!' Winnie snapped.

Mac smiled at her and wrapped his arms around her, hugging her to him. 'I know *you* do – you are a lovely person and I'm very happy to know and love you – but not everyone is as kind and open as you are.'

Winnie hugged him back tightly knowing that what he said was true and that unfortunately there were people within her own family who were just like that, who

270

judged and looked down on people because of their backgrounds and beliefs.

She pulled away slightly so that she was still cradled in his arms but could see his face. 'Mac, my parents will probably come to the investiture and I'll introduce you to them, but only as a colleague. I think it's best we still keep our relationship a secret from them.'

He shrugged. 'If that's what you want, as long as you're doing it for the right reasons, not because you're ashamed of me.'

'You know I'm not!' She pulled out of his arms and started to pace up and down. 'I've told you before, it's only because I know what my mother's like and have had enough of her awful venom over the years to know that I don't want it directed at you. I want to protect you, darling Mac; please trust me when I say it is absolutely for the best.'

Mac held up his hands in surrender. 'All right, I understand. I'm curious to see your mother for myself.'

'From what you've told me about your mother, mine is the polar opposite, so prepare yourself.'

'What about Connie, is she going?'

Winnie shook her head. 'I wish, but there are only two tickets and my parents will have to have those.'

'I only need one for my mother, so Connie can have the other one. If you had her there she would be a support for you against your parents.'

'Are you sure? That would be wonderful, Mac. Thank you.' She threw her arms around him. 'Connie is an expert

271

at dealing with my mother – she's had plenty of practice over the years.'

Bletchley was only a short train ride from the convalescent home, so Bella was taking the opportunity to return to the place she'd fled from last autumn. Walking out through the station yard on her way to meet James, she recalled how she'd bolted back to the station from the tea room fighting back tears of anger and humiliation, believing that James had lied to her and thought so little of her. Thankfully it had all been sorted out and the untruths allotted to their rightful owner, the delightful Daphne, who had wanted James for herself and had done her best to split them apart. This time Bella was confident of James's feelings for her and she couldn't wait to see him again.

She hadn't even reached the place where they'd agreed to meet when she heard someone shouting her name and turned to see James pedalling towards her on his bicycle, his face a wide beaming smile of welcome.

'It's so good to see you,' he said, quickly dismounting and pulling her into a gentle embrace. He drew back a little, still holding on to her, and studied her face. 'How are you?'

'I'm fine, thank you, and all the better for seeing you.'

'Is the hospitality home helping?'

Bella nodded. 'Yes, I think so. It's lovely there and I'm thoroughly enjoying being out in the countryside again. I've even had a visit from my mother. It's certainly doing Frankie good. She's looking a lot better and she's seen

272

Stanley, which perked her up no end.' She paused. 'I'm not so sure I really needed a rest, though. There are plenty of civil defence workers who need it more than me.'

'Station Officer Steele wouldn't have sent you there if she didn't think you needed to go, would she? She's not one for pandering to people.' He gently touched her cheek. 'Remember, you were caught in a landmine explosion.'

She touched his hand. 'I know.'

'So just enjoy it and make the most of it, because you'll be back on duty soon enough.'

'I'm writing about it for my next article in the newspaper. I thought the readers might be interested in hearing how the Red Cross are helping civil defence workers to get better.'

'That's a very good idea. I'm sure they'll like it.'

'I hope so. I do love writing for the paper, it's a challenge and makes me think hard.'

'Who knows where it might lead one day,' James said. 'You might get a job on a newspaper after the war.'

Bella laughed. 'I doubt that, but I'm just enjoying it while I can.'

They started walking towards the centre of the town, Bella with her arm linked through James's free arm, him wheeling his bicycle along beside them.

'How's your work?' Bella asked.

'Same old stuff, pushing paper around. This war generates a huge amount of paperwork.'

'Station 75 produces its fair share of it. Station Officer Steele does a magnificent job of managing it, though I think Winnie struggled a bit when she took over for her while she was off. Being super-organised and keeping up with paperwork isn't one of your sister's strong points.'

'She'd agree with you there.' James grinned. 'I had a letter from her this morning: she's got the date for the investiture at Buckingham Palace and is worrying about what's going to happen there.'

'Well, she'll get her medal; there's nothing to worry about, surely?'

'It's not that, it's the possibility of our mother meeting Mac.'

'Ah.' Bella's stomach tightened at the memory of her own meeting with Mrs Churchill. 'She doesn't know about Winnie and Mac, so even if they should meet, there's no reason for her to think that he's anything other than Winnie's colleague.'

'I know, but Winnie's terrified that she'll know somehow and be awful to him. She can be very rude and unpleasant if she chooses.'

Bella sighed. 'I know.'

James frowned. 'You say that with feeling, Bella. I know she was rude not shaking your hand when you met her, but that was nothing; she can be much worse.'

'Yes, I know that as well.'

James stopped walking and looked at her, his eyes searching her face. 'What do you mean? Tell me, please.'

Bella bit her bottom lip. 'I wasn't going to tell you because it's all been sorted out. Connie helped me see sense.'

'Connie?' He frowned. 'What happened, Bella?'

Bella took hold of his hand. 'Do you remember when I went to get your mother's coat that day at Connie's house? While she and I were out in the hall she . . . well, she told me that I wasn't the right sort of girl for you, me being a former housemaid, and that you need to marry someone much more suited.' She watched as James's face clouded over. 'And she said that if I cared for you at all, I would end our relationship.'

'But you didn't.' His grey eyes looked anxious behind his spectacles.

Bella shook her head. 'No, I didn't, though I did consider it – I was so shocked and upset by what she'd said that it planted a seed in my head that perhaps she was right.'

'But she's *not* right.' James shook his head. 'I am so very sorry, my darling Bella, that my mother said that to you. It is unforgivable, rude and—'

'James.' Bella squeezed his hand. 'Forget about it. It didn't work – actually it made me even more certain about how much I like you. Connie told me to ignore what your mother said, because it's irrelevant and untrue.'

James smiled at her. 'I don't know what Winnie, Harry and I would have done without Connie in our lives.'

'She's one of the very best.'

'And so are you, Bella.' He smiled at her, then gently kissed her. 'You are the woman for me, and I have no intention of letting you go.'

'Likewise.' Bella beamed at him. 'So let's forget about

awful family problems and go and have that tea and currant bun that you promised me in your letter.'

'Certainly, and rest assured no awful Daphne will be there to spoil it this time.'

'Go on, off you go, Stanley. I know you're desperate to show Frankie around.' Bella's mother smiled warmly at the boy, who had sat so patiently and politely while they all had something to eat and drink at the big kitchen table.

Stanley grinned at her, then scrambled out of his seat, looking eagerly at Frankie.

'I'm ready.' Frankie stood up. 'Thank you very much for the tea and scones, it was very kind of you.'

Bella's mother bobbed her head. 'You're very welcome. It's lovely to have you come here to see us. Stanley's been desperate to see you again and to show you around; he's talked of nothing else.'

'Then let the grand tour begin.' Frankie held out her hand to Stanley, who took hold of it and led her towards the door. She was doing her best to be upbeat; she didn't want to show Stanley how she really felt inside, so sad and hollow as she battled to accept that her grandad was gone.

'Enjoy yourself,' Bella called.

Frankie turned and smiled back at her friend. 'I will.' Being here and seeing where Stanley lived was a balm to her; she could finally put images to what she'd only been able to imagine before. When she returned home, those would help her when she thought about the boy and wished they were together.

Outside, Stanley took her straight to the large garden behind the house. It was ringed on all sides by tall brick walls that created a sheltered oasis, capturing the sun and providing a perfect spot for growing food. No space was wasted; even the walls had fruit trees growing up them, espaliered branches laden with white and pink blossom stretching out in long arms across the brick. Rows and rows of neatly tended vegetables and fruit bushes were growing vigorously. Station 75's allotment would have fitted into this garden many times over.

'It's beautiful,' Frankie said, looking around.

Stanley beamed at her, clearly delighted that she liked it. 'Come and see this.' He pulled at her hand and led her across to the far wall of the garden, which had a long greenhouse built into the side. He opened the door and they went inside, where it smelled of warm earth and sunshine. He bent down and showed her some tender young plants. 'These are tomatoes.' He rubbed his finger and thumb gently on one of the leaves and held his hand up to her. 'Smell this.'

Frankie sniffed, and a sharp tang hit her senses, reminding her of the taste of tomatoes in the summer.

'These are baby cucumbers,' Stanley said, pointing out more plants.

Watching him move around the greenhouse so clearly at ease in his surroundings brought a lump to Frankie's throat. Stanley had come a long, long way from Stepney,

277

in both distance and lifestyle. He didn't spend his days here collecting shrapnel or playing on bomb sites; his nights weren't spent sleeping in an Anderson shelter that could be blown apart if a bomb fell on it. This place was so different from everything he'd grown up with and become used to when his home city became a war zone. Here he was learning new things and ways, and most importantly, he was safe.

'Are you all right?' he asked, frowning at her.

Frankie nodded and smiled at him, ruffling his hair. 'I'm just pleased to see you, and amazed at 'ow much you've learnt since you came 'ere. There ain't a garden and green-house like this at 'ome in Stepney.'

'I like learnin' new things, it's interesting. The lady who owns the house 'as taught me a lot. She says I've got green fingers.' He grinned. 'I told her I ain't but she said it means that I'm good at growing things.'

'Are you happy 'ere, Stanley?' Frankie asked.

He nodded. 'Yes, I am. I miss you but I do like it 'ere, a lot. If I can't be at 'ome with you, then this is a good place to be.' He paused for a moment and frowned. 'What will 'appen to me now?' he asked.

'What do you mean?'

'When the war's over and it's time for me to come 'ome, back to Stepney, where will I go?'

'You'll come back to our house in Matlock Street.' Frankie smiled at him. 'I'm still there and your 'ome is still with me, and it will be there waiting for you when it's safe for you to come back again.'

'And Ivy? What about her?'

Frankie shrugged. 'Well, she's still there, so with Ivy too, I suppose.'

Stanley looked anxious. 'As long as you're there.'

'I'll always be there for you, Stanley; you'll always 'ave a home with me, I promise.'

He smiled at her, clearly satisfied with what she'd told him. 'Do you want to see Primrose the cow? She's down in the meadow.'

'All right then, lead the way.' Frankie followed him, glad that he was happy with what she'd told him. She'd meant what she'd said: he would always have a home with her. It wasn't going to be easy, but she had to do whatever it took to keep the home fires burning because she was responsible for Stanley now, and he was a charge she gladly took on because she loved him dearly. Ivy, her other responsibility, felt more like a heavy burden, but she'd made her promise and had to stick to it. It was what her grandad had wanted, and she couldn't let him down.

Frankie hadn't heard a word from Ivy since she'd been injured; she hadn't come to see her in hospital or even sent a letter. She wasn't looking forward to going back to Matlock Street in a few days' time, but she had to do it for Stanley's sake. Keeping a home for him and Ivy was inextricably linked; she couldn't have one without the other. The important thing to remember was that she was doing it for Stanley.

*

Winnie felt like a mouse waiting for a cat to pounce as she walked through the gates of Buckingham Palace with her parents and Connie. She was convinced that her mother would somehow know that she and Mac were more than just colleagues and would be awful to him. Just as her godmother had predicted, her parents, especially her mother, had been delighted to accompany her to the palace, though she suspected it was more to do with being in the presence of royalty rather than because they were proud of what their daughter had done.

She looked around for Mac but couldn't see him in the throng of people being ushered inside. He was meeting his mother at the station and bringing her straight here, and then she'd be coming to stay at Connie's for the night later on.

Unlike for most of those being awarded a medal, it wasn't the first time Winnie had been to Buckingham Palace. Walking in through the doors reminded her of those awful months of the season when she'd come out and been presented at court with other debutantes. She'd hated every moment of the whole thing: the endless dances and tea parties, all of it in aid of finding a suitable husband, which certainly hadn't worked for her.

She recalled how she'd tried her hardest to convince her mother that it wasn't the right thing for her to do, but as usual Cynthia Churchill had cast her daughter's opinion aside and ploughed on with her own agenda. After that, Winnie had sworn never to give in to her mother's wishes again, which was one of the reasons she was here now getting a medal for her work as an ambulance driver.

Connie caught hold of her arm as they walked up a flight of thickly carpeted stairs to where the ceremony was to take place. 'Are you all right?' she whispered.

Winnie nodded. 'Just reliving the horrors of my coming out; being here has brought it all back.'

'Oh don't.' Connie shivered. 'I've buried mine away in some dark recess of my mind and shut a door firmly on the whole charade.'

Winnie started to giggle, earning herself a glare from her mother, who was walking along beside her father in front.

'Shh!' Connie said, her lips twitching with laughter.

'Have you seen Mac?' Winnie looked around as they entered the large, ornately decorated room where the ceremony was to take place. Rows of seats had been put out and were filling up with guests.

'Don't worry, he'll be here. You go and get ready and I'll keep a close eye on your parents,' Connie reassured her.

Winnie squeezed her godmother's arm. 'Thank you. I'm so glad you're here, it's made me feel a lot better, though I'm still terribly nervous. Look.' She held up her hand to show how it was shaking.

'You've met the King before. He's a nice man, nothing to worry about,' Connie said.

'It's not him I'm worried about, it's when Mother sees Mac. I've got this idea that she'll somehow know ...' She shook her head. 'It sounds ridiculous because there's no reason she should, but I've got this really uncomfortable feeling about when they meet.'

'She doesn't know.' Connie's blue eyes held hers for a few moments. 'Everything will be fine. I'll be there to keep an eye on things, so try to relax and enjoy being awarded a medal for what you did.' She smiled. 'For being so very brave.'

Winnie nodded. 'I'll try.'

'Good girl, now run along and get ready.'

Being presented to the King was a huge improvement on the last occasion. This time there was no flouncy dress, long white gloves or ridiculous ostrich feathers in her hair. Winnie felt comfortable in her smart blue silk dress and jacket, with one of Connie's hats at a jaunty angle on her head.

She was first to be called to receive her medal, walking with her head held high to where the King stood on a dais. She curtsied neatly and shook his hand.

'Congratulations,' the King said, smiling at her warmly. 'I'm delighted to present you with this George Medal in acknowledgement of your bravery in the line of duty.'

'Thank you,' Winnie said, taking her medal and smiling shyly back. Then she turned and made her way back to her seat while the next recipient went up to the dais.

It was heartening to hear the stories of the many people who'd been recognised for their brave deeds, among them a telephonist, a matron and a railwayman: so many different professions who were doing their bit and beyond for the war effort. Winnie felt honoured to be part of it, and especially so as she watched Mac go up to receive his own

George Medal, remembering the night of 29 December when infernos had raged across London and they had driven through fire to reach casualties.

Afterwards groups of people stood around chatting and Winnie took the opportunity to go and talk to Mac and meet his mother.

'Mother, this is Winnie,' Mac introduced her.

Mrs McCartney smiled at her and held out her hand, her eyes warm and friendly. 'How do you do? I've heard lots about you.' She lowered her voice with its rich Gloucestershire burr. 'Don't worry, I shan't give you away.'

'Thank you.' Winnie shook the older woman's hand, her cheeks growing warm, glad that Mac's mother seemed far more understanding than her own. 'I'm delighted to meet you and I'm looking forward to you coming to stay at my godmother's tonight. I hope you enjoyed the ceremony.'

'Oh, I did. I never thought I'd get the chance to go inside Buckingham Palace, or even come to London.'

'It's—' Winnie began but halted as a familiar voice called out.

'Margot, there you are, we're going for luncheon now.' Her mother appeared at her side.

Winnie's stomach clenched into a hard knotted ball as the moment she'd been dreading arrived. 'Mother, this is William McCartney – Mac – who also works at Station 75, and his mother who's come down from Gloucestershire for the ceremony.'

'How do you do?' Mac held out his hand, which Cynthia Churchill ignored, looking him and his mother up and down. Winnie knew what she'd be thinking, taking in their cheap clothes and Gloucestershire accent. Her snobbery was oozing out of every pore; she clearly considered herself far superior to these people before her.

'Good afternoon,' she finally managed. 'You're an ambulance driver as well; are you waiting to be called up?'

Mac looked at Winnie and she gave a slight shake of her head, but before he could say anything, his mother spoke.

'My son's a conscientious objector. He's doing his bit in his own way.' Mrs McCartney held her head high and looked proud of her son. Clearly this wasn't the first time she'd faced opposition for what he'd chosen to do.

'Really?' Winnie's mother only spoke a single word, but it was loaded with meaning, and combined with the look of sheer disgust on her face, there was no doubt how she felt about being in the presence of a conscientious objector.

'Yes,' Mac's mother said. 'He's proved how brave he is and has been rewarded for it. There are different ways of fighting a war and not all of them need a gun.'

Winnie's mother didn't respond. 'We're leaving in two minutes, Margot.' Giving the briefest of nods to Mac and his mother, she turned and went to find her husband.

'I'm sorry.' Winnie reached out her hand and touched Mac's, tears smarting in her eyes. 'She's . . .' She shook her head.

He squeezed her hand. 'You did warn me.'

Mrs McCartney leaned close and whispered, 'You can't choose your family, my dear. Don't worry, I've met plenty like her, and they don't frighten me.' She reached out and patted Winnie's arm. 'You're nothing like her, else my son wouldn't love you.'

A single tear slipped out and Winnie quickly wiped it away with the back of her hand. 'Thank you.'

'Winnie!' Connie came rushing over. 'Are you all right? I saw your mother come over and I couldn't get away from Sir Archibald.'

'She was as I expected.' Winnie did her best to smile. 'Mrs McCartney, meet my wonderful godmother, Connie.'

Connie held out her hand. 'I'm delighted to meet you and I'm looking forward to having you come and stay with us tonight.'

'Likewise,' Mac's mother said, shaking her hand. 'It's very good of you to put me up.'

'It's my pleasure,' Connie said, smiling warmly. 'I'd invite you to have lunch with us,' she lowered her voice, 'only I think some people might spoil it with their bad attitude.'

'Oh don't worry, William's promised me a tour of the sights,' Mrs McCartney said.

'I think a tour would be much more pleasant,' Connie said. 'Wish I could come with you. I expect you do too, Winnie.'

Winnie nodded and smiled. 'We'll make lunch as short as we can.' The thought of spending any more time in her parents' company than she absolutely had to wasn't in the slightest bit appealing. After her mother's performance just now, she'd rather not go at all. The only saving grace was that Connie would be there.

Bella watched as her mother expertly worked the flour and fat into breadcrumb-sized pieces, her strong fingers instinctively doing a job they had done so many times before.

'Do you want me to—' she began but stopped at a sudden insistent rat-a-tat-tat on the outside door.

'Can you get that for me, please?' her mother said. 'Ask them to come in if they need to speak to me. I need to get this finished and the Woolton pie in the oven or it won't be ready in time for tea.'

When Bella opened the door to see who it was, she immediately wished she hadn't, her stomach lurching in terror. The sight of the telegram boy standing looking awkward on the doorstep reminded her of what people called them: 'angels of death', on account of the terrible news they often delivered. Strangely, she felt sorry for him. It wasn't a pleasant job. People dreaded the sight of the telegram boy coming to their door, and it must show on their faces every time they answered his knock.

'Telegram for Mrs Belmont,' he said, handing the buff-coloured envelope to Bella. He touched the peak of his cap and quickly made for his bicycle, which he'd left leaning against the wall ready for a quick getaway.

She stood quite still watching him pedalling away, and then he turned the corner and was gone, but what he'd delivered wasn't; it was still there in her hand. Bella stared at it, studying her mother's name and address on the front. It was like a ticking bomb in her hand; its contents probably had the power to blow her family's life apart, to change it for ever. Something must have happened to Walter.

'Who is it?' her mother called from the kitchen.

Bella closed her eyes and tried hard to still the trembling that had started to shake her whole body. She had to go in and give the telegram to her mother.

'I'm just coming,' she managed to say, her voice sounding strained. With a heavy heart and feet that felt more lead than flesh, she went into the kitchen, painfully aware that she might be about to break her mother's heart.

Her mother was rolling out the pastry for the crust on the pie; she looked up, and without Bella needing to say anything, her eyes sought out the envelope in her daughter's hands.

'It's a telegram,' Bella said, needlessly.

Quickly wiping her hands on her apron, her mother reached out her hand for it, then paused as if gathering her strength. Pulling out the single sheet, she looked at it for a moment, and the blood drained from her face. Then she put her hand to her mouth and stifled a sob, the sound of it ripping into Bella's heart.

'Is it Walter?' she asked.

Her mother nodded and handed her the telegram, then leaned her hands on the table, her head hung low.

It was as if Bella had suddenly been doused with a pail of ice-cold water. She felt sick. She didn't want to know this. Walter couldn't be dead, it wasn't right. Reluctantly, but knowing she had to see it for herself, she read the words printed on the telegram.

REGRET TO INFORM YOU THAT YOUR SON SGT WALTER BELMONT IS MISSING IN ACTION AS A RESULT OF ENEMY ACTION ON 17/5/1940. LETTER FOLLOWS. ANY FURTHER INFORMATION WILL BE IMMEDIATELY COMMUNICATED TO YOU.

She stared at it, then read it again. He wasn't dead, not actually dead. He hadn't been killed, he was missing. Just missing, not missing presumed dead.

'I thought it was going to say that he was dead,' she said. 'He's still alive.'

Her mother looked at her, her eyes red-rimmed and her cheeks streaked with tears. 'They don't know he's still alive. He could be dead somewhere, they just haven't found him . . . ' She started to sob.

Bella put her arms around her. 'We've got to keep hoping he's alive and they'll find him. We mustn't give up hope.'

Her mother pulled out of her arms. 'My head's throbbing, I'm going to lie down. Can you see to the pie? They'll be wanting tea.'

'Of course, you go on. I'll take care of everything, don't worry.'

Her mother picked up the telegram and its envelope from where it lay on the table and without another word left the kitchen, her shoulders slumped, her once upright demeanour battered down with the news that her son was missing.

Bella sat down at the table, her mind starting to race with possibilities of what might have happened to Walter, where he might be right this moment. He might already have been found and be back with his unit, swatting the flies away and grumbling about sand in the food. *No*, whispered a voice in her head. *He can't come back, he really is dead.* She blocked the voice out; she wasn't going to listen to it. He wasn't dead, he mustn't be.

She stood up and started to fit the rolled-out pastry on to the Woolton pie, crimping it round the edges and using the leftover bits to make leaves to decorate the top, then put it in the oven to cook, all the time telling herself that Walter was still alive, he had to be. She wouldn't give up and accept he was dead, not now, not ever . . .

'Where's your mother?' Frankie asked as they all sat down to eat later that afternoon. The table was full, with Stanley, the two other evacuees and the Land Girls who worked there.

'She's got a bad headache, had to go and lie down,' Bella said.

'We'll save some pie for her,' Stanley said.

Bella nodded. 'Good idea, she'll probably be hungry later on.'

When she'd gone up to check on her mother earlier, the poor woman had been in a terrible state, clearly convinced that her son was dead. She took no comfort in the fact that he was missing. It was as if she'd already given up any hope of him being found alive. She had asked Bella not to say anything to anyone; she would tell them when she was ready, when she'd had time to get used to it.

Bella knew that she wasn't going to say anything to anyone either. If she kept it to herself and went on hoping that he would be found safe and sound, then it would be true. It had to be, because if she hadn't persuaded Walter to go back to the army – if he'd gone AWOL as he'd wanted to – then he wouldn't be missing now. There'd have been no telegram to shatter her mother's world. A trickle of guilt mixed in with the turmoil of fear and hope that swirled inside her.

'Are you all right?' Frankie asked quietly. 'You look pale.'

Bella pasted a smile on her face. 'Yes, I'm fine.'

Frankie smiled back at her and Bella felt guilty that she hadn't been honest with her dear friend, but Frankie had enough to deal with in her own life; she didn't need to hear about Bella's worries as well. This was something she was going to have to deal with on her own, show a bit of stiff upper lip like Winnie, while she hoped and prayed that another telegram with even worse news wouldn't need to be delivered.

Russell Square, near Connie's house, looked beautiful. The warm evening light was filtering through the fresh green leaves high up on the trees and the square felt like a calm oasis in the middle of war-torn London. Winnie sat beside Mac's mother on one of the benches, watching Trixie scamper around sniffing at the plethora of smells.

'Oh it's good to sit down and take the weight off my feet. I've walked miles today,' Mrs McCartney said. 'Seen so many things and places I'd never dreamed of seeing.' She smiled at Winnie. 'It's been a marvellous day.'

'I'm glad you've enjoyed yourself.' Winnie smiled back. 'I'm terribly sorry about what happened this morning. My mother's attitude was appalling.'

'There's nothing for you to apologise for, my dear.' Mac's mother patted Winnie's arm. 'I didn't let her spoil my day, and I hope you didn't either.'

'Well Connie and I left the lunch as soon as we possibly could without looking rude.' Winnie shrugged. 'I'm just glad that I followed my instincts and didn't tell Mother about Mac and me. He's so important to me and I don't want him to have to face a barrage of unpleasantness from my mother.'

'Oh don't you worry about him, he's quite capable of looking after himself and ignoring thoughtless jibes. He's had to put up with plenty ever since he signed up as a CO.'

'Did you try and persuade him to do otherwise?'

Mac's mother looked at her and shook her head. 'Gracious, no, my dear. He knows what he believes and I agree with him.' She paused for a moment, watching Trixie running around. 'But not everyone looked at it like that. He lost his job at the school and had white feathers sent to him.' She sighed. 'But he's stuck to his beliefs and I'm proud of him. And your Station Officer Steele thinks highly of him too.'

'You met the boss?'

'William took me to Station 75, I wanted to see where he worked, and Station Officer Steele invited me in for a cup of tea. She's a good woman, I liked her very much.'

Winnie smiled. 'So do I.' The boss had given her and Mac their shift off to go to the palace to get their medals. 'She runs our station like clockwork but she's kind when she needs to be.'

'Well she thinks a lot of you, I could tell.'

'We've had our moments in the past, clashing over broken rules, but we get on very well now.'

'William's much happier at Station 75 than he was at his last one.'

'Did he tell you it's not far from here, just a few streets away?' Winnie asked.

The older woman shook her head. 'He didn't say anything about it; probably wants to forget it.'

'As you can see,' Winnie threw her hands out wide, 'that station's patch is a lot grander than ours; they don't get sent to the docks or the East End.' She smiled. 'But I much prefer ours, it's more interesting, though it's been hit hard by the bombers.'

'That station might be in a grand area but some of the crew didn't have grand manners to match,' Mac's mother said, bristling slightly. 'They didn't have the decency to treat COs kindly. I would have liked to come down here and give them a piece of my mind.'

'What happened? Mac's never told me.'

'Some of the other crew were hostile to him, ignoring him, refusing to work with him. It was ridiculous, childish, bullying behaviour, and they should have known better.' Mac's mother sighed. 'The best thing to do was move stations and get away from it, because it wasn't going to stop while those crew members were still there.'

Winnie put her hand on the older woman's arm. 'I'm sorry he was treated badly, he really didn't deserve that, but I'm very glad he moved to Station 75. It was definitely their loss and our gain.'

Trixie came bounding up with a stick in her mouth and dropped it by Winnie's feet, her tail wagging as she looked expectantly for her mistress to join in with her favourite game. Winnie obliged, and threw the stick, sending Trixie scampering after it.

'She's a lovely dog,' Mac's mother said.

'Yes, everyone loves Trixie. You'd have to be hard-hearted not to.'

'So how did you come to join the ambulance service?' Mrs McCartney asked, picking up the stick, which Trixie had quickly returned, and throwing it again for her.

'After the Munich crisis, I thought I should be doing something just in case the worst happened. Since I could already drive, I thought it would be a good thing to train as a volunteer ambulance driver,' Winnie explained. 'After war was declared, I joined Station 75. My parents weren't very happy about it, but Connie helped them accept it, for the time being.'

'Didn't they want you to join the Wrens instead?'

'Or get married.' Winnie pulled a face. 'But their prospective husband for me isn't one I'd ever choose. So I'm staying exactly where I am. I love being in the ambulance service, and as long as they need me, I'll stay there.'

Mac's mother patted her arm. 'You're a brave young woman and I admire what you do. My WVS work is quite tame compared with going out in the middle of an air raid.'

'What do you do?'

'All sorts, whatever's needed. We do a lot with the evacuees in the area and run a clothing exchange for children's clothes and shoes. I knit for the troops as well. It keeps me busy.'

'The WVS are an absolute treasure, going out with their mobile canteens. I've had plenty of much-needed cups of tea from them when we've been out on call.'

'I enjoy what I'm doing,' Mac's mother said. 'The war's not a pleasant thing but it's brought me a lot of joy, I've made some good friends in the WVS and I've learnt new things. Every cloud has a silver lining . . . '

'You sound like Bella; she always says the war's made her life better. She was a housemaid before and hated it.'

'It's got women out of the home and doing things, proving they're just as capable as men in many ways. Women did extraordinary things in the Great War as well, only they had to stop when the men came home again and wanted their jobs back.'

'Well we absolutely can do things,' Winnie agreed. 'When we're given the chance.'

Chapter Eleven

'Have you seen this?'

Winnie pulled her head out from under the bonnet of her ambulance and looked at Sparky. 'Seen what?'

He held out the newspaper he'd just brought back to Station 75. 'They've started rationing clothes. See here.' He pointed to the announcement.

Winnie wiped her greasy hands on a rag and took the paper to read for herself. There it was in black and white: an official announcement from the Board of Trade stating that from today, 1 June, clothing and footwear would be rationed so that it would be fair for all.

'So it's coupons for clothes as well as food from now on,' Sparky said.

'They kept that secret,' Winnie said. 'Had to, I suppose, otherwise people would have gone crazy buying up anything they could. Look at this, though, it says you'll still be able to buy boiler suits without coupons, so you'll be all right.'

Sparky grinned, patting down the front of his navy-blue boiler suit, which he always wore for work. 'You should get yourself one of these, save messing up your own clothes.'

'We're supposed to be getting uniforms ... or so they keep saying. If we're going to be rationed on how much clothing we can buy, then I don't want to be using coupons on clothes for work. I'm going to ask the boss about this, she might know something.'

'Did you know about this?' Winnie put the newspaper down on Station Officer Steele's desk and pointed to the announcement. 'Does this mean we are going to get our uniform soon?'

Her boss read through the announcement and shook her head. 'It's as much news to me as it is to you and most people today. And no, there's still no news about our uniforms.' She shrugged. 'Do sit down, Winnie, you're looking rather cross.'

'I am.' Winnie plonked herself down on a nearby chair. 'It's bad enough our clothes getting ripped and covered in goodness knows what while we're on duty without now having to limit what we can buy with coupons. Will they be giving us extra coupons as we have to wear our own clothes for work because they *still* haven't given us a uniform?'

'I haven't heard anything about that, I'm afraid,

Winnie.' Station Officer Steele reached out and patted her arm. 'I know it feels very unfair, but we just need to be patient. I've been assured that we will get a uniform in time, but exactly when I can't say.' She smiled. 'Try not to get annoyed about it: it won't help and will just make you feel terrible.'

Winnie couldn't help smiling. 'I do get a bee in my bonnet about the uniform, or rather lack of it, sometimes, don't I?'

'Indeed you do. If it's any consolation, I'm in complete agreement with you, and bringing in clothes rationing is just going to make it harder for crew members. You might want to get yourself a boiler suit like the men wear, since they won't need coupons – it would keep your own clothes protected at least.'

'They're not very feminine, are they, but I might just do that. I could start a new trend.'

'Perhaps.' Station Officer Steele smiled. 'As you're here, Winnie, I'd like to talk to you about your three-month trial as deputy station officer. What are your thoughts on where we should take it from here? Has it been a terrible burden?'

Winnie considered for a moment. 'To be honest, it hasn't been anything near as hard as when you were off with the flu; that was difficult, having to make decisions and keep everything going. You make it look so easy.'

Station Officer Steele shrugged. 'It doesn't always feel easy, but I'm used to it and that makes it easier to deal with. So are you willing to make it a permanent thing?'

Winnie had a sudden urge to say no; the thought of such responsibility was heavy and unwanted. But if she thought about it rationally, the past three months hadn't been so terrible. The boss had given her some additional work to do – helping with paperwork and taking on more of the monitoring roles, checking that ambulances and equipment were ready, the occasional shift manning the telephone – but it hadn't been anything she couldn't cope with.

'Winnie?' Station Officer Steele's voice interrupted her thoughts. 'I have no doubt that you can do the job – you have proved that beyond any doubt over the past months – but I need someone I can rely on too. Is that you? I think it is, but only you know how you feel.'

'To be honest, my initial thought is to say no. I don't want any more responsibility beyond what I already have as an ambulance driver, but part of me thinks I need to be challenged and should push myself to do more – and I know I can do it.'

'I agree. You are a very capable young woman and, I think,' Station Officer Steele smiled, 'one who needs a little bit of pushing now and again. It's the teacher in me. I don't like to see talent going to waste.'

Should she do it? Winnie wondered. A voice whispered in her mind and her heart seemed to be in agreement with it. 'Yes, very well, I will carry on. It will be my privilege.'

'Jolly good. I hoped you would say that.' The older woman held out her hand. 'It gives me great pleasure to have you as my deputy, Winnie.'

'Thank you.' Winnie shook her hand. 'A while back I

would never have dreamed I'd agree to this; it was even touch and go at times if I'd still be allowed in the ambulance service because of something I'd done, or not done.' She smiled at her boss, who looked back, her own face warm. 'And here I am agreeing to take on more responsibility permanently.'

'I'm proud of you and jolly glad you've made that decision. We're lucky to have you at Station 75, Winnie. The place wouldn't be the same without you.'

Matlock Street looked the same, Frankie thought, standing at the end of it, only it wasn't and never would be again. She'd been dreading coming back, and now that she was here, she just wanted to turn tail and run, but she couldn't. This was where her family home was and she had no choice but to keep it going so that Stanley would have somewhere to come home to.

Walking past number 5, she saw the net curtain at the front window twitch to the side and Josie's beaming face appear. The older woman tapped on the glass and beckoned for Frankie to come in. Smiling, she turned back to her neighbour's front door, glad of a reason to delay her return to number 25.

Josie threw the door open and pulled her inside, enveloping her in a crushing hug. 'I've bin lookin' out for yer all morning.' She stepped back and looked Frankie up and down. 'Yer lookin' much better, got some roses in yer cheeks again. That country air's done you good. 'Ave you got time for a cup of tea?'

'Of course.' Frankie followed her through to her kitchen at the back of the house, which was identical in layout to the one at number 25, only Josie's felt warm and welcoming, the way the one at home used to when her gran was still alive, a warmth that came not from a fire but from a person.

''Ave a seat while I get the kettle on.' Josie busied herself making the tea. 'How's yer arm?'

'All right as far as I know – it's hard to tell with it encased in plaster.' Frankie sat down at the table. 'I'm goin' back to work tomorrow. I'm lookin' forward to it.'

'But you ain't goin' to be able to drive or go carrying people about on stretchers with it still in plaster, are yer?'

'No, but I'm sure there's something I can do. I don't want to stay at 'ome, I need to get back to work – I've missed it.'

'At least your crew mates have had a quieter time of it lately. There ain't been any raids since that terrible night. It's bin strangely quiet.' Josie frowned. 'I ain't sure if I prefer it when they come every night – at least we know what we're doing, straight to the shelter for the duration.' She shrugged. 'I end up lying awake 'alf the night waiting for the Moaning Minnie to wail.' She put two cups on the table and a plate of biscuits. 'I saved these for your 'omecoming.'

'Thank you, it's very thoughtful of yer, Josie, but you should give 'em to your children.'

Josie laughed. 'Don't you worry, I've saved some for them too.'

The kettle started to whistle and Josie warmed the teapot, then added fresh tea leaves and poured in the hot water.

'Fresh leaves as well, I am honoured.' Frankie smiled at her neighbour. 'Thank you.'

'Go on, 'ave a biscuit. It's only right you should be welcomed 'ome properly. I doubt you'll get any fuss made of yer at number 25.' Josie's plump face flushed and she clamped her hand over her mouth. 'I shouldn't 'ave said that.'

'Why not? I expect you're right.' Frankie took a biscuit. 'I certainly ain't expecting anything.'

'Ivy's only bin widowed a couple of weeks. I shouldn't say unkind things, it ain't neighbourly. She's took yer grandad's death hard.'

Frankie leaned over and laid her hand on Josie's arm, looking her straight in the eye. 'We both know what she's like; it's best not to pretend. Ivy ain't going to be easy to live with, but it's my 'ome and I've got to keep it going for when Stanley comes back.'

Josie covered Frankie's hand with her own. 'I'd 'ave you come and live 'ere, only I ain't got the room with all my lot.'

'I know you would, but number 25 is my 'ome. I've lived there all my life and I ain't goin' to let Ivy push me out. She won't be able to afford the rent on her own anyway, so she'll need me there to pay my share.'

Josie poured them both a cup of tea and added some milk from a bottle.

'Did yer see Stanley?'

Frankie smiled. 'Twice. He came to see me and I went to see 'im another day. It's a lovely place where 'e's stayin' and he's very 'appy there. I ain't bringing 'im 'ome till the war's over and it's safe again.'

They chatted for a while longer, till the biscuits were gone and the brown teapot drunk dry.

'I'd better go and face it, Josie.' Frankie stood up. 'No good puttin' it off any longer.'

'You're welcome 'ere any time, you know that.' Josie went over to the mantelpiece and picked up an envelope that was propped against the photo of her husband in his army uniform. 'Before you go, I need to give you this. I 'oped I'd never 'ave to, but . . . ' She held it out.

Frankie took it and stared at her name written on the front. She recognised the writing – it was her grandad's beautiful copperplate script. 'It's from Grandad?'

Josie nodded. 'He left it with me to give to you if . . . ' Her bottom lip trembled.

Frankie could feel her throat thickening with emotion.

'He told me he was going to leave another copy with Sergeant Jeffries at the police station, just in case this one got destroyed in a raid. I expect the sergeant will deliver 'is copy when he 'ears that you're back.'

'Has Ivy got one?'

'Oh no.' Josie shook her head. 'And she don't know nothin' about them either. He didn't want 'er to, he was very clear about that. Whatever's in there is for you and only you, and it was very important to 'im that you got it.'

Puzzled, Frankie put the envelope in her pocket to read later. She would have dearly loved to tear it open straight away, but something told her that it would be best to wait until she was on her own. If this was Grandad's last words to her, then it shouldn't be rushed or shared.

The smell of number 25 hit Frankie as soon as she opened the front door. It was just the same – the pervading odour of stale cigarette smoke, Ivy's trademark. Frankie's gran would have hated the way her home now smelled; she'd loathed the smell of smoke and would never allow anyone to smoke in her house. How different Grandad's two wives had been; they were poles apart.

Frankie walked slowly to the kitchen and paused in the doorway, observing Ivy for a few moments before the woman became aware of her. She'd let herself go. Her dark roots were peeping through her peroxide hair and it looked in need of a good wash and brush. Her face was pale, with no trace of her usual lipstick and rouge.

'Oh, it's you!' Ivy narrowed her eyes, glaring at Frankie. 'You've come crawlin' back, 'ave yer?'

'Yes, I'm back.' Frankie kept her voice calm. 'How are you, Ivy?'

Ivy looked at her suspiciously. 'I'm just bleedin' marvellous, ain't I? How d'yer think I am with Reg gone?'

'I miss 'im too.'

'Well I was 'is wife.'

'It's not a competition to see who misses 'im the most, you know.' Frankie could feel herself starting to tense, her blood pulsing faster around her body as it prepared for battle.

'Well you ain't even bin 'ere, living it up in the countryside.'

Frankie sighed. Nothing had changed. If anything, Ivy's attitude was even worse, now that Grandad wasn't here to smooth things over any more. There was no point in getting angry, though. It wouldn't do any good, would just feed the woman's bitterness. 'I'm going to unpack.'

Ivy shrugged. 'Do what you want, but don't expect me to run around lookin' after you. I ain't shoppin' or cookin' or waitin' on you.'

'I never thought you would,' Frankie said sweetly, wanting to add that it could work both ways, but she'd had enough of Ivy for now. Seeing the awful woman again made her promise all the more galling, but a promise was a promise and she had to honour it out of respect for her grandad, though looking after such a poisonous woman wasn't going to be easy or the least bit enjoyable.

Upstairs, Frankie's room looked just the same except for the layer of dust powdering the dressing table and mirror. Ivy clearly hadn't been in there to dust. Frankie threw open the window to let the fresh summer air in and looked down at the garden her grandad had so lovingly tended. It was looking ragged, with weeds growing unchecked in the vegetable patch. He would have been upset to see it like that; she'd have to sort it out, but first there was the envelope to open.

Sitting on the edge of her bed, she stared again at her

name, running her finger over it as if she would find some trace of him there, but there was none, just dried ink on paper. She quickly opened the envelope and took out the two sheets of paper inside.

The first thing she noticed was the date – 4 March. He'd written it not long after he'd come home from hospital. She read on.

My dearest granddaughter,
If you're reading this, then the worst has happened
and I'm gone. I'm sorry to have left you and I hope
that you'll keep carrying on, because that's what
you have to do. Life goes on and you have to as well.
Don't mope after me, live your life and be happy.
I know you'll look after Ivy and Stanley for me, I
have no doubt about that as you're a good and kind
young woman. That's not why I'm leaving this letter
for you. I'm writing it because your gran and I lied
to you and you need to know the truth.

Frankie stopped reading for a moment. What did he mean, lied? She quickly went on.

I hope you'll forgive us for not being truthful with
you. We thought it was for the best and it was what
your mother wanted.

The mention of her mother sent an icy finger trailing down her spine. She had rarely been spoken of while

305

Frankie had been growing up, and she knew very little about her. She was just a shadowy figure in Frankie's life, known only by a few anecdotes and her wedding photo, a young bride standing beside her new husband.

The next words jumped out at Frankie, making her gasp.

The fact is, your mother is not dead. What we told you about her having Spanish flu was true – she was very ill with it and we thought she was going to die. You were only a few months old and your gran took over looking after you, and by the time your mother was over the worst, you'd become very attached to Gran. Your mother was still very weak, so her parents came and took her home to Suffolk with them to recuperate. She wanted you to stay with us as you were settled and she couldn't care for you properly – she planned to come back and take over again as soon as she was fit and well.

When she did eventually come back, she couldn't settle. London wasn't her home, it was so unlike where she came from and it made her deeply unhappy. It was different when your father was alive, but with him gone she couldn't stay, she had to go back to where she grew up, and she left you with us because she saw how much we loved you and how you'd helped to fill the hole in our lives left by the deaths of your father and his brothers in the Great War. She sacrificed her chance to be with you, and we were grateful to her for giving you to us.

So why did they say she'd died? a voice shouted in Frankie's mind. Why lie to her all those years?

Your mother thought it best that you think of her as dead – she didn't want you pulled in two directions. She's never forgotten you. We wrote to her every year and sent her photos of you. She knows all about you growing up and now working as an ambulance driver.

If I know you, you'll be angry with us and I don't blame you. We lied and let you grow up thinking you were an orphan when you weren't. I'm sorry for that and it's why I'm leaving you this letter – so that you know you still have some blood family left and are not alone. You have your mother.

Frankie threw the letter on the floor and curled up on her bed, hugging her knees into her chest. He was right: she was angry, bloody angry. Furious. How could they have lied, how could her mother abandon her like that? Not all children lived with their parents, she knew that, but her mother could still have kept in touch, seen her from time to time, instead of letting her grow up with that empty, hollow feeling in her chest because, unlike so many of her friends, she had no mum or dad.

Scalding tears slid down her cheeks. She didn't know who to be most angry with: her grandparents or her mother. Her life had been built on a lie, and now that she knew the truth, it was as if the foundations of her world

307

had crumbled away to dust. How could her grandparents have lied to her all those years? She'd believed they were honest people, but she'd been wrong, so very wrong. Now they'd both gone, and that was bad enough, but leaving her this letter with its world-shattering contents was cruel. She'd rather not have known, but the lie was out now; there was no turning back.

She looked down at the letter that had thrown her already altered world into even more chaos. There was an address at the bottom of the page. She reached over and snatched it up, reading the words that told her where she could find her mother if she wanted to. But Frankie wasn't sure she ever would.

'You shouldn't pick them yet, they're not big enough.'

Winnie ignored Mac and prised the pea pod open, then carefully picked each of the small peas loose and tipped the whole lot into her mouth. As she chewed, the sweet flavour exploded on her tongue. They were simply delicious. Not wanting to waste anything, she then crunched on the pea pod until nothing was left except for the stringy bits from the side.

Mac looked at her, shaking his head. 'If you leave them for a few more days, they'll be much bigger.'

'I know.' Winnie broke off another pod. 'But they taste best when they're smaller. This is my last one.' She grinned at him. 'For now . . .'

Station Officer Steele had sent them down to the allotment to work for an hour, as all the jobs at the ambulance station had been done and the crews were sitting around waiting for a call-out. It was very quiet; there hadn't been a single call all shift. Since the last big raid, London had thankfully remained free of bombing and the workload of Station 75 had fallen dramatically.

After they'd finished hoeing between the rows of vegetables, they sat down to rest, leaning their backs against the moat wall with Trixie lying beside them dozing in the afternoon sunshine.

'This is lovely.' Winnie closed her eyes and tipped her face up to the sun. 'These are the sort of shifts I like, no air raids, no casualties, time to potter around the allotment.' She sighed. 'Bella and Frankie will be back at work tomorrow and everything will be in its right place again. I've missed them so much.'

Mac took hold of her hand. 'It's been strange without them. You three are quite a team – you keep me and Sparky well and truly on our toes.'

Winnie opened her eyes and looked at him. 'I thought the boss did that.'

'Her as well. Us blokes are under the female thumb.'

She laughed. 'You love it.'

Mac's face clouded and he looked uncomfortable.

'What's the matter?'

'There's something I need to tell you, Winnie.' His dark blue eyes looked troubled. 'And unless I'm very much mistaken, you aren't going to like it.'

Winnie's stomach clenched. 'Let me be the judge of that. Come on, spit it out.'

'I'm . . . I'm thinking of volunteering for bomb disposal.'

She stared at him, not wanting to believe what she'd just heard. 'You're what?'

When Mac repeated his words, it didn't sound any better the second time around.

Winnie snatched her hand out of his. 'Well you were absolutely right, I don't like it! Why the bloody hell would you want to do that? Are you mad?'

'No.' Mac spoke calmly. 'I've thought about it very carefully.'

'You've seen what they have to do when we had that UXB at the station. Bomb disposal crews sometimes get blown up.'

'Not always.' Mac shrugged. 'I know the risks. I spoke to them, remember?' Winnie recalled how he'd spent a lot of time with the bomb disposal men. 'Several of them were conscientious objectors – like me.' He reached across and took her hand again. 'I've been going over and over it, and I need to be doing something more.' He sighed. 'It's hard to explain, Winnie, but it's been growing on me for a while, and now that everything's gone quiet—'

'But they'll be back again!' Winnie snapped. 'Any time, perhaps tonight or tomorrow. Just because we've had no raids for a couple of weeks doesn't mean it's all over. When they do come back we'll be rushed off our feet again, every driver needed.' She looked him straight in the eyes. 'Being an ambulance driver isn't an easy option, you know that. Remember you were awarded the George Medal for doing it.'

'I know that, but it's just . . .'

They sat in silence for a few moments, looking anywhere but at each other. Winnie felt sick. She suddenly knew this wasn't just a discussion about whether he should join bomb disposal.

'You've already made up your mind, haven't you?'

Mac nodded. 'I've signed up. I've got to report for training at the beginning of August.'

Winnie jumped up. 'You're being ridiculous. Have you thought about me?'

Mac stood up and reached out to her. 'Of course I have. You are what makes it so hard to go. I don't want to leave you, Winnie, but I have to do it.'

Winnie sighed. 'I worry about you enough when you're out in air raids, but at least you're here and sometimes I'm out with you. Now you want to go away and dig up bombs that could blow up at any moment.'

'I worry about you too, you know. Ambulance drivers can get killed or hurt, they're not invulnerable.' Mac's eyes met hers for a few moments before she looked away.

'I only want you to be safe, Mac. If you truly want to go and do something else, why not join the Pioneer Corps or the Army Medical Corps instead?'

He shrugged. 'To prove myself, I suppose. Do more than I am now. Show I'm not a coward.'

'Of course you're not a coward!' Winnie threw her hands in the air. 'You have nothing to prove, Mac; you have a George Medal for bravery, for heaven's sake. You're being utterly ridiculous.'

His eyes searched hers. 'I hoped you'd understand.'

'Oh I understand all right.' Winnie took a step back from him, her hands on her hips. 'You've made up your mind because of some stupid male pride that you have to prove how brave you are, and in doing so will put yourself in unnecessary danger. If you're joining bomb disposal then it's over between us. I'm not going to spend my life worrying that you're going to be blown to bits at any moment.'

'Winnie, please . . . it doesn't have to be like that,' Mac pleaded. 'We can still be together, we can write and see each other as much as possible, depending on where I get posted to.'

She bent down and scooped up Trixie, who had woken and was whining at their raised voices. 'You've made your choice.' She swallowed hard against the emotion that was thickening her throat. 'And so have I.' She stalked away.

'Winnie, come back!' Mac called after her.

She ignored him, focusing all her effort on walking through a world that felt as if it had tipped on its axis and was blurring and distorting through her tear-filled eyes.

Bella sat by the front window of Connie's sitting room. Her fingers were busy knitting another sock for one of Connie's Red Cross parcels, seeming to work of their own accord as her mind drifted. She was doing her best to steer it away from the thoughts that had plagued her for the past few days. Where was Walter? What had happened to him? Was he alive? Or was he dead?

She'd gone over and over various possibilities until her brain ached and she felt emotionally wrung out. She still knew no more than what that dreadful telegram had said, and could frustratingly do nothing to find out anything more. For all her worrying, she was no further forward than when she'd first read the telegram back in her mother's kitchen.

'Damn!' She'd dropped a stitch. Using the spare needle, she managed to hook up the missing stitch through the small ladder that had formed in the sock.

The problem fixed, she stopped to look out of the window, craning her neck so that she could see to the far end of the street, but there was no sign of Winnie yet. She should be back soon. Bella was desperate to see her again, and to bask in the warmth of her friend's *joie de vivre*, which, she hoped, would allow her to put things into perspective. Being back at Connie's house would help her to stop dwelling and worrying so much. She wouldn't forget Walter, but she could do her best to carry on as normal, hoping that he was still alive and would soon turn up. And if he didn't, and the worst had happened . . . She gave herself a mental shake. There was no point crossing that bridge until she had to. *If* she had to. She would do what Winnie would do: keep a stiff upper lip, keep going and importantly keep it secret. Nobody else needed to know, not until there was something more definite.

A movement at the end of the street caught her eye. It was Winnie, pedalling along with Trixie sitting regally in the basket at the front of the bike, her golden ears streaming in the wind. Bella abandoned her knitting and hurried to the front door, flinging it open just as her friend dismounted at the kerb outside the house.

'Winnie!' Bella rushed out and flung her arms around her. 'It's so good to see you.'

Winnie squeezed her back, hugging her with one arm while she held on to her bicycle with the other, before stepping back and looking her up and down. 'How are you feeling? Better, I hope, fully rested and ready for work again?' She narrowed her eyes. 'You still look a bit pale. Are you sure you're ready to come back?' She suddenly laughed. 'Not that I want you to go away again. I'm absolutely delighted to see you back again, and so is Trixie.'

The little dog had been jiggling in the basket, desperate to join in the greetings, and almost threw herself into Bella's arms as she gathered up the wriggling ball of softness for a hug. 'It's good to see you too.' Bella laughed as the dog licked her hands with obvious pleasure, her tail wagging wildly.

'Take her in with you while I carry my bike down to the basement,' Winnie said.

'I'll go and make some tea and you can tell me about getting your medal and all that's been happening,' Bella said. 'I've missed you and being at Station 75, I want to know everything.'

Winnie's face suddenly clouded, and Bella was sure that her grey eyes looked over-bright, as if she was holding back sudden tears. She was instantly alert: something was wrong.

*

'So tell me about the medal ceremony,' Bella said when they were settled at the kitchen table, with a pot of tea made with fresh tea leaves in honour of her return.

'I think my mother enjoyed it far more than I did,' Winnie said after she'd explained what had happened at the presentation. 'Royalty, a palace, lots of bowing and curtsying, everyone dressed in their finest and on their best behaviour. It suited her perfectly.'

'Did she meet Mac?'

'Only briefly, and I introduced him as a colleague. His mother let slip that he's a CO and Mother wasn't at all impressed, so fortunately she didn't want to stay and talk to him.'

Bella nodded as she poured out two cups of tea and pushed one across the table to her friend. 'So what's Mac's mother like?'

'The polar opposite of mine. Kind, warm, friendly, you get the picture.'

'You'll have to tell your mother about Mac sometime, won't you? You can't hide your relationship for ever – sooner or later she'll find out.'

Winnie's face blanched and she looked down, suddenly showing great interest in fiddling with a teaspoon, her head and shoulders slumping forward.

'Are you all right?' Bella reached out and touched her arm.

Winnie took a deep breath and looked up, her eyes sparkling with unshed tears. 'There'll be no need to tell her about Mac, not any more . . . We've parted.' Two fat tears spilled over and ran unchecked down her face, plopping on to the oilcloth-covered table.

Bella stared at her, not quite taking in her words. It was so sudden and completely unexpected. Winnie and Mac were made for each other and were more likely to have announced their engagement than split up. 'What? Why?'

'He told me this afternoon that he's leaving the ambulance service to join bomb disposal.'

'Why on earth would he want to do that?'

Winnie stood up and started to pace up and down. 'Because apparently he's got some ridiculous notion into his head that he needs to prove himself.' Her voice was loud and angry.

Bella shook her head. 'There's nothing wrong with what he's doing now; we do an important job and it's not an easy one.'

'He's already joined up.' Winnie threw her arms in the air. 'Signed on the dotted line. He's got to report for training at the beginning of August.'

Bella felt shocked that Mac would leave Winnie because of that. 'Even if he's going away, it doesn't mean that you can't still be a couple. Didn't you tell him that plenty of couples are apart these days?'

'It wasn't his decision.'

'What do you mean?'

Winnie stopped her pacing and looked at Bella, hands on her hips and her chin trembling as she fought back tears. 'It was me. I finished it.'

Bella frowned. 'But why would you do that? I don't understand.'

'I don't want a relationship with someone whose job is digging up unexploded bombs. He could get blown up any day, and I'm not putting myself through that. It's hard enough worrying about him now; if he's working for the bomb squad it will be so much worse.' Winnie's face crumpled and she began to sob.

Bella rushed over and put her arms around her friend.

'Are you sure about this, Winnie? Lots of women worry every day about their men. Think about the wives and girlfriends of pilots – every time they fly, they must wonder if they're coming back.'

Winnie wiped at her eyes with her crumpled handkerchief. 'I know that, but I just can't do it. It's bloody stupid him leaving a good job to go off and do *that*. I'm not supporting him. He's made his choice and I've made mine.' She took a deep breath and stuck out her chin, a stubborn look on her face. 'If it means we part, then so be it.'

'Is that wise when you care for him so much?' Bella stepped back and held Winnie at arm's length, looking into her eyes. 'Are you sure you're not just being stubborn? Cutting off your nose to spite your face?'

Winnie narrowed her eyes. 'I've made my decision, Bella. If you'll excuse me, I'm going to have a bath.' She stepped out of Bella's grasp and headed for the door, then suddenly stopped and turned back to face her. 'I'm so sorry, I haven't asked you about your stay at the convalescent home and if you managed to see James while you were there.'

'It was lovely there, and yes, I did see James and it was wonderful to spend time with him, as it always is.'

Winnie nodded. 'I'm glad.'

'Go and have your bath, try to relax,' Bella said. 'It'll make you feel better.'

As she watched her walk away, she couldn't help wondering if her friend had made a huge mistake parting from Mac, but then who was she to judge when she had worries and secrets of her own? All she could do was support Winnie in the days and weeks to come, and hope that her fears over the dangers of bomb disposal didn't come true.

'If you're both sure about being back here before you're completely fit, then I shall put you on light duties. You won't be sent out to incidents or be expected to maintain an ambulance; it will just be office work and a bit of housekeeping suitable for your injuries.' Station Officer Steele smiled at the two young women sitting by her desk. Both of them had returned to work this morning, insisting that they wanted to be there. She admired them for it and completely understood their need. 'It's good to have you back at Station 75; it wasn't the same without you here.'

'Thank you for organising the stay at the country hospitality home,' Bella said. 'It was lovely and a real treat to get away from the war for a while.'

'You both needed it.' She studied their faces, glad to see that they had more colour in their cheeks than when she had last seen them, though there was still something not quite right with Frankie. Her eyes had lost their usual spark; they had a dull, sad look about them. Perhaps that was to be expected as she'd not long lost her grandfather, but something about her whole manner made Station Officer Steele uneasy. Was she returning too soon?

'Bella, it's almost time for tea break. Would you mind going to make the tea for the rest of the crew, while I speak to Frankie? But don't go carrying the tray downstairs; get one of them to come up and get it.'

'Of course.' Bella nodded and left the office.

Closing the door behind her, Station Officer Steele sat down facing Frankie. 'Are you quite sure about coming back? With your arm still in plaster you have every reason to wait until it's fully healed. I appreciate you wanting to be here to do what you can, but I can't help feeling that something isn't quite right with you, Frankie. Call it my teacher's intuition. Is something upsetting you that I could help you with?'

Frankie bit her bottom lip and stared down at her hands clenched tightly in her lap.

'You don't have to tell me if you don't want to, but sometimes it can help to talk, and I may well be able to do something about what's worrying you.'

The young woman remained silent for a few moments and then looked up, her eyes meeting her boss's. 'I'd much rather be here than at 'ome.' She reached inside the bib pocket of her dungarees and pulled out an envelope. 'A neighbour gave me this yesterday when I got 'ome. It's from my grandad – he left it for me in case . . . ' Her voice broke and she pushed the envelope across the desk.

Station Officer Steele looked at it. 'Do you want me to read it?'

Frankie nodded and returned her gaze to her lap.

As she read through the letter, Station Officer Steele immediately understood why Frankie looked the way she did. The news it contained was shocking. To have grown up believing one thing only to find that it was a lie when she'd just lost what she'd thought was her last blood relative must be hard to take in. But then perhaps it was good news – a ray of light in the darkness.

When she'd finished, she reached out and took hold of Frankie's hand. 'This must have come as a terrible shock to you.'

Frankie looked up and nodded, her blue eyes bright with unshed tears.

'But I think your grandfather did a wise thing leaving you this letter.'

'Do you? I don't.' The young woman shook her head. 'I wish he'd never told me. I'm so angry with 'im.' She paused, chewing her bottom lip as she struggled to hold back her tears. 'And then I feel so guilty for being angry with 'im.'

'I think anyone would feel the same way. It was a big lie.' She squeezed Frankie's hand. 'But it is a chance for you to find your mother, if you should wish to. Do you?'

Frankie shrugged. 'I can't 'elp thinkin' how she left me and let me grow up thinkin' she was dead.'

'I can understand that must feel terrible, but it might have been very difficult for her too. She sacrificed being

320

with you so that your grandparents had you to love after they'd lost their sons. That can't have been easy.'

'So why have no contact with me, why let me believe I was an orphan?' Tears spilled over and ran down Frankie's face. 'She could 'ave left me with Gran and Grandad but at least told me she was alive, just livin' somewhere else. Lots of children live with other family members, it ain't so rare.'

Station Officer Steele squeezed Frankie's hand. 'She must have had her reasons. Perhaps it was easier for *her* that way. But she did keep in touch with your grandparents; she must have wanted to know how you were. She didn't abandon you altogether, so she must have cared for you.'

'It would 'ave been better if Grandad 'ad never written that letter, if I'd never got to know about it.'

'It may seem like that now, but it might help you in the long term. It's done now and you can't go back to before, when you believed your mother was dead. Will you contact her?'

The young woman shrugged. 'I don't know.'

'You could at least tell her about your grandfather, otherwise she'll have no way of knowing what's happened to him. Then take it from there. Think about it, Frankie. There's no rush to do anything, but I think if I were in your shoes, I would write to her. It may not work out, but at least you would have made contact.'

'I don't know what to do. It feels such a mess. It was hard enough coping with Grandad getting killed, but finding out about this makes everything so much worse.'

'I know, but give it time, Frankie, you might come to feel differently. You've had two terrible shocks.' She smiled sympathetically. 'Remember, I'm here to help you; you can come and talk to me any time. And do think about writing to your mother.'

'I will.' Frankie stood up. 'I'll go and help Bella with the tea.'

'Don't forget this.' Station Officer Steele quickly folded the letter and put it back in its envelope.

Frankie took it from her, putting it back in her pocket. 'Do you want a cup?'

'Yes please, I'll be out to get it in a minute.' She watched the young woman leave, hoping that something good would come out of this for Frankie; that she'd make contact with her mother and wouldn't feel so alone. It even might help her deal with that awful step-grandmother.

'He's told her,' Sparky said, coming to stand beside Station Officer Steele at her lookout post by the common-room window, a steaming mug of tea in her hands as she looked down on the crews sitting in the sunshine out in the courtyard enjoying their own drinks. 'It didn't go down too well.'

'So I gather. I did warn him that he should talk to her about it first before he signed up. I knew she wouldn't take it very well.'

'She couldn't 'ave taken it any worse, put an end to things between them, which is a terrible shame – they were very well suited.'

She turned and looked at him, smiling. 'I never had you down as an old romantic, Sparky. You do surprise me.'

Sparky grinned, shrugging his shoulders. 'I 'ave me moments.' He sipped his tea. 'I tried talking to Winnie about it but she didn't want to know, said he's made up 'is mind and so 'as she. She wouldn't be shifted on it.'

'She's stuck her stubborn heels in, even though any fool can see it's hurting her. You only have to look at her to see how unhappy she is.' Station Officer Steele watched as Winnie, who had already finished her tea and was back at work, polished the same bit of ambulance bonnet over and over again, her mind clearly elsewhere. 'She's avoiding Mac like the plague. The poor man's miserable; he'll be glad to leave to get away from the bad feeling.'

'Couldn't you have a word with her, try and make her see sense? You are the boss, after all.'

'I would if I thought it would do any good, but I honestly think that whatever I said to Winnie wouldn't make any difference whatsoever. She's made up her mind, and if I'm honest, I can understand her reasoning. I don't agree with it, but it is her decision and hers alone.'

'Well it don't make for a good atmosphere amongst the crew. You could cut the air with a knife when they're in the same area.'

'I'm sure we can survive until he leaves, Sparky, we've been through a lot worse in the past few months. As long as it's not affecting their work, then I'm going to let it go, all right?'

'If you think so, boss.'

'I do. With any luck Winnie might see sense and forgive him before he goes.'

'Do you think she will?' Sparky looked hopeful.

'No.' She smiled. 'But we can hope, can't we?'

It was beautifully warm and sunny down at the allotment. Frankie sat cross-legged, eating her fish-paste sandwiches and looking across to Tower Bridge, which thankfully had survived the bombing so far and still spanned the river, standing tall and proud. Winnie and Bella had accompanied her and were sitting beside her, leaning against the wall of the moat eating their own sandwiches. Everything seemed wonderfully normal here, Frankie thought.

She closed her eyes and enjoyed the feeling of being bathed in sunshine, glad to be back here doing the job she loved and spending time with both her friends again. A warm glow of contentment radiated inside her, filling her with a sense of peace and calm, until it was suddenly jerked away from her as she realised that she'd forgotten for a few moments what had happened. She'd lost herself in what used to be normal, but the terrible truth now slunk back into her thoughts like freezing fog on a cold winter's morning, snuffing out the warmth and making her throat ache so painfully with emotion that she had difficulty swallowing her mouthful of sandwich. Her life had changed irrevocably; what she'd once believed had shifted on its axis and an uncomfortable new reality now hung over her. This was the new normal and she didn't like it one little bit.

Laying the rest of her sandwich back in the paper wrapping, she glanced at her friends, who both sat looking at her with concerned expressions on their faces.

'Are you going to tell us what's wrong?' Winnie asked. 'You're clearly very upset about something.'

'I'm fine.'

Winnie rolled her eyes. 'And I'm the Queen of Sheba. Come on, Frankie, it's quite obvious that something is troubling you. We can see it in your face and we want to help you.'

'Something's happened since we came home,' Bella said. 'You weren't like this while we were away.' She reached out and patted Frankie's arm. 'Please tell us so we can help you.'

Frankie sighed. 'You're not your usual self either, Winnie. What's the matter with you?'

Winnie and Bella glanced at each other. 'You'll have to tell her,' Bella said.

'Tell me what?' Frankie asked.

Winnie smiled, her pillar-box-red lipstick bright in her pale face. 'So it's to be confession time then, is it, ladies? Time to spill our secrets and share what's bothering us.'

Bella's face paled. 'Who's going first?'

'Frankie,' Winnie said. 'If that's all right with you?'

'Very well.' Frankie took a deep breath and began to tell them about her grandad's letter with its shocking news.

'Bloody hell!' Winnie said when she'd finished. 'And you had no idea at all?'

Frankie shook her head. 'No, I was always told she'd

died of Spanish flu and I 'ad no reason to suspect my grandparents were lying. Why would I?'

Bella laid a hand on Frankie's arm. 'What are you going to do?'

'Station Officer Steele thinks I should write to my mother, tell her about Grandad, see what 'appens from there.' She shrugged. 'But I'm so furious with 'im for lying to me and then I feel guilty for feeling like that about 'im . . .' Frankie's voice faltered.

Winnie leaned over and put her arm around her friend's shoulders. 'It's perfectly natural to feel that way. I'd be incandescent with rage.'

'I've been worryin' myself sick about promising to look out for Ivy when all along he was lying to me about somethin' so important. He let me down.'

'Well if I were you, I'd forget about that promise,' Winnie said. 'You've got enough to deal with without being responsible for that beastly woman.'

'Winnie!' Bella frowned at her. 'It's not your decision.'

Winnie looked sheepish. 'I know, I was only giving my opinion. Seriously, Frankie, no one would blame you if you stepped back from it.'

Frankie dashed away tears with the back of her hand and pulled Trixie into her arms as the little dog had come to sit on her lap. 'I know what you're saying, Winnie, but I ain't goin' back on my promise. I can't, as much as I'd like to, because it's what he wanted.' She sighed, stroking Trixie's butter-soft ears. 'I wish he'd never left that letter.'

'Are you going to get in touch with your mother?' Bella asked.

'I don't know what to do. I'm not sure if I want to know the woman who left me and let me think she was dead all these years.'

'But she is family,' Bella said. 'It might turn out to be a good thing that you've found out she's still alive. You could meet her. You might even like her.'

'Perhaps.' Frankie shrugged. 'I need to think long and hard about it. I really ain't sure what I want to do.'

'You can either forget all about it, try to go back to the way you were before you got the letter, or you can write to her,' Winnie said. 'It's your decision.'

'What would you both do?' Frankie asked.

'Write,' Winnie and Bella chorused, and then laughed.

'Only because I'm nosy and would want to know more: why and how, everything. It wouldn't necessarily mean I would want much to do with her if I didn't like her.' Winnie grimaced. 'But then I don't have the best experience of a mother-and-daughter relationship, do I?'

'It can't have been easy for her to leave you, and she was still interested in you growing up – she didn't cut herself off altogether,' Bella said. 'I'd give her a chance.'

Frankie looked at her friends and smiled. 'Very well, I'll write to her, but only when I'm good and ready. That's all, I ain't promising any more than that. All right?'

Bella grabbed Frankie's hand and squeezed it. 'Good, and we're here to help you – we'll do anything we can, remember that.'

Frankie nodded. 'I know. Thank you, I appreciate it.' Her bruised heart felt a bit lighter than it had; being with her friends and hearing their honest opinions helped. 'That's me sorted out then. Tell me what's 'appened to you, Winnie. You ain't done anything to upset the boss while we've been away, have you?'

'Of course not. I'm a reformed character now, deputy station officer and all that.' Winnie smiled, though it didn't quite reach her eyes. 'Mac and I ... well, we've parted ways.'

'What?' Frankie stared at her friend. 'But why?'

'He's leaving to join bomb disposal, so that's the end of it.' Winnie looked down at her hands as she spoke. 'He's determined to go and do his bit, but I'm not going to wait around for him to be blown up, so it's the end, my decision not his.'

'Oh Winnie!' Frankie put her hand on her friend's arm. 'He must be upset about it.'

'So am I!' Winnie snapped. She held up her hand. 'I'm sorry. I'm just not prepared to wait around worrying myself silly that he's going to be blown to smithereens any day. We all know it happens to bomb disposal crew, so don't try to convince me he'll be all right.' She did her best to smile, but her chin wobbled, betraying her feelings. 'So that's my news. Come on, Bella, tell us something to cheer us miseries up.'

'Well I do have something nice.' Bella smiled, her cheeks dimpling prettily. 'Remember that journalist who went out on call with me and Frankie? I wrote a little piece for him in April and it was published in the *War Illustrated*.'

'What? Why didn't you tell us so we could read it?' Winnie said.

Frankie looked at her, her eyes narrowed. 'I think we did, Winnie. Remember that afternoon in the common room when Sparky pointed out an article in the paper?'

'Yes.' Winnie nodded. 'But that didn't have your name on it . . . ' She paused and grinned. 'You used a nom de plume – what was it?'

'P. Harper. Harper was my mother's maiden name,' Bella said.

'Why didn't you tell us?' Frankie asked.

Bella sighed. 'I wasn't sure I could do it and I didn't want to look a fool if I failed.'

'You'd never look a fool,' Winnie said.

'You did it, and very well.' Frankie put her arm around Bella. 'And you've been doin' it since then as well, ain't you? I've read some more of the articles about working at an ambulance station; they were very good, true to life, and I liked the funny stories especially.'

Bella nodded. 'I was asked to write a fortnightly article and the boss was happy for me to do it as long as I don't use real names. The longer it was a secret, the harder it became to tell you, I thought you'd be cross I'd hidden it from you.'

'Oh Bella, we've all been guilty of holding on to secrets. Yours is rather wonderful,' Winnie said. 'You clever old thing.'

*

'Cooeeee! Only me,' a voice called from the hall.

'Come through, Josie,' Frankie shouted back as she finished drying the plate and putting it away in the cupboard.

'Hello, ducks. I just saw Ivy go past on 'er way out so I knew it was safe to come round.' Josie held up an envelope and smiled. 'You've 'ad a reply.'

Frankie's stomach plummeted into her shoes. She wasn't sure whether to be pleased or to wish it hadn't come. It had taken her several weeks before she'd been ready to write to her mother – she'd needed time to get used to the idea that she was still alive after years of believing her dead – and then it had only been the briefest of notes informing her of Grandad's death and explaining about the letter he'd left for her. Her mother had clearly replied straight away.

She stared at the envelope with her name written on the front in unfamiliar writing. What was inside? Would there be answers to the many questions she wanted to ask? Would the letter tell her why her mother had abandoned her and insisted on the secrecy so she'd grown up thinking she was an orphan?

'You all right, ducks? Only you've gone right pale.' Josie pulled out a chair from the table. ''Ere, sit down.'

Frankie did as she was told. 'I'm just a bit shocked to see it 'ere, that's all.'

Josie laid the envelope on the table in front of her. Frankie had asked her mother to send her reply to her neighbour's house to avoid any awkward questions from

330

Ivy, whom she hadn't told about the letter her grandad had left her.

'Shall I make yer a cup o' tea?' Josie offered.

'No thanks, I'm fine.'

'Do you want me to stay with you while you read it, or clear off and give you some privacy? I don't mind either way.'

'I think I'd best read it on my own, if you don't mind, Josie.' Frankie smiled at the older woman. 'I really appreciate you 'aving the letter come to yours and bringing it round, but I think I need to be on my own. I don't know how I'll . . .'

'I understand, ducks. You know where I am if you need me. I 'ope it works out for yer, I really do. You deserve to 'ave someone there for yer. I'm sure that's what your grandad wanted, why he wrote that letter instead of letting the secret die with 'im.'

Frankie nodded. She'd spent a lot of time talking to Josie about the revelation that her mother was still alive, trying to work out how she felt about it. Josie had helped her slowly temper the anger she'd felt towards her grandad. He'd lied to protect her. He hadn't been a bad or deceitful man, and Frankie was sure he would rather have been honest with her.

'Come and see me later if you feel like it.' Josie laid a hand on her shoulder and then left, closing the front door quietly behind her.

Left on her own, Frankie stared at the envelope for a few minutes, her mind whirling with the excuses her mother might make for the way she had behaved, the revelations the letter might contain . . . She swallowed hard against the lump in her throat that lodged there every time she thought about whether her mother had had more children – brothers or sisters Frankie had never known about. Of course it might contain nothing of that, and merely be an acknowledgement of the brief letter she'd sent informing her mother of Grandad's death. She'd purposely left out how angry she felt, given no indication of how hurt she was, no offer of an olive branch, because that had to come from her mother, the one who'd left and not come back.

It was no good tormenting herself with what-ifs and maybes. Frankie grabbed the envelope and ran upstairs to the sanctuary of her bedroom, where she could read the letter without the risk of Ivy suddenly returning and catching her.

Sitting down cross-legged on her bed, she took a deep breath and slit the envelope open with her finger, pulling out three folded sheets of paper. As she opened them out, a photograph fell into her lap. She snatched it up, her heart thudding hard in her chest as she stared at the family captured in it. Standing outside a house was a man, a woman and three children – the two girls looked around thirteen and sixteen and there was a younger boy about Stanley's age. Her eyes settled on the woman. She'd seen her before, standing next to Frankie's father in the only photograph of her parents that she had. It was her mother. She reached out and touched her face and then pulled her finger back as tears distorted her vision, making the black-and-white image before her dance and shimmer.

Laying the photograph aside, she picked up the letter and took a deep, steadying breath before she began to read.

Dear Stella,

Your letter came as a shock to me. I'm very sorry to hear that Reg, your grandfather, has been killed. He was a good man and I'll never forget the understanding and kindness he showed me. I'm very glad that he left a letter for you, otherwise the knowledge that I'm still alive would have died with him.

Thank you for writing to me. I know you didn't have to and could so easily have ignored your grandfather's letter, forgot that you ever knew I existed, but you didn't and I am very grateful for that because it gives me the chance to explain myself and what I did to you.

Frankie stopped reading for a moment, preparing herself for what was coming next. The knowledge that her mother was alive had barely left her thoughts since she'd read her grandad's letter. Painful as it was, she needed to know why her mother had left her and let her believe she was an orphan. Her heart thudded hard as she realised she was about to find out the answers to her questions, answers that had the power to either hurt or heal. She couldn't be sure which, and the uncertainty and anxiety was excruciating, but there was only one way to find out.

I'm sure the news that I was alive must have come as a complete shock to you. I know that your grandparents kept their word and told you that I'd died. That wasn't easy for them, but they did it for me and so that they could keep you.

There hasn't been a single day that's passed when I haven't thought of you, my firstborn daughter, and wished that things had been different, that I could have brought you home to Suffolk with me after I'd recovered from my illness, but I had to do what I thought was right at the time – right for you and for your grandparents. In the time they'd been looking after you they'd formed such a strong bond with you. You had brought joy back into their lives after they'd lost your father and his brothers. I couldn't rob them of that, but neither could I stay in London. It wasn't my home and I couldn't live there.

It was the hardest decision of my life, and there were many, many times when I wanted to come back and snatch you away from them and bring you home to be with me where you belonged. But that would have been cruel, and I think your father would have been happy that his parents were raising you and that you had made them happy again.

Cutting myself off from you seemed like the best thing to do. I thought it would remove the temptation *to come back for you if you grew up thinking I was dead. Though I couldn't completely break away, I asked your grandparents to write to me once a year and send a photograph so I could watch you grow up from afar, and it made me happy to see your smiling face and to hear how you were doing.*

Frankie remembered how Gran had insisted that she have a photograph taken every year, dressed up in her best. Now she knew why.

I'm sorry that you grew up not knowing the truth and believing that both your parents were dead. I know that you were very well cared for by your grandparents and were happy with them, and that has given me comfort over the years when I have regretted what I did. Nothing can turn the clock back and I hope that perhaps we can now be given another chance to get to know each other. I think that is what your grandfather wanted; that's why he left you the letter, so that you know that you are not alone. You have me.

The writing swam and distorted before her eyes and a tear fell on to the page, making the ink pool and run. Frankie wiped her face with the back of her hand. The remains of the gut-wrenching anger she'd felt towards Grandad was dissolving. The letter had revealed how it hadn't been easy for her grandparents to lie to her, but they had done it for her mother. It was a relief to know that. Feeling angry with Grandad had been difficult when she'd loved him so much. But as for her mother . . . the anger was still there. She didn't know her, so there was no love to temper her fury. And now her mother was offering an olive branch – what should she do? Did she want to get to know her? Her mother had abandoned her, but this letter showed it hadn't been an easy choice, and was one that she regretted. What would she herself have done in the same situation? Frankie wondered. She shook her head. These questions, with their impossible answers, were giving her a headache. There was still more to read.

Let me tell you something about my life. Two years after I returned home, I got married again, to Bob, who I'd known all my life. He's a farmer and we have three children – Lizzie who's seventeen, Eve who's fourteen and eleven-year-old Robert.

So she had two sisters and a brother. Frankie took a deep, slow breath to calm the way her heart was whooshing the blood around her head. She'd wished so hard for siblings when she was a child, envious of her friends who always had someone to play with and on their side. Now she actually had some of her own. An unexpected dart of jealousy stung her – they'd grown up knowing their mother. She hadn't.

She picked up the photograph and looked closely at her siblings' faces, studying them for any similarity to herself. The older girl and boy looked like their father, but the

336

younger girl resembled their mother, her face similar to the one Frankie saw when she looked in a mirror. She had the same hair and face shape, the same eyes and nose, and although she couldn't be sure from the black-and-white image, she might have the same auburn hair too. But while they might share blood and similar features, these children were strangers to her.

Her eyes were drawn to the final lines of the letter.

I would very much like to see you, Stella. I could come to London and meet you. Please write back to me and if you would like to meet we can arrange a day and place. I hope you can forgive me for what I did all those years ago. I don't regret giving joy to your grandparents, but I do wish I hadn't been such a fool as to cut myself right out of your life.

Your loving mother

Frankie leaned back against the wall and closed her eyes. What should she do? *Meet her*, whispered a voice in her head. The thought of it was terrifying. What if she didn't like her mother? What if her mother didn't like her? What would her grandparents advise her to do?

She knew the answer straight away. Grandad had left her that letter for a reason, and she should take her chance to meet her mother and get to know the family she had never known existed. But not quite yet, she wasn't ready. She needed time to think about what the letter had told her, time to get used to the idea of having sisters and a brother. She had had too many shocks in the past weeks, and she wasn't going to rush anything. Her mother had waited twenty years to see her; a bit longer wouldn't hurt.

Ward Three at the Queen Victoria Hospital in East Grinstead was as busy and noisy as the last time Winnie had visited. Music blared from the gramophone and one of the patients was doing his best to persuade a nurse to dance with him. Winnie looked around for her brother and spotted him sitting nursing a glass of beer.

'Harry!' She walked over to him, smiling. 'How are you?'

'Hello, old girl, what brings you here?' Harry said, a swathe of bandages across the middle of his face leaving his eyes and mouth visible above and below it. He'd had another operation, this time to try and rebuild what was left of his nose.

'I thought I'd come and see how you are.' She studied his face for a moment. 'How's the nose?'

'Couldn't say. I presume it's under there somewhere. The boss said the op went well, so I'll take his word for it. Care for a glass?' He held up his beer.

'No thanks.' Winnie sat down on a nearby chair.

'Have you brought your gong to show me? I heard from Mother that she and Father accompanied you to the palace.'

'Yes, she enjoyed it.' Winnie rolled her eyes. 'And no, I didn't bring it.'

Harry chuckled. 'Course she did, it's just the sort of thing she likes.'

'Harry, I need to do your obs.' A pretty, dark-haired nurse arrived, speaking with a beautiful sing-song Welsh accent. 'Who's this then?' she asked.

'I'm his sister,' Winnie said.

'The ambulance driver? Harry's told me all about you. You got the George Medal, didn't you?'

'Hush now, Meredith, we don't want my sister to get big-headed. She's—' The nurse silenced him by sticking a thermometer in his mouth and winked at Winnie.

It seemed odd to hear her brother calling the nurse by her first name, but that was the way it was in Ward Three: normal hospital conventions didn't apply.

'Come to see how he's doing, have you?' Meredith gently took hold of Harry's wrist to measure his pulse.

'I thought I'd better check on him, I hope he is behaving himself.'

'Oh, he has his moments.' Meredith smiled sweetly at him.

Winnie was surprised to see how her brother responded, his eyes twinkling back at the nurse. She could tell that he was desperate to say something but couldn't with the thermometer clamped between his teeth.

'Right, let's see how you're cooking then.' The nurse removed the thermometer, checked it and quickly recorded the reading on Harry's chart.

'Am I warm enough for you?' Harry asked.

Meredith raised her eyebrows. 'You'll do. Right, blood

pressure next.' She deftly wrapped the cuff around his arm and inflated it, listening with her stethoscope. All the while Harry sat still and obedient, his eyes on the nurse.

Satisfied with the reading, Meredith added it to his chart. 'Well you're in tip-top shape, Harry, so I'll leave you to talk to your sister.' She turned to Winnie. 'It was nice to meet you.'

'And you,' Winnie said.

Meredith gathered up her equipment and with a nod went to attend to the next patient. Harry watched her go.

'She's lovely,' Winnie whispered to him.

He turned and looked at her and nodded. 'I think so.'

'Ah, so it's like that, is it? Are you sweet on her, dear brother?'

Harry shrugged and did his best to smile, his scarred skin stretching tightly around his lips. 'Perhaps.'

'No perhaps about it.' Winnie had never seen her brother look at a woman like that before. He'd always been popular with the girls but had never settled on one, preferring to enjoy himself and go out with many. Was he falling for someone at long last?

'Mind your own business, old girl, and leave me to mine. And don't say a word about it to Mother.'

'Don't worry, there's no danger of that happening.'

'I take it you still haven't told her about Mac?' Harry asked.

'No, and there's no need to now anyway.'

Harry stared at her. 'What do you mean?'

Winnie looked down at her hands. 'He and I parted ways a month ago.'

'What? But why?'

She sighed. 'Because he's joined bomb disposal and starts his training at the beginning of August.'

'So, what difference does that make to you and him, apart from not working in the same place any more, obviously?'

'The difference is that I'm not willing to hang around worrying and waiting to hear that he's been blown up, so I told him if that's what he's decided to do, then we're finished, I . . .' Her voice cracked.

Harry shook his head. 'What the bloody hell did you do that for?'

She glared at him. 'Because I . . .'

'Are you happy, old girl?' Harry touched her arm with his scarred hand. 'If you are, then perhaps you did the right thing, but from the look of you I'd say you're down-right miserable about it.'

Winnie's throat thickened and she dared not speak for a few moments. 'I miss him terribly and . . . I do care about him, very much, but it would be utterly beastly thinking he could be blown up every time he goes out.'

'Then you are being a stubborn fool. You could get blown up out in your ambulance, you know, don't forget that. He could get blown up, but he might not.' He paused for a moment, a look of pain flashing in his eyes. 'If there's one thing getting fried has taught me, it's that life is extremely precious and you've got to grab every

341

moment of happiness you can ...' He sighed. 'Because no one knows what's ahead of them, whether you'll even get a tomorrow with this bloody war on.'

Winnie nodded, sniffing back sudden tears. 'Mac might not want to be with me any more after I was so unkind to him.'

'He might or he might not, you won't know until you try, will you? So are you going to?' Harry asked, his grey eyes peering out above the bandages.

'I'll think about it.'

'Do that, but don't leave it too late. Talk to him before he goes or you might not get another chance. Grab your happiness while you can.'

'Pull over here, Winnie,' Bella shouted to her friend as she braked and brought her bicycle to a halt near St Paul's Cathedral.

Winnie came to a stop a few yards ahead of her and turned back. 'What's the matter?'

'You.' Bella marched towards her, pushing her bicycle along the pavement. 'Come on, we're going to sit on the steps and have a talk. What I have to say won't take long.'

Winnie sighed, but did as she was asked, bumping her bicycle over the kerb and following her friend.

Bella leaned her bicycle against the wall and lifted Trixie out of Winnie's basket. 'Come on, sit down here.' She sat with the little dog on her lap, stroking her soft golden ears. 'Right, are you going to tell me what's the matter?'

'What do you mean?' Winnie said.

'We haven't got time to mess around, Winnie, or we'll be late. There's something bothering you. You've been very quiet since you went to see Harry. Is he all right?'

Winnie nodded. 'He's fine. Sweet on some pretty Welsh nurse, which is a first for him; it's usually the other way round.'

'So what is it then?'

'Do you know, you are being exceptionally bossy, Bella. You're not normally like this. I wouldn't be surprised if there wasn't something bothering *you*.'

Bella's cheeks grew warm. 'Look, Winnie, I'm worried about you, that's all. You're my dear friend and you haven't been the same since you and Mac split up. You've been moping about for weeks and now you're even sadder. I'd like to help you if you'd let me, if there's anything I can do.'

'Well there isn't!' Winnie snapped, and then immediately held up her hands in submission. 'I'm sorry, that wasn't fair. I know you're only trying to help, but the fact is, the only person who can do that is myself, and I'm not sure if I'm brave enough to give it a try.'

'Brave enough to do what?' Bella probed.

Winnie sighed. 'To ask Mac to forgive me and to start again.'

Bella stared at her. 'You want to try again with him? But that's marvellous. What's made you change your mind?'

'Harry. He told me to grab what happiness I could, because you never know, I'm as likely to be blown up in my ambulance as Mac is by a UXB.'

'He's right. We all need to hang on to whatever happiness we can these days. So when are you going to speak to Mac?'

Winnie leaned forward, elbows on her knees, her head in her hands. 'I don't know.'

Bella put a hand on her shoulder. 'If you don't ask, you'll never know how he feels. I think he'll want to try again – he's been going round looking thoroughly miserable since you split up and probably can't wait to leave.'

'I'm scared he'll be angry and won't want anything to do with me again.'

'Perhaps, but I doubt it. Look, why don't you go down to the allotment when we have some free time, and I'll talk to Mac and send him down to see you.' She nudged Winnie so that her friend sat up again. 'Then perhaps you two can sort out your problem and both be happy again.'

'Do you think he'd come?' Winnie asked.

'I can't promise anything, but it's the best idea we've got, unless you can think of anything else.'

Winnie shook her head and flung an arm around Bella's shoulder. 'Thank you.'

Chapter Twelve

Concentrate, Winnie reminded herself as she nearly took out the leaves of another beetroot with her hoe. She needed to focus on the weeds and stop worrying about whether Mac would appear.

Trixie lay sprawled out in the sunshine nearby, apparently asleep. She suddenly started and sat up, her tail beginning to wag from side to side before she leapt up and ran off. Winnie turned around and felt her stomach somersault at the sight of Mac walking towards her, with Trixie skipping joyfully at his heels. He'd come. She shielded her eyes against the sun, trying to see the expression on his face, but she couldn't make it out. There was no way of preparing herself, but the fact that he'd come was a good sign, wasn't it?

'Bella told me you were down here,' Mac said as he reached her.

Winnie nodded, her mouth dry. 'What else did she tell you?'

'Well . . .' Mac nudged at a felled weed with the toe of his boot. 'She told me that you regretted what you'd done. That you'd made a mistake.'

'I do. And I did.' Winnie's voice came out in a squeak. She cleared her throat and held her chin up high, looking Mac directly in his beautiful dark blue eyes. 'I'm so sorry for what I said to you, I was wrong, stupid and selfish . . . and I wish I hadn't done it now. I . . . I love you and I don't want you to go, but if you do I will still love you and never stop.' There, she'd said it. She chewed on her bottom lip waiting for his response.

Mac reached over and took the hoe out of her hands, letting it drop to the ground, then he held his arms open wide and with one long stride she fell into them. Closing her eyes, she rested her head on his chest breathing in the familiar scent of him, soap and essence of Mac.

He dropped a kiss on to her hair and held her tight. 'I love you too, Winnie. I never stopped. I was angry and disappointed and hurt by what you did, but I understood the reason behind it . . . even if I didn't agree with it.'

Loosening her arms she looked up at him. 'I was so afraid of losing you, that you'd get blown up, but no one knows what's in the future. The war's not over and there's nothing I can do to stop it, but I'm not going to let it ruin what we have. I don't want to let another day pass without having you in my life.' She paused, looking into his eyes. 'That's if you'll forgive me. Can we start again?'

'We can do better than that.' Mac's eyes held hers. 'Marry me, Winnie, be my wife.'

She wasn't sure that she'd heard him correctly. 'Say that again.'

'Marry me.'

She stared at him, the blood fizzing through her veins as what he'd asked her sank in, then her answer shouted out loud and clear from her heart and was echoed by her head. She nodded. 'Yes, yes please.'

Smiling broadly, he picked her up and swung her around, making Trixie bark and gambol around his feet.

'I was scared you'd say no,' Mac confessed as he put her down. 'But I thought it was worth the risk.'

Winnie took his face in her hands and kissed him gently. 'I'm so glad you asked me, I'm wonderfully happy.' The awful heavy weight that had settled over her since they'd parted had gone; it was like the sun coming out again after a thunderstorm. 'When shall we get married?'

'As soon as we can, before I go if we can arrange it. Why wait?'

'Let's grab our happiness,' Winnie said. 'Hold on to it and never let it go, no matter what happens.'

Station Officer Steele waited for silence. 'I'm sure that I speak for all of us here when I say how delighted we are that Winnie and Mac,' she smiled at them standing together, arms around each other, 'have announced their engagement.'

'At least it'll stop them being so bloomin' miserable

and tetchy now they've seen sense,' Sparky shouted out, making everyone laugh.

'Indeed, they both suffered during their thankfully temporary parting.'

'And so did we!' Sparky added.

'We're all happy and relieved that you're back together, and I'd like to propose a toast, in tea.' She held up her mug, glad that the pair of them had seen sense. Love between two people was a precious thing, and even more so in wartime, when no one knew what the next day would bring. 'To Winnie and Mac, wishing you both all the happiness in the world.'

All the crew members echoed her words, holding up their own mugs in salute to the couple, and once they'd taken a sip, everyone broke into loud cheers and clapping.

'Thank you,' Mac shouted out. 'We both apologise for being miserable so-and-sos. We're feeling much better now.'

'So when's the wedding?' Sparky asked.

'As soon as possible.' Winnie smiled happily. 'If we can get a special licence, we'll get married before Mac leaves.'

Station Officer Steele watched as Winnie and her friends chatted happily about the forthcoming wedding, talking about where it might be, what she'd wear and whether they'd have a honeymoon. It reminded her of the excitement and utter joy she herself had felt when she'd become engaged during the Great War. They'd been planning their wedding for her fiancé's next leave, but the day had never arrived. He had been shot at dawn by his own side just weeks before they should have become man and wife. After surviving countless battles and muddy trenches, her beloved man had crumpled and couldn't take it any more, but instead of helping him with rest and care, the British Army had seen fit to cure him with a bullet.

A dart of pain sliced through her, surprising her with its sharpness. The years had helped dull the agony of her fiancé's death, but clearly it could still rear its ugly head to hurt her. Slipping quietly away, she went into her office and sat down at her desk, where she started to fiddle about with bits of paper as if she were doing some work, all the while breathing slowly and deeply to calm her galloping heart and dampen down the urge to weep for what she'd lost.

What would her fiancé have been like now if they hadn't shot him for desertion? Would they still have been as much in love as they were then? She hoped so. The bond they'd had was strong; he'd been her soulmate, the one who'd understood her, and she him. He was utterly irreplaceable. Like so many women of her generation, she'd remained single as much through choice as through the depleted number of men left after the killing had stopped.

The memory of trying on her finished wedding dress flashed into her mind. She'd had the beautiful lace gown made for her by a gifted seamstress in a small French village near to where she'd been based with her ambulance unit. Her friend and co-driver, Elsie, had gone with her for the fitting, and she'd felt such joy and excitement wearing it, knowing that the next time she did would be her wedding day. But that day had never come and the dress had remained unworn. It now lay wrapped in tissue paper and stored in her wardrobe, a sad reminder of what never was.

Winnie could use it! The thought popped into her mind. With clothes now on ration, it would be hard for her to buy a wedding dress or even enough material to make one. Of course she might not like it, or it might not fit her, but it could be altered and . . . Station Officer Steele smiled. The idea that her dress might be used, that it might be worn by a young woman who reminded her so much of her younger self, gave her a warm glow.

Pushing back her chair, she went over to her office door and called out, 'Winnie, can I speak to you a moment, please?'

The young woman left the group she was talking to and came over. 'Is everything all right, boss?'

'Yes, I've had an idea. Come and sit down a minute while I tell you.' She waited until Winnie was seated and then spoke. 'What I'm about to say is just an offer, and if you don't want to accept it then I won't be offended. I know how important it is that you feel happy about your wedding day.' She paused for a moment. 'You may already have one, but in case you don't, I would like to offer you my wedding dress. It's unused, and you could wear it as it is, alter it as you wish, or not use it at all. It's entirely up to you. Only with clothes rationing now in force, it will be harder to get a dress. I . . .' She stopped as Winnie reached out and touched her arm.

'Thank you, that's such a generous offer, but . . .'

Station Officer Steele smiled, doing her best to ignore

the swell of disappointment rising in her chest. 'I understand, you have your own plans. It was just a thought.'

'No, you misunderstand,' Winnie said. 'Are you absolutely sure you want to offer me your dress? It's a precious reminder of your fiancé and what should have been.'

'I'm quite sure. It's lain in its box for too long and I would be delighted to see it being worn.'

Winnie smiled, her grey eyes bright with tears. 'Then I would be very honoured and happy to wear it, though it might need altering to fit me.'

Station Officer Steele nodded, not daring to speak for a few moments. 'That's settled then, and we'll find a seamstress to do any alterations.'

'I'll ask Frankie, she's an expert with a sewing machine. I'm going to ask her and Bella to be my bridesmaids. I've got some silk dresses that can be altered to fit them.'

'I'll help you as much as I can,' Station Officer Steele said. 'I'd like to offer my flat as a place to do any dressmaking and alterations.'

'Thank you, that's very kind of you.' Winnie shook her head. 'I can hardly believe we're talking about wedding dresses now, when this morning Mac and I weren't even a couple.'

'Well I'm very glad we are.' The older woman reached out and touched Winnie's arm. 'You two are so well suited and should be together. I'm delighted you've both seen sense. Love is a precious thing and should be treasured, especially in times like this.'

*

'Winnie! Telephone call for you,' Bella's voice called up the stairs.

Winnie had heard the telephone ringing down in the hall, but had ignored it, hoping someone else would answer it as she pulled dresses out of her wardrobe, considering each one as a possible bridesmaid dress for either Bella or Frankie, taking into account their hair colour and complexion.

Laying the dress she was holding on the bed, she ran downstairs with Trixie following at her heels.

'Who is it?' she whispered to Bella as she handed over the receiver.

'Harry,' Bella said, smiling. 'He wants to know what you've been up to.'

'Did you tell him?'

Bella shook her head. 'Oh no, that's your news.' She grinned and then scooped Trixie up in her arms. 'I'll take her out in the garden for a bit.'

Winnie smiled her thanks and spoke into the telephone. 'Hello, Harry, is everything all right?'

He ignored her question. 'Have you talked to Mac yet?'

'Yes.'

'Well, what happened? Did he say yes?'

'Not exactly.' Winnie smiled to herself, enjoying teasing her brother.

'What do you mean by that?' Harry sighed. 'Just tell me what he said, old girl, for God's sake, I've been wondering what's going on and worrying about you.'

'You worrying about me?' Winnie laughed. 'Are you

352

going soft and becoming more in tune with your emotions around that sweet Welsh nurse?'

'Just tell me.'

'Mac asked me to marry him.' She paused for a moment, spinning out her tale. 'And I said yes.'

There was silence for a few moments, and then a piercing whistle and a whoop of delight. 'Thank God for that!' Harry's voice boomed out of the receiver. 'See, it was worth you swallowing that stubborn streak of yours, wasn't it?'

'Go on, you can say I told you so, I don't mind.'

'I don't need to.' His voice was gentle. 'I'm happy for you, truly I am.'

Winnie's eyes filled with tears at his words. Emotion wasn't something the old Harry had ever seemed to give in to, but since he'd been shot down and suffered so much, he'd changed, and rather for the better, she thought.

'Thank you. I'm extraordinarily happy about it. It feels right; we feel right together.'

'Good. So when's the wedding?'

'As soon as we can arrange it, before Mac has to report for training.' The thought of him going away made her stomach tighten, but she ignored it. There'd be time enough to dwell on missing him. 'We'll get a special licence. I hope you'll come.'

'Try and stop me.'

'You can bring that lovely Welsh nurse if you'd like to,' Winnie offered.

353

Harry laughed. 'I may just do that.' He paused. 'Have you told Mother yet?'

Winnie's stomach clenched again. 'No.'

'Well you're going to have to, old girl.'

'I'm over twenty-one, I don't need their permission to marry.'

'No, but you have a duty to tell them. Anyway, they'll want to be there.'

She laughed. 'I'm not so sure about that, Harry. When they find out I'm going to marry a conscientious objector ... well, you can imagine how they'll be. You could see Mother's disgust when I introduced her to Mac at the investiture. She had no idea then that he and I were a couple.'

'You're going to have to tell them, you can't avoid it.' He sighed. 'If they choose not to come to the wedding, well that's their loss.'

Winnie worried at a loose thread on her blouse. 'I know what you're saying is right, Harry, but it's not going to be easy.'

'You're a brave woman. Remember, you go out in the middle of air raids,' Harry reminded her. 'You can tell them.'

'I'd rather go out in an air raid any day.'

'Look, I'm going to have to go. I'm happy for you, old girl. Write and tell me when the wedding is as soon as you can, and I'll be there. Goodbye.' He was gone.

She replaced the receiver and sat down on the bottom of the stairs to think. Harry was right, she had to tell her parents, but she knew it would be like poking a stick into a wasps' nest and she wasn't looking forward to the repercussions. She stood up. She'd go and do it now, write a short letter to her parents telling them she was getting married, and post it before she left for today's shift, and then she would wait for the fallout to begin.

Chapter Thirteen

Frankie had never been as nervous as this before in her life. Not when she took her driving test, nor when she started work at Station 75, or even when driving out in the middle of an air raid for the first time. Waiting here now beat all of those times.

She paced up and down, avoiding bumping into the throngs of people passing through Liverpool Street station – servicemen balancing kitbags on their shoulders, people going about their everyday business – all the while keeping an eye on Platform 10, where the train was due. It should already have been here, but had been delayed like so many trains these days, no doubt forced to wait for more important trains to pass through, carrying troops or bombs to wherever they were needed.

The longer she waited, the stronger the urge to turn tail and run grew. It would be so easy to slip away and blend back into the busy streets of London, to just go and get on with her life, forget about Grandad's letter and the discovery that she had sisters and a brother and that the woman who had given birth to her was still very much alive. But if she ran now, she'd never know what her mother was like . . .

The steaming arrival of the engine pulling up alongside Platform 10 with its line of coaches behind caught her attention. She was here. Frankie's heart was racing as she quickly glanced at the exit out on to Bishopsgate. If she hurried, she could be gone before her mother saw her. The image of her grandad flashed into her mind. He would want her to stay, and she knew that she must. Frankie was no coward, and as hard as this was going to be, she had to see it through no matter what happened.

Standing a little way back from the ticket collector, she watched as the passengers came through, handing their tickets in. She recognised her mother the moment she saw her queuing up. She hadn't changed much from the photograph Frankie had of her as a young married woman. As if she knew she was being watched, she looked over at Frankie and their eyes locked for a moment. Without thinking about it, Frankie raised her hand and waved, and her mother smiled back at her and hurried towards her.

'Stella.' She stopped in front of Frankie and nervously held out her hands to her. 'I'm so very happy to see you.'

Frankie let her mother take both her hands. 'Hello.'

Her mother studied her face for a few moments and

smiled. 'I was worried you'd change your mind and wouldn't be here.'

'I nearly did,' Frankie confessed. 'I felt like running away.'

'I know this isn't easy for you, but I hope ... well ...' She paused, gently squeezing Frankie's hands. 'Should we go and have a cup of tea somewhere, then we can talk?'

Frankie nodded. 'There's a buffet over there.' She led the way, glad of something to do, and of a chance to get used to being with her mother. It was strangely overwhelming to think that after all the years of believing her dead, she was actually here beside her.

Walking along, she was very aware of her mother beside her. She was a few inches shorter than Frankie but had the same colour eyes and hair, and their features were so similar, there was no doubt that they were mother and daughter.

'So,' her mother said when they were settled at a table by the window of the buffet, cups of steaming tea in front of them. 'How is your step-grandmother? She must be heartbroken to have lost your grandfather.'

'Ivy?' Frankie shrugged. 'She's the same as ever, I suppose. Not sure heartbroken is the way to describe how she is. The most important person in her life is herself. She's nothing like my gran – the complete opposite in fact.'

'I was sorry that your gran died,' her mother said. 'She was a gentle, kind woman.'

'Well Ivy's not.' Frankie looked down at the teaspoon she was fiddling with before returning her gaze to her mother's face, looking her directly in the eye. 'Did your husband know about me?'

Her mother nodded. 'Bob knew right from the start. I told you in my letter that I'd known him all my life; we went to the same village school, were in the same class. He knew I'd married your father and he knew about you.' She paused, biting her bottom lip. 'But my other children don't know.'

Frankie's stomach twisted, and she folded her arms, hugging them tightly around her. Was she a guilty secret? 'Why didn't you tell them?'

Her mother shrugged. 'I don't know. It was easier not to, I thought they might think badly of me . . . ' She shook her head. 'I'm not ashamed of you, please don't think that. Of myself, but not of you.' She looked at Frankie, her blue eyes glistening with tears.

'Are you going to tell them?'

'Yes, when I get home.' She reached across the table and laid a hand on Frankie's arm. 'I hope that perhaps you'll come and visit us, meet your sisters and brother.'

Frankie turned and stared out of the buffet window, watching the people going past but not seeing them properly as her mother's words sank in. Did she want to go and meet her siblings, and see where her mother had run back to when she'd left her behind in London?

'There's no rush, you could come whenever you wanted to. It's up to you, but you'd be very welcome. I know Bob would be pleased to meet you.'

Frankie had to fight a sudden urge to bolt out of

the buffet. Meeting her mother here had been difficult enough, but to go and meet her family – sisters and a brother who had no idea she existed – was another thing altogether. They might not be quite so welcoming.

'What do you think?' her mother asked, her eyes hopeful.

Frankie shrugged. 'I'm not sure. I'll need to think about it.'

Winnie held tightly to Mac's hand as they approached the Dorchester, her heart feeling heavy and her stomach so scrunched up that she felt sick. She glanced at her watch once more, anxious that they shouldn't be late, knowing her mother's pet hate for tardiness.

Mac pulled at her arm to bring her to a halt and turned her to face him.

'Will you please try to relax? She can't stop us marrying, whatever happens in there, remember that.' He gently kissed her lips and smiled at her, his blue eyes gentle and kind.

'I know, I know,' she sighed. 'It's just … my mother's a fierce opponent and still has the ability to put the fear into me. Whatever she says, I'm going to marry you,' she gently cupped his face with her hand, 'but part of me still quakes at her disapproval.' She paused, fighting back tears. 'What really worries me is her being unkind to you, because you don't deserve it.'

'Don't worry about me, Winnie. I've faced plenty of unkindness since I chose to be a CO and I can assure you that nothing she says won't have been said before, but I know I did the right thing for me and I can hold my head up because of that. If she chooses not to come to our wedding, then it's her loss.'

Winnie nodded and took a deep breath. 'Come on then.' Her voice sounded far braver than she felt.

Normally when Winnie's mother took tea at the Dorchester, she sat at a table near the centre of the room where she could watch other people and more importantly be seen herself, but today she was sitting at one of the more discreet tables, tucked away behind some potted ferns, where it was more difficult to be seen and heard. Winnie felt herself bristling. Her mother was clearly preparing for battle, and in that case, so was she.

Giving Mac's hand a final squeeze of support, Winnie plastered a neutral, pleasant look on her face as they approached her mother's table.

'Hello, Mother.' She tried not to breathe in too deeply, as the scent of Chanel No. 5 always had the ability to trigger memories of facing her mother for various misdemeanours throughout her childhood, a time when she had had no say and was in the control of her parents. Now of course she was an adult, fully responsible for herself, but still capable of being affected by unhappy memories.

As always, her mother checked her watch first to ensure she hadn't been kept waiting, and then looked at Winnie. 'There you are, Margot.' Her eyes slid over her daughter's shoulder to Mac but she said nothing to him.

'Good afternoon, Mrs Churchill.' Mac stepped forward and held out his hand, which the older woman ignored.

'Do sit down.'

Winnie felt her blood starting to fizz with anger at her mother's rudeness. She caught Mac's eye as he pulled out a chair for her and he gave a small shake of his head, obviously well aware of how she was feeling.

'I've taken the liberty of ordering tea already. They shouldn't be long,' her mother said.

They sat in silence for a few moments, and Winnie was relieved when the waitress arrived. She helped her offload the tea things, aware of the glare her mother gave her for helping the staff, considering it not the done thing when it was the woman's job to serve.

'So,' her mother said as she poured the tea. 'Where has this ridiculous notion of you marrying come from?'

Winnie passed a cup to Mac and took one for herself, biting down on her tongue to stop a retort from bursting out, knowing that if she were to stand any chance of coming out of this meeting with a sense of dignity, she needed to keep calm.

'We love each other and we want to get married and spend the rest of our lives together,' she said, adding milk from the little jug and gently stirring it in with a spoon.

Her mother laughed, a brittle, mocking sound. 'You *think* you are in love, Margot, but love is very overrated. Marriage is for the long term, and choosing a husband should take many things into account: background' – her icy blue eyes came to rest on Mac, who stared straight back at her – 'education, beliefs, moral values . . . ' She left her last words hanging in the air, as good as any physical punch, then took a genteel sip of tea.

Winnie reached out for Mac's hand under the table and held on to it tightly, her blood fizzing and coursing around her body as she felt her temper starting to boil. 'If . . . ' she began, but Mac squeezed her hand to stop her.

'Mrs Churchill,' he said, 'I understand that you are concerned about who your daughter is marrying – any parent would be – so let me tell you something about myself and my family. My father was a clerk for the local council and my mother a teacher before she married. I followed her into the teaching profession and taught at the local school until I joined the ambulance service. My moral values wouldn't allow me to kill another man – that's why I am a conscientious objector.'

Winnie watched as her mother visibly winced at those last words.

Mac went on. 'But I do not believe in sitting back and doing nothing to help the country, and that's why I joined the ambulance service and am going on to work in bomb disposal. I am not a coward or a shirker, just someone who cares for fellow people and cannot harm them.'

Winnie's mother looked as if she had a bad smell under her nose. 'Where would the country be now if every man had your attitude?'

'It's a free country; every man and woman has the right to choose for themselves,' Winnie said. 'Take that away and we'd be the same as Hitler, who has robbed people of their liberty and choices.' She turned and smiled at Mac. 'I'm proud of Mac and that he stands up for what he believes in.'

Mac squeezed her hand under the table.

'The fact remains, it is a most unsuitable match for you, Margot,' her mother said, turning her full attention on Winnie as if Mac wasn't there, keeping her voice low. 'You have been raised to marry someone of a similar background who can support you in the manner you are used to.'

'I don't care if Mac isn't rich, Mother. He's a far more decent person than many of the so-called eligible young men that you've foisted on me over the years.' Winnie didn't bother to lower her voice, and her mother looked around uncomfortably to see if anyone was listening.

'I'm going to return to teaching after the war and we'll be fine,' Mac said.

Her mother suddenly looked at him, her eyes narrowed. 'If you truly care for my daughter, then you would do the decent thing and walk away rather than dragging her down to your . . .' she paused, searching around for a word, 'level.'

'How dare you?' The words were out of Winnie's mouth before she could stop them. 'I am going to marry Mac, and it will make me the happiest I have ever been in my life.' She stood up, pushing her chair back with such force that it fell backwards with a clatter, causing a hushed silence to fall over the room as everyone looked to see what the fuss was about.

Mac stood up and righted the chair. 'You are welcome to come to our wedding,' he said.

Winnie's mother was furious, her jaws clamped tightly together and her eyes flashing. 'I will *not* be attending.' Her voice was clipped and cold.

'Very well.' Leaving her mother sitting ramrod straight, her fingers clutching her teacup so tightly her knuckles stood out white, Winnie grabbed Mac's hand and stalked out of the room. She was aware that many eyes were on them, but she didn't care. So many of these people were like her mother, bothered more about how much money someone had, what their family background was, than about what they were like as a person and how they conducted their life. Her mother had made her choice and so had she.

'We should never have come!' she said as they marched out of the hotel doors and back on to the street. She looked up at Mac, her eyes stinging with tears of anger. 'I'm so, so sorry about the way she treated you. I can't believe . . . ' She sighed and waved her arm in the air. 'Actually I can. I'm appalled and ashamed of the way she behaves. She lives by all these ridiculous rules, with her pompous airs and graces, but perhaps she should look at the way she treats people.' She stopped to take a breath.

Mac smiled at her, taking her hands in his. 'It's all right, Winnie. I didn't expect her to be welcoming or happy about me marrying her daughter, and I know that being a CO makes people react in different ways. She's as much entitled to her opinion as I am to mine.'

She shook her head. 'I don't know how you can be so forgiving of her. I'm bloody furious.'

'Let it go, Winnie. Don't let it spoil things. We met her, she had her say, we disagree, but the important thing is that we're still getting married, your mother's disapproval hasn't changed that. If she changes her mind, then she's welcome to come.'

'Humph! I'm not so sure I'd welcome her,' Winnie said.

'Come on, Winnie, be the better person,' Mac reminded her. 'She probably won't come, but if she does, then welcome her.'

Winnie sighed. 'I'll try.' She suddenly laughed. 'You are such a good, kind man, Mac, did you know that? Certain members of my family could learn an awful lot from you.'

He shrugged. 'Come on, let's put this afternoon behind us and go and see about getting this special licence – that is, if you still want to get married before I leave.'

'Oh, I do,' Winnie said. 'I've never been so sure about anything in my life.'

'Winnie! Please keep still!' Frankie said through a mouthful of pins.

'I'm trying to,' Winnie said.

Station Officer Steele smiled at the two young women, Frankie kneeling on the floor carefully pinning the hem of the dress while Winnie stood on a chair, towering over everyone else in the room. It was wonderful to have them here at her flat for the dress fittings; she was thoroughly enjoying having her normally silent home brought to life by the energetic and joyful young women. Bella had already had her fitting and gone to change out of her bridesmaid's dress in the bedroom.

'Would you mind 'olding this bit, just so?' Frankie asked her, showing her where she needed the fabric gathered so that she could pin it.

'Of course.' Station Officer Steele gently took hold of the lace and recalled her own fitting with the French seamstress so many years ago. Afterwards, she and Elsie had giggled at how the woman had managed to hold a conversation with them while sporting a mouthful of sharp pins clamped between her teeth.

'How much longer?' Winnie asked.

'I'll just finish this bit,' Frankie said, deftly pinning the fabric so that it fell just as she wanted it, 'then you can take it off and I'll tack it in place before we do a final fitting. When we're completely 'appy with it I can machine it.'

'Thank you so much, darling Frankie. I know I'm not a very patient person and I do appreciate you altering the dress for me.' Winnie looked at Station Officer Steele. 'And also your fabulous generosity in lending it to me in the first place.'

'I'm very happy that it's going to be worn by a bride; it was what it was made for,' Station Officer Steele said. 'You look beautiful in it, Winnie. It's perfect for you.' Her gaze met Winnie's and held it for a few moments.

'Thank you,' Winnie whispered, her grey eyes bright.

Station Officer Steele patted her arm and nodded.

'Right, that's it.' Frankie inserted the last pin and stood up. 'Now be very careful taking it off – do you want me to 'elp you?' She held out her hand to Winnie as she climbed down from the chair, taking care not to stand on the folds of material making up the skirt of the dress.

'No, I'll be careful, I promise you,' Winnie said. 'I don't want to have to be pinned again.'

'But you can't manage all the little buttons on the back on your own, Winnie.' Bella had come back into the room carrying her bridesmaid's dress, which she carefully laid over the back of an armchair. 'I'll help you; the last thing we need is you struggling and ripping the dress. We don't have time for Frankie to mend it.'

Winnie held up her hand. 'Of course, you're absolutely right, Bella.'

'I know I am.' Bella smiled at her friend. 'This way then.' She opened the door for Winnie and turned back to wink at Frankie before following their friend out.

'What about your dress?' Station Officer Steele asked Frankie. 'Is it ready?'

Frankie nodded. 'I thought it would be enough to deal with Winnie and Bella's 'ere. I got my neighbour Josie to 'elp me with mine.'

'Very wise. There isn't a lot of time to get everything ready. At least they've got the special licence now so the wedding can officially go ahead.'

'That's one more thing ticked off the list.' Frankie deftly threaded a needle with cotton and got to work tacking around the hem of Bella's dress.

Station Officer Steele sat down on the sofa. 'Have you heard any more from your mother since you saw her?'

Frankie looked at her. 'She's sent me several letters and keeps asking me to go and visit. She suggested this coming week, but I can't go then.'

'Why not?'

'Because of the wedding, I need to get these dresses finished. I can go some other time.'

'Are you sure you're not using that as an excuse?'

Frankie shrugged. 'I'll go sometime, it ain't urgent.'

'Forgive me if I'm prying here, but do you *want* to see her again?'

'I ain't sure. Part of me wants to know more but another part feels . . .' She bit her bottom lip. 'I feel angry that she let me grow up thinkin' I was an orphan, especially when she's got other children who live with her. I ain't sure what to think and perhaps it's best to just forget I ever found out about her.'

Station Officer Steele leaned over and put her hand on Frankie's arm. 'I don't think you could do that now you've met her, could you? Aren't you curious to meet your sisters and brother?'

'A bit,' Frankie admitted. 'I keep thinkin' about it: should I go or not. It's driving me crazy.'

'Sometimes worrying about something is worse than the thing itself. You might feel better if you go and meet them and find out for yourself. Then you'd know for sure instead of tormenting yourself with questions you can't answer.' She smiled at the young woman. 'There's only one way to find out, and that's to do it.'

'Do what?' Winnie asked as she and Bella came back into

the room, carefully carrying the wedding dress between them.

'Frankie's been asked to go and visit her mother and her family next week,' she told them.

'That's marvellous,' Bella said, smiling.

'But I can't go,' Frankie said. 'I need to finish the dresses.'

'Yours is already done,' Station Officer Steele said, 'and if I put you on dressmaking duty on tomorrow's shift, you'll definitely get these two finished in plenty of time.'

'But what about my work?' Frankie said.

'Thankfully things are still quiet, so I'm sure we can manage. You can find a quiet spot in the women's rest room to work so Mac won't see the dresses, and then you'll be free to go and see your mother before the wedding.'

'That sounds like a marvellous idea,' Winnie said. 'I would feel terribly guilty if you didn't go because of me. How long would you go for?'

'Only one night. I wouldn't want to stay any longer in case it was terrible.' She shrugged. 'Anyway, I can't go havin' time off work; it ain't my turn for a holiday.'

Station Officer Steele put her hands on her hips. 'My dear girl, by rights you shouldn't even have gone back to work so soon after you'd broken your arm. Having a couple of shifts off to go somewhere important won't be a problem at all. In fact, as your boss, I insist you take the time off.'

Frankie stared at her for a few moments and then sighed. 'Why do I feel that you're all gangin' up on me and whatever reason I come up with for not going you'll 'ave an answer to?'

Winnie laughed. 'I don't think you can wriggle out of it, darling Frankie. So are you going?'

'Very well then, but only if the dresses are finished,' Frankie agreed.

Chapter Fourteen

Frankie put her suitcase by the front door, ready for a quick getaway. What she had to say to Ivy wasn't going to go down very well, and there was certain to be a row about it, so it was just as well she was going away for a night. Bracing herself, she went into the kitchen, where Ivy was in her usual place in the armchair.

'I thought you were goin' to work?' Ivy said, not looking up from the *Picture Post* spread on her lap.

'I'm not goin' today, I've got some time off.'

Ivy looked up, narrowing her eyes. 'What for?'

'I'm goin' away for a night.'

'Where to?'

Frankie took a deep breath to prepare herself. 'To my mother's.'

Ivy snorted with laughter. 'Gawd, you need to see a doctor more like. Yer mother's dead, been dead for years.'

Frankie shook her head. 'She ain't dead, she lives in Suffolk with my stepfather and their children. I'm goin' to visit them.'

Ivy stared at her for a moment and Frankie could see her trying to work out what was going on. 'Reg told me she was dead, died of Spanish flu when you were a baby. That's why they brought you up – it was either they took you in or you went to an orphanage.' The last few words dripped venom, as if she wished Frankie *had* been dumped in an orphanage.

'That's not what actually 'appened. My mother left me 'ere with my grandparents.'

'Where's all this come from?' Ivy asked.

'Grandad left me a letter tellin' me all about it,' Frankie said. 'He wanted me to know.'

'He never told me,' Ivy blustered. 'I was 'is wife, why didn't he tell me?'

'It wasn't really any of your business, was it?'

'Where'd you get this letter then?'

'It doesn't matter,' Frankie said. 'Before I go, I need to talk to you about the rent. We're going to struggle to pay it without Grandad's wages comin' in. I can't afford to pay all of it on my own, so you're going to 'ave to get a job, otherwise we'll 'ave to move out.'

Ivy glared at her for a few seconds and then exploded. 'I pay what I can out of Reg's pension. I'm lookin' for a job.'

'Well look 'arder,' Frankie said. 'Otherwise you'll be lookin' for a new place to live.'

'Don't you talk to me like that. Reg would be furious to hear you speakin' to me like that . . .'

Frankie walked away, leaving Ivy ranting and wishing again that she didn't feel obliged to honour the promise she'd given Grandad to keep an eye on the vile woman. If it hadn't been for that, she would have been free of her now. As it was, she was supporting her, paying more than her fair share of the rent to keep the house going for when Stanley came home, but she couldn't sustain that for ever, not when Ivy was sponging off her like the clinging plant she was named after. It was time for the woman to start paying her way.

Several hours later, Frankie was feeling sick with apprehension as she stared out of the bus window at the passing Suffolk countryside. Following the instructions her mother had sent her, she'd caught the train to Ipswich and then switched to a bus for the final leg of the journey, asking the driver to tell her when they got to the village where her mother lived.

It was beautiful countryside, the land gently rolling, a world away from the streets of Stepney where her mother had found it impossible to settle. She must have felt as alien there as Frankie did out here. How would she feel herself if she came to live here? Would she be able to cope with such a drastic change?

'We're nearly there,' the bus driver called out, his Suffolk accent sounding odd to her ear.

'Thank you,' she replied, her heart quickening its pace.

She spotted her mother waiting at the bus stop by the village shop before they'd come to a halt. She was looking anxious too. This wasn't going to be easy for her, introducing the daughter that her other children had never known existed to her family. Frankie wasn't sure whether to feel pity or anger; her emotions about this whole business were still a complicated mess. Station Officer Steele had been right when she'd encouraged her to come here and find out for herself. Hopefully it would put an end to the worry and torment that had plagued her about her unknown family.

'Hello.' Her mother smiled warmly at Frankie as she climbed down the bus steps. 'It's good to see you again.' She opened her arms and Frankie allowed herself to be embraced in an awkward hug.

'Thanks for coming to meet me,' Frankie said, stepping out of her mother's arms.

'I'm glad to, gives me a chance to have you to myself for a little while.' Her mother spoke quickly, slipping her arm through Frankie's as they started to walk. 'The others are looking forward to meeting you and I probably won't get a word in edgeways once we're home.'

'What did your ... other children say when you told them about me?' Frankie asked as they walked along. Her mother hadn't elaborated on that in her last letter, only writing that she'd told them.

'Well, they were ...' she paused, 'shocked.' She sighed, 'But that's only to be expected. And Lizzie was angry at first. She's been used to being my eldest, so to find out she wasn't really . . . ' Her mother shrugged. 'She's a head-strong girl and just needs to get used to the idea. I'm sure she'll be fine when she meets you.'

As a child Frankie had often dreamed of having brothers and sisters, but in her imagination they'd been the best of friends, always looking out for each other. Clearly in real life it might not turn out the same way. From what her mother had said, it sounded as though one of her sisters had taken against her before they'd even met.

'What about the other two?' Frankie asked.

'Eve's excited about having another older sister. She and Lizzie don't get on, so she's hoping the two of you might. And Robert, well he's as easy-going as his father.'

'What about your 'usband?'

'Bob's happy that you and I are in touch again. As I said, he's always known about you, and how hard I . . .' Her mother stopped.

'I'm glad he don't mind.'

By the time they arrived at Rookery Farm, Frankie's stomach had knotted itself so tightly it felt like a heavy weight of dread inside her. She was wishing she'd never agreed to come here when the door of the farmhouse burst open and a slight girl with hair the same colour as her own came running out and rushed towards them, stopping a few yards away with a shy smile on her face.

'Hello.' She spoke softly. 'I'm Eve. Welcome to Rookery Farm.'

Frankie was instantly disarmed by the girl's genuinely warm welcome.

'Told you Eve was looking forward to seeing you,' her mother said, gently squeezing her arm. 'Are the others indoors?' She directed the question to her youngest daughter.

'Yes, but I couldn't wait. I've been watching for you,' Eve said, not taking her eyes off Frankie. 'Your hair's the same colour as mine and Mum's.' She beamed. 'Lizzie and Robert have got Dad's hair colour.'

'Enough chatter, young lady. I expect your sister's ready for a cup of tea and something to eat,' her mother said.

Frankie stared at her, momentarily stunned at being referred to as 'your sister' for the first time ever. It felt strange but oddly nice.

Inside the house her mother introduced her husband, who was tall, with dark brown wavy hair and kind hazel eyes. 'This is Bob.'

'I'm glad to meet you, you're very welcome here.' He held out his hand for Frankie to shake.

'Thank you.' She smiled at him, glad that he seemed genuinely welcoming.

'And this is Robert,' her mother said, propelling a min-iature version of Bob towards Frankie from where he'd been hiding behind his father.

'Hello,' he said, his eyes briefly meeting hers before he looked away again.

'And this is Lizzie.' Her mother smiled encouragingly at her other daughter, who had been standing, arms folded, watching Frankie's every move from the moment she'd walked into the kitchen a few minutes ago. She hadn't said a word, but there was no mistaking the hostility in her face. 'Lizzie, say hello to your sister.' Her mother's voice had an edge to it.

Lizzie glanced at her mother, her eyes narrowing, and receiving a stern glare in reply, then turned to Frankie and spoke, her voice cool and in complete contrast to Eve's greeting outside. 'Hello.'

'Good, so now we've all met each other, we'll have some tea. Sit yourselves down.' Frankie's mother started to busy herself at the stove, which was giving out a gentle heat into the room.

Following Bob's lead, Frankie sat down at the table, which was set with what looked like the best china and freshly baked scones and a sponge cake. Someone had gone to a lot of trouble here. Eve sat next to her and Lizzie opposite, still staring at her, her arms still firmly folded across her chest.

'Must be very different for you here in the countryside,' Bob said.

Frankie nodded. 'I ain't used to so much green around me. We used to go 'op picking in Kent every year and I liked that.'

'I'd be like a fish out of water in London,' Bob said. 'Is the bomb damage bad? I don't think they tell us everything in the paper or on the wireless.'

'You don't want to be talking about that,' her mother said, putting cups down on the table.

'I don't mind.' Frankie was grateful to have something

to talk about; it helped distract her from the fact that she was sitting with people who were family and yet who were also strangers to her. 'Yes it is bad, whole areas are bombed to smithereens.' As she told them about the damage, she was aware of Eve and Robert listening to every word she said. 'Do you have any raids here?'

'Ipswich gets them,' her mother said, sitting down at the end of the table. 'You can see the bombers going over and the sky glows orange over the city.'

'It's been like that sometimes in London,' Frankie said, accepting a piece of cake from the plate that Eve offered her.

'You drive an ambulance, don't you?' Eve asked.

Frankie nodded as she chewed her mouthful of delicious cake. 'I do.'

'Do you get scared?' Robert's voice piped up.

'Robert!' their mother said. 'Don't be so nosy.'

Robert's face flushed. 'I'm sorry.'

Their mother leaned over and ruffled his hair. 'Good boy.'

A sudden pang of jealousy sliced through Frankie as she watched the affectionate gesture. Her mother had never done that to her as a child. She struggled to fight down an overwhelming urge to cry for what she'd missed out on. But she had had love from her grandparents in its place, and plenty of it. She couldn't rewind the past. Pasting a smile on her face, she looked at Robert. 'It's all right, I don't mind. Yes, I do get scared sometimes, especially if I'm out in a really heavy raid.'

'What's it like being an ambulance driver?' Eve asked.

'It's different every day, you never know where you'll be sent or what you'll see.' Frankie was glad to talk about something she was so familiar with and happily answered the wide variety of questions about her work that both Eve and Robert fired at her, all the time aware that Lizzie was sitting silently watching. She might not have said a word, but it was clear that her reaction to Frankie was unfriendly. Lizzie didn't want or welcome her here.

'It sounds like a tricky job to me, going out in the middle of raids,' Bob said, standing up. 'You're brave to do it. If you don't mind, I'd better get back to work. Come on, Robert, you can help me with the milking.'

'Would you like anything else to eat?' her mother asked.

'No thank you, I've had plenty. It was a real treat,' Frankie said.

Her mother smiled at her and then turned to Eve. 'Why don't you take your sister on a tour of the farm?'

Eve smiled and stood up. 'Come on then, Stella. I'll show you where everything is.'

'All right.' Frankie smiled back at the girl – her sister – whom she had taken an immediate liking to. 'Lead the way.'

Outside, she could hear a dog barking. 'That's Jess helping to bring the cows in for milking. She always does it,' Eve said.

'How many cows 'ave you got?' Frankie asked.

'Ten. They're Jerseys, they give the best creamy milk, good for making butter.'

Frankie frowned. 'I'm a townie, Eve. I ain't got no idea what a Jersey is.'

Eve giggled. 'I forgot. They're beautiful cows, with big brown eyes. Come on, the best way is to show you.'

Eve led her through the farmyard to where a five-barred wooden gate stood open. 'They'll come through here to the milking parlour in a minute.'

They did have beautiful brown eyes, Frankie thought when the cows came waddling through the gate a few minutes later, their heavy udders swinging from side to side.

'You can have a go at milking if you want,' Bob called as he walked past at the rear of the herd.

'Go on, you should try it,' Eve urged her.

'I ain't sure if . . . ' Frankie began.

'You don't know until you try, do you?' Eve took hold of her hand. 'Come on, come and watch and see if you want to have a go.'

Frankie shrugged. 'Why not?'

Inside the milking parlour, the sweet smell of hay mixed with the warm smell of cow, and to her surprise, Frankie rather liked it. She watched as Bob and Robert went through the preparations, washing down the cows' udders and teats before both sitting down on small stools, positioning metal pails and starting work. The first streams of milk hitting the bottom of the buckets made a plinking noise that soon vanished as the level of the milk rose, a beautiful creamy colour with froth on top.

'Do you want a go?' Bob asked.

'Go on.' Eve gently pushed Frankie towards him, and before she could protest, she was sitting on the stool, closer to a cow than she had ever been in her life. She could feel the warmth coming from it on her cheeks.

'Right now, you need to pull gently and squeeze, like this.' Bob demonstrated.

Frankie took hold of a teat between her fingers and thumb and tried to do as Bob had shown her, but nothing happened; no milk came out.

'Try again, a little harder this time,' Bob encouraged her.

She pulled and squeezed again, and this time a small stream of milk came out.

'See, you can do it,' Eve said.

'Of course you can,' Bob said. 'Keep going.'

Frankie did, marvelling at the stream of milk, but her fingers and thumb soon started to complain, aching at the unaccustomed movement. She had to stop and wriggle her fingers. 'I ain't used to this.'

'You've done well for your first time,' Bob said. 'You can help us with the rest of the herd if you like.'

Frankie stood up, shaking her head. 'It would take me till tomorrow at the rate I go.'

'And I need to show her around the farm,' Eve added, tucking her arm through Frankie's.

'What 'appens to all the milk?' Frankie asked as they walked out of the milking parlour.

'We keep some to make cheese and butter, and the rest goes into churns and is picked up from near the gate. It goes to Ipswich for people to drink there.'

Eve's tour around the farm was full of information as the younger girl chatted away. She'd lost her initial shyness and was keen to show Frankie everything, from the pigs to the chickens, the beautiful shire horses grazing in the meadow and even a brood of swallow chicks in a mud nest under the eaves of the house.

Sitting on top of the gate looking down on the meadow, through which a lazy river was flowing, Frankie had to ask Eve the question that had been bothering her. 'What's the matter with Lizzie? Your . . . our mother said she was angry when she found out about me.'

Eve pulled a leaf out of the hedge at the side of the gate and started to shred it. 'She was.' She sighed. 'Lizzie's a bit . . . she's bossy and likes her own way, only she don't always get it. She wants to leave and do something else instead of working on the farm, join the ATS or the WAAF.'

'She's only seventeen, she's not old enough yet,' Frankie said.

'Dad said no even if she was old enough.' Eve put her hand on Frankie's arm. 'I'm sorry she hasn't been very welcoming to you, but the rest of us are happy you're here. I couldn't believe it when Mother told us about you. I thought that I might have a nice sister at last.' She put her hand over her mouth, her face turning pink. 'I shouldn't have said that.'

'I'm glad you're 'appy about me.' Frankie paused, watching a pair of birds skimming low over the meadow. 'I weren't sure if I should come 'ere or not. Until a few weeks ago I thought my mother was dead and 'ad no idea about you and the others.'

Eve smiled at her. 'I'm glad you know now. It's exciting having a new sister. You could come and live here with us.'

Frankie stared at her; she hadn't even considered that. Would she want to leave the East End and come and live here with her new-found family?

'It would be lovely, what do you think?' Eve looked at her hopefully.

'I don't know, I ain't thought about it, but I can't leave my job,' Frankie said, trying to let the girl down gently. She'd agreed to come and visit for one night only; the idea of moving here, away from all she knew and loved, was out of the question, because she was still a long way from forgiving her mother for what she'd done.

'Well maybe one day when the war's over,' Eve said.

Frankie couldn't sleep. It might have been the strange bed, the hooting of owls out in the trees or more likely the fact that her mind wouldn't stop going over the day's events that was keeping her awake. She'd come here to find out about her family and to probe at how she felt about her mother. So far, she'd liked what she'd seen of these people, who had welcomed her and seemed happy to have her here. All except Lizzie, who had remained silent in Frankie's company and avoided her as much as possible for the rest of the day. Perhaps that was just as well, Frankie thought; better for her not to say anything than unleash the feelings she so clearly harboured about her new sister.

Slipping out of bed, Frankie went over to the window and pulled the blackout curtains aside, looking out at the farmyard bathed in moonlight from the full moon that hung in the sky like a lantern. It was a bomber's moon. She hoped it wouldn't be guiding any bombers over London tonight.

The thought of London made her smile, it was her home, the place she felt at ease and knew so well, its streets and smells and busyness. Coming here to the peace and greenness of the Suffolk countryside had at least helped her to understand how strange her mother must have found it living in Stepney. How difficult, too. Not everyone was able to settle in an alien place after growing up somewhere completely different. But that didn't excuse her mother for leaving her behind and letting her think she was dead all those years, a voice whispered in Frankie's mind. Coming here she'd gained sisters and a brother, but she'd also seen what she had lost. She'd never had the chance to have the easy, loving relationship that her siblings had with her mother. Forgiving her for denying her that and letting her grow up an orphan wasn't going to be easy. It was going to take time and might even prove impossible.

Chapter Fifteen

Winnie had never thought she'd feel nervous on her wedding day; it wasn't an emotion that she normally entertained, but it had crept up on her and grabbed her firmly in its arms. She was very nervous, and she didn't like it. It wasn't how she was supposed to feel; today she should be brimful of happiness and excitement, not feeling like she wanted to turn tail and run away as fast as she could.

Turning on the bath taps, she tried to fathom out what was wrong with her. Why was she feeling this way? It wasn't that she'd changed her mind and didn't truly want to marry Mac, because she did, very much. She had no doubts about it at all; it was the right thing for her to do. Becoming Mac's wife would make her very happy. So feeling this way just didn't make sense. She was certain about what she was going to do, and yet this ridiculous, unsettling, unwanted feeling was tormenting her, making her feel sick and strung out and very far from a radiant bride-to-be.

When the water level reached the regulation four-inch mark that Connie had painted around the inside of the bath, she turned off the hot tap and poured in some of the precious rose bath oil that her godmother had insisted she use. Swishing it around with her fingers, she watched as the pale pink oil swirled and tumbled through the water, gradually blending in and sending up a heavenly scent to perfume the bathroom. It should have calmed and soothed her but it didn't.

Perhaps the warmth of the water would help. She was about to slip off her silk dressing gown when there was an insistent scratching and whining from the other side of the bathroom door. Trixie. The thought of her darling dog made Winnie smile, and she opened the door just wide enough for her to come inside.

'Hello, Trix.' She scooped the animal up in her arms and sat down on the wicker chair, settling the little dog on her lap. Unusually quiet and still, Trixie leaned against Winnie, looking up at her mistress steadily with her big, liquid brown eyes. It was as if she understood how Winnie was feeling and wanted to help. To comfort her. Trixie couldn't say anything, but she was giving her support the best way she could. Wrapping her arms around her, Winnie cuddled her dog to her, forgetting everything except the here and now, the two of them together in the steamy, rose-scented room. It was like a little oasis and

Winnie felt herself growing calmer, her nerves gradually melting away.

She wasn't sure how long they sat there – it could have been just a few minutes – but however long it was, she felt soothed by Trixie's presence, calmed and much more peaceful.

Trixie sat patiently next to the bath while Winnie sank into the warm water, making the most of those precious four inches. By the time she emerged from the bathroom, with Trixie trotting at her heels, she was ready, her normal confidence and sense of purpose back in place, and grateful for such loving devotion from her beloved dog, who'd known how she was feeling and had come to rescue her.

'I thought you might 'ave turned into a mermaid in there,' Frankie said, springing up from where she and Bella had been sitting on Winnie's bed, waiting for her.

'Just having a long soak,' Winnie said. 'A prerogative of any bride-to-be.'

Frankie narrowed her eyes. 'Hope you're not wrinkled up like a prune. Let's 'ave a look at yer hands.'

Winnie obliged, turning her hands over to show her friend. 'There's little chance of that in four inches of water. I'm here now, so let's get ready.' She paused, looking at her two friends, who were already dressed in their bridesmaid's dresses and had done their hair and make-up. 'You both look lovely. Those colours really suit you.' The emerald-green silk of Frankie's dress beautifully complemented her fair skin and auburn hair, while Bella's wine-red gown brought out the gloss and shine of her dark brown curls. They made a stunning pair.

'Connie helped us to get ready,' Bella said. 'Now it's your turn. We'll do your hair first.' She pulled out the chair in front of the dressing table. 'Do sit down and we'll get to work.'

Winnie did as she was told, putting herself into her friends' capable hands.

'Are you ready, old girl?' Harry smiled at Winnie, holding out his arm for her to take. They were the last two left at the house, all the others having already left to walk to the church. 'You really do look very beautiful.'

'Why thank you, kind sir, and yes, I'm ready.' Winnie curtsied gently, taking care not to catch the hem of her wedding dress.

'You sure you don't need a quick snifter of Connie's medicinal brandy? She's already given me a dose and said I could treat you to one if you needed it.'

'What, and turn up to take my vows smelling of alcohol? I don't think so.' She smiled, slipping her arm through Harry's. 'I don't need anything, I'm not in the least bit nervous now.'

'Well I am.' Harry opened the front door and led her down the steps into Bedford Place, turning right towards Bloomsbury Square. 'I've not given my sister away before.'

'You'll be fine.' She gently squeezed his arm. 'Thank you for doing this for me, I do appreciate it.'

'We couldn't have you walking down the aisle alone.' Harry nodded his head at some passers-by who had stopped to watch their procession down the street. 'I did my best to persuade Mother and Father to come, but . . .'

'It's all right, Harry. If they choose not to, then it's up to them. I invited them and told them I'd like them to be there, but if they can't bring themselves to approve of me marrying Mac, then I have to accept that.' Winnie smiled brightly. 'I'm not going to let it spoil today. I have you and Connie and James here, and all my friends, the people I care for and who are happy for Mac and me. That's what matters.'

'You're a strong, brave woman,' Harry said. 'Mac is fortunate to be marrying you.'

'I think I'm the lucky one. He's a good man and I fool-ishly almost let him go till you showed me the error of my ways.'

'Someone had to make you see sense.' Harry stopped walking and looked at her, his grey eyes bright in his scarred face. 'You helped me when I needed it, helped me to keep going. I couldn't stand by and let your stubborn-ness get the better of you.'

Winnie's eyes suddenly smarted with tears. 'Enough of this talk, you'll make me cry, and I don't want to turn up at the church red-eyed, it wouldn't do.'

'Come on then, old girl, let's get you to your wedding.' He glanced at his watch. 'You're five minutes late already. Mac will be starting to think you've changed your mind.'

'Never,' Winnie said, matching Harry's pace as they turned into Bloomsbury Way and hurried towards St George's church, where Frankie and Bella were waiting for them on the steps leading up to the main door.

'All set?' Bella asked as she and Frankie did a last-minute check on her dress and veil.

'Absolutely.' Winnie smiled at them. 'Mac is here, isn't he?'

Frankie rolled her eyes. 'Was there any ever doubt that he'd be here? The man loves you, Winnie. He's crazy about you.'

'And Sparky's got the ring,' Bella added. 'He's taking his best man duties very seriously.'

'Ready then?' Harry said. 'You can still make a run for it, you know, it's not too late.'

'Very funny, dear brother, now walk me down the aisle quick before I grab someone off the street to do the job instead.'

Harry saluted her. 'Yes, ma'am.'

Winnie linked her arm through his and paused for a moment at the open door. She glanced behind her at her two dear friends, who smiled and nodded back encouragingly, then took a deep breath and stepped forward as the organ launched into the piece of music she had chosen for her walk down the aisle – 'The Arrival of the Queen of Sheba', which Connie had found so very funny but had managed to persuade the vicar to allow to be played. She was vaguely aware of people on either side of the aisle turning to look at her, smiling warmly, but her eyes were firmly fixed on Mac. She could tell by the way he was standing that he was trying hard not to look round, but when she was just a few yards away, he gave in and turned towards her, giving her a beaming smile and a look of pure love that she returned in full measure as she came to a halt by his side.

'Ready, Mrs McCartney?' Mac asked.

'Yes indeed, Mr McCartney.' Winnie kissed his lips. 'Husband of mine.' The ceremony was complete, the vows exchanged and a ring given, and now that the necessary marriage certificate and registers were signed, they were free to go, to walk back down the aisle and step out into the world as husband and wife.

Holding tightly on to Mac's hand, Winnie beamed broadly at the familiar faces in the pews, but the sight of two figures sitting isolated in the back row wiped the smile from her face and almost brought her to a halt. Mac kept her going, his hand squeezing hers, willing her support and love as they passed the straight-backed figures of her parents, who weren't smiling at her and who looked as if they would rather be anywhere else than at their daughter's wedding.

'They came,' Winnie whispered to Mac as they passed through the doors. 'I didn't think they would.'

Mac didn't get a chance to reply, because a mighty cheer went up from a guard of honour waiting outside. Most of the crew members from Station 75 had slipped out of the church while they'd been signing the marriage register and now stood in two rows down the church steps, holding their steel helmets aloft to form an archway.

'Three cheers for the bride and groom,' someone called.

As they hip–hip–hoorayed, Mac and Winnie ducked their heads and walked through the tunnel of helmets.

'Many congratulations, my dears.' Station Officer Steele hurried over and showered them with a swirl of confetti. 'I wish you both the greatest happiness together.'

'Thank you,' Winnie said. 'And thank you for my dress.'

'You're very welcome. I'm honoured that you wore it. You're a beautiful bride and I'm only too glad to have been able to help you.'

The rest of the guests had come out of the church now and were swarming around the steps. Winnie looked around for her parents but couldn't see them.

'Harry.' She grabbed her brother's arm. 'Did you see them? They're here, they came.'

Her brother nodded. 'About time they saw sense. I had words with Mother about coming the other day.'

'Really?' Winnie stared at him.

He shrugged. 'She needed to be told.'

'So where are they now? I want to talk to them,' she said.

Harry looked around. 'I don't know.'

'Congratulations!' Mac's mother, her arm linked through Connie's, beamed at them. 'May you have many, many years of happiness ahead of you.' She reached up on tiptoes and kissed Winnie's cheek. 'Welcome to the family, my

393

dear. I'm very happy that my son has found such a lovely wife and I've got myself a delightful daughter-in-law.'

'Thank you.' Winnie put her arm around the older woman's shoulders and hugged her to her, meeting Mac's eyes as he smiled lovingly at her. 'I promise I'll always do my best to look after him.'

'I know you will,' Mac's mother said.

'Come on, Mr and Mrs McCartney, time for some photographs.' James arrived at Winnie's side with his camera strung around his neck. 'I've managed to get hold of a roll of film to record the momentous occasion when Mac was brave enough to take on my sister. So come on, let's get some pictures taken and then we can get back to Connie's to celebrate.'

'Good idea.' Mac smiled at Winnie. 'We need a photograph to show our grandchildren one day.'

'Steady on, old chap,' Harry said. 'You've barely been married five minutes.'

Standing in front of the church doorway beside Mac, Winnie smiled happily as James took photographs, some with the two of them on their own, others with Mac's mother, Frankie, Bella, Harry and Connie, who held Trixie in her arms. The little dog had come along with her godmother and had been perfectly behaved. He even managed a picture with everyone who'd come to see them get married standing on the steps of St George's, the pillars of the church providing a stylish backdrop. But there were none taken with her parents in. Winnie didn't see any sign of them and had no idea where they were. It was as if they hadn't come; they certainly weren't taking part in recording her marriage for posterity.

'So how do you feel?' Mac asked as they led the procession of wedding guests back to Connie's house. 'Happy?'

Winnie nodded and smiled at him. 'Very. I wasn't sure that being married would make me feel any different, but I do.' She paused. 'It's like I'm now part of something bigger than just me.'

Mac squeezed her hand. 'You've made me very happy.'

Their wedding procession was attracting quite a lot of attention from passers-by, who smiled, cheered and clapped. 'You're creating quite a spectacle around the respectable Bloomsbury neighbourhood,' Mac said. 'I don't imagine you get a lot of brides walking themselves to and from their weddings around here; they're more likely to ride in a fancy car.'

'That would have been a waste of precious petrol when the church is just a few minutes' walk from the house and it's such a beautiful summer's day. Besides,' Winnie smiled at her new husband, 'I like to go my own way in life.'

Mac laughed. 'Oh I know that. Though you did promise to obey, didn't you?'

'Yes . . . but only if I agree with what you tell me to do.'

Mac shook his head. 'Did I ever tell you how irrepressible you are?'

'Several times, as I recall,' Winnie laughed.

'It's part of what I love about you.'

*

Back at Connie's house, guests were mingling and enjoying cups of tea and sandwiches. Winnie took her godmother to one side. 'Did you see them?'

'Who?' Connie asked.

'My parents. They were sitting at the back of the church but I haven't seen them since.'

Connie nodded. 'I noticed them as we walked out. They wouldn't catch my eye, though they knew I was looking at them.' She put her hand on Winnie's arm. 'I'm sorry, I don't know where they are now; they haven't come back here.' She sighed. 'But at least they came to the church and saw you married, that's something. They didn't look terribly enthusiastic, but they can truthfully say they attended their daughter's wedding.'

Winnie nodded. 'I suppose so. It would have been worse if they hadn't come at all. I wish they'd come along here or at least spoken to me outside the church, though.' She shrugged and looked around her at the smiling faces of her friends and colleagues, who all seemed to be enjoying themselves. 'But perhaps it's just as well they're not here now; they might have put a real dampener on the fun.'

'I think you're right.' Connie nodded. 'Just enjoy yourself, darling Winnie. You have the dearest husband and today is your wedding day. Don't let the narrow-mindedness of two people spoil it for you.'

Winnie threw her arms around her godmother and hug ged her tightly. 'Thank you, Connie, you are a shining light of my family and I don't know what I'd do without you.'

'You and I understand each other,' Connie said. 'I'll always be there for you.'

'I know, thank you.'

*

'Piece of cake, Sparky?' Bella offered him the plate of wedding cake. As with most wartime weddings, Winnie and Mac's cake wasn't a traditional fruit cake, but a sponge made from donated rations of butter and sugar.

'Thank you.' Sparky took a piece and bit into it, nodding his head in approval. 'Very nice.'

'Are you enjoying yourself?' Bella asked.

'I am, and it looks like everyone else is an' all.'

The dining room with its table pushed to one side was abuzz with happy conversation and laughter. Frankie and Alastair were talking to Mac's mother; Station Officer Steele had a group of ambulance crew from Station 75 in fits of laughter about a tale of her exploits driving an ambulance in the Great War.

'Even Hooky's having a good time,' Bella whispered, nodding her head towards the normally bad-tempered attendant, who was laughing at something Harry was telling her.

'I never thought I'd ever be invited to somethin' in one of these 'ouses.' Sparky leaned towards Bella. 'It's a lot bigger and fancier than my little terrace 'ouse, that's for sure.'

'And the house I grew up in too.'

'Bella, there you are.' Connie came hurrying over to them. 'There's a telephone call for you.'

397

'I didn't hear it ringing,' Bella said. 'Though that's not surprising with the amount of chatter going on in here.'

'I'll take that for you.' Connie held out her hand for the plate of cake.

'Thanks.' Bella passed it over and headed for the door, smiling to herself as she heard Connie offering Sparky a piece and him accepting it as if he hadn't already had one.

Out in the hallway, she picked up the receiver. 'Hello?'

A choked sob came down the line. 'I've had a letter.'

'Mum, is that you?'

'Yes. He's alive, Walter's alive.' As her mother's voice came down the wire, Bella slumped on to the stairs, the news having made her legs wobble underneath her and her heart pound in her chest with sweet relief.

'Where is he? Is he coming home?'

'No, he's a prisoner of war, so it says in the letter. Further details about where he is will follow. We'll be able to write to him. He's not dead, he's not dead!' Her mother's voice cracked and she started to sob.

Fighting back her own tears, Bella did her best to soothe her mother across the miles. 'It's good news, Mother, he's out of the war now and away from the fighting.'

'I know, it's just the shock, that's all. I'll let you know as soon as I hear where he is. You'll write to him there, won't you?'

'Of course.'

They talked for a few more minutes, and when they

ended the call, Bella slumped forward with her head in her hands and finally let her tears fall. The weeks of worry and waiting were over. Walter wasn't missing; he wasn't dead, but captured and now a prisoner. The relief was immense.

'Bella!' Frankie called.

She heard her friend's shoes tip-tapping across the tiled hall floor but didn't look up.

'Whatever's wrong? Connie said you'd had a telephone call.'

Bella nodded. 'It's Walter.' Her voice came out hoarse and strangled, but before she could say more, she heard the door to the dining room open and close and more footsteps hurrying over to her.

'What's happened?' It was Winnie.

'Come on, let's get you into the library,' Frankie said.

Bella didn't protest as her two friends put their arms under hers and eased her up on to her feet, then led her to the quietness of the library and settled her down in a leather armchair.

'What's happened, Bella?' Winnie asked kindly, holding Bella's hand in hers. 'Whatever it is, we'll help you all we can.'

Bella did her best to smile, but her mouth betrayed her in a wobble and tears started to flow again.

Frankie fished out a handkerchief from a hidden pocket in her dress and handed it to her. 'It's clean.'

'Thank you.' Bella took it and dabbed at her tears, taking slow breaths to calm herself down. 'Walter's been missing in action and Mother's just heard what's happened to him.'

'Since when?' Winnie asked.

Frankie put her hand on Winnie's arm. 'Let her finish.'

'Remember that day we went to see Stanley and my mother when we were staying at the country hospitality home?' Bella asked.

Frankie nodded.

'Well, a telegram came while you were out in the garden with Stanley, informing Mother that Walter was missing in action. We've been waiting ever since to find out if he'd been ... killed.' She paused and swallowed hard. 'Today Mother had a letter to say he's alive and a POW.' She looked at her friends' astonished faces. 'He's alive.'

'That's marvellous news.' Winnie squeezed her hand. 'I'm so glad he's safe, but ...' she frowned, 'why on earth didn't you tell us he was missing? Why keep it a secret?'

Bella shrugged. 'I thought it was for the best. I know you would both have done everything you could to help me, but I wasn't the only one with problems and worries to deal with. You'd just split up with Mac and Frankie was grieving for her grandfather and then found out about her mother. I couldn't add the burden of any more worry on to that.'

Frankie threw her arm around Bella's shoulder and hugged her tightly. 'It would never have been a burden, Bella. We're there for each other, always. You shared our worries and we should have been sharing yours.'

'She's right, Bella. I understand why you did it, but you really shouldn't have spared us. It might have given me a jolly good kick up the backside and made me stop feeling sorry for myself.' Winnie grinned. 'So no more secrets from each other, and that goes for all of us, no exceptions.'

Bella nodded. 'I'm sorry, I thought I was doing the right thing. No more secrets from now on.'

'You too, Frankie,' Winnie said.

Frankie nodded. 'No more secrets.'

'Last few buttons – I'm nearly finished,' Frankie said, working her way down the row of tiny silk-covered buttons at the back of Winnie's wedding dress. 'There, that's it, all done. Ready, Bella?'

Bella nodded, and together they picked up the hem of the silk and lace dress and gently peeled it up and over Winnie's outstretched arms.

'Thank you.' Winnie wriggled free of it and stood there in her pale pink silk cami-knickers. 'If I'd tried taking it off on my own, I'd probably have ripped a hole in the lace and had the boss after me. She told me she's going to keep it as Station 75's wedding dress in case anyone else wants to use it.'

'Is anyone else planning on getting married?' Frankie asked, carefully arranging the dress on a hanger and starting to fasten up the buttons on the back to help keep it in place.

'Not to my knowledge, but you never know.' Winnie grinned. 'If you'd told me a few months ago I'd be getting married in July, I'd have thought you were crazy.'

'You're not regretting it, are you?' Bella asked, handing

her the blue silk dress that she was going to wear to go away on honeymoon.

'Of course not.' Winnie stepped into the dress, carefully putting her arms through the sleeves and turning her back for Bella to do up the buttons. 'Not one little bit. It feels right to be married to Mac, like a union, part of something bigger than just me.' She shrugged. 'It's hard to explain.'

'Things will be different from now on,' Bella said, fastening the buttons.

'What do you mean?' Winnie asked.

'You're a married woman now, and Frankie and I aren't.' Bella's voice sounded strangely strained.

Frankie glanced at her. Bella's face was flushed and she looked as if she was going to cry.

Winnie spun around and caught hold of her hand. 'I might be married, Bella, but as far as I'm concerned, you and Frankie are still my best friends. That hasn't changed at all, and it never will.' She paused, taking a few deep breaths to compose herself, and then went on. 'I'm going to need you both more than ever after Mac's gone to join his new unit. Who else is going to give me a jolly good telling-off if I mope about? I know I can trust you two to tell it to me straight.'

'Oh don't worry, we'll be letting you know if you do go all maudlin on us,' Frankie said. 'Won't we, Bella?'

Bella nodded, looking happier. 'Of course.'

'And I'll still be living here with you and Connie,' Winnie said. 'It will hardly be any different at all, except that Mac will come and stay here when he gets some leave.' She held out her arms to her friends and the three of them hugged each other tightly.

'Come on, we need to finish getting you ready,' Frankie said, sniffing back tears. 'Or you'll miss your train.'

'Has Mac told you where you're going?' Bella took hold of Winnie's shoulders and gently turned her around to finish doing up her buttons.

'No, only that we're leaving from Paddington,' Winnie said. 'I don't mind where it is as long as we've got a few precious days together before he has to report for duty . . .' Her voice cracked.

'Aye, aye, Bella, she's starting to go maudlin on us, we can't have that,' Frankie said. 'Here.' She picked up Winnie's pillar-box-red lipstick from the dressing table and handed it to her friend. 'Reapply this, and stiff upper lip, Miss Churchill . . . ' She laughed. 'Sorry, Mrs McCartney. Don't waste thoughts on what's to come; just enjoy the moment. You have a handsome husband waiting downstairs to whisk you away on honeymoon, so get cracking.'

Winnie stared at her for a moment and then broke into a beaming smile. 'See, Bella, I absolutely do need you two to sort me out. Yes, you're quite right, Frankie, it's an emotional day but I need to show a bit of stiff upper lip.'

'So get that lipstick reapplied then,' Bella said.

Winnie raised her eyebrows, then threw her head back and laughed. 'Thank you, my darlings, you are the best friends a girl could ever have.'

'Likewise,' Frankie said, holding out Winnie's hat for her to put on.

A few minutes later, Winnie was ready. She looked stunning in her beautiful pre-war peacock-blue silk dress, which complemented her honey-blonde hair and peachy complexion, topped off with a jaunty hat borrowed from Connie.

'How do I look?' she asked, twirling around. 'Will I do?'

Frankie looked at Bella and grinned. 'Shall we tell her?'

Bella shrugged. 'What, and let her get all big-headed on us?'

Winnie frowned, turning to peer down at the back of her legs. 'Have I got a ladder in my stockings?'

'No.' Frankie hooked her arm through Winnie's, nodding for Bella to do the same on the other side. 'You look wonderful, a beautiful bride. Mac is a lucky man.'

'This way.' Bella grabbed Winnie's suitcase and, still arm in arm, led her towards the door. 'You have a husband waiting and we'll see you when you get back.'

Outside, Frankie and Bella stood arm in arm, watching as their dear friend and her new husband said their goodbyes to their guests. Everyone had spilled out of the house on to the steps and the pavement near the taxi that was waiting to take them to the station. Station Officer Steele and Sparky were throwing confetti, and the ambulance crews from Station 75 were clapping and cheering, giving them a rousing send-off.

Pausing by the taxi door, Winnie turned and looked back, then raised her hand and smiled warmly at her two friends, sending a silent message that the three of them understood perfectly. They both smiled back and returned her wave, knowing that their friendship was truly one that would stand the test of time and whatever life threw at it.

Acknowledgements

It's been a delight to write more about the lives of Frankie, Winnie and Bella and to have the support of the magnificent team at Sphere. Thank you to Manpreet Grewal, Maddie West, Tamsyn Berryman, Jane Selley, Bekki Guyatt and Clara Diaz for your expert guidance, care and hard work bringing the book together and launching it out into the world.

Thank you to my agent, Felicity Trew, who is brilliantly intuitive and supportive and with whom it's always such fun to mull over the lives of the East End Angels, working out how their stories will unfold.

Thank you to the Imperial War Museum and London Metropolitan Archives for access to their precious archives which are so fascinating and inspire my writing. Also to the Norfolk Library Service for providing so many research books.

My writing friends are a constant source of fun, laughter, good advice and support. Thank you all, especially the Norfolk members of the Romantic Novelists Association, who are a fabulous bunch.

The feedback from readers of *East End Angels* has been truly heartwarming. Thank you so much to everyone who has read the book and taken the time to share their thoughts in reviews – I appreciate each and every one. It's always great to hear from readers, so do please get in touch.

Finally, thank you to my family who understand what it takes to write a book. David, Isobel and Tom, you are all utterly wonderful and thank you for all you do to help me make it happen.